THERE'S NO HIDING IN CYBERSPACE

....

Web
of
Betrayal

A Novel

Clare F. Price

....

CFP MediaGroup, LLC   Sacramento, California

Cover Design by BespokeBookCovers.com
Interior Design by Chinook Design, Inc. (chinooktype.com)
Edited by Elizabeth Hennies
Copyedited by Zoë Bird
Author photo by Joy Porter Photography

Published in the United States of America

ISBN: 978-0-9903723-0-1 (pbk)
ISBN: 978-0-9903723-1-8 (ebook)

CFP MediaGroup

Experience Web of Betrayal

We live in a digital age. This book chronicles the birth of that age. So, how could we resist using Internet technology to immerse you, the reader, further into the story and the times?

We couldn't, of course! Scattered throughout the book you will find links and QR codes to help bring the 1990s back to life and deepen your connection to the characters. These links and QR codes will lead you to the people, places, music and events that we hope will make this a more engaging reading experience.

If you'd like, start here by scanning the QR code below with your mobile device* and visiting the book's Website (www.webofbetrayal.com). Enjoy!

*On some devices it may be necessary to first install a free app to read QR codes.

PROLOGUE

THE DAY ARNOLD TOLLIE BURNED ALIVE WAS ORDINARY IN EVERY other respect.

It was business as usual as Toby Eastman unobtrusively parked his Piper Super Cub at the far end of the jungle landing strip just outside Cali. Toby instinctively chose secrecy over exposure whenever possible. He adapted like a chameleon, blending naturally into any background or situation. This trait had served him well in the past and it would do so again today.

Arno—as Toby called Tollie—was late. Arno was often late. Toby habitually threatened to take off without him; it was an empty threat and they both knew it. Toby and Arno protected each other in this jungle just as they had when they served together in Vietnam. It was Arno who had arranged for Toby's introduction to Colombian drug lord Enrique Valdez when Toby needed cash and connections and didn't care where he got them.

Toby walked to the edge of the landing field, peering down the path. Nothing.

The chatter of monkeys and screams of macaws above heightened his awareness of the silence on the trail. *Come on, Arno,* Toby thought, as impatience slid into nervous irritation. It was more than the flight delay that made Toby nervous this time. Arno was taking chances again, the way he had when they'd run drugs in 'Nam. Nothing too big or too obvious, just a little bit off the top here and there. It was stupid and risky but Arno seemed to think he was invincible. Invincibility, Toby knew well, was not a factor of the human condition.

First Toby heard the footfalls, then the grunts and groans. Valdez's men were walking down the trail. They were half-pushing, half-carrying Arno, bound and gagged, between them. Arno was barely walking. His face was pulverized.

Toby dove behind a stand of mangroves, watched, and waited. Arno was a big man. It took four of them to drag him to the open field where the bush pilots landed, where his death would serve as a warning to any other pilots who thought they could steal from Valdez.

They staked him spread-eagle to the ground and began cutting holes in his clothes, exposing naked skin with the dispassionate precision of a surgical team. Arno writhed in the tight ropes as they dipped frayed sections of his clothing in kerosene. Kneeling, one of them massaged Arno's hair with the oil as if for a shampoo.

Their methodical preparations, Toby realized with a sickening lurch in his stomach, were meant to avoid an explosive conflagration that would end quickly. They favored an excruciatingly tortuous burn that would slowly melt living flesh from bone. A human torch.

As Toby waited through the night, unable to escape the sight, the smell and the screams, a human torch was exactly what Arnold Tollie became.

December 18, 1993: Palo Alto, California

The fire crackled. A tongue of flame broke free, reigniting dying embers, warming the room. Toby leaned back in his chair, took a small sip of his brandy and glanced around the tight space. Henry Rhodes's bachelor's quarters held the same comfortable clutter that Toby remembered. A sagging green sofa and two wingback chairs faced the now-cheerfully crackling fire. An oversized bookcase against the wall held evidence of Henry's two passions–volumes of the classical literature he loved and, in a testament to Henry's thirty-five years of gainful employment, a wide range of computer manuals.

Henry sat in the other armchair, his feet barely reaching the floor. Like his home, Toby thought, enjoying the constancy, Henry hadn't changed much in the last eighteen years. He was a small man, now sixty-two, rounded from his enjoyment of food and drink. His eyes closed in pleasure with his first sip of brandy.

"It's good to see you, Toby," Henry said. "I enjoyed all those letters, but it's not the same as a real visit. Are you back in the Bay Area for good?"

"I'm not sure yet. What about you? Have you been traveling much?"

"Not as much as I'd like. I thought when I retired I'd have more time, but my consulting has almost become a full-time job."

"The secret's out, Henry–everyone's finding out how good you really are. Of course, there were some of us who always knew it," Toby replied, allowing himself another small sip of brandy.

Despite the warmth of the fire and the brandy coursing through his veins, Toby knew he couldn't afford to relax; not until he had the computer disk back safely in his possession. He touched the glass to his lips once more and then pushed it aside, watching with pleasure as Henry finished his first drink.

"And how are your boys?" Toby asked.

"I've got a couple of boys who are real crypto-wizards. Give even you a run for the money," Henry said, chuckling mildly as he set down the empty glass.

Henry referred to all the young engineers he'd shepherded through the company as "his boys," even the women. Although Henry had been a talented software programmer in his own right, his company soon recognized he had an even greater ability to mentor the young college recruits they hired. Henry still kept in touch with most of them. Toby had been one of Henry's boys, once, though his tour of duty in Vietnam had given him a later start than most of the others.

"I've got pictures. Would you like to see them?"

Toby nodded.

Henry disappeared into his bedroom and returned with a large manila envelope. He peered over Toby's shoulder as Toby flipped through the pictures of a recent camping trip. Toby remembered those camping trips. This one was in Yosemite, with El Capitan visible in the background. Two young men stared at the lens. The young Asian man stood stiffly, uncomfortable in front of the camera. The impish smile on the other boy, a chubby-faced blond wearing a blue and white rugby shirt, tugged at Toby, snagging him with memories he thought he'd laid to rest years ago. Memories he could not afford to indulge, especially now.

"They look like great kids, Henry," Toby said as he studied the prints.

"Smart, too. Like you. But I keep them on their toes. I've still got a puzzle game or two up my sleeve," he said.

Henry sat down, poured a second glass of brandy and enjoyed a large swallow. He began talking about the old days, about the puzzle games, and how the competitive contests to crack encrypted computer code had helped discipline young minds like Toby's and, in turn, had given Henry's company valuable insights into the emerging field of cyber security. The reminiscences were flowing as freely as the brandy. Another time, Toby thought, he could relax and enjoy them, but not tonight. Too much was at stake. Henry finished the last of his brandy with a flourish and stood, reaching for the bottle and Toby's half-filled glass.

"No more for me, Henry. I have to go," he said, rising. "I really just came to pick up that disk I sent you a few weeks ago."

Henry looked up at Toby embarrassed, his smile sheepish. "I know you told me keep that one strictly confidential, Toby. But your puzzles are always the best. It was just too tempting."

"What do you mean?" Toby asked, forcing a casualness he did not feel.

"I couldn't crack it. I tried, but it was beyond me."

Toby smiled, starting to relax. "I'll send you another. But I need this one back, tonight."

"I don't have it," Henry said.

"What?" Toby fought to keep his voice calm.

"When I couldn't solve it, I sent it to the boys to see what they could do with it." Henry's tone was mildly irritated, as if Toby had forgotten who was the student, and who the master.

Toby's mind spun, recoiling at the Hobson's Choice Henry's recklessness offered him. The one man he thought he could trust had betrayed him.

"Henry, that disk wasn't just another puzzle," Toby said vehemently. "That disk has information on it that belongs to some very powerful men."

All the color drained from Henry's face. "What kind of information?"

"Useful information, but only if you know what to do with it."

Henry's eyes blinked rapidly. He looked at Toby as if he'd never seen him before. "Toby, what have you gotten yourself into?" he asked, his voice cracking.

"Nothing I can't get out of. As soon as I get the disk back, everything will be fine." Toby offered him a comforting smile. "You know me, Henry. Just tell me where the boys are and I'll fix it," he cajoled.

Henry gave Toby a concerned look. Then he turned, picked up pen and paper and rapidly scribbled names, email addresses and phone numbers. "I'm sorry, Toby," he said, handing over the note.

You're sorry? Toby queried silently. *It's too late for sorry.* His mind flashed back briefly to the jungle, and the odor of the lump of burning flesh that had once been a man. The tension started in his neck and shoulders. Adrenaline kicked in, and with it the same rush of excitement and danger he'd always felt in the jungle right before the kill. Staring at his mentor, Toby felt uncontrollable rage explode inside of him, spouting like lava from an active volcano.

"You stupid old goat," he snapped. "Why didn't you do what I told you and keep that disk secure?"

Henry stood before him frozen in shock. His mouth sagged open in fear and protest. Toby understood his distress. The young recruit Henry had known wouldn't dare speak to him that way. But Toby was no longer that man, if he had ever been. He reached into his pocket and palmed his stiletto, opening the blade. As it caught the bright light of the fire, Henry gasped. His expression changed rapidly from surprise to comprehension soaked with dread.

"Who are you?" Henry whispered, backing away. "What kind of animal have you become?'

Toby stared mercilessly at the man who had been his closest friend. Then, in one cat-like movement, he stepped across the room and grabbed Henry by the neck, pressing his fingers against the carotid artery. As the body went limp, Toby shoved his knife into the man's back. The force of the thrust penetrated the kidney, twisting upward toward Henry's heart. Black-red liquid oozed from the small wound, staining both their shirts.

The body shuddered and slumped against Toby. He stepped back letting it slip to the ground in the widening pool of its own blood.

His task completed, Toby paused, panting from exertion. Drawing a deep calming breath, he looked around the room investigating the scene, ready to cover his trail. He picked up his glass and swallowed the remaining brandy. A reward for a job well done. Then he pocketed the used glass and the photographs.

As he moved around the body lying lifeless on the floor, he glanced back for one last look. Henry's eyes stared at the ceiling in surprise. A stream of pink blood trickled down his jaw.

The sight stopped him. His clean and uncomplicated exit from the house was suddenly impeded by a pull he hadn't experienced in years, maybe since he'd sat under Henry's tutelage at the company. Leashed by fleeting but honest remorse, he returned to the body and tenderly closed its eyes.

"I'm sorry, old friend. I truly am," he whispered, his lips brushing against Henry's ear. "But if it hadn't been me, it would have been them."

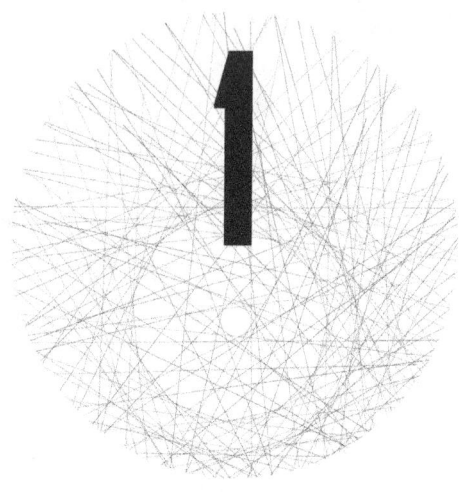

THE NOISE. IT WAS ALWAYS THE FIRST THING PETER ELLIS NOTICED about Las Vegas. The chaotic clamor of bells, chimes and music—punctuated by the occasional shriek of a joyful winner—could be heard even in the jetway.

Just inside the gate, Peter dropped his travel bag and rubbed his temples. It was a futile attempt to block the insistent clang of metal on metal as slot machines doled out just enough change to keep their patrons wedded to the handle. The flight from San Jose, though mercifully short, had been miserable and overcrowded. He'd been forced to jam his six-foot, two-inch frame into a middle seat, his knees at his elbows.

"God, I hate this town," he grumbled. He swung his travel bag over his shoulder and started to make his way through the congested terminal. The taxi line stretched for what seemed almost a quarter of a mile—meaning that it would be at least an hour before he could get to the hotel for a much-needed shower and drink. With more than 120,000 people expected in town for the Consumer Electronics Show, this was just the beginning. *Get used to it,* he told himself grimly. *It's going to be a long three days.*

Despite the convention crunch at the airport, the registration lines at the Las Vegas Hilton were mercifully short, and Peter made it to the hotel bar in record time. Like most veteran convention reporters, Peter made stops at the popular hotel lounges part of his daily routine. Not only was conversation in the relaxed atmosphere of the bar likely to yield its fair share of tips; many an overenthusiastic product engineer had been caught leaving details of his company's latest design efforts on the back of an abandoned cocktail napkin.

 Sliding into a velveteen seat, Peter took in the scene. The <u>Hilton's gaudy bar</u>, so reminiscent of the 1970s, with its hot-pink chairs and, red glow-in-the-dark cocktail tables set on a muddy pink and brown carpet, was proudly pretentious in a way that only the leisure suit crowd could truly appreciate.

A leggy young blonde, wearing a black silky miniskirt barely long enough to cover the essentials, arrived to take his drink order. She stood pen poised, giving him the kind of sidelong glance women often used when they were pretending not to stare. Studying the drink menu, Peter ran a long aristocratic finger down the side of his Grecian nose, tapped it against his cleft chin then looked up, letting his deep blue eyes drifted over her before ordering. "Dewars, neat. Water back."

She scribbled, nodded and smiled. She had a sweet smile. Peter rewarded her with the infectious boyish grin that usually got him whatever he wanted. He just hadn't decided whether he wanted her—yet. He studied her shape as she hustled toward the bar then turned back the pre-convention scene.

Expectation, excitement and urgency pulsed through the crowd's chatter like an electronic signal through a packet switch. So many familiar faces, belonging to acquaintances, colleagues, even some Peter had called friends and most of whom he hadn't seen in months. Peter took a sip of the Scotch the waitress set down before him and wondered what his reception would be, now that he was back in the game. A trio of business reporters from the *Valley* huddled around the back corner of the bar, congenially trading shots and war stories. Nate King from the *Merc* looked up and offered a cursory nod in

Peter's direction, a bland look that held no invitation.

Peter nodded back, considering even that brief acknowledgment to be a breakthrough of sorts, as a tall angular woman in a red pantsuit rushed past his table. She stopped short directly in front of Peter and whirled, turning on the young associate trailing behind her. "You idiot! What in the hell did you think you were doing?" she demanded.

Chin pressed to his chest, he stared down at her Jimmy Choos and mumbled. "My job. I was just doing my job."

She hit back with a withering look and a sharp retort. "Well, you screwed it up. As usual. You're worthless! How did I ever get stuck with you?"

July 9, 1993: Palo Alto, California

"Get your ass in here, Ellis," Adam Boswell, the *Valley Tribune*'s publisher yelled the moment Peter walked into the office that Friday morning last July. He glanced at Tina Basco, the *Trib*'s office manager. She looked as perplexed as he felt. It wasn't the kind of reception a top investigative journalist gets after breaking a major story. The paper, with its banner headline, "TriCorp Execs Hide Product Flaws from Gov't Buyers," lay on the corner of Tina's desk.

She shrugged. Peter turned the corner and stepped inside Boswell's office. As he took in the scene, his confusion intensified. Boswell stood behind his desk, his cut-glass features etched with fury. He was flanked by a grim-faced Ben Carter, the *Trib*'s managing editor. When Peter looked beyond his editor and saw the tall, patrician-looking woman in the red Chanel suit, his insides turned to jelly. She fixed him with a belligerent, uncompromising stare of utter contempt.

"Hello, Margaret," he said.

"Peter." She nodded with no break in the rigidity of her features.

"Do you two know each other?" Adam asked, his reedy, high-pitched voice even more painful to Peter's ears than usual.

"She's my sister," Peter replied, watching Margaret closely. He knew that whatever game was being played here, she was in control of it.

Peter felt the tension in the room ratchet up a notch. Adam's face, hot pink when he entered the office, turned blotchy red.

"What's this about?" Ben demanded. Ben's job as managing editor was to protect his reporter and his story. Peter, staring at what he knew would be a brutal confrontation, would need every bit of that support.

Margaret ignored Ben. Stepping forward and taking command of the room, she spoke directly to Peter.

"You didn't know TriCorp was one of ours, did you?" she asked, marking the company as a client of their father's law firm, Ellis, Blackwell and Barnes. Margaret ran the New York office of the global corporate litigation practice.

"It's irrelevant. I was just doing my job," Peter retorted.

"And rather badly, it turns out," she said, her tone implying what Peter had heard her say to his face many times before: "like the rest of your miserable little life."

She reached into her briefcase and pulled out several sets of thick documents, turned toward Adam and began her prosecution.

"The story you published in yesterday's *Tribune* asserts that my client, TriCorp Systems, is facing major production delays in the release of its newest graphics chip and lying to the federal government about it. That story is pure fabrication and I'm here to ensure that my client suffers no business or revenue loss because of this reporter's negligent actions." She pointed in Peter's direction.

"Peter?" Ben interjected.

"I stand by my story, Ben. I have solid proof."

"Let's talk about your proof, shall we?" Margaret said. "Starting with your first accusation, the product delays. Nonexistent!"

She fanned a set of TriCorp documents across Adam's desk. "These are the engineering roadmaps. As you can see each milestone was signed off as completed on the required due date by the team lead."

Adam and Ben, leaning in for a closer look, exchanged glances.

Peter kept his eyes trained on Margaret. She held out her right hand, and a young man Peter hadn't noticed before passed her another set of documents. She gave these directly to Ben and turned her venomous gaze back to Peter.

"Secondly, you accused my clients of distributing flawed chips. I've just handed your editor twelve Q&A reports, each signed by a different test engineer. Twelve people, Peter, two of them federal test engineers. Did they all lie? Is this one of your cute little conspiracy theories?"

"Not a theory, Margaret, facts. What I live by," Peter snapped.

She laughed. "Like the fact that the TriCorp executive team tried to hide the nonexistent product delays and flaws from their customers? The federal government? Then explain to me why three separate federal design inspectors signed off on the sample test run before taking delivery?"

She tossed the inspection reports on Adam's desk. Peter stared at the forms. The yellow highlighted signatures almost burned his retinas. This can't be happening, he thought miserably, struggling to frame his thoughts. He felt himself begin to collapse under the weight of Margaret's formidable presence, just like he had since he was four years old.

Ben stepped up and presented Peter's case valiantly. "We've got memos and emails that tell a completely different story: missed engineering milestones, rejected Q&A reports, and this," Ben handed another set of papers to Margaret. "An email from TriCorp's COO to Peter's source, demanding he bury the flawed Q&A reports. So yes, we do believe they were lying. And for the record, having been a reporter at the *Washington Post* during Watergate, I've seen my share of government conspiracies." Ben finished with a determined glare at Margaret, while Peter stood next to him mute, heart racing, breathing shallow, wishing that he had the courage to confront Margaret himself. Just this once.

"Clearly someone is lying here, but it is not my client," Margaret said, turning the full force of her anger on Peter. "Let's talk about your sources, shall we?"

Like any good prosecutor, she saved the most damning evidence for last. "We have good reason to believe that Mr. Ellis accepted these documents knowing they had been fabricated and used them anyway. And how do we know this?" She paused dramatically, scanning the room, letting her gaze linger on Adam.

"Because we know who his sources were, and we know that both of them had accepted positions with ReedLogic, TriCorp's biggest competitor before providing Mr. Ellis with this conveniently damning information."

Dropping the documents on the table with what sounded to Peter like the thud of a large book closing, she said: "The bulk of these emails came from ReedLogic, not from TriCorp."

Ben picked up the first email, showed it to Adam, then to Peter. The company logo was missing, but the header Margaret had highlighted in yellow showed the emails' point of origin as ReedLogic. She had accused Peter of the worst crime a reporter could commit—knowingly rigging a story.

"It's doesn't matter where those emails come from. The information was accurate," Peter protested, sounding weak and defensive even to his own ears.

"The evidence proves otherwise," Margaret said crisply.

Peter watched in horror as both Adam and Ben folded. Margaret saw it too. She turned toward Peter, eyes riveted on his face, immensely enjoying the wounds she'd inflicted.

This is what it feels like to be stoned, he thought. The floor shifted beneath his feet. Margaret's face blurred as his pupils constricted and the pounding in his temples increased. His stomach clenched. He took a step back to avoid losing his balance.

Margaret turned back to Adam and issued her demands. "We want a complete retraction, a new, accurate story written by someone else on your staff, and a personal apology in writing from Mr. Ellis here, or we will file a multimillion dollar law suit against the *Valley Tribune* this afternoon."

Adam didn't even put up a fight. He ordered Peter to start working on his apology immediately, and readily agreed to the rest of Margaret's demands. As Peter turned to leave the room, he saw triumph in his sister's eyes.

• • • •

"You know those two were working for ReedLogic?" Ben asked him later that afternoon.

"They weren't, at least not when we started talking. But I should have kept checking. First rule of a whistleblower source is, know their angle," Peter said, glancing at Ben.

Ben nodded. "Adam wants you fired."

"I figured as much," Peter replied. "I guess I'll start packing my stuff."

Ben held up his hand for Peter to wait. "You're a good reporter, Peter. But you cut corners here and you got burned." Pausing, Ben eyed him. Peter felt his chest constrict.

"Still, this smells like a setup to me," Ben continued. "I've seen it before. I told Adam we'd investigate, and I've asked him to give you another chance."

Peter felt his knees go weak with relief. "You won't regret it."

"Be careful," Ben warned. "Play it safe."

As it turned out, Peter didn't have much of a choice. Word spread. His sources dried up. Even good friends started avoiding his calls. In a matter of days, he went from star reporter to editorial pariah, lucky to get a few column inches in the back of the business section. It stayed that way for six long months.

Then, to top it off, his girlfriend dumped him. To her credit, she stuck with him long after everyone else had deserted him, though in his anger and disillusionment he rebuffed her attempts to console him. His bouts of heavy drinking scared her. Finally, she told him she just couldn't take it anymore; and he watched her go.

It was okay, he thought at the time. Women weren't for regretting. She could be replaced.

Except Jessica surprised him. She'd left an unexpected void. In his glitzy world of socialites, drama queens, gold diggers and party girls, Jessica stood apart. With her solid Midwestern roots, unpretentious, no-nonsense style and unshakable belief in her own self-worth, Jessica offered him the respect he craved and the stability he needed. She was his rock, as immutable as the mountain peaks she loved to climb. Jessica, he realized too late, was the one he did regret losing. The woman he couldn't easily replace.

It was the continuing ripple effect of the TriCorp debacle that had caused him to react so badly when Ben ordered him to Vegas to cover CES. He saw it as one more kick in the balls. *Back to trades for you, Peter. Whatever made you think you were a real reporter?* Now, sitting in the Hilton bar, he realized that, rather than punishment, Ben was really offering him a shot at redemption.

"Hey, Ellis," a booming voice called from across the floor. Heads turned. Charlie Sheffield, a large-boned, chubby-faced man sporting a black goatee, was threading his considerable bulk between the tight tables with ease, face beaming with delight. Peter grinned and waved, grateful for the prospect of Charlie's cheerful company. It might help purge his mind of troubling memories. He knew Charlie's boisterous manner grated on the nerves of many of the Valley's elite, and that it was probably responsible for Charlie's lack of success in some quarters; but Peter had always found him a good friend and an entertaining companion. Then again, Peter had also known Charlie longer than most. They had been classmates at Harvard, and had stayed in close touch over the last nine years while Charlie finished his MBA and Peter had gone to New York to pursue a freelance writing career.

Charlie squeezed himself precariously into the chair opposite Peter and ordered a dry martini. "Didn't expect to see you here."

"I'm pinch-hitting. The other guy broke his leg skiing."

"Oh," Charlie nodded. "That's it then. I wasn't sure, when I got your call."

Like the others, Charlie had distanced himself professionally when the TriCorp scandal broke. Peter took the invitation for a friendly drink in public as one small sign that things might be starting to thaw.

"What about you?" Peter asked.

"Scouting, as always. Gotta let my clients know what's hot and what's not," Charlie replied. As vice president of the Archer-Evans Group, a merger and acquisition consultant to some of the Valley's top investment firms, Charlie's income—more importantly, his portfolio—depended on his ability to gain and trade valuable information.

"Anything I should know about?" Peter asked, an eyebrow cocked in Charlie's direction.

"Check out Delta Software, multimedia gaming software. Very hot. Get an interview with their top programmer, Brian Tucker, if you can. They're on someone's acquisition list," Charlie added with a wink.

Yeah, Peter thought, *yours*. He figured Charlie would use him to generate some good press so he could juice the price of a deal and increase his finder's fee. Hey, that was the game. He was glad to be back in it.

You talking to anyone at Draco Communications?" Charlie asked, changing topics.

"Yeah, Alex Kavanagh, their new marketing guy," Peter replied.

Charlie took a quick sip of the martini the waitress had just delivered and leaned toward Peter. "Could you check something out for me?"

"Sure," Peter agreed enthusiastically. Charlie had given Peter his share of tips over the years and Peter was glad to return the favor, especially now that he needed all the friends in the industry he could get.

"I've heard Draco's got a new cable box in the hopper. Supposed to be a cable box on steroids, two hundred channels, something like that, with Internet access built into it."

"Really? I've been hearing rumors about these Internet set-up boxes for a couple of years now, but as far as I know no one's ever got a functioning one out of the lab."

Charlie shrugged. "I'm not hearing this from the engineers, Peter. I'm hearing it on the investment side. The money guys are getting ready to throw some serious cash into this. Draco, with all their cable outlets and programming, could be real winner.

"You know everybody's all hyped about the infobahn and what it'll do for business," Charlie continued. "All those legal documents and medical records flowing from one end of the earth to the other. Big advances in education, yadda yadda, yadda."

Charlie waved his right hand in the air. "It's pissant compared to where the real gold is, and that's the consumer. You hook the Little Old Lady from Pasadena up to the Internet, now that's the mother lode. If Draco's out in front on that one, I'd like to know about it."

"So would I," Peter agreed, certain that Charlie had clients who were either developing something like it or looking to invest in a company that could. "I'll call you after I meet with their marketing guy, okay?"

"Appreciate it." Charlie said, standing.

Peter glanced at his watch. Still an hour and a half to kill before the hospitality suites opened. He got up, started toward the horseshoe-shaped blackjack tables and froze.

Standing less than fifty feet away, her face partially obscured by a row of dollar slots, was Jessica Brennan. Peter stepped away from the blackjack table, staring intently at the face he had half-hoped, half-dreaded he would see. She was thinner than he remembered, but her vibrancy was undiminished. Transfixed, he studied her as she strolled through the casino to the house phones and picked up a receiver. As she talked, her smile brightened. The last time he'd seen her look like that, she was standing in his living room, holding an expensive glass of Cabernet.

July 7, 1993: Menlo Park, California

It was early evening, the night his TriCorp story hit the front page and slid across the wires. His first big scoop for a daily paper hit the wires. It didn't get much better than that, Peter thought, smiling as he unlocked the door to his townhouse in Menlo Park. He noticed the aroma of garlic, mushrooms and red wine; and there was Jessica, standing at the door with a wine glass in her hand.

"Surprise!" Her smile was as bright as he'd ever seen.

He really was surprised. "I thought you had a class tonight."

"I couldn't let you celebrate your first big scoop all alone." She offered him the glass.

He collected the wine and a kiss. "What are we having?"

"Guess." She chuckled, eyes shining with pleasure.

Peter took a whiff, let the scent linger in his nostrils and smiled. "Chicken Marsala."

She nodded. "And tiramisu. Which I made myself," she added proudly.

She'd recreated the special meal they'd shared at that little Italian bistro in SoHo. Their first real date. The same dinner he'd made for her the first night they'd made love. Peter took a deep breath that ended in a contented sigh. His heart was full. Taking a sip of wine, he started to follow her into the kitchen. Then he noticed the brightly wrapped package on the dinette table.

"What's this?" he asked, pointing.

"Open it."

He put down his wine glass, tore into the wrapping, pulled off the ribbon and held up a framed copy of his TriCorp story. Jessica smiled at him, respect and admiration lighting her features. "I'm so proud of you, Peter."

As those six little words—words he'd never gotten from anyone else—sunk deep into his soul, he felt complete.

The memory faded as he ran his finger instinctively across the jagged scar on his palm. The scar was a permanent reminder of how, in a drunken rage two days later, he'd smashed the picture frame against the fireplace, slicing his hand as the glass shattered in a thousand little pieces around his feet.

Jessica hung up the phone and picked up her purse. Peter was sure that Ben had offered him a chance for redemption with this trip to Vegas; as he studied Jessica's profile, it hit him that restarting his career was only one step in his restoration. Without Jessica back in his life, he would never be fully whole. He stepped up from the casino floor and stood directly behind her.

"Jess," he called, just loudly enough for her to hear him.

Her back stiffened. She turned and faced him.

"Hello, Peter," she said in a neutral tone.

"Hi Jess. What a surprise. You look great." He gave her a bright smile and watched her face soften.

"Thanks, you too." she replied, extending her hand with a cautious smile. A gold heart-shaped locket hung around her neck. The locket was new. He wondered where it had come from and, more importantly, from whom.

"How about a drink? We could catch up a bit," he asked.

"Not tonight. I've got plans, and a trade show to cover just like you do." She gave him a cool look.

"How about tomorrow? Six okay?"

"Tomorrow's even worse. You know how manic these trade shows are." She pulled her purse up onto her shoulder, ready to depart.

"C'mon Jess. One drink. Ten minutes." He held out his hand, smiling as invitingly as he knew how.

Jessica hesitated. Peter waited, willing her to surrender to his charms.

"Okay, one drink."

He hid a triumphant smile and fell in beside her as she edged forward. A jackpot alarm sounded next to them and a tubby middle-aged woman in powder-blue polyester stretch pants jumped up to grab a coin container, almost knocking Jessica down.

Instinctively, Peter reached out to steady her. "You okay?"

"Fine," she said, stepping ahead of him as they walked across the casino to the lounge. The Hilton's lounge was near the back of the casino, right off the hallway that led directly to the convention center. It was a popular thoroughfare. Peter took a table in a private corner, hoping that no one they knew would spot them. He wanted Jessica all to himself.

"How have you been, Peter?" she asked after they had ordered their drinks.

"Doing ok."

"Good." She sounded genuine. "I've haven't seen much of you lately."

He knew she meant his byline and was asking how things stood. He saw it as a good sign. "Things are picking back up."

"I'm glad."

The waitress returned with their drinks; Scotch for Peter, Chardonnay for Jessica. Masking his interest with a sip of Scotch, he studied her carefully. She had the same trim figure, the same attractive, confident face with hazel-green eyes, the same high cheekbones and sensuous lips that he remembered and now sorely missed. Through her silk blouse he saw a hint of white lace bra. His fingers twitched. He longed to caress those nipples again. It had been too long.

"It's great to see you. How have you been?" Peter gave her a winning smile, got a halfhearted one in return. He refused to let it deter him.

"Busy."

"I noticed. That was a great series you did on all the new ecommerce startups."

"Thanks." She smiled, took a sip of wine, and visibly relaxed.

"You really think people are going to do that much shopping online?" he asked.

"I do. As long as it's secure. It's easy and convenient. There's a guy in Seattle who's launching an online bookstore. I have an interview with him next week."

Peter shook his head. "Oh, that will never work. Books need to be held and smelled and felt. The crackle of fresh pages when you open up a new book—you can't get that online."

"Maybe it wouldn't work for you," Jessica laughed. "I couldn't pry you out of book store with a crowbar."

Peter gave her a jaunty grin in return. "Guilty as charged. It's good to hear you laugh, Jess." His voice softened. "I've missed that. I've missed a lot of things."

He paused, watching as she pushed a loose strand of her

auburn hair behind her ear. It was a gesture he'd always found alluring. Leaning forward, he covered her hand with his. "Have dinner with me. The least I can do is save you from the all-you-can-eat seafood buffet."

Jessica laughed briefly, catching the joke, and withdrew her hand. "I can't. I have plans, remember." She studied him over the rim of her glass.

"What are you doing here anyway?" she asked finally. "I thought the point of joining the *Trib* was to get off the trade show grind."

"Was and is, but the guy who was supposed to be here broke his leg skiing. So here I am with the rest of the herd, waiting breathlessly to see what David Lockwood is up to."

"Yeah. And it better be good. He's got a lot to make up for after that Falcon debacle."

"Redemption can be a long road," Peter said quietly, studying her. Guilt flickered briefly across her face. Maybe she was sorry she'd dumped him after all. The thought bolstered his confidence. Jessica was the first woman he'd ever tried to win back, and he was on shaky ground. How could he tell her how much he'd missed her exuberant laugh, their private jokes, her strength and stability when he felt the world closing in, without looking foolish or needy? He cleared his throat.

"Jessica, I know I didn't handle the whole TriCorp thing well. It got ugly and that was my fault. But things are different now. Maybe we—"

She shook her head, refused to meet his eyes. "There are only so many times you can say 'leave me alone' before people give you what you ask for."

"I never said that," he protested.

"In words, no, but in actions, yes, you did. You pushed all of us away—me, Tim. Everyone who tried to be there for you."

The disappointment in her eyes sliced through him. Words fled. He stared at her, struggling to recover his equilibrium. "I know," he whispered, so quietly he wasn't sure she even heard him.

She sat silently for a moment, then glanced at her watch. "It was good to see you, Peter, but I really do have to go," she said, standing. He rose quickly and stood next to her.

Putting his hand lightly on her arm, Peter offered her his sweetest smile. "Have dinner with me. If not tonight, while we're here. Or soon. We can get to know each other again. Put TriCorp behind us."

Her eyes grazed his face as she stepped back. "It's too late. I've moved on. I'm involved with someone else."

She fingered the locket at her throat. It was as if, Peter thought, she held it as a talisman against any charms he might still possess. "Besides," she added. "I heard that you moved on, too. Someone named Sherry? Cherie?"

"It wasn't important," he replied with a shrug.

He got a cold, knowing smile in return. "We never are," she said, with a sad shake of her head. "Goodbye, Peter."

Jessica turned and walked across the casino floor. He watched her leave.

"Too late, my ass," he muttered darkly. "Look out, whoever you are, because you don't stand a chance."

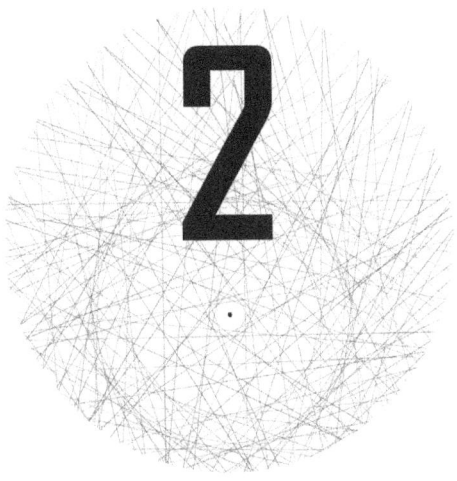

2

AT EIGHT-THIRTY THE NEXT MORNING, PETER WAS ALREADY TIRED, angry and running late.

His seven-thirty breakfast meeting at the Mirage was a no-show. In his pre-TriCorp days, Peter would simply have been pissed off and put the PR flack who set up the meeting on his *Do Not Resuscitate* list. But now, filtering this meeting through the lens of his public disgrace—as he did everything these days—he couldn't help but wonder if he was being avoided.

Get a grip, he told himself, as his cab driver tried vainly to reach the convention center doors in stalled traffic. Several AT&T buses hugged the curb and disgorged dozens of passengers, all wearing the venerated globe logo. Three black stretch limos fanned out behind the buses, turning the traffic behind them into a funnel with no endpoint in sight.

Five of them—Peter and four others from the Mirage—had packed inside a cab meant to hold three. It was the only transport available, and the driver would be expecting a big tip for breaking the seating rules. Peter glanced at his watch. He had seven minutes to get inside the hall: he wasn't going to make it. Lockwood's keynote was the main reason he was in Vegas. He pulled a twenty-dollar bill out of his wallet and handed it to the guy seated next to him.

"I'm walking," he said, pushing open the car door and jumping out of the cab into the milling crowd. He sprinted the half mile toward the convention center entrance, grateful that years spent on tennis courts gave him the leg power. Following the arrows pointing to the main hall, Peter dashed through the corridor, bobbing and weaving through the interlocked mass of humanity as best as he could.

The keynote was always a popular event, and it was going to be especially crowded this year. In an industry that prided itself on the youth and quantity of its demigods, David Lockwood topped the list. Lockwood was one of a handful of visionaries who had shaped the industry before IBM and Microsoft changed the rules. Like Gary Kildall of Digital Research, and Steve Jobs and Steve Wozniak of Apple, Lockwood's Trxton Computer Corporation produced an innovative personal computer that had educated and entertained thousands of people who, in the ordinary course of events, would never have had access to the padlocked mainframes and minicomputers that dominated corporate business worldwide.

Peter glanced at his watch. With only three minutes left to get around the rotunda to make the event, it was going to be close. Brushing past a group of Japanese businessmen in dark suits and thin ties, Peter picked up his pace. People jammed the doorways. The hall was packed.

A blue-suited security guard saw the badge and yellow "Press" ribbon pinned to Peter's jacket and waved him through a side door. Peter dashed down the steps to the front section marked PRESS and found an empty seat. He paused before sitting, picked up the white plastic 3-D glasses on the chair and held them toward the gray-haired man in the adjoining seat with a curious look.

The man shrugged. "Who knows? It's Lockwood."

Peter tucked the glasses in his breast pocket and settled into the seat, breathing deeply and trying to decompress from the hard run through the rotunda. Shifting forward, he surveyed the crowd, hoping to locate Jessica. She was seated three rows in front of him, and was chatting breezily with a reporter from *Time Magazine*. Peter felt a cold stab. If that was the new boyfriend, he was going to have to step it up. That guy was good. Really good. He already had a Pulitzer. Shaking off his concern, Peter refocused his attention on the stage as the roar of the crowd greeted Lockwood's arrival.

The stage curtains parted to reveal David Lockwood standing center stage, his only prop a slender white Grecian column upon which rested a gray laptop.

• • • •

As the applause reached a crescendo, Toby Eastman slipped into a seat in the back row and studied the man who had ruined his life. Tall, slender and bearded, dressed in his trademark jeans and navy blue turtleneck sweater, Lockwood looked much younger than his thirty-nine years. A single blue light illuminated his face. He stood still for a few seconds, allowing the crowd to praise him, then held up his hand for silence. "Good morning. I'm David Lockwood."

The crowd tittered. Around Toby, men and women—many of them worth millions themselves—hunched forward in rapt attention.

"Every year the crowds at CES get larger and the dreams get bigger. Who here has a big dream?" Lockwood asked. As he scanned each section, hands thrust toward him as if the very act of holding out a hand in Lockwood's direction could change one's fortune.

"Sycophants," Toby snarled, looking at the mesmerized faces. He'd expected salutations and fanfare from the gullible press, but the adulation from the crowd in the hall was far beyond anything he could have imagined. His stomach churned.

Lockwood stepped to the edge of the stage. "Congratulations to all of you who are willing to dream big. Now more than ever, this industry is on the verge of amazing things. The Internet, like the personal computer, will change everything. The way we work, the way we live, and most importantly, the way we think. It will take the courage and tenacity of great men and women to make it happen."

Behind him, oversized video screens flashed a picture of Lockwood's crude sketch of the original Trxton Personal Computer—four white lines with a grid of squares like tiny teeth, resembling an attached keyboard and set against a blue background. It was the same sketch that had appeared in the company's ads for years. Applause swept through the crowd. Toby stared unflinchingly at the screen. As always, the tension began in his neck and shoulders, preparing him for battle. Yet here, in this civilized hall of commerce, Toby could neither fight nor flee. His immobility drove up the tension in his nervous system. Behind his eyes, enlarged capillaries throbbed in blood-driven rage. Despite the pain, he refused to avert his eyes from the picture—the symbol of his humiliation, his mark of Cain. That sketch had exiled him from his rightful place on the Trxton development team.

Lockwood stared out across the audience, face solemn, hands clasped. "And I applaud all of you for your dreams," he paused. "But children dream. So do drunks on bar stools. It's not enough to dream. Each of you must decide for yourselves what you are willing to pay to make your dream a reality."

Lockwood moved to the pedestal, rested his hand on it. "For many of you, the challenge will be too great, the walk too long, and the dream too distant. A chosen few, the brightest and the best among you, will reach a pinnacle of success beyond what any mere mortal has the right to achieve, and I salute you. To those whose hunger to reach that peak eclipses any barrier, defies any limitation, resists any opposing force, I offer these three principles of life. First, excellence at any cost."

The images on the screens changed to photos taken from the Trxton Development Lab in its glory days. The vintage, late 1970s photos showed small gray terminals and shining green LCD screens with black cable snaking around the sides, attached to a row of servers. Racks of test equipment shone as if polished by a careful hand. Long worktables were free of clutter, software manuals meticulously arranged.

Something in Toby's brain snapped, and he was hit with a wave of dizziness. He had only been in that lab once, eighteen years ago, but in those ten minutes his life had been irrevocably altered. In one grainy image, young engineers with long hair, sideburns and droopy moustaches leaned against the terminals, staring unsmiling at the camera. David Lockwood stood in the center of the team with a clenched jaw and fiery eyes. The men's expressions all sent the same message. *We are ambitious people, serious about changing the world, and we don't need celluloid for preservation.* Their product would ensure their immortality.

Toby pressed his arms against the chair to hold his body vertical as he scoured the screen for the one face conspicuously missing: that of Lockwood's partner, Devon O'Reilly. The true genius behind the Trxton PC, O'Reilly had written both the operating system and the innovative graphical user interface, the first of its kind in the industry.

"But did Devon get the credit?" Toby muttered at the screen. "Of course not. There's only room for one ego in the room, David, and that's yours. Too bad that ego cost you ten years of your life," Toby added with a snicker, recalling, with immense pleasure, the failure Lockwood's Falcon Project had been.

Lockwood stepped forward, hand raised. The entire crowd shrank back in unison as a large bird of prey thrust itself at them through the video screen: a lone Peregrine Falcon, legs tucked, wings spread, tail fanned, stark against a cloudless blue sky.

"Second, embrace your failures. For those of you who think there will be no Valley of Death, no wilderness journey, think again. It will happen, and it will happen to you."

The crowd gasped. Lockwood's Falcon Project, a high-end graphics workstation, was rumored to be a Sun killer when it was announced in 1988. Government, military and educational institutions had lined up en masse for the rights to own Lockwood's next big thing, but despite the millions Lockwood and his investors had poured into developing the product, it had never made it past the early test stage. That started the whispers in the engineering community that Lockwood had lost his touch. He had always been obsessively private. The very public failure of Falcon drove him into total isolation.

In exile, fettered to the Valdez cartel, Toby rejoiced that Lockwood's own ego had dealt him the death-blow that Toby had been unable to inflict. Now Lockwood was back, intent on not on resurrection, but transfiguration. This time, Toby vowed, he would finish the job.

Predator to predator, Toby studied the vigilant eye of the Falcon, appreciating its ruthlessness and power. The Falcon killed with speed and dexterity, by catching its prey unawares and that, Toby thought with ironic self-satisfaction, was the fate awaiting Lockwood. A fate only Toby could deliver. Toby turned his attention back to the man. On stage, Lockwood continued to lecture his apostles.

"When failure happens, embrace it," Lockwood preached.

Yeah, David, we know your shit doesn't stink.

"Call the failure to you. Learn its life lessons. Let it teach you, and in the end, it will not control you. You will control it."

On screen, the Falcon turned its head, looked down and dived. It landed gracefully on the outstretched glove of a falconer.

The falconer. David. Really? Bend nature to your will? Toby chuckled. *Only you would be oblivious to the reality that all that stands between you and the agony of those talons sinking deep into your flesh is a thin piece of leather—a covering far too flimsy to protect you from justice, so long overdue.*

The crowd erupted, its dissonant applause ringing in Toby's ears. Lockwood waited for silence. As the crowded quieted down, he continued.

"We all know what personal computers can do. We've been teased with all sorts of promises for world-changing breakthroughs from the so-called information highway and this new World Wide Web; changes in education, entertainment, and medicine. But why just change the world?" Lockwood asked, walking to the edge of the stage.

"Shift the Universe: Stop time. Suspend gravity. Break the laws of physics. Make the impossible, possible."

Lockwood lifted a pair of 3-D glasses from the pedestal beside him, and held them out toward the crowd. "It won't be too long before these will be totally unnecessary, but for today, please humor me and put on your 3-D glasses."

· · · ·

Peter pulled the glasses from his breast pocket. As he pushed them up the bridge of his nose, the hall lights went out. Lockwood stood silent on the stage, the small bluish spotlight focused on his face lending him an ethereal presence. He stroked the keys of the laptop with practiced ease. After a frozen moment, the screens exploded with the roar of the sea and the magnificent curl of a deep ocean wave.

"Ladies and gentlemen, the discovery of America," a booming voice announced.

As the wave tumbled toward the audience, a 3-D hologram of Columbus's Santa Maria burst out over the first ten rows of the hall. Somewhere in the back of the crowd, the applause began in earnest.

The ship faded, the screens shifting from sea to earth to sky as a 3-D hologram of the Wright brothers' airplane lifted gracefully into the air. Suddenly, the airplane began spinning wildly, out of control, twisting toward certain impact with the earth. Just before the inevitable crash, the plane faded into a 3-D image of Apollo 11 landing on the moon.

The audience roared as they recognized the image of Neil Armstrong stepping lightly from the lunar module and planting an American flag on the moon's surface. Watching the audience's enthusiastic reception from the stage, Lockwood allowed himself a small, self-satisfied smile.

"I'm glad you liked it," he shouted above the cheers, stepping forward as the screens behind him faded to black and the hall lights came up.

"But remember, these discoveries are part of the past. With the power of the Internet that lies before us, the real excitement is yet to come. If you are going to be anything, be disruptive. Shift the Universe."

Lockwood raised his right hand and the screens sparked once more: a brilliant blue and white star exploded into the audience and disappeared.

The crowd erupted with applause.

"This will be the talk of the show," Peter's seatmate proclaimed, adding his voice to a crowd already buzzing with excitement.

"Mm," Peter replied. He could see tomorrow's headlines and he wasn't buying them. He was positive Lockwood's smug smile had taunted them with a message of some sort. Peter picked up his notebook and sketched all he could remember of the three holograms.

Holograms captured, Peter suddenly remembered his appointment with Draco Communications. *Oh, shit,* he thought, glancing at his watch and scrambling for the exit. *I'm going to be late.*

· · · ·

Hurrying through the crowded aisles of the sprawling exhibit hall filled with hundreds of booths, Peter thought the scene bore a striking resemblance to a Middle Eastern bazaar. It was as if every out-of-work magician, dancer and pitchman had found employment for the duration of the show. They competed admirably, but ineffectively, for attention with the helium-filled pandering of the computer and electronics companies. Their colorful visions of brave new worlds were offered with all the adroitness and candor of Persian rug dealers. Access to the Internet was everyone's favorite magic carpet ride.

Wandering past the Panasonic booth, Peter refused proffered leaflets from both a Bengal tiger and a Mighty Morphin Power Ranger. The traffic jam at E3 Computer, which was offering free trials of its virtual reality machine, was unavoidable. Finally, Peter spotted the looming presence of Draco Communications.

The forty-by-sixty-foot, three-story-high Draco booth was one of the largest and tallest on the trade show floor. In a nod to Las Vegas itself, the <u>Draco logo</u>, a green and yellow abstract of the Dragon constellation, blinked in neon boldness at the top of the towering booth structure. Peter had to crane his neck to see it.

The booth contained four rooms divided by thermoform vinyl partitions. The one closest to the walkway, meant to draw in curious passersby, was styled as a tribute to Route 66 and hung with photographs taken along the venerated route. A video clip from the 1960s TV show of the same name ran in a loop in the background with Nat King Cole's recording of the <u>famous theme song</u>. A classic blue

<u>1966 Corvette convertible</u> roadster parked in the center of the display would be raffled off for charity at the close of the show. Peter made a mental note to buy a ticket for that one.

The next room was set up as a mini-theater, complete with wide-angle viewing screen and chairs for about thirty people. People took seats for the next presentation while the pitchman on stage began his sound check.

Peter turned the corner and faced the large demo room. A half dozen Unix workstations were strategically placed on the green and white Draco-logo-embossed carpet. Animated salespeople holding brochures stood at attention beside each workstation, eager to tell the Draco information highway story to potential customers. Peter kept walking toward the private conference rooms at the back of the booth, where the real business of the trade show was done.

"Alex Kavanagh, please." Peter handed his card to the booth bunny at the Plexiglas reception stand. She sashayed off and returned with a medium-sized man in his mid-thirties, slightly paunchy, with hair receding at the temples, aviator glasses and a too-bright smile. He wore his red polo shirt, with the trademark Draco logo, tucked into dark khaki pants.

"Hello, Peter," Kavanagh said, extending his hand.

Kavanagh's grip seemed unusually tense. Peter put it down to the stress of the job. Kavanagh was new to the executive suite, having just been promoted to Vice President of marketing three weeks earlier. Kavanagh's rise to VP from field marketing rep in less than six years was meteoric. Peter, who had followed Kavanagh for most of his career, considered him no more than a capable mid-level marketer. Yet he knew Kavanagh was acutely ambitious and gifted with exceptional political skills, a combination which often trumped talent and merit in a company with the size and reach of Draco.

Kavanagh ushered Peter into a small suite barely large enough to contain a small conference table and a large viewing screen. In one corner, a programmer sat in front of a workstation awaiting Kavanagh's signal to begin the demo. Peter and Kavanagh sat down and took bottles of water from a tray in the center of the table.

"If it's okay with you, Peter, I thought we could run the demo and then I could answer any questions you have."

"Sounds good," Peter replied. He pulled out his notebook and pen and focused his attention on the screen.

"What if you could run a meeting from paradise," the narrator began, as video images flooded the screen: a man stood on the balcony of a tropical beachfront hotel, waves lapping the shore in the background. Dressed in white shorts and a Hawaiian shirt, he smiled at his laptop. Faces of colleagues from China, India and the United States arranged in checkered video squares smiled back.

"What if you could buy concert tickets from a cash machine or a whole cart of groceries with just one swipe of your credit card?" the narrator asked. A busy family, kids tugging at their parents' clothes, zipped through the supermarket checkout line in less than a minute, stopping only long enough to swipe a credit card on a small square box attached to the cash register.

"What if you could watch your local sports team playing on live TV, and pause the action to get some more popcorn?" the announcer continued. Peter smiled at an image of kids bouncing on a couch and rapidly punching a remote control, starting and stopping the action of a football game as a bemused mom and dad returned from the kitchen with an overflowing bowl of buttered popcorn.

"What if you could watch your favorite TV show, and, if you like the dress the actress is wearing, you could point, click, and purchase it right on the spot?"

A fashion model twirled across a crowded dance floor while a picture-in-picture inset highlighted her dress, jewelry and shoes. Icons under the inset allowed video viewers to point and click to order in their own sizes and colors. One last click and the screen flashed SOLD as an in-home delivery date popped up on the screen.

"Your World. Your Way. Draco Communications."

 The screen faded to black. Peter turned to Kavanagh. "Impressive, Alex. I want it. So when can I have it?" (See the 1994 AT&T "You Will" Ads)

"It's 1994, Peter," Alex replied. "You'll have it before you know it."

"You want to be a little more specific," Peter said, knowing full well that most of the applications Draco was touting here were years if not decades away. "Realistically, you guys are laying pipe."

"If by laying pipe you mean creating the fiber optic backbone we need to send digital signals across the country, then yes, we're laying pipe. We've got about half our SONET backbone finished and it'll be completed by the end of the year," Alex agreed.

"Okay, so you're making progress on the foundation, the roadbed, what about the rest of it?" Peter asked.

"We've got several strategic alliances in the works. We'll be announcing those in the next few weeks. Stay tuned."

"That wouldn't be the cable partnerships with Comcast, TCI and Phillips, would it?" Peter asked. Alex's face shifted from its bright smile to a look of wary appraisal. He was clearly unprepared to respond to Peter's direct query.

"You know I can't pre-announce anything," Alex replied, his tone implying that Peter's questions should stay within the limits of

Draco's canned vision of the brave new Internet world. Alex took a pull on his water bottle and refocused his attention on Peter.

"Anything else I can answer for you?" he asked.

That was my warm-up. If you didn't like that one, you'll like this one even less, Peter thought as he prepared to go straight for the jugular.

"Just one more thing. Let's say, just for kicks, that you do get some cable partners. Then the key question is how are you going to get those applications to the consumer? They need a way to access all those goodies on the information highway. And I'm hearing that access is through Horizon."

Alex's jaw clenched briefly. He relaxed it and smiled a little too broadly. His face took on the expression of an indulgent uncle humoring a bright but confused child.

"Horizon," he said, rubbing his chin and furrowing his eyebrows as if in attempt to recall a name he'd never heard before. "I don't know what you mean."

"I'm surprised you haven't heard of it since it's an Internet ready cable set-top box that you've got in development. I understand it provides two hundred cable channels and runs both analog TV and digital Internet signals from the same box," Peter replied, putting the facts that he'd collected in front of Alex, gauging him for his reaction.

Alex threw back his head and laughed. "Really, Peter, where do you come up with this stuff?"

Peter was determined to get some kind of confirmation he could use. "Okay, let's leave the mythical Horizon out of it for a minute," he said, checking his notes.

"You're showing sophisticated global video conferencing on that demo. You've got movies and TV on demand, correct?"

"Yes."

"Okay, I buy that. Now, tell me how it works?" Peter asked innocently.

Alex sidestepped the noose. "I'll have to set you up with an interview with one of our engineers. I can do that next week."

"Fine. But let me just confirm one or two things, Okay?"

"If I can," Alex replied. His body stiffened. He was clearly on alert now.

"Let's start with current broadcast technology," Peter said. "It's all analog. Whether you use old school rabbit ears or a cable box, the signal generated is like a wave. Just like a wave on the beach, it flows in and out, which is why pictures on different channels don't look the same, one is brighter and louder, another less so. The bottom line is that analog signals are unpredictable, right?"

Alex nodded slowly. Peter could tell he had no real understanding of the technology he was marketing. Peter's estimation of Alex Kavanagh, already low, dropped another notch.

"The Internet is digital. Computer code is simple, 1s and 0s, which means it is easier to control and easier to create exactly the image you want—a sharper, better, higher-definition image. Digital signals are precise, correct?"

Peter was throwing the technology at Alex fast, hoping to catch him off-balance. From the cautious expression on Alex's face, Peter thought he was succeeding.

"Because the analog signal is an unpredictable video wave and the digital signal is precise computer code, the two signals aren't compatible," Peter continued. *Now comes the punchline*, he thought.

Alex's reaction to this would tell Peter a lot about how far he could get with the story. He hoped to push Alex into an admission that could be used on the record.

"If you're going to offer video conferencing or movies on demand on a TV and a computer at the same time, you're going to have to convert analog signals to digital, aren't you?" Peter asked.

Alex refused to take the bait. "I'd help you if I could, Peter," he said, standing. "But really, that is a question for our engineers. As I said, I'm happy to arrange an interview."

Peter stood and faced him. "Horizon is the converter box you need to do the analog to digital conversion," he stated.

Alex's smile veered toward a smirk. "I hate to tell you this, Peter. But you've been misinformed."

Peter caught the inference in Alex's tone, calculated to remind him of the embarrassment of TriCorp. "I don't think so. I've got great sources for this," he replied.

"Well, we do know how undependable sources can be at times," Alex said pleasantly, opening the conference room door.

"It happens," Peter agreed with a faint smile, swallowing the angry retort he wanted to deliver, and extending his hand. "Have a good show."

This time there was no mistaking the tension in Kavanagh's grip.

"Alex Kavanagh, you just made the biggest mistake of your career. If you think you can fuck with me and get away with it, think again," Peter muttered, giving vent to his anger and frustration as he walked back across the trade show floor. Pulling his cell phone from his pocket in mid-stride, he punched Charlie Sheffield's line. He got voicemail.

• • • •

Two hours later, showered, freshly shaven and dressed in brown loafers, khaki pants, button-down shirt and navy blazer, Peter headed down to the Hilton's mezzanine level to make the rounds of the hospitality suites. He joined the throng headed into the Tymelink suite.

Peter glanced around the room, looking for Jessica, but he didn't see her or anyone else he knew.

Tymelink had spared no expense. On one side of the room, a piano man played popular show tunes on a baby grand. The bar in the center was staffed by three young, black-vested bartenders. They mixed and poured drinks at a rapid pace for the thirsty trade show crowd. Peter stopped and grabbed a Scotch. A large buffet table, displaying a wide variety of seafood, vegetables, exotic cheeses, soft breads and hot hors d'oeuvres, beckoned to him with enticing aromas that reminded him he hadn't eaten since breakfast. He grabbed a small plate of assorted canapés as two men, one rotund, the other crowned with a large halo of fuzzy whitish blond hair, passed him on their way to the food.

"So, Jimmy, how's the show going for you guys?" the portly man asked, piling his plate high.

"Great. We're really giving Microsoft a run for the money this time around," Jimmy Fuzzyhead replied.

"Glad to hear it," his friend said, popping a large stuffed mushroom into his mouth. "Say, did you ever catch up with Brian Tucker?" he asked, still chewing.

Peter's ears pricked up. The name rang a bell. It took him a minute to recall that Brian Tucker was the programmer Charlie had suggested he interview. In the rush of the day, he'd forgotten to follow up on Tucker. Peter edged closer as the two men continued down the buffet line.

"No, I haven't seen him," Jimmy Fuzzyhead replied. "I've really got to find him. I've still got his package at my booth. It's from Henry."

"Are you serious?" the fat man asked. His voice held a level of urgency and concern Peter couldn't help but notice.

"Would I kid about a thing like this, under the circumstances?" Jimmy Fuzzyhead asked, his tone somber.

The two men dropped their voices. Peter leaned as close as he could without appearing obvious. A woman backing away from the bar bumped into him, sending a spout of liquid into the air and down the front of Peter's jacket.

"Aw, damn," he said, setting down his drink.

"Oh, I'm sooo sorry," the woman gasped. She reached over, collected a handful of napkins and offered them to him.

"Forget it," Peter said. He took the napkins and dabbed halfheartedly at the spot while he scanned the room, hoping to relocate Jimmy Fuzzyhead and his rotund friend. They had disappeared; but in the interval, Alex Kavanagh had entered the suite and was headed for the bar. Peter looked around for an escape route, but Alex's progress was blocked almost immediately by Esther Gibson, a well-known, widely avoided industry pundit. As she grabbed Alex's arm, the brilliant blue stone on her finger caught the reflected light of the chandelier and twinkled with dazzling flashes of white light. Peter chuckled at Alex's predicament and refilled his Scotch. When he turned back, Esther was gone and Jessica stood in her place.

The look of adoration on Jessica's face as she gazed at Alex pierced Peter's body like tiny needles, turning his nerve endings into pinpricks. He watched, motionless, as Alex and Jessica exchanged intimate looks. Alex slid his arm around her waist, pulled her close and kissed her affectionately and possessively. Glancing up from the embrace, Alex caught Peter's eye and smiled. A conqueror's smile. He took Jessica's arm and they walked out the door.

The din of the party and the technobabble of the surrounding conversation suddenly became intolerable. Stomach swirling, Peter pushed through the crowded room and out of the hotel, greeting the cold, biting wind with enormous relief. Neon flashes seared his eyes as he walked down the strip. He spotted an empty cab.

"Where to?" the driver asked as Peter slid wearily into the backseat.

"Anywhere there's a good bar. Where I can get a real drink."

"How about the Hard Rock Café?"

"No. Somewhere quiet. Where the locals go. Where I won't see anyone from this damn industry."

The cabbie looked into his rearview mirror.

Peter sunk lower into the backseat.

"I got just the place," the cabbie said, turning left on Spring Mountain Road.

He pulled up outside a one-story brick building long past its prime. Peter handed him a few bills and walked inside.

The cabbie knew his trade. The long, curved saloon-style bar was as seamed and weatherbeaten as the faces of its regulars. A half-dozen blue-jeaned, cowboy-booted patrons stopped talking and eyed Peter as he leaned against the bar in his blue blazer and khakis. Peter stared back, nobody moved, and eventually the locals resumed their tribal gossip.

"Dewar's, neat," Peter said, hesitating for a brief moment. "And a pack of Camels," he added.

The bartender handed over the drink and the cigarettes. "Matches?"

"Yeah, thanks." Peter lit up and inhaled, gratified by the taste of his first cigarette in more than three years. He paid his tab and took the drink and cigarettes to a back table, away from the hubbub of the bar.

Alex fucking Kavanagh. How could she? Jessica is one of the smartest women I know. How could she fall for a manipulative weasel like Kavanagh? Peter downed the Scotch in two gulps trying unsuccessfully to rid his mind of the look of adoration he'd seen on Jessica's face. It made him wonder if he knew Jessica at all. If she was worth the energy he'd planned to expend win her back. He put out his cigarette in three angry stabs at the ashtray and lit another.

I'm wasting my time. Women really are just good for one thing.

The lone cocktail waitress sauntered by, raising her eyebrows at his empty glass. He nodded and she returned quickly with his refill. As she placed the glass on the table, her gaze lingered a moment before retreating. Peter ignored the look. It was easy to do. He'd been getting that look from women since he was thirteen, and by the time he was sixteen he'd coined a name for it. He called it the Fuck-Me-Look. He'd long ago stopped counting the number of times he'd been able to convert that look into personal gratification.

Sipping the fresh drink, he paused and studied the waitress's rhythm as she meandered through the bar tidying up the tables. She was attractive in a hard, self-possessed way that had appealed to Peter before. Her routine completed, she turned and smiled again. Peter raised his glass and accepted the invitation.

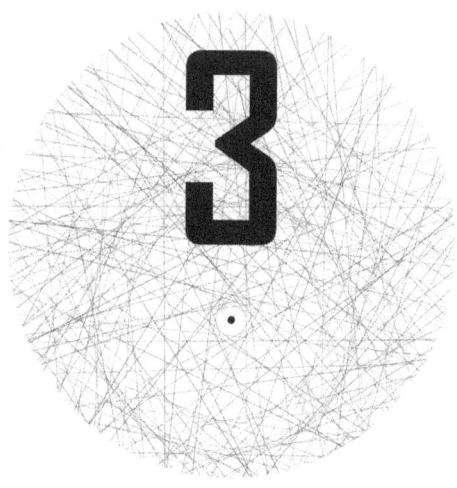

3

PETER AWOKE TO THE SOUNDS OF RUNNING WATER AND SOFT OFF-key singing, and a persistent pain that felt like a hammer pounding on his temples. He grabbed a pillow and curled it around his ears in a vain attempt to ward off the intrusion of all three.

The peace only lasted a few minutes. "You said not to let you sleep too late. It's already seven," she said.

"Did I say that? Forget it. Bad idea," he mumbled.

"Get up, Peter," she demanded, in a voice too similar to his nanny's for comfort.

He stretched and opened his eyes. She stood by the bed naked except for a white towel wrapped around her head. She looked older than she had last night. He could tell that she kept in shape, but now he noticed the lines on her neck and a sag to her breasts that betrayed any claims of youth. She was older—a lot older—than his twenty-nine years. Not that he cared. She was as innovative as she was skillful, and he had enjoyed himself immensely. Judging from her responses, he had no doubt she had been captivated by his performance.

"Morning," he grinned, running a lazy hand along her inner thigh.

"Don't start," she said, laughing. As she retreated, the towel slipped from her head. She was a redhead. *Like Jessica*, he thought. She grabbed the pack of Camels from the nightstand. Putting two cigarettes in her mouth, she lit them both and passed one to him. He took the cigarette, inhaled deeply and straightened his back against the headboard.

He watched her as she traveled nonchalantly about the hotel room sipping coffee and collecting various articles of her clothing. She knew he was watching, so she took her time slipping into her thong and the silky, cock-teasing miniskirt she'd worn in the bar, striving to remind him, with her calculated gyrations, of the pleasures they had just shared. It worked. Peter considered skipping the trade show altogether and staying where he was for the rest of the morning.

"Where the hell is my blouse?" she muttered, pawing at a chair.

He reached down on his side of the bed and handed it to her.

"I had a great time," she said as she buttoned up.

"So did I."

"I have one question, though."

Peter braced himself. He generally preferred to be the one asking the questions.

"Who's Jessica?"

"What?"

"You called me Jessica three times last night. Not that I minded. You made up for it in other ways, but I'm curious."

Peter sucked on the last of the cigarette and tossed it in the ashtray.

"My ex-girlfriend. Very ex."

"Important? The love of your life?"

He shrugged, ignoring the sharp pain in his gut.

"Not by a long shot. I bumped into her by accident yesterday, and I guess she was on my mind."

"Oh. I see," she said, one eyebrow arched.

He stood up and pulled on his shorts. "You hungry? How about breakfast?"

"No. I've got to go. I got to get my kid off to school." She paused as she placed her hand on the door knob. "Well, you know where to find me."

"I sure do."

Peter leaned over and gave her a quick kiss as she opened the door and left the room. Sauntering into the bathroom he relieved himself, then grabbed a cup of coffee from the little pot on the counter. Back in the bedroom, he picked up the phone and dialed. Tina Basco, the *Tribune*'s office manager, responded.

"Hi, Tina. It's Peter. Ben around?"

"Sorry Peter. You just missed him. Adam wants to talk to you."

"Tell him I'll get back to him, okay?"

Tina lowered her voice. "I can't, Peter. He knows you're on the line."

"Okay. Tell Ben I called and put me through."

Ten seconds later, Peter heard the profane bellow of his publisher, Adam Boswell.

"Ellis, what the fuck are you doing down there? Poking every babe on the chorus line?"

"Not exactly," Peter said, swallowing his irritation as the pounding in his temples increased.

"Well, did you happen to notice a couple of headlines from the trade show you're supposedly attending? The *San Francisco Chronicle*, 'Lockwood Wows CES attendees'. The *San Jose Mercury News*, 'Lockwood Back in the Limelight.' What did we have from you Ellis? A paragraph on Lockwood, and then a bunch of techno-weenie crap about some new futuristic cable box that runs two hundred TV channels," Adam scoffed. "We are not a trade weekly. We are a daily business paper."

"My story was a preview of what Draco Communications could be developing. It's news," Peter snapped. "Those Lockwood stories were performance reviews. Lockwood did a great smoke and mirrors act and everyone jumped up and down. There was nothing in either story about what he's really doing."

Peter paused and heard Boswell confirm his guess with a grunt.

"I, on the other hand, have a line on his new project. With

details." Even as the words left his mouth, Peter regretted giving in to his ego and promising Boswell a story he had very little chance of delivering.

"Yeah, well, okay," Boswell said, a twinge of grudging respect in his tone. "Get the copy in by four. You're on a short leash, Ellis. Remember that," he said, disconnecting.

As if I could forget it. Peter sighed, sat down on the bed and took another sip of coffee. He pulled out his notebook and flipped to his notes on Lockwood's presentation. A quick scan confirmed his belief: he had nothing.

Me and my big mouth, he thought, trying to reconstruct Lockwood's presentation in his mind. The pounding in his head made it impossible. He drank some more coffee and hoped that his hangover would wear off by noon.

Get the copy in by four, Adam had demanded. *Good luck*, he thought. He tossed the notebook aside and stared at the stark hotel room wall. Everybody was going to be chasing this story, including Jessica, and she was almost as good a reporter as he was.

April 6, 1992, Palo Alto, California

Early that Monday morning eighteen months ago—April 6, 1992, to be exact—he'd found the three issues of *Computer Industry News* lying on his chair, tied with a red ribbon. In the five months that Jessica had been at *CIN*, she had scooped him three times, including today. He'd been here for more than four years, and had earned his reputation as the most aggressive reporter in the California bureau. No one had ever scooped him more than once—until Jessica. He picked up the magazines and carried them into Jessica's office. She greeted him with a confident smile.

"You're on a streak. How about lunch to celebrate?" he asked.

Jessica gave him an amused look. "Is this a keep your friends close, but your enemies closer kind of thing?"

"Something like that." He grinned back. "You won. I lost. Loser buys. That would be me." His smile brightened with the invitation.

She hesitated briefly before responding. "Lunch is fine, as long as we go Dutch."

He got the message. Colleagues, nothing more. It was then that he set out to win her heart, but his real chance didn't come until a few months later at *CIN*'s annual summer meeting in New York.

Thursday was the only free night, and most of the California crew was headed out for pizza. Peter asked Jessica if she wanted to have dinner in Manhattan. She'd told him on the flight in that she was hoping to see New York, but they'd been stuck in meetings in Manhasset all week. This was her one and only chance, so he wasn't surprised that she took it. The Italian bistro in SoHo was percisely what he wanted: quiet, casual and charming.

"The rumor mill's in overdrive about the big announcement tomorrow," Jessica said, as the waiter placed a platter of Chicken Marsala in front of them. Jessica dished Peter's half onto the empty plate the waiter had provided and slid it toward him.

"What big announcement?" Peter asked, playing it cool. She rewarded him with a conspiratorial grin. "Like you don't know that they're announcing the new California bureau chief and it's you."

Peter's eyebrows shot up. "Where'd you hear that?"

She took a bite of her chicken before answering. "This is really delicious," she said, her tone teasing.

"Jessica."

"That's what reporters do. Find stuff out. Care to comment?" Her eyes twinkled. He hadn't noticed just how green they were until now.

He knew who the new bureau chief was, and it wasn't him. He wondered if she would be disappointed, and was surprised to realize that he cared. "Not me," he said, shaking his head.

Her face fell. "I'm sorry, Peter. That's too bad." She did look disappointed, but not in him. She looked disappointed for him.

That's a new one, he thought.

"It's okay," he said, taking a forkful of chicken and mushrooms. "You're right. This is delicious."

"You would have been great for the job," she insisted.

Peter paused for a sip of wine, considering his answer. He could tell her to forget it. That it didn't matter to him, which was true enough. But the genuine warmth and concern in her eyes invited him to confide in her. Uncharacteristically, he decided to give her a real answer.

"They offered. I declined."

It was Jessica's turn to be surprised. "Why? It's a promotion. More money."

He shrugged. "I don't want to sit behind a desk. I like being in the field, breaking stories. It's the rush of being on the front lines." He leaned toward her, expression earnest. "I take a management slot, I'm stuck in the trades. I want to be on a big daily. Someday, maybe, *The Wall Street Journal*."

He'd never shared that dream with anyone before. She looked suitably impressed as she raised her wine glass with a bright smile. "Well, here's to living the dream."

Peter touched his glass to hers. As he allowed her accolades to warm him, Peter began to consider that he had finally found someone who understood him, and would give him the respect he deserved.

He thought he was over her. But Vegas was turning out to be an emotional minefield. Memories of Jessica now intruded on him in embarrassing ways, at unexpected times. Like last night. He had never, ever called a woman by another's name. The slip skewered his pride. He sighed, refilled his coffee cup, swallowed the memories with the coffee and forced himself to focus. He had until four o'clock to file something on David Lockwood, and he had absolutely no idea where that story was going to come from.

• • • •

It was early, and traffic on the trade show floor was light. Most of the decorated booths were empty, standing in wait for the day's carnival action to begin. Delta Software had a small, nondescript booth at the back of the convention center. As he approached, Peter noticed a trio of salesmen joking in one corner. In another, a systems engineer was testing the booth's computer equipment.

Peter walked up to the sales trio.

"Hello," he said. "I'm looking for Brian Tucker. Is he around?"

"Tucker? I don't know him. He in marketing?" one of the salesmen asked with a customer-ready smile.

"Engineering, I think."

"Oh. You better try the home office. You got the number?"

Peter shook his head and reached for the business card the salesman waved.

"Thanks," he said, turning away.

Peter strolled over to a vacant corner and pulled his new cell phone out of his breast pocket. He'd gotten his hands on an early release of Motorola's latest model, the <u>MicroTAC Elite</u>. At 3.9 ounces versus twelve to sixteen ounces for most cell phones,  it was the lightest and most advanced cell phone of the day. It was the first to include an integrated phone book and automated voicemail; important tools of his trade, Peter had decided, even if it did cost him more than six hundred dollars.

He punched up the number for Delta Software. In short order he learned that Tucker was out of the office this week, but that the receptionist could not—or would not—say where he was or when he would return. Peter flipped the phone closed with a sigh. *What a waste,* he thought. Ten to one this Tucker character would be popping by his booth any minute. Peter made a mental note to check the booth once more before the end of the day and promptly forgot about the errant engineer.

Feeling the press of humanity as the trade show filled to noisy capacity, Peter automatically looked for breathing space. He hated the penned-in feeling crowds gave him. Glancing around, he noticed a small man with a pencil-thin moustache enjoying a private cigarette at a corner table.

"Mind if I join you?' he asked, wandering over and pulling his pack of Camels out of his breast pocket.

The man shook his head and buried his nose in his exhibit guide to avoid further conversation. Peter shrugged, lit his cigarette and puffed slowly, trying unsuccessfully to shed the images of Jessica that continued to haunt him.

As the reluctant bystander, he relived Jessica's adoring smile, Alex's possessive kiss, and the brilliant white flash of Esther Gibson's sapphire ring lighting them as if bestowing a hallowed blessing on their union.

Peter opened his eyes and sat up straight. In his mind's eye, Lockwood raised his right hand and the screen behind him sparked in finale as a brilliant, blue and white star exploded into the audience and disappeared. A smile tugged at the corner of Peter's mouth. "You clever bastard," he chuckled. He'd gotten the message. He still didn't know what it meant, but he knew how to find out.

Tossing aside his cigarette, Peter flipped open his cell and dialed. A moment later, he heard the familiar, irritated "Yeah?" that signaled he'd reached Tim Dupree, his most trusted source and closest friend.

"Tim, it's Peter. Can you do me a favor?"

"So what else is new?" a bored-sounding voice replied, accompanied by the nonstop clatter of a keyboard. Tim only stopped programming for life-threatening emergencies and tennis.

"I'd do it myself, but I can't get on the Internet from here," Peter said.

"Okay," Tim replied. "What's up?"

"Data search on David Lockwood. The noise level here is that he's launching a new company. I think it's either home or education related. That's about all I've got."

"Peter, I'm very good. But this is not 2001 and this workstation is not HAL. So you want to be a little more specific. Some keywords would help," Tim said sardonically.

Peter chuckled. "Yeah, okay. 'Lockwood' and any of these: 'education,' 'discovery,' 'interactive multimedia.' And Tim? This may be a real long shot, but try 'Sapphire,' too."

"Sapphire? Is that a code name?"

"It might be. Does it ring a bell?"

"Sort of. I'll ask around the engineering groups. We've got a few ex-Trxtonites here, maybe someone's heard something."

"Great. Thanks. Call me as soon as you can. I'm on deadline."

"Yep." The line went dead.

Peter sat back down at the table, pulled a cigarette from his pack and lit it. He took out his notebook and flipped back to Lockwood's presentation. He studied the three holograms that Lockwood had chosen: the Santa Maria, the Wright Brothers, Apollo 11.

"I'm missing something," he muttered. "I know I'm missing something, but what?"

Peter looked at the holograms from every angle and jotted down every thought that occurred to him. He had a talent for pulling facts from unconnected places, seeing the hidden picture emerge, connecting the dots. It made him very good at his job. If he worked at this one long enough, he was sure he could find the message Lockwood sought to hide. *Discoveries, firsts, breakthroughs; the technology-changers of their day*, he thought, running each frame independently in his mind's eye.

Whatever Lockwood was building, Peter knew, he would consider it to be all of those things. Maybe that was the message Lockwood was sending: *Hey, I'm great. I've got the technology game-changer, and none of you are smart enough to have a clue as to what I'm really doing.*

That would be vintage Lockwood, all right, Peter thought, as he reran the entire film again in his mind, frame by frame, searching for the pattern.

"Ladies and gentlemen, the discovery of America."

As if they were one continuous image, Peter recalled the appearance of Columbus's Santa Maria sailing the ocean, the Wright brothers' airplane as it lifted gracefully into the air, then tumbled and faded into the 3-D image of Apollo 11 landing on the moon.

Nice presentation, Peter thought for the hundredth time. The way those holograms moved across the audience caught everyone by surprise. Those smooth transitions from one image to the other.

Peter tossed his notebook aside. The realization was as welcome as a Royal Flush in a high stakes poker game. He grabbed his cell phone and redialed.

"Tim, It's Peter. I've got it. I know what Lockwood is doing. He's doing video. Internet streaming video."

"Nope," Tim snorted. "It can't be done. We've tried. Everybody's tried. Technology's not there yet. We're two, maybe three years away."

"Tim, listen to me. It's the only thing that makes sense. He showed these amazing holograms, and they moved like video from his laptop. Seriously. His laptop."

"Yeah, well, IBMers were playing around with holograms in the 1970s. It's all smoke and mirrors, Peter. BFD."

"But these holograms weren't static projections. They moved, together, in one continuous motion. Motion pictures, Tim. Internet video."

"Impossible," Tim countered. "Can't be done."

"Exactly," Peter said. "The voyage to the New World, airplane flight, lunar landing—they couldn't be done either. Until they could. Every technical problem has a technical solution, right?"

"Of course."

"Lockwood's brilliant enough to find a breakthrough solution to a technical problem no one else could, isn't he?" Peter asked. The keyboard had stopped clacking. Tim was listening closely.

"Yeah, so?" The first shade of doubt appeared in Tim's tone. It gave Peter more confidence that he was on the right track.

"I think he did. That's what those holograms signify. They weren't just pretty pictures to wow the crowd. They were examples of Internet streaming video. Tim, you had to be here. I know I'm right. I've got the real story," Peter declared.

Tim was silent, thinking, piecing it together methodically and, Peter hoped, coming up with the same answer he had.

"So what if you are right?" Tim asked. "You can't run with a story like that. Not without a competent engineer on the record to back you up. Nobody will believe you. You'll be a laughingstock in the Valley. It'll be worse than TriCorp. No one in the engineering community will ever talk to you again."

Peter's fingers tightened around the phone. His breath quickened. Tim was right. He felt the weight of reality hit him.

"Tim," he spoke rapidly. "Ask around your Trxton buddies again. Find someone who knows something. Someone I can talk to. Please."

"I'll try," he said. "But don't count on it."

Peter tried in vain to shut out the doubt in Tim's voice.

"I did find out one thing, though," Tim added. "You were right about Sapphire. It's a code name. I hope that helps."

"Yeah, it does. Thanks, Tim."

Peter stood up, stretched and grabbed his briefcase to head back to the Hilton and work all his Valley contacts. The Valley was a gossipy place. Someone had to know something.

"Excuse me, did I hear you say you were looking for Brian Tucker?"

Peter turned and faced a young man in his early twenties with blond hair pulled back in a ponytail. He glanced at Peter as he pulled at the wispy moustache brushing his lips.

"Yes, I am."

"I thought I saw you at our booth this morning. I work for Delta. What'd they tell you?"

"At the booth? That I could reach Brian at the office, but so far…"

"Well, they're lying."

"Oh?" Peter resisted the urge to pull out his notebook. The guy looked nervous enough already. *So, there is a story around this Tucker guy*, he thought.

"Brian's disappeared. No one knows where he is."

The young man's voice dropped to a whisper. He looked anxiously around the convention floor and back to Peter.

"Look, how about if I buy you a cup of coffee and you fill me in?" Peter asked, placing his hand lightly on the young man's arm.

He paused and focused on Peter's badge. "You're a reporter aren't you?"

"Peter Ellis with the *Valley Tribune*."

Peter extended his hand and waited patiently for his companion to identify himself. He stared at Peter, his expression apprehensive.

Finally, he thrust a fine-boned hand at Peter. "I'm Joe," he said. "But no last name," he said. "I could get in trouble talking to you."

"I don't need your name at all," Peter replied, steering him toward a nearby green and white umbrella that signaled the presence of a beverage cart. They collected their drinks—coffee for Peter, a Coke for Joe—and sat down at the closest table.

"Papers find people, don't they? Without the police being involved?"

"Sometimes."

Joe tugged absentmindedly at his moustache. "It's just that I'm really worried about Brian this time."

"What do you mean this time?"

"Well, the first thing that you should know is that Brian has done this kind of thing before."

"Often?" Peter asked.

"No, just once. Almost a year ago. He left the office around two a.m., and then he didn't come back for three days. Everyone, especially the product marketing guys, freaked because—" Joe stopped abruptly. Peter held his breath, willing him to continue.

"You see that demo we're doing? The new 3-D video game?" Joe asked pointing. Peter nodded.

"Well, that's about ninety percent due to Brian. Without Brian Tucker, Delta would be just another me-too product company instead of having a shot at the big time. So when Brian disappears everyone freaks, right? Well, three days later he's back without a word to anyone. No explanation. He just starts coding again and everyone is thrilled. No one even asks why.

"Now he's gone and done it again. We were supposed to room together at Circus Circus. But Brian never showed up and he's not at the office either. Forget what they told you about that."

"Could I take some notes?" Peter asked. "It'll help me remember."

Joe nodded and Peter pulled out his notebook. "Do you know if Brian had any problems at work or home recently?" he asked. "Anything suspicious?"

"There was one odd thing," Joe replied, stroking his moustache, lost in thought. He turned back to Peter and spoke rapidly, in a hushed tone.

"About a month ago, around the middle of December, Brian turned into a zombie. He walked around mumbling something about not getting his last puzzle. No one had any idea what he was talking about and he sure as hell wouldn't explain it.

"Then about a week ago he started working like a machine. He got that demo we're running over there finished in about three days. I guess everyone pretty much thought he was over his zombie phase. Or they hoped so, anyway."

Joe shrugged. "That's all I know." He studied Peter intently. "Think you can find him?"

Peter reviewed his notes. "And you don't know what he meant by this puzzle? The one he was looking for?

Joe shook his head and stood.

Standing, Peter reached in his pocket and handed Joe a card. "If you think of anything else, call me, okay?"

Joe nodded. He paused again, then asked, "If you find out anything, can you let me know?"

"Sure, but I'll need to know how to get in touch with you."

"Oh, yeah." Joe smiled slightly, and pulled out a stained and well-thumbed business card. He looked a little embarrassed at its condition.

"I don't use many of these," he said.

"Yeah, I know that one," Peter agreed. "I've got a good buddy at Sun Microsystems and I doubt he even has a card. Thanks for your time. I'll let you know."

They shook hands and Joe disappeared into the trade show throng. Peter turned in the opposite direction, trudging wearily through the convention center corridor to the bank of hotel elevators on the mezzanine floor. The corridor was deserted. The trade show was in full swing. It was 2:30 pm, ninety minutes before his deadline and, as Tim had so directly reminded him, he didn't have squat for copy. As he walked, he left another message for Tim and a half dozen others who were equally plugged into the industry grapevine.

The elevator doors opened. Peter stepped inside, pushed the button for the thirty-second floor and slumped against the back wall of the elevator. He checked his phone again. The "no messages" light in his voice mailbox was maddening.

He heard the commotion as the elevator glided to a stop at the fifth floor. The doors opened to reveal a woman and two men, their voices raised in heated discussion, and Peter heard what sounded like a final command:

"Not now. I need time to think," David Lockwood barked, holding up his hand to his entourage as he stepped inside the elevator, alone.

He glanced in Peter's direction, face tight, clearly agitated. Then he focused his attention on the blinking white numbers indicating the upward progression of the elevator. Peter saw "30" lit up in the elevator's push-button wall plate. They had just passed the fifth floor. Peter had twenty-five floors to make his pitch.

"Mr. Lockwood. I'm Peter Ellis, with the *Valley Tribune*. I really enjoyed your keynote yesterday morning." Peter's tone was respectful. He wanted Lockwood to know he understood that he was in the presence of greatness. Lockwood gave no indication that he had heard a sound.

6,7,8. Three floors slipped away.

"Those holograms were particularly impressive," Peter added, receiving a curt nod in return. Peter breathed an inward sigh of relief. He'd gotten Lockwood to respond. *First hurdle down*, he thought. Peter watched the white circles light up counting down the seconds he had left.

10,11,12

"Personally, I liked the blue and white star at the end. It reminded me of a sapphire."

In of his peripheral vision, Peter saw Lockwood's jaw tighten slightly.

"I did some checking and I believe that you've got a new Internet set-top box in development. Code name 'Sapphire.'"

Lockwood refused to acknowledge the statement. He shifted his weight from one foot to the other and stared straight ahead.

"But not just any Internet set-top box. Yours is the real technology breakthrough. It runs a video signal across an IP network instead of through a satellite or cable connection. Internet streaming video. The first of its kind."

Lockwood's head swiveled in Peter's direction, his expression scornful. "Ridiculous. You don't know what you are talking about. It's impossible."

Peter ignored the sarcasm. "Unless it is. Shift the universe: stop time, suspend gravity. Make the impossible, possible."

Lockwood leveled his laser-like eyes at Peter and Peter felt the raw power of his presence. "Congratulations. You were paying attention." Lockwood's tone was mocking. He turned away and resumed staring at the numbers marking the upward progression of the elevator.

15, 16. The numbers flashed.

"I got the message. I know what you're doing."

Lockwood chuckled. "I doubt that."

Why because I'm a dumb ass reporter and not a brilliant engineer?

"I got it from the holograms."

18,19

"How?" Lockwood demanded, after several more seconds had elapsed.

Peter glanced at Lockwood. Lockwood stared back, his features a mix of suspicion and curiosity. Peter could see that the technocrat in Lockwood forced him to ask the question. Lockwood had to have a technical explanation to satisfy himself that Peter was merely guessing, and hoping Lockwood would be foolish enough to give himself away. Peter knew then that he had read the man correctly.

"Three points," Peter responded, fighting to keep his voice calm against the rapid beating of his heart. He had one chance to get this right.

20,21

"First message you sent: all of those holograms illustrated firsts, the technical breakthroughs of their day. They'd never been done before. They were impossible. They couldn't be done until Columbus, the Wright Brothers and Armstrong proved they could. Whatever you're doing, Mr. Lockwood, has to be a true technology breakthrough. It's something that only you have the vision, the innovation and the skill to do."

Lockwood acknowledged Peter's point with a slight nod of his head.

"Interesting. Naïve but interesting. Do you have any other brilliant insights to share?" He focused on Peter, reengaging that mind-bending, iron will Peter had experienced earlier. Peter fought for confidence and pressed forward, ignoring the flashing elevator orbs.

22,23.

"Second message: those holograms moved out over the heads of the audience. Most holograms are static projections. If they move at all, it's herky jerky. Your holograms moved smoothly. Not just pictures. Moving pictures. Video.

"Plus, they flowed together, one image faded seamlessly into the next. Not the kind of start-stop you'd expect to see with static holograms pieced together for some special effect. You demonstrated digitized video streaming over an IP network in real time. True Internet streaming video."

Peter turned toward him now meeting his gaze unflinchingly. Lockwood's eyes narrowed.

"I liked the third message the best," Peter continued. Beads of sweat had formed under his collar, coating the back of his neck.

24,25. The numbers flashed.

"Each of those holograms was more than a technical breakthrough, though that was impressive enough. They also opened up a new universe: Columbus, the New World; the Wright Brothers, aviation; Armstrong, interplanetary exploration. Internet streaming video, especially the video on demand that everyone is waiting for, opens up the Internet to the consumer universe. It's the killer app," he said with conviction.

Peter heard a sharp intake of breath, indicating surprise and consternation. He had scored the right points. Now he had to get Lockwood to admit it. That would require finesse and luck.

"In a couple of years we'll be able to watch movies on our laptops. Everybody's been promising this stuff. You're the only one who's actually done it." Peter finished his summation and looked expectantly at Lockwood.

Lockwood regarded him suspiciously. "You got all that from the holograms?"

"Yes. One question, Mr. Lockwood, just one. Am I right? Yes or no?"

Peter knew that the binary question (yes/no; on/off) was the only hope he had of confirmation. Lockwood would never volunteer a detail. At this point, a company executive would have evaded him; a marketing dweeb would have tried to spin him. Lockwood was an engineer. Peter was betting that the engineer in Lockwood would feel compelled to answer a direct binary question. Lockwood leaned against the back of the elevator. His expression was vague, his raw power contained. They passed the twenty-eighth floor. To Peter's heightened sense of awareness, the elevator appeared to be traveling faster now. Sweat poured down his back.

"Sapphire. Internet streaming video. Yes or no?" Peter asked again.

29, 30

The elevator slowed toward its stop. In three seconds, Lockwood would walk out of the elevator, step into the hallway and take Peter's career with him. As the elevator doors slid open, Lockwood turned toward Peter, his brown eyes so intense Peter felt as if they were boring a hole in his skull. "I'll give you some free advice. Follow the old saying, and write about what you know."

Capping the statement with a cryptic smile, Lockwood exited without another word.

Peter entered his room and tossed his briefcase on the bed.

Lockwood had thrown down the gauntlet. *If you think you know what I'm doing, report it. If you've got the stones for it, hang it out there, and see if you're really as smart as you think you are. But be prepared for the consequences if you're wrong.*

There is a Valley of Death, Lockwood had warned in his keynote. Peter had been through that valley once and nearly lost his career. He slumped on his bed, staring at his empty laptop screen. Did he have the courage to risk it again, on a bigger story, with more at stake, and only his belief that he could read between the lines of Lockwood's statements for corroboration? Did he have the stones for it? There was only one way to find out.

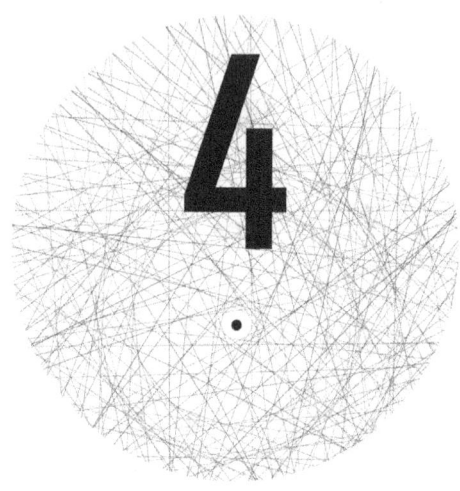

PETER'S STORY ON DAVID LOCKWOOD'S SAPPHIRE PROJECT SCOOPED everyone, including the *Wall Street Journal*. Lockwood's caustic comment was meant to intimidate, to undermine his confidence in his own reporting; and in the murky shadow of TriCorp, it almost worked. But Peter persisted, found a songbird, a source who could confirm the details about Sapphire on the record and convinced Ben to publish. When the story hit the wires, the publicity forced Lockwood into the open. He talked to the networks and national news magazines. Though Lockwood still hadn't returned any of his calls, it was only a matter of time, Peter mused, as he pulled into the parking lot of the *Valley Tribune*.

The paper took up the entire third floor of an older brick building on Hamilton Avenue. With its airy garden courtyard and wrought-iron staircase, its architecture attempted a blend of utilitarian office space and California mission style, and partially succeeded. Peter whistled as he hit the stairs at full speed. He was still feeling the afterglow that breaking a major story like Sapphire gave him.

Tina greeted him with a warm smile. "Congratulations," she said, handing him his messages. A few more solid wins like Sapphire and his career would be back on track. Then, he thought with satisfaction, he could leave the *Tribune* for one of the bigger dailies.

Won't bother me to leave this place, Peter thought, glancing around the modest lobby. Boswell had purchased the paper three years earlier and had done some remodeling. Peter didn't think the new bright orange chairs and oak-laminated tables in the lobby were much of an improvement over the old furnishings. He considered the minor awards the paper had won, proudly displaced in the lobby: a joke compared to what was possible for staffers on the big dailies. Peter himself was aiming for nothing less than a Pulitzer or two—within the next couple of years.

Could be worse, he reminded himself as he headed down the glass partitioned hallway to his cubbyhole office. At least the paper made a little money, and, thanks to Ben's formidable presence, the reporters didn't have to suck up to advertising the way they did at some of the other local papers.

Besides Adam had helped the staff immensely by replacing the ancient IBM Selectric typewriters that had dominated the newsroom for decades with a network of Macintosh computers, linked to each other and to the Internet. Peter, for one, applauded the choice, and was eternally grateful he didn't have to deal with Windows.

He entered his office, hung up his leather jacket and tossed his messages on his desk. The desk was littered with numbers and names written on bits of paper and crammed manila folders stacked high, waiting to be filed. Yellowing copies of newspapers like the *Wall Street Journal* and *San Jose Mercury News* were stacked in one corner. A spare tennis racket and Nike duffel bag were tossed in the other. A framed and signed photograph of Andre Agassi winning his 1992 Wimbledon men's title hung above his desk. An expensive, nautical brass wall clock and a couple of Cape Cod sailing prints were the only other adornments in Peter's otherwise nondescript quarters. He settled into his chair and flipped on the Mac, scanning his emails, looking for some response to the dozens of calls he'd made about Draco Communications' Horizon project from the trade show. He was inches away from another breaking story. He just needed one person to go on the record.

The Internet set-top box war between Lockwood's Sapphire and Draco's Horizon is going to be brutal, Peter thought with enormous satisfaction. Lockwood the renegade engineer versus Draco, the corporate titan. Peter was delighted to have a better than ringside seat at the confrontation. His role in chronicling the blow-by-blow, if he played it right, would virtually guarantee his future as a well-known and highly respected business journalist and win him his ultimate prize—an editorial position on the *Wall Street Journal.*

The hunt enthralled him, as always; the more competitive the better. To win as a journalist meant he needed to break open the product details on Horizon—so far no one had—but he was holding his breath. Even more importantly, he had to put the heat on Draco, and keep it there as the Horizon project moved forward from development to roll out. That meant putting the heat on Alex Kavanagh.

Peter chuckled softly as he walked through his notes on both Horizon and Sapphire. The directions the two products were taking epitomized their creators. Lockwood's Sapphire Project, with its ability to stream video in real time and on demand, would bring the broadcast picture quality of TV to the home computer through the Internet. It was a technology breakthrough, future focused, cutting edge, an engineer's dream product. All the cool kids would want Sapphire. But it would be years before Sapphire-like functionality would be affordable and widely available enough to appeal to the average consumer.

Horizon, by contrast, was a safe bet. It was a hybrid set-top box able to bring TV into the Internet Age by bridging the old analog world and the emerging digital one. By converting analog TV signals to digital, Horizon would allow people to run both their TV and their Internet-connected computer from a single system similar in look and feel to their current cable box. Consumers would be comfortable with the Horizon set-top box because it would move them slowly in baby steps, to an unknown world. Draco's Horizon was a safe, predictably profitable, business play by a global conglomerate intent on expanding its market domination.

Peter picked up the phone and dialed, cajoling sources, trading favors and tracking down leads until at last, with a tip from Charlie, he got what he needed.

Draco Communications Developing TV–to–Internet Converter Box

Horizon vs. Sapphire: Let the Internet Wars Begin

By Peter Ellis, Tribune *staff*

In a bold move to dominate the emerging battle for control of the information highway, Draco Communications has begun development on an Internet set-top box, code name Horizon. Horizon will compete directly against Sapphire, the new Internet set-top box created by David Lockwood. Lockwood's Sapphire Project is the first product of its kind to offer Internet streaming video...

"Hey, Ellis. You ever heard of a beat list?"

Peter swiveled his chair in the direction of the voice. Sam Parker perched on his crutches in the doorway, right leg raised to keep his weight off his cast. Sam was tall and thin, with a prominent Roman nose and fiery dark eyes. Dressed as he was today in a bright pink t-shirt and black jeans, Peter thought he looked like a flamingo. A very angry flamingo. "Morning, Sam. What's up?"

"Draco Communications, that's what's up," Sam replied, hobbling into Peter's office and slamming the door. "Draco is my company or have you conveniently forgotten?"

"I got a tip at the trade show. I figured I'd check it out."

Sam pulled himself up on his crutches. "We had a deal. You got ninety-eight percent of the hot companies in the Valley and I got the other two. Draco was one of my two," he snapped, swaying slightly.

"I would have brought you into it, but it heated up faster and hotter than I figured."

"Like hell you would."

"Listen, Sam—"

"No! You listen!" Sam interrupted. "I'm tired of you grabbing my headlines and getting away with it."

Peter felt his blood pressure rise. He knew the only way Sam would have had the story on Draco was if the *Merc* had published it first. Since they'd split up the beat a few weeks ago when Sam joined the *Trib*, Sam had written nothing but puff pieces on Draco. Peter was tempted to tell Sam he didn't have the balls to be a reporter and to try a career in PR. But he controlled the impulse and adopted a conciliatory stance. Sam was tight with Adam, and Peter didn't need the grief.

"Okay, you're right. I should have brought you into this, but my key source is an old college buddy of mine. He wouldn't feel comfortable talking to anyone else. You've got sources like that, Sam. We all do. Can we just forget about this?"

Sam mulled that over. He looked mollified for a moment, until his expression hardened. "No. You're still poaching, Ellis, no matter how cleverly you try to explain it. From now on, stay out of my way."

Sam wheeled around, opened the door and hobbled away. Peter shook his head and told himself that Sam would never last. Then he picked up his pack of Camels and headed down the hall.

"Peter, can I see you a second?" Ben called as Peter passed his office.

Ben was a medium-sized, broad shouldered man in his early fifties with keen brown eyes and a smooth style of speech reminiscent of his native Virginia. An experienced, hard-nosed editor Adam had recruited from the *Washington Post*, Ben routinely demanded and got the best from his small reporting staff. As he entered the office, Peter saw Adam standing beside Ben, his face tight and angry. Peter sighed, shoved his cigarettes in his pocket, closed the door and leaned against it.

"Ben, I'm asking you to hold this fucking story. We can't print a story this farfetched about Draco Communications. They're one of our biggest advertisers." Adam's voice had a caustic edge.

He turned and faced Peter, tugging irritably at his trademark suspenders. Peter studied him impassively. Peter always found Boswell's starched white shirts and matching suspenders and bow tie—they were paisley, today—amusingly pretentious in the casual *Tribune* offices. Now, as he stood fuming at Ben and Peter, his wardrobe made him look ridiculous.

"I was just looking over your Draco story. You sure about this?" Ben asked calmly.

"I've got three sources, Ben. All very trustworthy."

"We're not running this," Adam stated flatly.

"We have to run it," Peter insisted. "Ben, I pulled in just about all my markers to get this story. What more do you want?"

"I," Adam said slowly, emphasizing the personal pronoun, "want more proof. Get someone to go on the record. Get a name to go with this fucking story or forget it. We're not running anonymous sources. Especially from you," he added for emphasis.

"I can't do that. My sources all work with Draco. If they went on the record, it'd be like chopping their legs off at the knees." Peter took a step toward Adam. Almost involuntarily, Adam stepped back, but he caught himself and held his ground, fixing Peter with a belligerent stare.

"We'll let you know," he barked, striding out of the office.

Peter watched Adam's back disappear. He turned to face Ben.

"You didn't do yourself any favors there," Ben said.

"C'mon, Ben. A little tension between publishing and editorial never hurts," Peter replied.

Ben wasn't smiling. "That's not the real issue. Sam came and talked to me about this story. He has a legitimate gripe."

"We worked it out."

"I'm glad to hear it, but Sam's not the only one on my staff who's complained lately. I know you think you have something to prove, but I want you to go easy."

"I do have something to prove, don't I, Ben?"

Ben stared hard at Peter and slowly nodded. Peter saw the concession and moved in.

"Then let's be honest. Sapphire and now Horizon. They're red hot and they're exclusives. Sam isn't complaining because I'm in his territory. He's complaining because I'm getting stories that he'd never get in a million years."

Ben sighed. "You're missing the point. You're a good reporter, Peter. You may be my best reporter, and some big city editors would probably ignore the games you've started playing again. Some might even reward you for it. But this is a community newspaper."

Don't remind me, Peter thought sourly. Ben tossed Peter a look of disappointment, almost as if he could read his thoughts.

"I want to see that sense of community in my staff. Including you, understand?"

Peter started to respond but Ben was just getting warmed up.

"The trouble with you is that all you see are the headlines. When they break. Where they run. 'Page One' or nothing. You've never once stopped to see that the real story isn't the headline. It's the people behind the headline. The 'human' in 'human interest.' Until you do, you'll never be half the reporter you think you are."

Peter gritted his teeth and responded the way Ben expected. "I understand."

"I hope you do because I've got something here that you can really sink your teeth into. Word has it that MediaBuilders is on an acquisition binge. Check it out." Ben thrust a page of scrawled notes at him. Peter felt his stomach clench; a bitter taste swamped his tongue.

"I can't cover MediaBuilders. Give it to Sam."

"You mind telling me why?" Ben queried.

Peter hesitated, framing his answer. Then he looked Ben straight in the eye and gave him the bad news. "MediaBuilders is one of my father's firm's biggest clients. My sister Margaret is their corporate counsel."

"I see," Ben said. He looked as disappointed as Peter felt.

Peter didn't blame him. No one with Peter's ambitions would turn down coverage on a company like MediaBuilders—unless they had to. It was just as obvious to Peter that Ben didn't relish another run-in with Margaret. For most people, one unpleasant encounter with Margaret was enough. Peter had dealt with it all of his life.

Ben shook his head. "Sam's not ready for this one. If you can't do it…" His voice trailed off.

"Sam and I will make it work," Peter insisted. "I'll back him up, make sure we get what we need. Okay? But let's keep it between us. Sam doesn't need to know."

"Okay, Peter," Ben agreed. "Just know I'm counting on you."

Peter nodded. He'd disappointed Ben with TriCorp and Ben had given him a second chance when most other editors would have tossed his butt out the window. More importantly, Ben showed Peter that he believed in him. He wanted to keep Ben's respect, but if he didn't play the MediaBuilders game right, he knew that losing Ben's respect would be the least of his worries. Leaving Ben's office, he stopped just long enough to collect his cigarettes and head for the patio. It was forty degrees outside, still threatening rain.

He struck a match, lit a Camel and inhaled deeply, seeking escape from fragments of childhood memories that still cut like shards of glass: a carelessly thrown ball, a broken vase, a hard slap across the face from his ever-vigilant sister; a second, even harder for being so weak as to cry. He recoiled at the thought of a confrontation with Margaret over MediaBuilders. With everything she had at stake there, it would cost him more than a blow to his career and ego. It could cost him everything he had.

Peter tossed the cigarette butt and the memories in the sand bucket near the back door and walked up the stairs into the production department. Earlier in its history, when it was a larger more profitable paper, the *Tribune* had its own printing press like the bigger dailies. These days, the cavernous production room housed only layout, the classifieds, the photo lab and the paper's frustratingly incomplete morgue files.

It was two in the afternoon, and the production team was rushing to meet the four o'clock deadline that applied to everything except the front sections of the paper. Peter ignored the frantic activity and checked layout for the business section. Thanks to Charlie's willingness to back up his specs privately with Ben, Peter's Horizon story was running. The story would surprise all the other local papers. He would probably make the wires for the second time this week, and Ben would be pleased despite his bullshit lecture about community.

As he headed down the hallway, Peter saw Sam about to enter his office.

"I've been looking for you," Sam said as Peter approached.

"It's too late. The Horizon story is in layout."

Sam shrugged. "Actually, I wanted to talk to you about Media-Builders. You had any lunch?"

"Not yet."

"Want to go for a pizza?"

Peter studied Sam's face; his facial muscles twitched in an expression stuck somewhere between glee and suspicion. He and Sam had started on neutral ground; not friends, but not enemies either. Peter had never been concerned about making friends with other reporters. The job came first. That had been true even when the other reporter was Jessica. Despite the Draco Communications sparring, Sam was making a friendly gesture. Or maybe, Peter thought, he'd made it, when he'd suggested Sam for the MediaBuilders assignment. Either way, he was hungry. "Yeah, okay. I'll meet you downstairs."

• • • •

The wind slapped their faces as they headed across the street to Mama Jo's Pizzeria. The aroma of garlic, tomatoes, onions and spices that greeted them as they entered the restaurant was a welcome relief from the dank day. They ordered an extra-large deluxe pizza, with coffee for Peter and a Coke for Sam, and slid into a booth by the fireplace. A kid who looked like he was still in high school sauntered over a few minutes later and unceremoniously dropped the pizza between them.

"Let's talk about MediaBuilders," Sam said, picking up a large piece of pizza and taking a generous bite.

"Okay, what do you want to know?"

"The straight scoop." Sam was studying him. *Fishing for*

something, Peter thought, although he couldn't imagine what. He pulled a piece of pizza from the tin plate and took a few bites.

"It seems pretty straightforward to me. MediaBuilders wants to set itself up for the information highway. They've got the programming content covered with the studios, newspapers and magazines they own. But not much else. They've got lots of holes to fill if they want to be a really big player so they're on a buying spree, collecting companies to fill in the gaps in their strategy." Peter started in on a second piece of pizza. He was trying not to sound condescending. *Sam should know this stuff*, he thought.

"That's not what I mean," Sam answered, shaking his head for emphasis. "You could have knocked me over with a feather this morning when Ben gave me this assignment. I asked myself, what's the deal here? Why is Peter Ellis of all people walking away from one of the biggest stories of the year? Could be he's had a pang of conscious over poaching that Horizon story?"

"I didn't poach that—"

Sam waved his hand at Peter for silence. "I don't care anymore. It's over. MediaBuilders, that's different. I couldn't figure that one out at all. So I started checking around."

Sam stopped talking, took another piece of pizza, finished it in three bites and grabbed another. Peter stared at Sam's jaws as he chewed.

"You know, I always wondered about you, Peter," Sam said, a strand of cheese clinging to his chin. "I was curious about the Porsche, the expensive clothes, the townhouse in a fancy Menlo Park neighborhood. All that on just twenty-two thousand a year? It didn't add up."

Peter felt queasy. The pizza he'd just eaten wasn't sitting so well, now. His family business was his and his alone. That was the reason he didn't use his full name as his byline. Sam wiped the cheese from his chin with a napkin, then wadded up the napkin and tossed it aside. "But now I know, Peter Andrew Ellis III. You don't use your full name, do you?"

"Too many letters," Peter replied.

"Whatever. I found out that Daddy is a big-time corporate lawyer in the city, and there's family money as well."

"Some."

"Some," Sam snorted. "Your family is on the Forbes 400."

"What's your point, Sam?"

"It explains your sudden lack of interest in MediaBuilders. Your father's firm does most of their legal work."

Peter relaxed a little. "Makes sense, doesn't it?"

"Sure. Except I called a lawyer friend in the city. He's totally plugged in, but I surprised him this time. He said he didn't know Andrew Ellis had a son."

Peter felt the rupture deep inside. Carefully sutured wounds split open, burning. He smothered the feeling quickly, with a chuckle. "I guess that says a lot about the quality of your sources, doesn't it?"

Sam's face blanched. He glared at Peter. "Bastard," he growled.

Peter regarded him coolly. "I believe we've established that's not the case."

Sam turned a brighter shade of red and a bead of perspiration formed on his upper lip. Peter figured he'd made his point, and offered the olive branch. "Look, I didn't plan to cut you out of the Draco story. It just happened. But MediaBuilders is a fair trade, isn't it? Let's call a truce, do our jobs and we both win, okay?"

Sam regarded him suspiciously. "Yeah, sure. Now you want to play nice? Or maybe Daddy's got his thumb on the trust fund?"

Peter stood up abruptly. "MediaBuilders is still my company. I was doing you a favor. You don't want it? Fine. I'll ask Ben to assign it to someone else. And for the record, I don't have a fucking trust fund."

He threw a few bills on the table and stomped out of the restaurant before Sam could grab his crutches. The drizzle had turned to rain. The rain soaked his clothes and extinguished every cigarette he tried to light as he trudged down the street trying to escape the words: *"He said he didn't know Andrew Ellis had a son."*

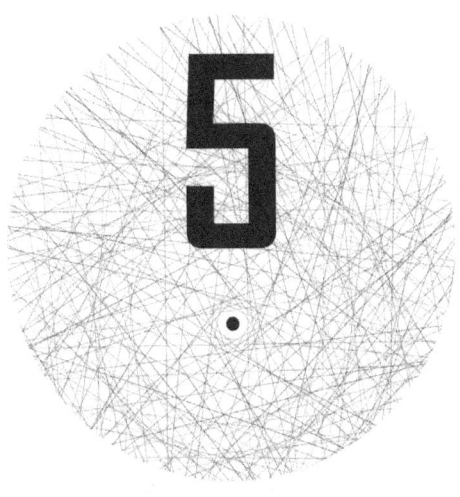

AT PRECISELY NINE-THIRTY A.M. THAT WEDNESDAY, TOBY EASTMAN entered the lobby of Draco Communications' engineering and manufacturing facility in Cupertino, just down the street from Apple's corporate headquarters. The building was typical of the area, a four-story white wall and glass rectangular office complex. In front, surrounded by formal garden beds, was a twelve-foot sculpture of the Draco logo.

Toby glanced around the busy lobby. In its center, three young women worked the large circular reception desk, handing out visitor badges to the customers, suppliers and partners that made Draco's global supply chain hum. At each corner, overstuffed brown leather chairs and mahogany tables invited private conversation. Video screens built into the walls ran demos of Draco's latest products and services.

Engineering was on the fourth floor, secured from public entry by coded keypads only employee badges could open. Toby fingered the newly-issued employee badge on his belt loop. He was Jake Mullens, VP of Engineering. As he waited for the elevator, Toby studied his reflection in the polished doors, liking what he saw. He stood just under six feet with the broad chest and arms of a wrestler.

The surgeons had concentrated on his face. They had narrowed his nose, widened his lips and lengthened his chin. The thick, jet-black hair of his youth was now silver. The alterations had been subtle, but effective. No one who knew him as Toby Eastman had yet raised an eyebrow at Jake Mullens. His persona intact, his cover story airtight, he was about to assume command of the only engineering team in the Valley capable of driving David Lockwood to his knees. Toby rubbed his hands in anticipation as he entered the elevator, letting his smile linger as he rose to the fourth floor.

Toby strolled into the large, rectangular conference room and took his rightful place up front. The Horizon development team, all eighteen of them, were there waiting. They had been waiting for at least a half an hour. He had kept them waiting on purpose, because he wanted them on edge; and he could see from the sea of fidgeting bodies and pinched faces in front of him that he had achieved his first objective. The door at the far end of the room opened and Toby watched Alex Kavanagh, VP of Marketing, sit down at the opposite end of the oblong black and chrome conference table. Toby leaned casually against his own small table at the front of the room. His relaxed posture was calculated to lull the team into a false sense of security.

"Good morning," he said smiling. "I'm Jake Mullens, your new VP of Engineering. I thought I'd start out by telling you a bit about myself. I've spent the last ten years as a troubleshooter for DEC, rescuing failing products and engineering teams. As I'm sure most of you know DEC has needed its fair share of rescuing in the last few years," he added to nods, smiles and a few snickers from the engineers.

Digital Equipment Corporation (DEC) was the undisputed market leader during the reign of minicomputers in the 1970s and early 1980s, but the shift to faster, higher capacity Unix workstations from companies like Apollo Computer and Sun Microsystems had ended DEC's dominance by the mid-1990s.

Toby's carefully crafted cover story was perfect. Everybody knew somebody who worked at DEC and when they checked, his role as troubleshooter would be impossible to trace. Troubleshooters were the hired guns of the industry; in and out and on to the next project, often without ever appearing on the company's employee roster.

"But the problems at DEC are nothing compared to what I'm seeing here," his voice rose and hardened. He stood up, placed his hands on the conference table and leaned forward, glaring at the team. Only one of the engineers—and Alex—had the courage to meet his eyes.

The energy in the room dissipated like a vapor as the door opened. Jake's admin walked in and carefully placed a white envelope in front of each member of the Horizon development team. Hands reached forward.

"Just a minute," Toby commanded. "We'll get to those."

Hands pulled back and the team turned toward him in curious expectation.

"As of this moment you are all fired," he said, watching with satisfaction as the entire room burst into noisy protest: gasps, shouts, yelps and demands for an explanation. The faces staring at him were a rainbow of colors from bright red, to sickly pink, ashen and corpse-like white.

"What the hell is going on here?" one engineer demanded to the nods of his fellow team members. "You can't do this."

"I can and I did." Toby turned his piercing black eyes on the young engineer. The engineer's courage fled. Toby motioned for silence. He had them in complete submission, exactly where he wanted them.

"Good. Now we can move forward. In your packets you'll find your official release from the Horizon team, a check for the salary and severance you're entitled to, and a piece of paper with the date and time for a one on one meeting with me. That's your opportunity to convince me that I should hire you back," Toby said, looking at each team member in turn.

"If anyone wants to take their severance and leave, do it now," Toby said, and he watched four members of the team get up and exit the room. He was gratified to see that they were his weakest links, the ones he already planned to replace. He had four others in the room he couldn't afford to lose. They knew it now, too—instead of layoff notices, they'd received bonus letters in their packets. The other ten were solid players, most of whom he would keep if they shaped up and started performing as a disciplined unit. Toby could see he had his work cut out for him.

"All right, you can go now. I'll see you at your one-on-ones," he said, as his team filed out of the room. It would take about a nanosecond for his edicts to hit the local engineering grapevines, which was just fine with him.

"Alex," he called out as Kavanagh prepared to leave with the others. "Do you have a minute?"

Alex froze for a moment and then turned around slowly, signaling his displeasure at the interruption of his schedule with stance and attitude.

Neither of them planned on a long, drawn-out discussion. Both Alex and Jake worked directly for Draco CEO Win Davis, which left Alex with the mistaken impression that Jake couldn't touch him.

"A little harsh, weren't you?" Alex asked.

"You've missed two code freezes and are about to miss a third," Toby responded. "What did you want me to do, coddle them?"

"No. But alienating the entire team is overkill."

"Your team," Toby said, with emphasis on the *your,* is sloppy, lazy and undisciplined. Intimidation is the fastest way to whip them into shape."

"You're going to lose some good people," Alex predicted.

"That's my problem," Toby replied. "Your problem is, we are moving the Horizon intro date up to March thirtieth. That gives you two and a half months to be ready to roll."

"What!" Alex exclaimed. "That's not your call."

Toby ignored the outburst. "I cleared it with Win."

"Look, Mullens I know you've got a hard ass reputation, but you can't just show up and toss everything this team has done for the last six months out the window."

Toby had checked out Alex, as he had the entire team, and knew him to be a weak-willed opportunist, eager to build his reputation on the backs of those who had really earned the glory. *Just like Lockwood and Lieutenant James.* The memory started to pull Toby in a direction he couldn't afford to go; not here, not yet. He squelched his building frustration and turned to Alex with a sardonic smile.

"As I told the engineers, I can and I did. Win knows I can deliver. With this team, that'll be a new experience for him."

Alex's jaw clenched. "I've been delivering."

"You've spent all your time spinning bedtime stories about some mythical Internet fantasy world without any fucking idea what it takes to get it done. I'm here to win the real Internet Wars not sell fairy tales."

"Screw you. You can build the greatest fucking box in the world if the customer doesn't want it, it's shit," Alex sneered. "Marketing drives the features on Horizon. That's straight from Win. I've done the customer research. I've mapped out the competition."

"A hell of a lot of good that does if the competition knows what we're building before we build it." Toby responded, his tone mocking.

He pulled a batch of *Valley Tribune* newspapers out of his briefcase and tossed them on the table in front of Alex. The Horizon headlines glared accusingly.

"This reporter." Toby paused and read the byline. "Peter Ellis. Knows a helluva lot more about our development plans than he should. You own that."

Alex took a step toward Toby. "I don't control the media."

"But you do control our message and our message is spinning out of control. Where is he getting these details?" Toby demanded.

"Ellis is aggressive, connected and well sourced," Alex replied. "He broke Lockwood's Sapphire story, too."

"Excuses! All I get from you people are excuses." Toby felt a dark spike of anger. No one on this team, including Alex, seemed to understand the size of the stakes here. Throwing Lockwood in his face infuriated him.

"Okay, Alex. Ignore him. It's your ass. Ask yourself where your career is going to be if the next story Win reads from this Ellis character is all about the development delays we've been having.

Because it looks like that's exactly where this guy is headed."

Toby stared hard at Alex's face, watching as the anger evaporated and was replaced by a faint flicker of fear.

"Find his sources. Shut him down," Toby commanded.

"I'll take care of Ellis," Alex flared. "I know his Achilles' heel."

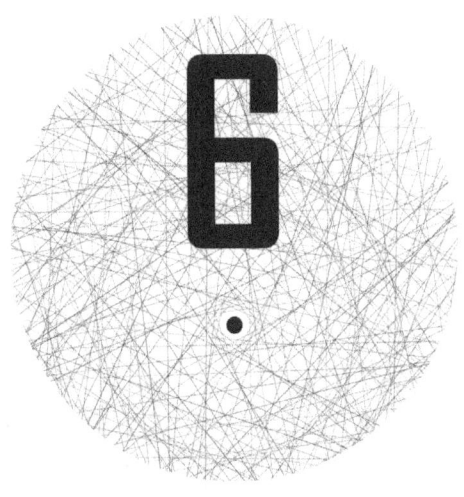

6

January 15, 1994: Hillsborough, California

TIM DUPREE BOUNCED THE TENNIS BALL TWICE AND SERVED. PETER rushed the net and stretched, but the ball arched erratically, bounced twice, and landed untouched on the court.

"That's the match, Ellis," Tim called, as if Peter needed reminding. He was playing badly, too aggressively, too intent on winning and naturally losing in the process.

"Not your day, is it, bro?" Tim laughed, trotting up to the net. Peter won more often than he lost, and Tim was enjoying the turnabout.

Peter shook his head. "Nope. Let's take a break."

"We've got the court for another hour. We've got time for another match."

"Great. Let's take fifteen, and then we'll get back to it." Peter opened the side door of the court and sat down on the nearest white wooden bleacher.

The Racquet Club had twelve regulation-sized courts, and on this perfect, mid-January Saturday afternoon, every court was full. The air was fragrant with the perfume of early pink blossoms, and the oaks ringing the courts waved softly in a light breeze. White, puffy clouds dotted the azure sky.

Tim flopped down next to Peter. The two were a study in physical contrasts. Peter was lean, muscular and tall. Tim was three inches shorter, with a thick waist and heavy legs. What most people noticed first about Tim was the startling shock of white, just above the brow, in his ponytailed black hair. Peter leaned back and let his arms and legs dangle across the bleachers. He closed his eyes and turned his face to the warmth of the sun.

"You're getting old, man." Tim snickered. "It's those cancer sticks you're smoking again."

"If they were good enough for <u>Murrow</u>, they're good enough for me," Peter replied, without opening his eyes.

"The guy died at fifty-seven," Tim reminded him.

"That gives me another twenty-eight years to enjoy my life," Peter responded. "That's probably enough. So, dude, quit stalling, what's that tip you've got for me?"

Tim had sent him a tantalizing email message after lunch confirming the match for four-thirty p.m. and promising him a very hot tip. Peter needed the tip. He owed Ben something hot and nothing he was tracking had panned out. So here he was, counting on Tim to help him out once again. If he chose to, Tim could rightfully take credit for more than a half dozen of Peter's biggest stories including the scoop on Sapphire.

"So what's up?" Peter asked again.

Tim peered at Peter, a hint of a smirk framing his lips. "It's about Horizon. The development team is in shambles. Hardware and software teams are pointing fingers. It looks like they've lost about three weeks of development time, and your buddy Alex Kavanagh is taking a lot of heat for it."

"Couldn't happen to a nicer guy," Peter said, grinning. So far, everything had gone exactly as planned. He was on top of the Horizon coverage in the Valley. He was just about to launch his campaign to win back Jessica. The cloud from TriCorp had all but disappeared. Life felt good.

"Yeah, they just brought in some new VP of Engineering, some major hard ass straight out of DEC to clean things up," Tim added. "But that's not all—"

"Excuse me. Are you guys using this court?"

Peter glanced up and into the deep brown eyes of an athletic, well-endowed brunette who stared back down at him, racket in hand. She wore a pink polo shirt embossed with the Racquet Club logo. A matching pink visor shielded her eyes from the sun.

"We're taking a break, but we have the court for another hour," Peter said, making a quick appraisal and liking what he saw. She was slender yet nicely curved, unlike some of the women he'd seen around the club who looked positively anorexic.

"Would you mind if my friend and I warmed up for a few minutes?" she asked.

Peter glanced over at Tim who shrugged.

"Be my guest," Peter said. The pair trotted over to the net. The brunette's tennis partner was a short Asian girl. Peter watched with casual interest as the girls rallied the ball. As the brunette reached to return a lob, Peter admired the supple, strong lines of her physique. Her bronze tan was a perfect complement to her amber-colored hair, which brushed her shoulders as she moved in the rhythm of the play. Peter was sure she wintered somewhere.

"Nice forehand," Tim said, nodding her direction.

"Nice ass too," Peter said enjoying the scenery.

"You're hopeless, man." Tim replied, shaking his head.

"Beats sitting in front of a CRT screen at two am."

"I'm not as fond of casual encounters as you are."

"I'll take my chances," Peter replied with a shrug. "You said there was something else about Horizon I should know?"

"Oh, yeah, and this is really good, too." Tim leaned forward.

Just then, the girls finished their warm up and wandered back over.

"Thanks so much," the brunette said, standing in front of Peter.

Peter glanced around the courts. They were all still full.

"It doesn't look like you've got a court yet. Do you want to play some doubles?" he asked, standing up and stretching.

He noticed her take a good long look at him. His face crinkled into a grin as he pushed back the lock of wavy brown hair that had fallen across his forehead. She gave her friend a quick glance. "Sure," she said with a warm smile. "I'm Jordan, and this is Grace. And you are?"

"Peter and Tim," he replied, as the foursome took their positions on the court.

Both teams played two up, a signal that the girls were prepared to be aggressive at the net. Jordan served first. The strength of her serve surprised him, and he had to move quickly crosscourt to return it. Grace caught the ball on the bounce and played a perfect drop shot that landed just over the net in front of Tim. The girls had the advantage at the start and they kept it, winning the first two games handily. Peter and Tim battled back for the next game. The competition increased as they traded wins, until Jordan and Grace finally had them, winning three of the five sets to take the match.

Another couple grabbed the court as soon as they finished play. Peter and Tim followed Jordan and Grace on the path to the clubhouse.

"Well, Tim, we got our heads handed to us today," Peter said, as Tim nodded in agreement.

Jordan looked over at him with an amused glint in her eyes and a wicked grin on her face. "We had fun," she said.

You really like to win, don't you, Jordan? he thought, returning her smile with a bright white one of his own. He found that kind of competitive streak appealing.

They stopped in front of the club. The century-old clubhouse, with its looming white pillars, Greek revival architecture and pavilion-style entrance, always reminded Peter of an antebellum mansion; a little too pretentious for his taste, but the club had the best courts in the area and that mattered to him.

"Can we buy you ladies a drink?"

Jordan shook her head. "We've got to run."

She dug into her sports bag, pulled out a business card, scribbled on it, and handed it to Peter. "Call me if you want to play again," she said, turning with Grace and heading for the south parking lot. Peter tucked the card into his breast pocket as he and Tim headed for the opposite side of the club.

"You going to call her?" Tim asked as they walked to their cars.

Peter shrugged. "I'm more interested in chasing that Horizon story right now." He stopped and leaned against his car door. "Can you chat now or do you want me to call you later?"

"Now's fine," Tim said, savoring the moment. "The big news is that Devon O'Reilly is joining the Horizon development team."

"Seriously? David Lockwood's ex-partner?" Peter unlocked the car, grabbed his cigarettes and lit up, ignoring Tim's look of disgust.

"Yep."

Leaning against his car, Peter paused to process that information. Lockwood and O'Reilly were the wunderkinds behind the Trxton PC. Lockwood's forte was developing the hardware, O'Reilly's the blazingly fast operating system and applications.

The acrimonious end to the famed Lockwood-O'Reilly partnership, on the eve of the introduction of the Trxton PC, had fed industry gossip mills for years. To Peter's knowledge no one had ever had the real story. O'Reilly joining Draco added major artillery to Draco's position in the Internet Wars.

"What's his role?" Peter took a final pull of his cigarette and tossed the butt on the ground.

"Not sure. Probably software."

"That narrows it down," Peter said with a laugh.

"Yeah, you're welcome," Tim countered.

"No offense, Tim," Peter replied, giving his friend's shoulder a quick pat. "You know how much I appreciate your help. Tell me, what does O'Reilly do best?"

"He wrote the graphical user interface for Trxton."

"I thought Lockwood developed the interface."

"That's what a lot of people think. Lockwood sure likes to take the credit. But that interface was O'Reilly all the way," he said, scowling.

Peter wasn't surprised by the intensity of Tim's response. He knew Tim idolized Devon O'Reilly.

"So, if I had to guess I'd say O'Reilly's writing the interface for Horizon," Tim added. "It's a critical piece of the software."

"That's a real coup for Draco," Peter muttered almost to himself. He opened his car door and got in. "Thanks Tim. I'll call you when I get something, okay?"

"Sorry, Peter. I won't be around." Tim smiled, a Cheshire cat smile. "I've got a date."

January 15, 1994: Menlo Park, California

Peter spent the rest of Saturday tracking down every lead, rumor and nugget of intelligence he could find on O'Reilly. By three-thirty p.m. he had everything he needed except a response from Draco. He grabbed a cup of coffee, and headed back into his home office to pound out a final urgent message to Kavanagh and the Draco PR team asking for comment, reminding them of the deadline and following up with calls to their cells. Then he called Ben.

"What have you got?" Ben asked.

"Head is, *O'Reilly Joins Draco: The Internet Wars' Next Big Battle.* I'm leading with O'Reilly joining the Horizon development team at Draco. His skill set, the graphical user interface and software applications. How the game changes."

"Okay, good start."

"Below the fold, it's Horizon versus Sapphire," Peter continued, reading from his notes. "Play up the two ex-partners on opposite sides in the Internet Wars, and how each is critical to his product's success. Finish with the history of the Lockwood-O'Reilly partnership. I've got a profile on O'Reilly to run as a companion piece."

"You get comment from anyone at Draco?"

"Not yet. I've left about a dozen messages."

"Give it till four. Then file," Ben said, disconnecting.

"Will do."

Peter finished the story, eye on the clock, and filed it at four p.m. He was especially proud of this one. This week, for the first time in history, the *Valley Tribune* was publishing an online edition. It was the first paper in California and possibly the country to do so, and Peter's story on Devon O'Reilly would lead the coverage.

January 17, 1994: Palo Alto, California

"Close the door," Ben snapped as Peter entered his editor's office Monday morning. The vein on Ben's temple throbbed; his face was contorted. As he stood there in front of Ben's desk, Peter could feel the heat rising off of him.

"I just got off the phone with Alex Kavanagh. He's challenging your story on Devon O'Reilly. He says O'Reilly is not on the Horizon development team. He wants a retraction. He's faxing his statement over now." Ben paused and glared at Peter.

"Damn it, Ellis," he continued. "What the hell are you playing at?"

Peter felt the bile rise in his throat. It almost choked him before he forced it back down. He met Ben's stare with a hard one of his own.

"That's bullshit, Ben. I sourced that story. Everything in there is attributed and on the record. I called and emailed Kavanagh and his PR people twenty times for comment and got stonewalled."

Ben picked up Peter's copy and thrust it toward him. "You sourced it, alright. You sourced everything except the core fact this story was built on. No one in here confirmed that O'Reilly had joined the Horizon team or what he was doing there," Ben jabbed his index finger into the paper. "It's all background."

Ben got up from behind his desk, paper in hand. Peter met him eye for eye. He was determined to stand his ground on this one. He started to speak, but Ben's scowl convinced him to let Ben's anger run its course.

"I'll tell you what you did. You got a hot tip and you ran with it. You built the story around it without nailing down the core facts. Admit it." Ben tossed the paper on his desk. "You put this paper and me at risk on an uncorroborated tip."

Ben's eyes bore into him. Peter winced. He felt the moisture in his armpits. Ben had been in the business too long. He knew every trick. Peter had sourced O'Reilly's profile just as Ben claimed, with the linchpins of the story Peter's gut and Tim's educated guess. Peter had gambled and he lost.

He had been willing to take the risk because it was Kavanagh, and he wanted it bad. But now his balls were in a vise, and he was the one who put them there. He struggled to find his voice, for some explanation that would mollify Ben. In the end all he could do was own up to it.

"I didn't source it as well as I could have," he admitted.

"Not good enough," Ben said, cooler now, his anger beginning to dissipate.

Ben edged away from Peter as if he didn't want to share the same air. He moved back behind his desk, retaking his editor's chair.

"What are you doing here, Peter?" Ben asked, his tone now more weary than angry. "What's driving you? Do you really want to be a reporter? It's not like you need the money."

A gentle knock on the door interrupted Peter's interrogation. Tina walked in slowly head down and handed Ben a single sheet of paper. She refused to look at Peter; she simply turned and quietly left the room, closing the door behind her.

Ben read the fax aloud:

Draco Communications has issued this statement to refute the facts in the story, "O'Reilly Joins Horizon Development Team by Peter Ellis," published on Sunday January 16, 1994. Devon O'Reilly is not now, nor has he ever been, a member of the Horizon development team. Draco Communications has, on occasion, consulted with Mr. O'Reilly as an expert in Internet communications and security. We demand a retraction and apology from the Valley Tribune *in the next edition of the paper including its new online edition.*

Ben faced Peter with renewed anger. "He's asked for a retraction and he's entitled to it. You're going to write it."

Peter nodded. He reached for the fax, but Ben tossed it on his desk. Peter felt the energy in the room shift from anger to regret.

"I'm as much to blame for this as you are," Ben muttered, chiding himself. "I let you get away with this. You had a great streak going. I gave you a pass on this one. I shouldn't have."

"This was entirely my fault. I own it. I was stupid. It won't happen again."

Ben's next move would tell him whether he still had a job. His arms and legs ached from tension, but he refused to give in to the pressure to sit as he waited for Ben's decision.

"That's what I heard the last time," Ben replied, with a sad shake of his head. He studied Peter carefully. Peter could see Ben was weighing his options. He'd be justified in firing him now. Adam and Sam would not be the only ones happy to see Peter go.

"I accept your apology," Ben said after several tense minutes. "That's two strikes, Peter. Don't bring me another story that's not sourced to your shorts, understand? Because if you do that story will get spiked and you'll be out on your ass before you can spit."

Peter heard the words as if from a distance. His limbs were frozen, but his mind was working at warp speed, thinking hard about the fax. He stared past Ben almost as if he were in a trance. Ben, Peter sensed, read his silence as capitulation when the opposite was true. His mind pulled the facts of his story together from all directions, testing assumptions, realigning the evidence. This was too neat a play to be a coincidence or a simple mistake on his part.

He was sure that Alex Kavanagh, the master manipulator, had set a trap for him. Granted, he'd taken the bait. But the trap had to be there. Peter hated the thought, but he probably had Jessica to thank for it. She knew how he worked. She knew most of his sources. Not that he believed for a minute that she would knowingly give him up. Could Kavanagh learn what he needed to know through some adroit pillow talk? Peter was convinced that he could and did. The right whispered rumors repeated to the right people would get to Tim and through Tim to Peter. If he didn't know it before, he knew now; he was engaged in a full-scale war with Kavanagh, and it was personal. Peter had to win or it would cost him the driving force of his life—his career.

"Peter, are you okay?" Peter heard Ben ask as if through a deep fog. When Peter opened his eyes, not realizing he had closed them, Ben's expression was a mixture of puzzlement and apprehension that surprised Peter.

"I should start working on that retraction." He reached for the fax.

Ben pushed it across the desk, watching Peter closely. Peter acknowledged Ben's evident concern with a nod, and went back to his 'thinking place," as he called it. He had a gift of discernment and interpretation that enabled him to excel as a reporter: the uncanny ability to see through people, understand their motives and find the secrets they were trying to hide. Peter had learned early in life that his gift spooked people. He learned to keep it well hidden, and to use it only when he needed it. It was the reason he was able to decipher David Lockwood's holograms and unlock his secret. It would serve him equally well now, as he strove to expose Kavanagh's artifice.

Peter focused all his energies on the fax. He read it three times while his mind parsed every word, every nuance, seeking the lie or the half-truth buried there. Then he saw it. He grabbed a pen, aware that Ben was still watching him with a baffled expression on his face. Taking pen to paper, Peter crossed out a few words and circled the four critical ones, drew a line between them to highlight the message and slid the fax back across the desk.

"You see it, don't you?" he asked Ben, hunching forward. "It's a simple title change. Maybe O'Reilly isn't 'officially' on the development team, but he's the next best thing. He's a consultant to Draco on Internet communications and their Internet communications strategy is all about Horizon."

Ben nodded as he studied Peter's handiwork. Peter felt his excitement build. "Here's the retraction: *In our story we mistakenly named Devon O'Reilly as a member of the Horizon development team. In fact, Mr. O'Reilly is a consultant to Draco in Internet communications, the cornerstone of which is Draco's Horizon Project. The* Tribune *regrets the error.*

"It uses Draco's own words to tie O'Reilly directly to Horizon.

Sorry we got the title wrong, guys. What do you think?" he asked, looking expectantly at Ben for confirmation.

Ben smiled. "That's good. Very clever. Absolutely accurate."

Peter started to laugh. This would surprise, even embarrass, Kavanagh. Next time, maybe he'd think twice about trying to take Peter down. Ben dropped the fax, running his hand through his thick silver hair. "I can't let you off the hook completely. You made a big error in judgment."

"I know Ben and I regret it."

Ben took a parting shot: "Stop cutting corners or you'll regret it even more."

Peter stiffened at the rebuke. "There's just one more thing you need to know." His voice was low and ice cold, a north wind aimed directly at Ben.

"You asked me if I wanted to be a reporter. I haven't wanted to be anything else since I was a junior in college. I gave up everything, and I mean everything, to pursue this dream. What's driving me? I'll tell you. To be out there, on the battle lines. To be free to expose the lies and seek the truth. No one, not Alex Kavanagh, not even you, Ben, is going to stop me from finding The Truth."

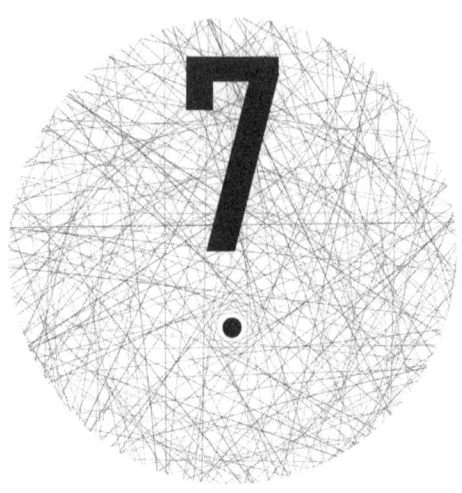

January 17, 1994: Dallas, Texas

THE INNER LOBBY OF DRACO COMMUNICATIONS HEADQUARTERS IN Dallas was vacant and so quiet, that Monday morning, that Toby could hear the clock above the reception desk tick off the seconds. He was waiting for a private meeting with Win Davis, a quiet word with the CEO before Alex Kavanagh and the rest of the executive team arrived.

The clock chimed, marking the six o'clock hour. Toby surveyed the ornate lobby. The corporate offices of immensely profitable companies all maintained the same casual air of powerful arrogance, he thought, amused. The lavish décor served as a constant reminder of the wealth and privilege accorded those blessed by the single-minded pursuit of profit. Two floors below, most of Draco's employees toiled in gray cubicles. The offices on the thirty-third floor were private, the hallway conversations subdued, the furnishings elegant. The goal was to impress customers and creditors alike with the immutable force that was Draco Communications.

Yet even this sanctuary wasn't protected from the poisonous presence of David Lockwood. Lockwood's smiling face stained the covers of all three of the magazines on the coffee table in front of him. Toby picked up *Venture Beat* and felt the bold black type assault his eyes and his ego. In the cover photo, Lockwood was smiling. Lockwood had worn an arrogant, supercilious smile like that the day he slammed the door in Toby's face and ended his career.

Toby's anger increased. The pressure in his chest was intense. Hatred consumed him. His fury was white-hot. He clutched the magazine. A crease appeared on the cover, right between Lockwood's eyes, and traveled downward, splitting his lips. Toby wanted to kill Lockwood, to spill his blood; a righteous killing, in anyone's book.

He wasn't aroused by the act of killing. He knew men who were. He was not one of them. He didn't kill for the thrill, for power, or for bloodlust. He killed dispassionately, expediently, and only when he had no alternative.

He could only remember two killings he'd actually enjoyed, memories he still savored: those of his cousin Earl and of Lieutenant James. Both men had died badly, begging for their miserable little lives. Earl Junior at fifteen was hardly a man, and could be excused for his limb-numbing terror when facing down the barrel of a gun. Not Lieutenant James.

Fucking Annapolis graduate, Toby muttered to himself. His fingers drummed the coffee table. His mind restlessly sampled the spaces between past, present and future. He was staring at David Lockwood's face, but the eyes that stared back belonged to Lieutenant James.

Tall, blond, Lieutenant James strutted around the base in his dress blues like he was at some fucking garden party instead of lost in hell. The lieutenant, a fourth-generation Navy man, was always surrounded by a fawning crowd of officers and wannabes. They listened, enraptured, as he claimed victories he hadn't won; they applauded him for abusing power he'd never earned.

Toby despised him for it. They should've stationed the little prick in Hawaii so he could down Mai Tais with the ladies and share war stories inherited from his father, Toby told his buddy Carl Perkins at the time. Carl laughed and warned Toby to be careful. Toby listened to Carl and left Lt. James alone, until the day he stepped over the line.

Toby followed him to the whorehouse in Saigon that night on instinct. He knew the lieutenant was going to see Mae, Toby's favorite, and that he was in a foul mood. Mae's room was a large one at the very back of the house, with a closet and a window that opened onto the alley. Toby slipped into the closet and waited while the lieutenant had a few drinks.

The pair entered the room thirty minutes later, bodies pressed together. Mae was already half undressed. Lieutenant James had one hand on her exposed breast, massaging a nipple. The other hand held a drink. Once they were inside the room, she pulled away from him and began to dance. She twirled around the room, long black hair flying, joyfully discarding her clothing in celebration of the fact that— for one more day—she was still alive. The lieutenant stripped and stood watching her, getting harder as she danced near him. Watching her from the closet, Toby was getting hard himself.

The lieutenant grabbed at Mae playfully as she came closer. She wiggled away, laughing. He took a wobbly, drunken step toward her and stumbled. She laughed harder. It made him angry. He grabbed her arm and squeezed. She struggled to break his hold. He slapped her face. She choked back a cry and struggled harder to free herself from his grip. He hit her again. As Toby watched the welt rise on her face, he unsheathed his knife. She managed to break the lieutenant's hold and ran from the room. The lieutenant was at the door in an instant, determined to follow her.

Toby had to work fast. Moving from inside the closet, he threw his arm around Lieutenant James's neck and held the tip of the knife to his chin. The lieutenant was too drunk to react quickly. He swayed under the pressure of Toby's hold. Toby pressed the knife against the lieutenant's soft white skin, drawing blood.

His knees buckled. Toby let him drop to the floor and smiled, enjoying the sight of his swaggering commander on his knees in a whorehouse, his dick shriveled, mouthing apologizes for hurting the girl, pleading with Toby to let him live.

Then Toby heard noises in the hallway. People were coming. Toby grabbed Lieutenant James by the hair and quickly, silently slit his *throat. Then he slipped through the window and into the night. There was only one rule in the jungle: survival. Cunning, duplicity and camouflage were the skills that ensured it.*

Toby glanced once more at Lockwood's picture. Lockwood had something in common with Lieutenant James, Toby thought, feeling his anger dissipate. Maybe Lockwood hadn't inherited his wealth, but he hadn't earned it either. He'd stolen it and Toby was determined to make him pay.

The sound of the door opening broke into Toby's reverie. Toby glanced up, putting the magazine down, as Win Davis walked up, motioning Toby into his office. At seventy, Davis still maintained the taut, muscular body and short haircut suited to a Marine Lieutenant Colonel. Retired from active duty for more than twenty years, he led Draco as he had his battalion in Vietnam and expected nothing less from his top executives. Toby's own exemplary service in Vietnam, embedded into his cover story, gave him a deep bond with Davis that non-military men like Kavanagh could not share. Toby intended to use that advantage today.

Ushering Toby inside, Win nodded for him to take a seat. Win's office in Dallas was the power center of Draco, and it showed in every detail: the blue oval carpet on the floor, embossed with the familiar Draco logo in green; Win's massive desk, a Spanish colonial piece, fronted by two large wing-backed leather chairs. Original oil paintings of three key battles for Texas's independence—Gonzales, The Alamo and The Battle of San Jacinto—decorated the walls. The massive conference table was hand-carved, dark oak with leather chairs. Toby noticed the strategy packets were already in place. The rest of the team would arrive shortly.

"Are you on schedule for the Horizon rollout?" Win asked, taking his customary seat behind his desk.

"Yes, we've made up the time those early delays cost us. We've had two successful alpha tests. Moving into phase I beta in about two weeks so we can make phase II early customer beta by March first," Toby replied.

"Excellent." Win's smile creased his deeply tanned face. "You've made a crack unit out of that slipshod outfit," he added. Toby accepted the compliment with a modest nod of the head.

"I'd like to move up the Horizon intro to March Sixteenth."

Win looked surprised. "We've already pushed the date once, Jake. Moving it up again is going to put some serious pressure on marketing. What's your justification?"

"Lockwood is moving faster than we thought. We need to beat him to the market."

"I'm not as concerned about Lockwood as you are."

Toby started to reply. Win cut him off.

"I know he's got the 'hot box' as all the media are saying. But he's got no backing. He's self-funded and he's got a tiny band of loyal programmers trying to compete against us," Win said. "He'll fail."

Toby narrowed his eyes, buying time to think. Despite his reputation as a superb military strategist, Win was making the classic mistake of a power player: he was discounting the fanatical commitment of the underdog.

"Naturally, Lockwood's resources are nothing compared to ours. However," Toby dropped his voice, "we both know what a small band of loyalists can do when highly motivated."

Toby shifted his eyes to Win's painting of <u>The</u> <u>Battle of San Jacinto</u>, the decisive battle of the Texas Revolution when a small group of outmanned and outgunned Texans led by Sam Houston defeated the vast Mexican army, and paved the way for Texas independence.

Win furrowed his brow and pursed his lips, his typical thinking pose. "I'm open to it. Let's discuss this at the strategy session," he said.

Toby had the concession he needed to get the issue on the table. He was saving the rest of his ammunition for the staff meeting— when Alex would be present.

Both men stood and moved toward the conference table as the

rest of the executive team filed into the room. Toby nodded to Alex and the others, though when the last man entered the room, Toby felt his throat constrict. Devon O'Reilly.

O'Reilly knew Toby and knew him well. They had worked together at Hewlett Packard for years and were friends as well as colleagues. O'Reilly was the one who had asked Toby to join the original Trxton development team and who had defended him, unsuccessfully, against Lockwood's crusade to expel him. Toby saw Devon as a comrade-at-arms despite his lack of military service. If one person in the industry could expose Jake for the impostor he was, it was Devon O'Reilly. Toby wondered what in the hell O'Reilly was doing here.

"Gentlemen," Win said, when they were all seated. There were no women executives in Win's inner circle.

"I'd like to introduce to you Devon O'Reilly."

O'Reilly raised a lazy hand as Win continued: "As I'm sure you know, Devon was the cofounder and developer, with David Lockwood, of the original Trxton Computer. He is also the founder of a successful software application company," he added to nods around the room.

Toby consciously avoided O'Reilly eyes as he mentally shuffled through his options. "What many of you may not know is that Devon is also an Internet security expert," Win continued. "As our information highway strategy continues to develop security is going to be increasingly critical. I've personally asked Devon here to join us to help us make sure our Horizon product line is as secure as possible. If we are going to ask consumers to shop with us through the Internet, we must ensure that their money is in safe hands."

Win looked at Devon. "Devon, is there anything you'd like to say before we begin?"

Devon stood and turned toward the team. At six foot three and two hundred and fifty pounds, O'Reilly defied all industry stereotypes of the undernourished, over-glucosed software programmer. He looked more like the hulking stevedore his immigrant grandfather had been than the math wizard-turned-programmer he had become.

O'Reilly rose and began speaking, looking at each member of the team in turn. As O'Reilly spoke, Toby trained his eyes unflinchingly on him. O'Reilly would have to call him out; he was not going to give in to fear or apprehension.

"From what I've seen, your approach to the information highway dwarfs the competition and I look forward working with each of you," O'Reilly wound up, returning to his seat.

"Jake," Win said turning toward him. "You have the floor."

Toby stood and pressed a button on the console in the center of the conference table. A white screen dropped down. Toby pushed a sequence of buttons and a series of pictures appeared on the screen.

"There are many players in the information highway game, but only one that counts," he said, flashing the first photo on the screen—a red and black-scripted logo. "MediaBuilders."

Win stiffened at the name of his most notorious competitor. Even though they all knew the subject of today's strategy session, no name invoked more animosity within Draco than MediaBuilders.

"MediaBuilders is looking for the same golden goose we are: the consumer. But they have an entirely different approach. We're focused on providing access—the connections and the outlets that consumers need to use the Internet. MediaBuilders is primed with content. They have tons of content: TV stations, movie and TV studios, newspapers, magazines, recording artists, theme parks. And they are on a buying spree. They are buying more content— video game companies, multimedia assets, movie studios. The list goes on," Toby explained.

"Good for them," Alex said. "So they have content. What are they going to do, send it through the air?" Snickers erupted around the table. Alex had scored the first point.

"No, Alex," Toby replied. "They're doing what we're doing. What any smart company would, filling their holes. They've got deals in the works with Sprint, MCI and several European and Asian cable companies to carry their content."

Toby reset the video screen. "Before we get into the weeds on the acquisitions they're making, let's look at the team."

The first photo to appear onscreen was of Jonathan Blaylock, MediaBuilders' CEO. Blaylock was a striking man, with a large head framed by a thick mane of white hair. His deep black eyes and sharp, hooked nose reminded Toby of schoolroom pictures of the American eagle.

"So far, Blaylock has been hands-off on this operation. He's leaving the information highway to his trusted lieutenant, Victor Henderson," Toby said, clicking the remote and moving to the next picture.

"Henderson runs operations on this side of the Atlantic. He is responsible for the deals and the dealmakers. Blaylock has given him the signet ring, so Henderson is the one we need to follow to see where MediaBuilders is going next. And," Toby added to dramatic effect, "Henderson has eyes on us."

Toby looked around the room. He had everyone's rapt attention. "These next two are the soldiers. Charlie Sheffield is the bird dog."

The screen showed a large-boned, chubby-faced man sporting a black goatee smiling at the camera.

"Sheffield is the acquisitions specialist. He finds the deals and she vets them." Toby clicked and the screen cut to a tall honey-blonde wearing horn-rimmed glasses and a black pantsuit.

"Margaret Ellis is head of the New York practice of the global corporate litigation firm of Ellis, Blackwell and Barnes. She's corporate counsel to MediaBuilders and a trusted ally of both Blaylock and Henderson."

"Did you say Ellis?" Alex asked abruptly. "Any relation to Peter Ellis?"

Toby shook his head. "I don't know."

"It's a common last name," Win said with a dismissive wave of his hand. "Get to the point."

Toby watched Alex hunch forward, intent on the photo of Margaret Ellis. It took him a moment to remember that Peter Ellis was the reporter who'd been dogging them on Horizon. *Worth looking into,* he thought. Win began drumming his fingers on the table and Toby quickly moved on.

"This is the team we have to stop if we are going to achieve dominance on the information highway and here's how we are going to do it." Toby tossed up a graphic of MediaBuilders' recent acquisitions.

"MediaBuilders is driving from the top down. They've got a false sense of security about their cache of content. They need a lot more infrastructure than they think."

"They talked to me about security," Devon interjected.

Win eyeballed him. "You chose the right side." Devon nodded in assent. Win turned back to Toby.

"They got anything like Horizon?" Win asked.

"No. Some of their cable partners are working on versions of an Internet set-top box, but none of them are even close to Horizon," Toby replied.

"What about Lockwood?" Alex asked. "He's out in front with his box."

Devon erupted in loud laughter. "David work for MediaBuilders? Not bloody likely. David dances to his own tune. No meddling corporate partners need apply."

Devon looked hard at Toby. "Don't you agree, Jake?"

All heads turned in his direction. Toby inhaled and studied Devon. Devon's face was open, seeking confirmation from an engineering colleague likely to know Lockwood's modus operandi.

"I agree. Lockwood will bring Sapphire to the market as an independent. He's still looking for redemption from that Falcon debacle. I've got my eye on him in case he makes a surprise move."

"So, what's your plan for MediaBuilders?" Win asked.

"Follow the bird dog and the lawyer," he said, pointing to a picture of Charlie and Margaret with Henderson standing beside them, each holding a glass of champagne. They appeared to be celebrating a recent acquisition. *The last easy one they'll get,* Toby thought. He turned to face the room.

"Know who they want and what they're willing to pay. Then either buy the company out from under them or force them to pay a debilitating price for ownership," he explained. "We've got a great scouting team and an ample war chest ready."

"Give Blaylock a taste of his own medicine," Win grunted approvingly. "Good plan."

"That brings us to the last item on the agenda, the Horizon roll-out," Win said, inclining his head in Alex's direction. "Alex, what have you got for us?"

Alex stood and took the floor, clicking through a PowerPoint slide show highlighting the new logo, brochures and tagline that Draco had premiered at the Consumer Electronics Show two weeks earlier.

"Is there anything here we didn't see at CES?" Toby asked.

Alex shot him an irritated look. "Of course. We'll have real customers talking about their experience with the product and several new applications that we are finalizing now. I've reserved the hall at Moscone Center for the introduction on March thirtieth with a press party following at the Modern Art Museum."

Toby glanced at Win. Win nodded and Toby zeroed in on Alex. "We'd like to move the intro up to March sixteenth. Engineering will be ready to go."

Alex was flabbergasted. It took him a few seconds to recover from the end run. He gave Win a worried look that spotlighted his weakness. Toby relished the impact.

"Not possible, Alex whined. "Our timeline is precise. There's no justification for this change."

Win glowered in his direction. "I'm with Jake on this one. Get it done. That's all gentlemen."

The team rose in unison and started to file from the room. Toby saw Win call Devon to the side for a private chat. Alex stormed up to him, red-faced and fuming.

"What the hell was that all about?" he demanded.

Toby let him stew for a moment before answering in a calm, measured tone he knew would infuriate Alex even more.

"Lockwood is out in front of us. He'll be launching soon and we've got to beat him to the punch. He's already got the brain-dead media eating out of his hand." Toby reached over and shut off the projector and screen.

"Speaking of which, you did a hell of a job shutting down that reporter."

"I got the *Tribune* to print a retraction," Alex snapped in his own defense.

"It was pissant and you know it. Basic message: so sorry we got Devon O'Reilly's title wrong. You didn't get Ellis to back off Horizon at all. He wrote up the product delays in detail, which I warned you about."

"That was accurate," Alex said in the same whiny, complaining tone. It took effort for Toby not to put a fist in his gut.

"What the hell does that have to do with it? Have you ever heard of a smear campaign?" Toby asked. "To top it off I got a call from my admin this morning that Ellis wants to set up an interview with me, and that you suggested it." Toby's tone was menacing.

"Looks like I'll have to do your work for you," he said, turning his back. He watched in his peripheral vision as Alex slunk quietly out of the room.

Perpetual victim, Toby thought in disgust. Win caught his eye and motioned him over to join his conversation with Devon.

"Devon has some great ideas for integrating security code directly into the operating system for Horizon and speeding up software development," Win said as Toby joined them. "I want the two of you to collaborate very closely on this. As of now, I'm putting Devon on your development team."

Toby's plan had been to keep a safe distance from Devon to reduce the chance of exposure. So far, Devon gave no sign of familiarity; but even with his physical alteration it might take just one small slip on Toby's part—an unguarded reference to the old days, a gesture or even his working style—to trigger Devon's memory and lead to catastrophe.

Win had foiled his plans. Now he and Devon would be working side by side, day and night. It was like being back in the jungle, where threat was a constant companion and vigilance his only real weapon. Weariness flooded him. He wanted the chase to end. He thrust the feeling back, stepped up and shook Devon's hand.

"Welcome aboard," he said.

Devon returned his shake with a powerful squeeze and a steady smile. Yet in his eyes, Toby was convinced he saw a tiny flicker of recognition.

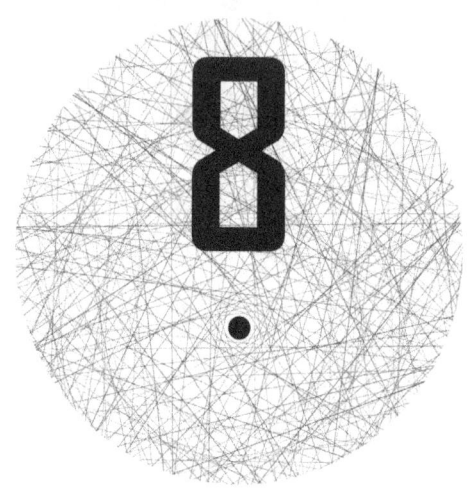

January 18, 1994: Palo Alto, California

Sam knocked on Peter's door late Tuesday afternoon. "Got a minute?" he asked, poking his head through the open door.

Peter glanced up from the papers littering his desk. "Yeah, sure," he said.

Sam, newly liberated from his cast, was dressed in his standard modified grunge garb, baggy cargo pants with oversized zipper pockets and a black *No Fear* t-shirt big enough for two of him. A gold stud dotted one earlobe. He pulled a spare chair up to Peter's desk.

"Can we talk about MediaBuilders?"

Peter nodded. He'd been pleased with Sam's coverage of the company so far. Sam had dutifully reported on all the company's activities without breaking any real news. No embarrassing headlines to worry about. No potential confrontations with Margaret to dread.

"MediaBuilders just acquired another company, PointNClick. They do ecommerce software." Sam pulled a press release out of his pocket and handed it to Peter.

Peter read the release, wishing things were different and the coverage was his. He'd kept away from the MediaBuilders action, as promised, but the acquisitions Victor Henderson had made so far didn't add up and Peter was intrigued. There was something going on behind the scenes, and Sam wasn't going to figure it out. Even Sam seemed to realize he was out of his depth.

"They're on a real feeding frenzy, aren't they?" Sam stared at the press release resting on Peter's desk as if he hoped it would impart some wisdom that had escaped him so far.

"Looks that way."

"Yeah." Sam nodded.

"I can't seem to figure out the pattern. Not yet anyway."

"Sure there is one?" Sam's discomfort was palpable.

Peter nodded, looking up at Sam. "Positive. Tell me more about PointNClick."

Sam read straight from the release: "They say they will 'plan, roll out and operate your Internet ecommerce solution from creating the online store to revenue generation.'" He dropped the release and added, "They build custom Web sites that look like cool boutique stores."

Peter scanned the release. "You know, Sam, it's hard to believe that CERN put out the first Web page less than a year ago: April 30, 1993, to be exact. Now there are thousands of Web pages out there and all these companies using the Web to create this new ecommerce market.

"Really?"

"Yeah. So, what else does PointNClick do?"

"They handle all the back-end stuff: ordering, shipping, payment, accounting, customer management. They even take credit cards."

"Custom back-end infrastructure," Peter mused. "Very sophisticated. How many customers do they have?"

"I don't know."

"They're live right? Not in beta or anything?"

"I think so," Sam said, scanning the press release. "It doesn't say."

Peter was frustrated that Sam needed so much hand-holding. Then he chided himself, remembering he promised Ben to help the kid out. "Let's take a look. What's the URL?"

Sam gave it to him. Peter turned to his Mac and pulled up the Website.

"They look real," Sam said.

"Lots of pretty pictures," Peter agreed. "But nothing about customers or installs, which they should be bragging about. This stuff is so new, people need to have confidence that it really works. But does it? We don't know." Peter turned around and faced Sam. "And we need to know."

Sam looked hard at Peter, hesitating, as if he were making a tough choice.

"MediaBuilders has a big press conference tomorrow in San Francisco. Want to come?" he asked, after a pause.

Peter nodded, giving Sam some extra reassurance. "I've been reading your stuff. It's good by the way, in case nobody's told you that. I doubt I could do better."

Sam smiled, letting the compliment sink in.

"You know," Peter continued, "since you've got MediaBuilders and I've got Draco, maybe we could share information on a few things."

Sam's face immediately turned from pleased to wary. He was prepared to read Peter's compliment as a trap.

"This is strictly for my coverage of Draco," he emphasized, for Sam's benefit.

"I'm convinced that the real battle in the Internet Wars is between MediaBuilders and Draco with everybody else, including David Lockwood, caught in the crossfire." Peter opened another window on his monitor and pulled up his chart. Sam leaned over for a closer look.

"Wow," Sam said, wide-eyed, studying the chart. "Where'd you get all this stuff?" His tone was both impressed and respectful.

"Just research," Peter shrugged. "Why don't I walk you through it and we can compare notes, okay?"

"Yeah, sure," Sam replied eagerly.

"The acquisitions both companies are making in content, Internet infrastructure and security scream a direct power play for

Component	Media Builders	DRACO	Options
Applications	**Need**	**Need**	Games, shopping, office
Content, Media	Have	**Need**	Studios, TV, Radio, Newspapers
E-Commerce; online shopping	**Need**	**Need**	Need to find companies.
Access—Set-top box	**Need**	Have	**WHAT? (MB) Horizon (Draco)**
Cable TV	Have	Have	Cable partners
Security-Encryption	Have	Have (in development)	Devon O'Reilly (Draco) MB?
PIPE-SONET	**Need**	Have	Integrated wireless, voice, Internet and TV

dominance. Draco is driving from the bottom up, starting with their huge telecommunications infrastructure. MediaBuilders is top down. They've got the content and now, with this PointNClick buy, they have a potential ecommerce solution."

"What about the Internet set-top box? Draco has Horizon. MediaBuilders doesn't have anything yet, do they?" Sam asked.

"That's a great question to ask Victor Henderson when you interview him."

Peter's cell buzzed. "Hey, Charlie," he answered when he heard Charlie Sheffield's voice.

You coming? Sam mouthed as he backed out the door. Peter nodded and turned his attention back to Charlie.

"Quick question for ya," Charlie said. "Did you ever get anything on that programmer I asked you to check out, Brian Tucker from Delta Software?"

Charlie's normally boisterous voice held a level of agitation that surprised Peter.

"Not yet. Let me give them another call."

In fact, he'd forgotten all about Brian Tucker—as he did most stories that didn't pan out. He'd made a few calls to Delta, came up empty-handed and dropped it. Charlie's call and his evident concern renewed his interest.

"Appreciate it. Lemme know as soon as you can," Charlie said, and disconnected.

Peter picked up the office phone and punched up Delta Software. "Brian Tucker, please," he said when the receptionist answered.

"May I tell him who's calling?"

"Peter Ellis with the *Valley Tribune*."

"Just a minute, please," she said. The line went to piped music.

Peter held on, wondering as he waited what was making Charlie so anxious about Tucker. Charlie played with the big boys, the CEOs and CFOs, the VCs. For him to care about a small-time programmer was definitely unusual.

A click on the line broke into his thoughts. "Hullo, Peter," a warm female voice greeted him. Her tone and style immediately marked the woman as a public relations conduit for Delta.

"You were calling about Brian Tucker?" she asked pleasantly.

"No, I was calling to talk to him. Is he around?"

"Brian Tucker has left the company. We'll be issuing a press release this afternoon."

"Would you mind telling me where he went?" Peter asked.

"He left the company for personal reasons. I'll fax you the release now if you'd like."

"Thanks."

They disconnected. Peter immediately redialed Delta. "Joe Simmons."

"Hold please."

"Yep?" Joe answered the phone with the same degree of enthusiasm Tim always exhibited. Engineers were all the same, Peter thought. Next time he'd email.

"Hi Joe. It's Peter Ellis with the *Valley Tribune*. You and I talked at the Consumer Electronics Show a couple of weeks ago. About Brian Tucker," he prompted into the silence. "And his puzzle games."

Peter heard a quick intake of breath. "Look, I don't know you, okay? Forget my name and Brian's. Don't call me again."

The phone banged, reverberating through Peter's eardrums. Peter replaced the receiver slowly, his mind spinning. He knew one thing for sure: the last person in the world he was going to forget about now was Brian Tucker.

He redialed Charlie. "Hey, Charlie, it's Peter. Brian Tucker has left Delta Software."

"Shit! Where'd he go, do ya know?" Charlie demanded, clearly agitated.

"I don't, but I promise you I'm going to find out."

Peter's cell buzzed. "Got another call. Let you know when I get something." Peter said, flipping the phone open.

"Hello, Peter."

He shifted back in his chair, lowering his voice to mask the pleasure he felt at her call. "Hi Jess."

He'd left a half a dozen messages since CES. She'd finally answered one. Persistence paid off. He smiled.

"I'm sorry it took me so long to get back to you. I've been out of town. I'm glad you called. I've been thinking about you, too."

Her voice rippled through him like the charge from a hot wire. He worked at sounding casual. "Maybe we could have a drink or lunch, catch up a bit?"

"Are you on deadline?" she asked. He imagined her pushing a strand of hair behind her ear as she talked, a gesture that had always charmed him.

"Done for the day. Why?"

"Can you meet me at the beach? Now?"

"Yeah, sure."

The phone was still warm from the sound of Jess's voice as Peter pocketed it, grabbed his keys and headed out to meet her.

January 18, 1994: Half Moon Bay, California

They parked next to each other on Mirada Road at the Waterfront Coastside trailhead. They had had many of their best talks while walking this trail, watching the setting sun melt into the ocean. He felt encouraged that she had chosen this path for the first real talk since their breakup. She walked beside him in tight jeans and a baggy orange V-neck wool sweater. Her spicy orange blossom scent, the one that still haunted him, mingled with the fresh air and flowers. Jessica spoke first. "You've been on quite a streak. First David Lockwood, then Horizon. Looks like you're golden again."

"Yeah, I've had a good month. They both hit the wires."

"I noticed that." She smiled.

"We're not really here to talk about David Lockwood, are we?" he asked as they meandered along the path. Jessica's hand dangled at her side. As he started to reach for it, she stopped, turned and faced him. "I didn't like the way we left things in Vegas." She was giving him that direct look, the one that always made him feel exposed, and suddenly all he could think of was how badly he'd blown it when he tried to talk to her in Vegas. He fumbled for speech. Only she could liquefy his nerves like this.

Jessica stepped into his silence. "You wanted to talk. I didn't let you. I want to hear what you have to say."

He moved closer to her, finding his voice. "When TriCorp exploded in my face, I spun out of control. It took me a long time to recover, but now my life's back on track. I wanted you know to that."

"I'm glad." She tilted her head, studying him. "So what are you saying?"

"That we can put TriCorp behind us. Like you said, I'm golden again. And we were good together, weren't we?"

"We had our moments." A slight nod of her head, and a half-smile was all the encouragement he needed. He took another step toward her. Though they had not yet touched, he could feel the pulse of her body in the narrow space between them.

"What was your best moment?"

"Being here. Talking. Being open and honest with each other." She gave him a sideways glance. The wind blew a strand of her hair across her face. He reached up and brushed the hair away, letting his fingers linger on her cheek for a moment. Jessica's face was flushed; from the wind or the conversation, he didn't know and didn't care.

"You know, this place is so special. To both of us. I miss you, Jess. I miss us." He leaned toward her.

She stepped back, refusing to meet his eyes. "I know. I felt it in Vegas and then when you left me all those messages. I knew I couldn't …" Her voice trailed off.

"That's why I asked you here. Because I knew this was the one place where you might be able to hear me. I know how much you love it here. The times we came closest to a real conversation, it was always here. And we really do need to talk." She took a deep breath that ended in a heavy sigh.

He felt her drawing from the deep reservoir of courage she possessed. He braced himself. "I'm not going to like what you have to say, am I?"

"No. I don't think you are. TriCorp wasn't my reason for leaving. It was my excuse to leave."

His throat constricted. "What do you mean your excuse?"

Jessica looked away, up to the hills, and back at him with a frank gaze. He'd always admired her frankness, except now, when it was directed at him. "It wasn't working. Not for a long time. I just didn't know how to tell you. Then TriCorp happened, and it made it easier to walk away."

"Why? I don't understand."

"Too many walls. Not enough bridges." She looked quiet, sad even, but resolute.

"What the hell is that supposed to mean?"

"Like today. If we met at Starbucks or a restaurant, or, God forbid, a bar, I knew all I'd get from you would be maneuvers. Social transactions, I think you like to call them."

"It was never like that with you."

"Sure it was. Any time I brought up something you didn't want to talk about, you'd turn on that boyish charm of yours and tease me out of it." She half smiled. "You remind me of Denny when you do that."

Her smile faded and, face impassive, she looked up at him. "Or you'd seduce me. And no one is better at that than you."

"Hey."

She continued as if she'd hadn't heard him. "Or, you'd shut down and disappear so deep inside yourself. I'd end up feeling rejected, like a failure, because the man I loved—" His head jerked toward her.

She nodded. "Yes, loved—was in a very dark place and I couldn't help him. I thought that if I gave you enough time and space, you'd open up to me. But you never did."

The disappointment, judgment and accusation he saw in her eyes hit him hard. "You fear people too much, Peter, and you can't build a relationship based on fear."

Peter glared at her, his jaw clenched. Jessica's cheeks turned pink, her lower lip trembled. "I'm sorry. I didn't mean that."

"Yeah, you did."

Peter turned his back on her and walked to the edge of the dune. The fact that she was right only deepened his feeling of isolation. He watched the pattern of the waves rise from the sea, form a white, misty cap and break against the sand. She reminded him of those waves; full of energy, yet constant and enduring. He wasn't ready to give up on her yet. He turned and faced her with a hopeful smile.

"I heard you, Jess. I heard every word you said. I can change, if you'll show me the way." He held his hand out to her. She pursed her lips the way she always did when she was thinking. He heard the call of a gull over the whoosh of the waves as he stood in front of her, waiting for her response.

"Can't we just walk and talk some more? Please?" he asked after a few more moments of silence.

She hesitated, then offered him a tentative smile. "Okay."

They edged down the steep trail to the sandy beach. He took off his tennis shoes, tied them together and threw them over his shoulder. "What do you want to know?" he asked.

"Did you ever figure out what happened with TriCorp?"

He was grateful to her for the softball question. It would allow him to ease into this new, intimidating territory of true confessions.

"No. Ben advised me not to. He told me that he thought I'd been used and that it happened to good—even great—reporters. He also said he'd seen some of those same good reporters chase ghosts and flush their careers down the drain. They never found the answers and they lost everything else in the process."

She nodded. "Makes sense."

"Ben's smart. After all, he worked for *The Washington Post* for twenty years. He was around my age when Watergate happened. My run-in with TriCorp was nothing compared with what the professional politicians pull."

Smiling slightly, Peter looked out at the waves breaking against the shore. "Ben told me to focus on the future and rebuild my reputation, and I'd get through it."

Her face darkened. The guilt he'd seen in Vegas was back. "I wasn't there for you. I should have stood by you, but I walked out at the worst moment of your life. It doesn't say much about my character, does it?"

"I didn't blame you for that. You didn't have a choice. Not with New York hammering you the way they were. It would have cost your career."

"I had a choice. When people say they don't have a choice, what they're really saying is, 'I don't want to face the consequences of the choice I should be making'. At least that's what Denny always says."

"Sounds like something a priest would say."

"My brother's right, Peter. I didn't do the right thing." she insisted. She started walking again. He had to pick up his pace to catch up with her.

"I still feel guilty about leaving you when you needed me the most."

"No guilt here."

"I'm Catholic. We do guilt better than anyone." She bit her lower lip, eyes downcast in a penitent expression that sought absolution. That wasn't his job, he thought, but he gave it to her anyway.

"I forgive you. Let's forget about it, okay?"

She nodded and moved a step in his direction. He pulled her close, wrapping his arms around her in a tight embrace. His kiss caught the edge of her chin as she tilted her head toward him. She returned his kiss gingerly, then stepped back, breaking his hold. As they resumed walking, close but not quite touching, Peter felt some of Jessica's warmth evaporate.

"The truth is, we want very different things," she said.

"Not so different. We both want a successful career. A good life. Adventures. Freedom."

"That's all nice, but it's only part of it."

"What do you want, Jess? Just tell me and I'll get it."

She sighed. "It's not things, Peter. It's values. The two things that are most important to me are my faith and family, and neither of those matter very much to you."

"I didn't know faith was that important you."

"More than I realized."

"Tim's Catholic. Maybe I can borrow his credentials."

She shot him a warning glare. "Don't trivialize it."

"Didn't mean to."

"Alex and I have so much more in common. We're both Irish Catholic. We both come from big families. We both want a big family. I don't think that you want a family at all."

The sun hovered low over the ocean, tossing a light orange and pink tapestry across the sky. The tide was going out, the breakers softening, waves receding. To Peter it seemed as if they were pulling his second chance into their foamy depths. He had to give her some answers.

"It's hard to want something you've never had, and don't really understand."

Jessica's eyes widened. Mouth open, she stared at him.

"Yeah. I know. Real honesty." The humor in his tone didn't quite make it to his eyes. She looked at him expectantly. With a fleeting smile, he continued.

"Look. Jess. My sister shipped me off to boarding school when I was eight years old. I grew up around little boys and headmasters. As for family, all I ever saw of my father was taillights, away to Europe, India, China, off to build his empire." He turned away and felt her step closer.

"All I ever heard from my mother was 'I'm busy, Peter. I'll talk to you when I'm done.'" He looked at Jessica and shrugged. "Except she was never done. There was always another cause to champion and..." he paused, pursed his lips. "I was not one of her causes."

He shoved his hands in his pockets, stared at the mound of seaweed at his feet and continued, his voice barely above a whisper. "Margaret was angry, always so angry. I just tried to stay away from the heat."

He looked up at her. "Who would want to share that with anyone? Especially someone they cared about?"

Jessica's face filled with compassion and understanding. She took his hand, gave it a squeeze and released it. The gesture felt almost fraternal. Jessica's family, with her three big brothers who doted on her, was the center of her emotional universe. She never understood his silence. Now, he thought, maybe she would.

"Why does Margaret hate you so much?" she asked.

It was his fire walk; the question he dreaded most. It cut to the core of his self-worth. He had a dozen evasive answers on hand. Some were even close to the truth. He palmed one, ready to begin his narrative.

"I know you don't like talking about your family, Peter, but family's the most important thing. If we can't share that, we don't have anything."

She looked away to give him space. He studied her profile, her sparkling green eyes and pert pixie nose, imagined her in the heat of passion and the way things were for them before his world shattered. He tossed out the card he was about to play and eased toward the truth.

"How much do you know about a line of succession?"

Jessica puzzled the question. "Isn't it about deciding who inherits what?"

"Yes, and it typically favors boys over girls regardless of birth order."

"That's ridiculous." Jessica sniffed, rolling her eyes.

"I agree. As absurdly Victorian as it sounds, my family practices it. Has ever since my great-great grandfather founded the law firm in

1850 to help gold miners litigate their prospecting claims."

Jessica's eyes widened in surprise. "You're saying Margaret hates you because you were born?" she asked, shocked.

Peter nodded. It had taken him years to understand the depth of his sister's animosity and the motive behind it. Jessica's question sent him back to that place of confusion and rejection. Reeling from the emotional assault of the memories, he lost his footing and stumbled. Jessica reached over and steadied him. He gave her a wan smile, then forced out the words.

"She had a lot to lose. As the eldest child in a family of two girls, Margaret had the assumption of inheritance. I don't mean the money. I mean the power seat, and with it the claim on my father's affections. You see, with no boys, my father was raising her as his son. And she was the perfect candidate for the job. She reveled in our father's patronage, attention, tutelage, all of it."

Jessica was listening intently. Peter paused to gather his thoughts. The wind had picked up, sending a paper cup scooting across their path. The fog hung off the horizon. It would roll over the hills soon. Jessica shivered.

"Getting cold?"

"A little."

He took off his windbreaker and encircled her shoulders.

"The sun's setting. You want to head back?"

"Finish your story, Peter," she demanded.

Peter felt a chill that had nothing to do with the ocean breezes. He was suddenly apprehensive about the direction he'd taken, but he'd gone too far to stop now.

"Margaret had fifteen years to enjoy her status as heir apparent," he continued. "She gave it everything she had, too, exceeding every expectation my father had of her. Then, unfortunately for her, I came along. Everyone in the family knew what my birth meant. Especially Margaret. Because I had the right equipment, I got my father's name and the power Margaret expected to inherit. In her mind, it was stolen right out from under her by a brand-new baby boy."

He looked away, seeking refuge in the movement of the ocean

waves. Eyes moist, he blinked rapidly, swallowing hard to dislodge the lump his throat. Jessica walked beside him, breathing quietly, a comfort without intrusion. Peter was grateful for her tacit understanding.

"But she's the lawyer in the family. She's got the corporate job," she said finally.

Peter stepped into a receding wave. The gritty, wet sand pushed up through the seams of his toes and scoured the soles of his feet. Memories descended. He shuddered anew at the scorn and ridicule she'd heaped on him even as a child just for being in her way.

"Yeah. But only because I walked away. All I ever really wanted was to run my own life. That was the one thing my father was never going to let me do. Still, I think in the back of Margaret's mind there's this irrational fear that someday I'll change my mind and come running home. My father will kill the fatted calf and life as she knows it will be over. It'll never happen. I don't want any of it. Never did."

Although Peter had stopped talking, the ancient memories freshly reawakened consumed him. As his mind spun and his energy drained away, even Jessica's comforting presence felt claustrophobic. He walked ahead of her to the edge of the shore. The water lapped at his feet. The sun hovered just about the horizon. In its dying light, Peter watched a brown pelican dive deep and resurface with a beak full of wiggling fish. *At least somebody is having a good night,* he thought.

The mild surf suddenly erupted as a pod of gray whales surfaced, flukes dancing. Two calves butted against each other. A larger one swam between them, circling as they dove beneath the sea and disappeared.

Jessica hurried up beside him. "Did you see the whales? Weren't those babies cute?"

Peter nodded. He watched the sea rise and fall. Calm again. The whales were gone. The eagerness in her voice at the word "babies" smothered him. He looked out at the lapping waves, drawing strength from the eternity of the ebb and flow. The sun was an orange whisper on the horizon when he spoke again.

"I can't do it, Jess. I can't be the man you want. I can't be the suburban husband fretting over crabgrass and attending PTA meetings. It's not in my DNA."

She laid her hand on his arm. "I know. But I needed you to know it too. So we could both move on." Giving his arm a squeeze, she released him, looking up to the darkening sky. "We better hurry or we'll get caught here in the dark."

He watched until her taillights disappeared into the darkness. Then he unlocked his car. He grabbed a cigarette from his pack and lit it. The sun was gone. The fog rolled in and visibility shrank to a pinprick. Peter listened to the pounding of the surf as he inhaled, still reeling from the unexpected loss. The glowing ember of his cigarette was now the only light on the dark and deserted beachfront road. When he'd gotten all he could from the nicotine fix, he tossed the butt aside and methodically ground it to dust with the toe of his shoe, wishing he could do the same with the unrelenting memories of Jessica. She was under his skin. It was going to take a while, he thought, reaching into his car and retrieving his cell, but at least he knew where to start.

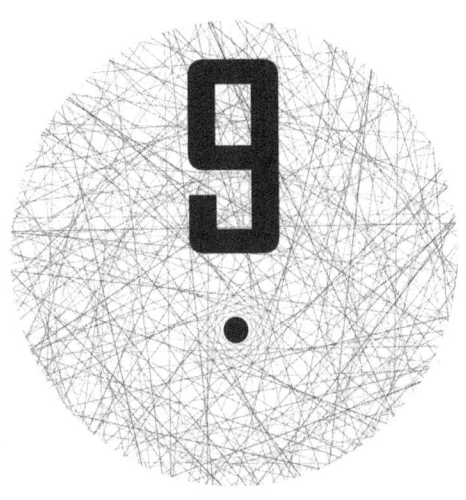

STARBUCKS IN MOUNTAIN VIEW AT SEVEN A.M., MIDWEEK, WAS not the best place for a quiet conversation. There wasn't a seat in the place. Peter and Tim stood sipping espressos and waiting for someone to vacate a table. Outside, the rain fell in solid sheets and broke hard against the large plate glass window. The sound mixed with the roar of the cappuccino machine, rock music from the speakers and the babble of constant chatter in the crowded coffee shop.

It was fifteen minutes before they were able to grab a small table by the window. Peter cleared away the used paper cups and paper pastry sleeves and sat down across from Tim. He suspected that the frown framing Tim's face had little to do with the crush of the Starbucks crowd.

"What's up?" Peter asked him.

"My group's getting re-orged again," Tim grunted. "Second time in six months. Barely get started on a project and they pull the plug. It's getting old, man. Wish these frigging directors would get their act together and figure out what they want us to do."

"You know where you're going yet?"

Tim shook his head. "Nope. Should know in a week or two."

"Why don't you look around?" Peter asked. "I know you've had some offers."

"I like Sun. Sun's been good to me."

And you hate change, Peter thought. Most engineers with Tim's skill set and experience chased the hot projects and moved every few years. Tim had been at Sun for nearly seven years. At least his stock options had to be good.

"Maybe it's time for a change," Peter suggested.

Tim shook his head again and Peter changed the subject.

"So, how are things going with Marie?" he asked, sipping his espresso.

Tim's face lit up. "Terrific. She's amazing."

"So, when am I going to meet this wonder woman?" Peter asked with a grin.

He knew next to nothing about the woman who had pulled Tim away from the keyboard. He knew her name, Marie Sanchez, and that she was a forensic accountant Tim had met at a Christmas party. That was it. Tim's atypical secrecy about his new girlfriend had piqued Peter's curiosity, especially since Tim had recently started missing their regular Sunday morning tennis match.

"One of these days. Why are you so interested in my love life?" Tim asked.

"Because this is the first time I've known you to have a love life," Peter replied chuckling. "Maybe I can give you a few tips."

Tim gave him a knowing look. "Don't think so, Peter. You don't have the best track record for maintaining a stable relationship, and that's what I'm looking for."

The barb hit too close to home, especially after last night's encounter with Jessica. Peter's face tightened, but he tried to shrug it off.

Tim was watching him closely. "Didn't mean it the way it sounded."

"I saw Jessica last night," Peter explained. "And it's over. Completely over." *Keep repeating it*, he told himself. *One of these days you'll actually believe it.*

"Sorry to hear that, man. I liked her."

Peter shrugged. "Way it goes. Say, did you ever get anything on Brian Tucker, that programmer I asked you about?"

"No. But I didn't really try that hard. Didn't sound that important."

"It wasn't. But now it is."

"Oh? How come?"

"I've been calling Delta since the show. Tucker's never around. I leave a number, end of story." Peter elected not to tell Tim that Charlie's frantic call had reengaged his interest in the missing programmer.

"So, yesterday when I called, I get a quick detour to PR and the flack's got a statement all prepared: Tucker's left the company. Personal reasons."

Tim shrugged. "Engineers change companies all the time. Industry's mobile."

"Thanks for the insight. The point is, I called Delta back and tried to talk to Brian's buddy Joe, and he acts like I can give him AIDS through the phone line. Barely draws a breath before he bails. This from a guy who was begging me to help him find his missing friend a couple of weeks ago."

"It's weird, all right," Tim agreed.

"Could you check around? I've got an itch, and I don't know anything about this guy except that he worked at Delta and he liked to play puzzle games."

"Puzzle games?" Tim leaned forward, expression intent. "Is that exactly how he phrased it?"

"Yeah. Why? Joe didn't know what Brian was talking about. Does it mean something to you?"

"Yeah. It does. Code games are real popular right now. There are a couple of bulletin boards on the Internet devoted to them," Tim explained. "I play 'em myself."

"Code games? What do you mean code games?"

"Well, lots of guys refer to breaking encrypted software as solving a puzzle or riddle."

"You've got my attention," Peter said.

"How much do you know about cryptography?"

"You mean Captain Midnight decoder rings, stuff like that?" Peter said with a smile.

Tim rolled his eyes in disgust. "Please. Cipher text is the result of encrypting plaintext using an algorithm called a cipher, so it's unreadable unless you're authorized to—"

"English translation, please," Peter requested. He could only handle so much code-speak.

Tim pushed aside his empty cup and opened up his comp book, sketching as he talked. Peter leaned over for a better look as Tim drew diagrams of various encryption schemes, how they were built, and how they were broken.

"Say you want to send a private message to a friend or keep some report confidential, you lock the information you want to send, called "plaintext," with a key created by a special software program. The "ciphertext" message contains all the information of the plaintext message, but it's not readable by a human or computer without the right key to unlock it. It looks like random gibberish to outsiders, so it's considered secure," Tim explained.

"What's the game?" Peter asked.

"Usually one guy puts out an encrypted message without a key. The only thing the other players have is the ciphertext. They have to figure out the encryption scheme for the key sequence. The first one in the group to figure it out and break the code wins. At least that's the way it works on the Net," Tim said, as he pointed his pen at the diagram and each step in the encryption process.

Peter absorbed the information as quickly as he could, trying to find a link between the puzzle games and Tucker's sudden departure from Delta. He figured there had to be a connection. "Then what happens?"

"The person who broke the code sends out a new message using a different encryption scheme and that starts a new round of play."

"Sounds exciting." Peter said, chuckling.

"It's the challenge. Bragging rights," Tim insisted.

The early Starbucks crowd had cleared out. It was eight-thirty, less than ninety minutes until the MediaBuilders press conference. Peter willed himself to ignore the ticking clock in his head and pay attention to Tim's explanation.

"What about disks?"

"You mean floppies?" Tim looked quizzical. "Everybody I know plays on the Net."

"In this case I think it is an actual disk," Peter said, pausing to recall his conversation with Joe at the show.

"Joe said Brian complained about not getting a puzzle—like it was something he expected to be sent to him. Then, when Jimmy Fuzzyhead showed up at the—"

"Jimmy who?" Tim interjected.

"Guy's got fuzzy white hair. Sound familiar?"

Tim shook his head.

"Well, anyway. He said he had a package for Brian from a guy named Henry. And no, I don't have an ID on him yet, either," Peter said, noting Tim's raised eyebrow.

"You can do these puzzle exchanges with floppy disks, can't you?"

"Yeah," Tim admitted. "But it would be a waste of time. It's Internet security that's important. It has nothing to do with computer disks. Sounds incredibly stupid."

Or incredibly paranoid, Peter thought.

"What about these Internet groups you mentioned? Maybe somebody in the group knows something about Tucker or the disk. Could you ask around?"

Tim nearly choked. "Not me, dude. Unless you know Brian's handle. The entire point of these groups is secrecy. No one uses their real name. They all use a handle. You want me to log on like some little lost sheep and ask if anyone's heard of Tucker? I'd get my ass flamed so royally I'd need to toss a bucket of water on my workstation just to cool it down."

"Okay, okay. But I've gone as far as I can without a break. All I got is that he worked at HP before Delta. I even dropped by Tucker's apartment last night, and the manager told me he'd moved out. He left a blind P.O. box in Palo Alto in case he got mail. Dead end."

"Could be he took a job out of the area," Tim suggested.

"Maybe. I just want to make sure I've covered every angle. Tucker and his encrypted puzzle disk are starting to bug me."

"Well, if you can get me Brian's handle, I'll check around. I doubt it means anything. Lots of guys play puzzle games to relax. Really, Peter. They're just for fun."

"I don't think so. Not in this case."

"Eh?"

"Brian's buddy Joe was nervous the first time he talked to me about Brian. Today, he about jumps out of his skin. It's not just Joe. Those two guys at the trade show were edgy too.

"When Jimmy Fuzzyhead says the package is from Henry, the guy he's talking to practically chokes and says, 'You're kidding?'. Then Jimmy says something like, 'Would I kid about this? Under the circumstances?' I don't even have a clue as to who Henry is."

Peter swallowed the last of his espresso and stared straight at Tim.

"There's a story here, Tim. I can feel it."

January 19, 1994: San Francisco, California

When Peter and Sam entered the ballroom at the Hyatt Embarcadero, it was already overflowing with press and broadcast media. Anything information-highway related was red hot, and MediaBuilders was widely viewed as one of the top players in the game.

The stage at the front of the room had the typical podium with an oversized view screen behind. The MB logo was the only image on the screen as Peter and Sam took seats near the side entrance. The photographers stood directly in front of the stage. The broadcast media, local TV stations and celebrity industry pundits got the prime center aisle seats. The big dailies, national and local, and the national industry press sat directly behind them. Smaller papers like the *Tribune* got the leftovers at the back or corners of the room. Peter felt a surge of envy watching the reporters from the *New York Times,* *Wall Street Journal* and *San Jose Mercury News* take their assigned seats in the front. He belonged up there with them.

Cameras clicked and lights flashed nonstop as Victor Henderson, VP of Operations for MediaBuilders USA took the stage. Henderson was a short, thin man with a fastidious appearance. His light gray eyes were hidden by heavy lids and gold-rimmed spectacles.

"Thank you all for coming," he began, in a clipped British accent. "The world is about to change and we are the ones changing it," he said. The screen behind him cut to what looked to Peter to be standard information highway hype.

Only a company like MediaBuilders could get away with showing a commercial like this before they fed us the news, Peter thought with distain.

The commercial ended and Henderson stepped up to the podium. "What's a highway if you have nowhere to go and nothing to do when you get there?" he asked. "MediaBuilders is taking the lead in providing the best content and applications for the information highway and today we are announcing a very exciting acquisition in the multimedia and video gaming space—Delta Software."

Peter startled at the mention of Delta Software, grabbed his notebook and pen and started writing as Henderson walked through the details of the deal, stopping short of the actual sales price. The screen behind him flashed through a company storyline of Delta Software, complete with smiling programmers and happy executives whose stock had now quadrupled in value. They were living the dream. Acquisition or IPO was the end goal of every Silicon Valley start-up.

Peter noticed Joe Simmons in one shot and wondered if Tucker was in there somewhere too. But Tucker was gone, and that made Delta far less valuable than it otherwise would have been, Peter mused. Brian Tucker's hasty departure and Joe's violent reaction to Peter's phone call now made perfect sense. Tucker seemed to Peter to be precisely the kind of programmer to jump ship to avoid being handcuffed to a conglomerate. Joe's vehemence had likely resulted from a management directive to keep quiet while the buyout was negotiated. Charlie was involved somehow too, Peter assumed, since he had pointed Peter to Tucker in the first place. But how? With MediaBuilders, or maybe their competition, Draco? He'd have to tread carefully there. Charlie was a stickler for client confidentiality.

Henderson finished talking and signaled for the doors to open. "Please join us for refreshments in the hospitality suite," he said, walking offstage toward the waiting broadcast cameras. He would do live interviews with CNN and local stations first. Print reporters had interviews scheduled throughout the afternoon. Sam had been lucky to get one of those slots.

Sam walked up and pulled Peter in the direction of the buffet table. "This is great," Sam said, viewing the table laden with shrimp, crab, pâté and other hors d'oeuvres with obvious pleasure.

"Yeah, it's a good spread all right," Peter agreed. "What time is your interview with Henderson?"

"One. We've got an hour to kill. What do you think he's up to?" Sam replied, glancing over as Henderson finished up an interview with Channel 4.

"I'm not sure yet. Remember the chart–MediaBuilders vs. Draco? MediaBuilders is content rich. Why buy another content company when they have so many other holes to fill?"

Sam popped a shrimp in his mouth while he considered Peter's question.

"I heard a couple of industry analysts say that MediaBuilders might go the partnership route now instead of more acquisitions. One guy I talked to said Draco was a good bet," he said.

"Yeah, that'll be happening," Peter chuckled.

Sam's eyes narrowed. "It sounds like a good move to me. Besides, that chart of yours shows that they have complementary holes to fill."

Peter sensed an undercurrent of resentment. Sam was reacting to a derisiveness he hadn't intended. Peter softened his tone.

"I can see them doing a partnership, Sam. Just not with Draco. Jonathan Blaylock and Win Davis hate each other."

"Really? Why?" Sam asked, obviously surprised.

"Six years ago, just about the time I started at *Computer Industry News*, Blaylock and Davis started a little partnership dance. This was way before the information highway noise, but everybody in the communications industry got excited about the move and proclaimed a brave new world. At the last second, Davis pulled out leaving Blaylock holding the bag. They sued and countersued for years. Their stocks slid. CEOs tend to hate that."

"Yeah. No joke." Sam snickered.

"Dear old Dad was thrilled. The law firm made a fortune in billings," Peter added, watching Henderson glide around the room shaking hands. "But that wasn't the end of it."

"What happened?" Sam asked, setting down his now empty plate on the edge of the buffet table.

"A year ago, Win Davis gets set to buy a little movie studio down in Burbank. He needs the programming to fill his cable channels, right?" Sam nodded.

"Well, Blaylock figures it's payback time. He jumps in and bids against Davis. Davis hikes his bid and they both put their dicks in play. The bidding war went on for months. Davis finally got the studio, but it costs him about four times as much as it was worth. No, I don't think those two will be playing corporate footsie anytime soon."

Peter glanced at his watch, gauging whether he had time to sneak out for a smoke before the interview with Henderson. *Too late*, he thought, as he saw Tom Patterson, Henderson's PR liaison approaching them.

"Peter, Sam, Victor's ready to see you now," Patterson said, leading them through the hospitality suite and down the hallway to a private room.

Henderson stood as they entered. As they exchanged business cards, Peter noticed Sam's hands were shaking. It was Sam's first big power interview, Peter realized. *Be cool, Sam*, he thought, trying telepathically to send some courage and confidence Sam's way.

Henderson glanced at the card Peter handed him, and back to

Peter with a puzzled expression. "Ellis? Any relation to Margaret Ellis?"

"She's my sister," Peter replied, watching Henderson try to hide his surprise. Peter nodded toward Sam. "It's his interview."

Henderson turned back toward Sam. "How does Delta Software fit into your overall strategy?" Sam asked.

It was a softball question, and Henderson gave a predictable non-response. Peter had no problem with that as an opener, though he was counting on Sam to ask the tough questions quickly. They only had twenty minutes with Henderson.

The trouble was, Sam's questions weren't getting any more challenging. Peter shifted in his seat. Sam had either forgotten or lacked the courage to ask the questions they had rehearsed. Peter could think of twenty questions he wanted to ask Henderson, about Horizon, Sapphire and the product war with Draco. Time was almost up when Peter heard Sam ask about how MediaBuilders was going to compete with Draco's Horizon.

"We're looking at several options," Henderson replied.

"But none are as good as Lockwood's Sapphire box, are they?" Peter asked, stepping into the interview seconds before it ended. Sam's mouth tightened. He shot Peter a warning glare. Peter ignored him. He needed answers to two questions and this was one of them.

Henderson turned toward Peter. "Sapphire is certainly one option we are reviewing. One of many, as I just said," he replied.

Peter was pleased. Henderson had confirmed they were looking at Sapphire and that was all he needed to know. Patterson stood, signaling that their time was up. Peter stayed seated, his eyes rooted on Henderson.

"Just one more question, if you don't mind. Why would MediaBuilders purchase Delta Software when Delta's top programmer, Brian Tucker, the one responsible for their biggest success, had just left the company?"

Henderson looked flummoxed. Either he didn't know Tucker was gone—unlikely, since the company had issued a press release yesterday—or he knew and didn't care, which made no sense to

Peter. M&A kings like Henderson always knew the true value of the assets they were trading.

Patterson took the question instead. "Brian Tucker was just one of Delta's top programmers. The company has a deep bench. He'll be missed, but his departure does not impact the intrinsic value of the company."

Bullshit, Peter thought. Sam was already standing, looking more relieved than annoyed. Peter stood to join him. As he shook Henderson's hand, Peter saw an unexpected wariness in Henderson's eyes.

Sam turned to Peter the minute they cleared the hallway. Peter was bracing himself for the reaming he knew was coming, so Sam's crestfallen look mystified him.

"I blew it," Sam said. "I didn't get to any of the questions we talked about."

"You got Henderson to admit they were looking at Sapphire."

"You did that," Sam pointed out. "I was too nervous."

"The first power interview is always the hardest," Peter replied sagely. "Mine was a complete disaster."

"How so?" Sam asked, with a sidelong glance.

"I'd just started with CIN when I got assigned to interview the new CEO of a software company, who happened to be a former cabinet member with the Reagan administration," Peter said, recalling the anxiety as if it were yesterday.

"I'm sitting in the lobby waiting for the guy and thinking, 'Dan Rather has interviewed this guy. Peter Jennings has interviewed this guy. Barbara Walters has interviewed this guy. What the heck am I going to ask him that he hasn't heard a thousand times?' I think it took me five minutes to stammer out my first question."

"Seriously?" Sam was laughing, disappointment dispelled. Peter, feeling an almost brotherly affection, was glad he'd brightened Sam's mood.

As they reached the lobby, Peter turned to Sam with one last piece of advice. "Be sure you charge at that MediaBuilders-Sapphire connection hard. You break something like that and it will make your career," he said.

"I will," Sam said.

No offense Sam, Peter thought as he left the hotel, *but just in case, so will I.*

January 19, 1994: Menlo Park, California

Peter met Jordan Langley at the <u>British Bankers Club</u> on El Camino in Menlo Park. The BBC, housed in a historic building that had once been a jail and later a library, was a popular hangout for their crowd. In keeping with the men's club feel, the gastropub featured a saloon-style bar and a restaurant. He stood in the foyer, scanning the room. He saw her sitting at a small round table in  front of the BBC's famous mahogany triple-arched Brunswick bar, under a large Tiffany stained glass window depicting Saint George the Dragon Slayer.

Jordan waved a lazy hand in his direction. He slid into the chair across from her and took a long, appreciative look. She was dressed in a white silk blouse that set off the creaminess of her skin, a red tartan skirt, black leggings and black mid-heel boots. A large pair of gold and reddish stone earrings and matching necklace added a dash of luster to her look.

"Great to see you again," he said.

"I'm glad you called." She responded with an enigmatic smile, meant to keep him guessing.

"What are you having?"

"Cosmo."

"Okay, this might take a minute."

Peter stood and threaded his way to the front of the crowded bar. While he waited for their drinks, he saw her pull her cell phone from her purse, chat briefly with someone and look back at him. Peter returned to the table with the drinks and sat down.

"So, what do I need to know about you, Peter?" she asked, a

soft smile playing at her lips. Her voice was warm, with a trace of huskiness that reminded him of Lauren Bacall.

"What would you like to know?" He took a swig of his Scotch.

"Hometown?"

Peter groaned inwardly. He knew where this conversation was going and he didn't want to go there. Jordan was playing the socialite game. She would ask the requisite background and credentials questions that would tell her exactly where he stood in the pantheon of her social circle. His initial answers would determine how far she'd allow the relationship to progress.

He hadn't played this game in a while and didn't want to play it now. He'd rejected those social constraints early on at Harvard and had no desire to be drawn back into the world of presumed position and privilege they demanded. The whole ritual irritated him. If he had to be judged, he wanted to be valued for his achievements, rather than some accident of birth over which he had no control.

Still, he had nothing else going on. Jordan had deep, soulful brown eyes, an engaging smile and a wicked backhand, and he badly needed a distraction from the nagging memories of Jessica. It couldn't hurt to play along for a while.

"Hillsborough," he answered. Old money, it told her.

"Schools?" she asked, the most predictable and critical question.

"Hillside School, Exeter, Harvard," he said, well aware that placed him near the top of her social pyramid.

"Such a cliché," she laughed, shaking her head and regarding him with an amused smile that suggested she found the expected exchange of breeding cards as ludicrous as he did. *Maybe she isn't so typical after all.*

"And where did you matriculate from?" Peter queried.

"Stanford, by way of Foxcroft. I'll get my MBA from Stanford in June."

"Oh, and I'm a cliché," he said with a wry smile.

"Point taken," she replied, taking a leisurely sip of her Cosmopolitan.

"So, what are you planning to do with that newly-minted MBA?"

"Become a corporate raider. I'll find damaged companies, buy them for a song, break them into pieces, fire all the people and double, possibly triple, the family fortune in the next five years."

He caught the daring gleam in her eye and decided he'd been right in assuming she was a bit of a renegade as well. It suited him just fine.

"I always wanted to be a pirate," he ventured in a conspiratorial tone.

"Perfect," she replied. "I'll take dominion over the earth, you can conquer the high seas, and we can rule the world together."

Peter laughed, a deep rich laugh that was at once intoxicating and freeing. A few heads turned in their direction.

"Too much work," he replied, slipping back into an easy flirtation, born of shared backgrounds, customs and experiences, with someone who also saw the total absurdity of it all.

"Ah, too bad," she sighed. "It could have been the start of a magical partnership."

She gave him a quick glance to gauge his reaction. He refused to take the bait, and responded with an impartial smile. When he'd called Jordan from the beach, he simply wanted a pleasant diversion for a couple of hours. The woman sitting across the table from him, toying with the plastic drink menu as she played him with her eyes, was not the type to be anyone's diversion—at least not for long.

"Actually, my own aspirations are much more modest as well. I'm looking at McKinsey, Bain and BCG. Any thoughts?"

"They're all good firms. I really haven't researched them. I heard Bain just went through a big restructuring, which can be problematic. On the other hand, they just put a woman, Orit Gadiesh, in a top spot. So that's encouraging for another woman, I'd think."

"Humm," she responded, giving his comments more weight than he expected.

"Why not Piper Jaffray?" he asked, recalling the card she'd given him had a man's name on the front and was from that firm.

She shook her head. "I don't want to work for Daddy."

"Why not?"

"Because it's a lose/lose situation," she said, taking a sip of her drink. Her face tightened. "You have to work three times as hard as everyone else to prove yourself and to avoid the taint of nepotism. Everyone wants you to fail and cheers—secretly or otherwise—if you do. Then, on Daddy's side, he can't even smile in my direction without catching some heat. It would put a strain on our relationship. Definitely a lose/lose."

She looked at Peter, her eyes intense. "I love my father too much to even consider it."

"Good reasons," he replied. He felt a quick stab of regret about his own family ties, but he'd lived with them long enough to know nothing would change.

"So, Peter, tell me what you do besides lose badly at tennis," she asked, voice light, flirting resumed. "Do you work?"

Peter laughed. "Yes, ma'am. I am gainfully employed."

"As?"

"Guess," he teased, taking a sip of Scotch waiting to see how she would react to the challenge.

"Lawyer?"

"That's the family business, not mine."

Jordan's eyes widened, amazed. "Ellis, Blackwell and Barnes?"

It was Peter's turn to be surprised. "Yes. Why?"

"My dad knows your dad," she said, smiling broadly, clearly pleased with the connection she'd discovered. Peter was less enthusiastic about the new twist and the uninvited intrusion of his family situation.

"Andrew Ellis, right?"

Peter nodded.

"My dad referred a client to him a few months ago. The client, a small business owner, was facing a huge product liability suit that could have wrecked the company he'd built himself from the ground up. Your dad's firm helped him save his business. Daddy was thrilled."

Her praise enlightened him. For a moment, through her eyes, Peter felt a touch of pride about his family's law firm and what it could accomplish for real people, not just faceless corporate entities. It was a new feeling and he wasn't sure what to do with it.

"So, not a lawyer," she said, breaking into his thoughts. "Doctor, maybe?"

"Serious aversion to needles. One more chance, Jordan."

"Can I ask questions?"

"Nope. I'm not making this easy on you."

"Nor should you."

She pushed her hair behind her ear and leaned forward, completely engaged in her quest. She studied him carefully, searching for some small detail, a hint that would give her a clue to his vocational identity. "Give me your hand," she said.

"Going to read my palm?" he asked, putting his right hand in hers.

"Maybe." She took his hand and turned it over.

"That's a nasty scar." She fingered the jagged cut on his palm. "What happened?"

"Broken glass." His hand tensed in hers.

"It must have hurt." She began to caress each finger from tip to knuckle. His body tingled in response.

"It did."

She gave his hand a light squeeze and pulled hers back to take a sip of her drink.

"See anything interesting?" he asked, his voice husky. He was still feeling the heat of her soft caresses.

She offered him a knowing smile. "Private detective," she said, "or a writer."

"How on earth did you come up with those?" he asked, a bit taken aback at the speed and accuracy of her deduction.

"First, when I asked you about the consulting companies, you said you hadn't done your research so I figured you liked digging for facts. You knew Orit Gadiesh had taken an executive role at Bain. That's not something anyone outside the industry would typically know. Plus, the big giveaway."

She took his hand again. "You have this little dent on your index finger." She moved her thumb across it, reigniting his body heat. "Which means you're usually holding a pencil writing something at the scene, not typing on a keyboard."

So which is it?" she asked, a triumphant gleam in her eye.

"Writer. Journalist, actually," he said, taking his business card out of his pocket and sliding it toward her. "With the *Valley Tribune*."

She took the card and stared at him in mock horror. "Not the dreaded media," she exclaimed.

"Guilty as charged," Peter replied, smiling, accepting the barb with good grace. "We're a community newspaper. I cover business and technology."

"Well, this changes things. Daddy rails against media constantly. I could never tell him I was dating a reporter."

Her tone was flat and there was enough likely truth in the words to chill him. He couldn't tell if she was teasing or serious. But he found he needed to know. She had charmed him with her fast repartee and her wicked grin. He intended to see more of her. He hated to think his career choice could change that.

"Your dad might not like reporters, but he reads us, doesn't he?" Peter asked.

"He reads the *Journal*," she said, taking a final sip of her Cosmo and pushing the empty glass aside.

"Well, that's where I'm headed." He thought he sounded a little too eager, dialed it back. "That's the plan, anyway," he added with a casual shrug.

"Well, that might make Daddy happy. But I'm disappointed. I want some adventure and risk." The twinkle was back in her eyes.

"I could always become a foreign war correspondent. Risk my life on the battle lines."

"Much better," she agreed.

"How about a refill?"

Jordan shook her head and stood. "I wish we could, but I've got this thing tonight. I told them I'd be late, but I have to at least make an appearance."

"Okay, another time."

He followed her as she slipped through the packed house to the street. They stood outside the pub, each waiting for the other to make the next move. "Thanks for the drink," Jordan said finally, starting to move past him toward her car.

"How about a match this weekend? I have a court reserved for Sunday at ten." It was the third week in a row that Tim had cancelled their regular Sunday morning game.

She demurred. "Sunday morning doesn't work. How about the afternoon, around three?"

"Yeah, sounds good." He stopped to unlock his car.

"Great, see you Sunday," she replied, stepping past him. He paused to consider the soft sway of her hips as she strolled along the darkened street. The streetlight cast her silhouette against the concrete. It was a voluptuous form. Worth remembering.

"What about dinner after?" he called, as she continued walking down the street.

"Only if you win," she called back without turning around.

January 19, 1994: Cupertino, California

Toby picked up the photos Henry had given him, thumbed through them studying the youthful faces. Michael Lee was the picture of suburban banality. In a couple of years he'd be changing diapers and extolling the virtues of his Weber grill. Toby knew he could take Lee anytime, in any place. It was Brian Tucker who worried him. Tucker had vanished without a trace. Toby knew all about disappearing. Even the pros left traces if you knew where to look, but Tucker was really gone. Toby stared at the cocky kid leaning casually against a red maple tree. A short, chunky blue-eyed blond in a striped rugby shirt, Tucker looked more like a refugee from a Beach Boys concert than a fugitive.

"Where are you?" Toby whispered. "And what in the hell have you done with my disk?"

January 23, 1994: Hillsborough, California

IT ALL CAME DOWN TO THIS. THIS SET. THIS FINAL POINT. EACH OF them had won two sets; now, in the tiebreaker, they had battled to deuce, advantage Peter. They had played long enough, hard enough and well enough to attract a small knot of spectators at the edge of the court. Peter corralled the last of his energy. He was tired and assumed Jordan was too, but nothing in her stance indicated it as she crouched for the serve. Neither of them was willing to give an inch.

Peter planned a topspin-slice serve with as much of a slice on the ball as he could manage. It was a risky move. Jordan had already shown an uncanny ability to put the ball exactly where she wanted on the edges of the court. A bad serve and she could easily finish him with a hard return. Their dinner date was riding on this serve. Peter had no doubt Jordan was serious when she said winning was the price of her company tonight. He just hadn't expected it to be this difficult.

He tossed the ball straight up, his knees bent, racket coiled back to force downward pressure on the ball. It sprang across the net toward Jordan's left, her weaker side. She caught it and volleyed it back to him. It was a weak return, giving him the chance to kick it back again to her left. Jordan wasn't caught out again. She returned the ball hard off the rise with a slice to the edge of the court. Peter could see it sailing past him. As he moved under the ball, he felt his leg slip, putting him slightly off balance. Jordan, prepared for the fast, hard return he favored, stood near the baseline, ready to move in any direction. His off-balance return tipped the ball on the edge of his racket. The lob landed gently, just beyond the net. She charged fast but too late. Game over. Peter had won.

"Well done," she called, trotting up to the net.

The small band of spectators broke out in mini-applause and scattered. Peter stepped up to the net. Jordan offered her hand in the obligatory shake. A few minutes later, gear bags in hand, rackets slung over their shoulders, they exited the courts together.

Jordan turned to Peter as they walked down the path toward the parking lot. "Congratulations. You get to buy me dinner," she said.

"In every universe I know, loser buys," he said, giving her an amused sideways glance.

"Really?" She turned and faced him, walking slightly ahead of him, her expression incredulous. A teasing smile rested on her lips.

Peter laughed. "When and where?"

"How about Ambiente?"

"Isn't that a dance club?"

"Yes, they've got a new DJ with a great house, techno and trance mix." Peter nodded sagely. Jordan's smile widened, amused by the confusion he wasn't succeeding at hiding from her.

"I was hoping for food," he said as they reached her car.

"They just opened a restaurant above the club. Spanish fusion. You'll love it." She pulled her keys from her sports bag and pushed the remote.

"Seven-thirty, okay?" she said, as he opened her door and she slid inside.

"Okay, but fair warning. I don't dance." He heard the remnants of her laugh as she drove away.

January 23, 1994: Palo Alto, California

Ambiente's was popular and crowded even on a Sunday night. People jammed the bar and spilled out the front entrance as Peter pushed his way through the masses and into the club. Blue and green laser lights illuminated the large chrome and black polished bar, where a young mixologist was doing his best to emulate Tom Cruise's *Cocktail* moves. Music thundered from six oversized amplifiers encircling the  dance floor as a neon-shirted DJ mixed the sound and announced the playlist. Peter recognized a popular dance song, "Push the Feeling On" by The Nightcrawlers, as he stepped cautiously through the gyrating dancers, trying to avoid an elbow in the ribs. The hammering sound and the fractured lighting were already beginning to take their toll on his nervous system. He rubbed his temples as he stood waiting his turn at the hostess station.

"How long is the wait for two?" he asked the hostess, when he got the chance.

"At least an hour, maybe more," she replied without looking up.

Peter grimaced and gave her his name, looking around to see if he could spot Jordan. He had just turned back toward the entrance when he felt a hand snake through his arm.

"Buy a lady a drink?" Jordan asked, lips nearly brushing his ear as she leaned toward him. Jordan's fashion-forward outfit, with its sleeveless, purple silk V-neck tunic cinched by a silver metallic belt over tight black pants, was catching more than a few admiring looks from the stud-hopefuls lining the bar. Peter steered her to a tiny table just vacated by a couple of underdressed and under-aged-looking coeds.

"Cosmo?" he asked. She nodded. The bartender was quick, and Peter was back with their drinks just as the DJ started a new set. Peter put the drinks on the table and started to sit. Jordan was still standing.

"Oh, "Inside Out." I love this one. Let's dance," she said, taking his hand and pulling him onto the dance floor before he could object. Everyone in club seemed to have the same idea. There wasn't an inch of space around them; everywhere, warm, sweaty bodies wiggled and hopped to mechanical voices chilled by the synthesized rhythms of bass and percussion. Peter bobbed and weaved as best he could boxed into a tight space, and he thought he was doing pretty well until he looked at Jordan.

She wasn't so much dancing as she was expressing the music. Her feet, even in black clunky heels, stepped nimbly to the sudden shifts in the throbbing bass line. Her hips swayed to the beat as if the drums were part of her body. She danced with such confidence and grace that Peter stopped moving, mesmerized by the sight of her. A whirling couple bounced against him and he pitched forward. Jordan reached out, caught his hands and steadied him just as the song ended. They walked hand and hand back to their table.

"You're amazing out there," Peter said, sitting down and taking a swallow of his Scotch.

"I do love to dance," she agreed. "You, not so much."

"I warned you." Peter reached in his pocket for his cigarettes and started to pull the ashtray toward him. Jordan reached over. Covering his hand, she shook her head. "I'd rather you didn't. It's not good for you."

"Yeah, I know." He pushed the cigarettes back inside his pocket and glanced at his watch. Dinner was still at least thirty minutes away. Jordan's head tilted toward the music flowing from the dance floor. The flicker of the green lasers highlighted her face as she stared over his head. She sipped her drink vacantly so lost in the music Peter began to wonder if she realized he was there.

She put down her drink and refocused on him. "I have an idea," she said rising as a new song began. "You'll like this."

He groaned as she pulled him back onto the dance floor. She put her hands on his shoulders and looked directly at him. If her brown eyes weren't so captivating, her mouth so seductive …

"Keep your eyes on mine and relax."

"Easier said than done," he mumbled.

"Don't think of it as dancing. Think of it as tennis. You move like a cat on the court. Imagine we're volleying the ball."

She stepped back as the tempo changed. Peter took a cautious step forward.

"Remember, volley the ball. Eyes on me."

That last part wasn't hard to do. She stepped to the right, he followed her. A couple of more quick turns and he got the hang of it. He felt his body relax and flow with hers. She twirled around him and pressed the length of her back against his chest, her hips wiggling against his groin. The sensation rocked him. He almost lost a step but recovered as she broke the embrace and stepped back, eyes lit with pleasure, mouth puckered. The music stopped, and as the applause rang out around them, he pulled her close and kissed her, a long lingering kiss that blocked out the harshness of the lights and sounds. He caught the scent of jasmine as her hair brushed his face.

The DJ's voice broke their concentration. "Okay, folks, we're going to take a little break now and—" The DJ stopped speaking abruptly as the doors to the club swung open, necks craned and people stepped back and gasped in surprise. International supermodel Adin stepped into the club, entourage of glitterati in tow, the flashes from hundreds of paparazzi in the doorway lighting her way. She paused, poised, looking the crowd over as she gauged the level of adoration in the room.

Peter studied the incredibly long legs extending from her white lace micro-minidress as she strolled across the dance floor. As she walked by him, he couldn't help but recall her practicing that now-famous runway stroll for him in their dank and dingy New York apartment; except, at that time and place, she was usually naked.

As Adin turned her head in Peter's direction, her eyes widened in recognition and she flashed her trademark cover girl smile at him, ending the connection with the barest wave of her hand. Peter acknowledged her flash of attention with a brief nod.

"You know her?" Jordan asked, as Adin and entourage headed toward a private room in the back of the club. Before she exited the floor, Adin turned back and caught Peter's eye with one final tiny smile.

"We dated when I lived in New York."

"You dated a supermodel?" Jordan's voice sounded astonished and uneasy.

Good, Peter thought. She'd had him off-balance since that first drink at BBC and turnabout was fair play. "I haven't seen her in years. I'd forgotten all about her."

"Well, she seems to remember you."

"I'm a memorable guy." He chuckled. Jordan arched a skeptical eyebrow in his direction. The encounter with Adin might have thrown her for a minute or two, but it didn't look like it was going to last.

"Ellis, party of two, your table is ready," the hostess announced.

The hostess led them up the stairs to the second floor. The restaurant was light and airy, with royal oak-caned tables and scallop-backed chairs. As they settled at a table by the window, the lights of downtown Palo Alto surrounding them, Peter felt the relaxed ambiance of a Barcelona seaside resort. Jordan placed their dinner order, while Peter studied the wine list. "Ravenswood Old Hill Zin," he told the waiter.

"So, the supermodel," Jordan said, expression intent, once the waiter had gone.

Peter shrugged. "There's really not much to tell. I knew her as Mollie Greenberg. She was a struggling actress, modeling on the side. I was a struggling journalist. We connected, kept each other warm. New York can be a pretty cold place when you're struggling to make it. Then her modeling career took off. I got the job at *Computer Industry News* and started traveling a lot. We disconnected. End of story."

Jordan looked perplexed. "What do you mean struggling?"

Peter tensed. He flashed her a megawatt smile he hoped would cover the unintended slip. "Struggling to get my career on the right path."

"Oh."

The waiter returned with their wine. Peter went through the traditional tasting ritual—testing the cork for moisture, tasting the wine—on autopilot, distracted thoughts swirling like the wine in his glass.

When Jordan had first alerted him to their family connection he'd started digging, and he didn't like what he'd found. Sid Langley and Andrew Ellis were more than business colleagues; they were friends, golfing buddies. *How much time do I have before Jordan mentions me to her father, before Sid Langley turns to my father on the putting green, joking about "our kids," and gets the...*

"How is the wine, sir?"

The waiter and Jordan were eyeing him expectantly. Peter looked up and nodded; the waiter poured them each a glass, and left. Jordan took a sip of the wine.

"Exquisite," she pronounced, smiling sweetly at him.

"I couldn't agree more." He smiled back, studying her, wondering how she would react to his news. If that would be it for them. Taking a long, courage-building pull on the Zin, he bought time. *Tell her now*, his conscious urged. "Look, Jordan, I—"

"Lobster ravioli for the lady." The waiter had returned and was setting streaming plates of food in front of them. "Paella for you, sir. Is there anything else I can get for you?"

"No. Thank you," Jordan said, turning back to Peter as the waiter retreated. "You were saying?"

Peter leaned back in his chair. "I have a past. We all do. Why don't you tell me about yours?"

January 23, 1994: Cupertino, California

Toby switched on his workstation monitor. No activity yet, but it was still early, just after eleven p.m. Usually Michael Lee didn't log on until after midnight, especially on Sunday nights.

The owner of the house Toby had rented in Cupertino was proud of his computer and told Toby he was free to use it anytime. Toby nodded and waved as the man and his wife left on their world tour.

Then, with a derisive laugh, he quickly chucked the owners' IBM 80486 PC, with its twelve-inch monitor and cheap ink jet printer, into the nearest closet and replaced it with one of his own: two Unix workstations, a high-speed printer and three phone lines for modems. A scanner monitored police calls. Waiting for Michael to log on, he checked each device in a carefully arranged sequence.

Surveillance had always fascinated him. In Vietnam, surveillance involved the high-tech art of the time. The Marines had taught him the skills he needed to navigate his plane through the jungle at night, to pinpoint targets with unfailing accuracy. It had sparked his interest in computers and the electronics that made such sophisticated surveillance possible.

Even as a child, Toby had always liked to watch. Watching, tracking and waiting were the most important skills in the ritual of hunting. His father had taught him that. Still, his father never knew that Toby had watched him, had hidden in the large oak tree by the kitchen window and watched the people entering and leaving his house. His dad was a very popular man. Toby especially liked to watch through the window at night when the men came to drink and play cards. He learned to recognize habits, patterns of behavior that told him who had won and who had lost, who was cheating and who was playing fair. People seldom changed their habits, but when they did they were the most vulnerable and easiest to catch. His father had taught him that too.

The workstation monitoring Lee's computer beeped. Toby turned his attention back to the screen. Michael was scanning his email, as he did every night. It was all work-related, as usual. They were testing a new chip design Tuesday morning about one a.m., could Michael handle it? the sender asked. Michael agreed, and logged out of email and onto the Internet. Toby studied the screen, expecting him to check the mutual funds listing. Instead, Michael invoked a series of commands that led him directly to a chat room. Michael had broken his pattern, and Toby reacted quickly. Clicking a few keys, he captured the screen image, downloading the series of commands Michael had used in case he needed to retrace Michael's steps.

The chat room Michael entered was private. Michael typed the password needed to enter the chat room unaware that Toby had piggybacked onto his system like a parasite, watching every keystroke he made. Toby found Michael's naiveté appalling. Henry had certainly been lax with this boy, Toby snorted, as he watched the conversation begin.

Now off the Internet, Michael reset his modem and logged on again. Toby watched in surprise and consternation as Michael completed a series of password exchanges with a Unix server in San Francisco and began downloading a series of files.

Acting quickly, Toby captured the sequence and watched as Michael logged off. He went into the bedroom to change his clothes and, twenty minutes later, he backed his BMW out of the garage and drove north. He ended up at a pay phone in Brisbane, near the Cow Palace. The line crackled and hissed as Toby deposited quarter after quarter in the box. In his ragged blue jeans, stained overcoat and black wool hat, he could easily have passed for one of the homeless huddled in the nearby doorways. The smell of stale urine assaulted his nostrils as he pushed more coins in the slot.

Somewhere in West Palm Beach, a pager number beeped. Toby fed it the numbers on the pay phone and waited for the phone to ring. The cartel needed him, he reminded himself. They were businessmen with corporations to run.

Not so different from MediaBuilders, Toby thought with a wry smile. His partners in Colombia packaged and sold entertainment. Some people used TV or the movies to escape from reality, others used white powder that came in cellophane bags. It didn't really matter to him.

The phone jangled. Toby picked it up, and was greeted by Carl's Southern twang.

"Carl, it's me."

"How goes it?"

"I've pushed up the Horizon release date. The heat is on all the players."

"Good." Carl sounded relieved, the warmth genuine. Toby was reminded once more that the bonds formed in 'Nam had not been broken.

"We've got another problem, though. I need your help." Toby filled Carl in on the details.

"I'll handle it." Carl paused. Then he added sharply. "This thing with Lockwood?"

"Under control."

"Don't let it get in our way. You make Valdez nervous again, there's only so much I can do."

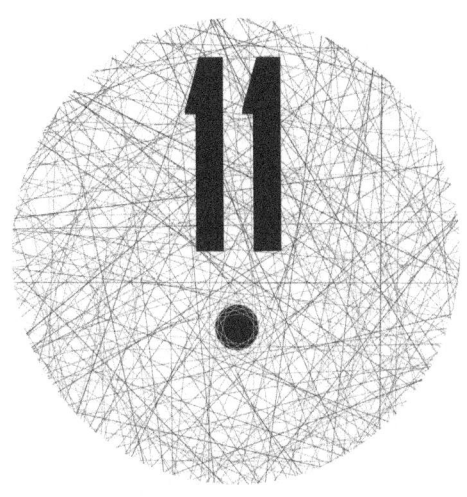

THE SCENE IN FRONT OF THE CONCRETE AND GLASS ADVANCED Micro Devices' building was chaotic. Six police cars were lined up on one side of the street. Bright yellow and black police tape prevented spectators from getting any closer than one hundred feet from the lobby doors.

Peter hurried up to the tape and flashed his press credentials at a young cop. A knot of print reporters stood in one cordoned-off section, waiting impatiently as the TV crews from two local stations set up to film the action. Peter joined the milling reporters, spotting Nate King from the *San Jose Mercury News*.

"Hi, Nate. Got any details yet?" Peter asked, stepping up beside him.

Nate nodded in Peter's direction. "One dead, two injured, gunshots, is all we've heard so far. They're going to get them out, and then talk to us."

The glass doors of the AMD building swung open. Paramedics emerged rapidly pushing two gurneys toward medical transport. The young Asian-American man on the first gurney mumbled incoherently as bright red blood soaked through his heavily bandaged leg. The paramedics loaded both gurneys into their vans, and, sirens screeching, exited the parking lot. The AMD doors closed again and the print reporters resumed their restless pacing while one of the TV crews began live coverage.

The doors opened a second time. TV cameras swung toward the action as the paramedics pushed a third gurney, carrying a green body bag, toward the second waiting medical van. This one was headed for the morgue. A medium-sized, balding man, his heavily lined face grimly set, followed the gurney out of the building. He looked up distractedly as a local TV reporter called his name and waved him over for an interview.

"Looks like Roger's got another tough one," Peter said to Nate, inclining his head toward Detective Roger Ferris, head of Santa Clara County's special crime unit.

"Yeah, and it looks like I've got time for a smoke," Nate snarled in disgust, as the Channel 7 TV team swarmed around the detective.

"Think I'll join you," Peter said. They leaned against the wall and lit up. A few minutes later, the TV crew started packing its equipment. Peter ground his cigarette butt into the pavement and joined the wave of print reporters surging forward, rabid for details.

"I'll give you the basic facts as we know them. Then open it up for questions," Ferris said, rubbing his leathery, moist face with his hand. "The robbery took place around three this morning. According to witnesses, two heavily armed men with semiautomatic weapons broke through the lobby. They went straight for one of the testing labs, where a shipment of microprocessors was being spot-tested for failures. They were after 80486 chips, and they knew exactly what they were looking for.

"They bound and gagged all three of the AMD employees. Two test specialists, Terry Chu and Calvin Briggs, were injured. Chu was shot in the leg. Briggs got a rifle butt in the teeth."

"What about the dead guy?" someone yelled out. "Who was he?"

"His name was Michael Lee. He's a company engineer. Apparently, he was here last night reviewing the test results. He was shot twice in the stomach."

"How'd it happen?"

"The details are sketchy. Chu and Briggs were face down on the floor. They can't tell us much. But it looks like Lee might have tried to be a hero and confront the assailants."

Nate's voice rose above the din. "There's been four of these robberies this year, Roger. What are you doing about them?"

"Following up every lead we get," Ferris responded. "That's all for now, folks. If you need anything else, you know where to reach me."

Peter chose not to join the mob chasing Ferris to his car. He knew Ferris well enough to know when he was through talking.

With the action over, the crowd scattered. Peter took one final look around. Out of the corner of his eye, he spotted a young woman leaning against the building, her faced marked with dried tears. Peter walked over.

"You okay?" he asked.

She nodded. "I just need to catch my breath. It's been a long morning. The police. All those questions and more to come," she added, her voice dipping to a whisper.

"I can imagine," Peter commiserated.

"I'm the one that found them," she volunteered.

"You were? I'm Peter Ellis, with the *Valley Tribune*. Could I ask you a few questions?"

She responded with a listless smile. "The police grilled me for two hours. Now I'm an expert at handling questions. What's a few more?"

"Thanks. I appreciate it. What's your name?"

"Nancy Dobson."

Peter listened quietly to her story. It would be a long time before Nancy would feel at peace again, if she ever could, he thought. He left his card and told her to call if she wanted to talk.

January 24, 1994: Palo Alto, California

"What do you have?" Ben asked Peter later, as Peter cradled his office phone.

"That was Ferris. I've got more details on the dead kid, Michael Lee. He was twenty-eight years old, worked for AMD for the last five years. Here's the tough part. He was a newlywed. Married about eight months."

"You talk to the wife?" Ben asked.

"I called. Someone, a relative I guess, is handing out the standard line. 'She's not talking to reporters.'"

"Okay, so how do you want to handle it?"

"Play up the violence and the death," Peter said. "Ferris said he was surprised at the level of violence. No one has been hurt in the other robberies. Lee was shot in the stomach. Ferris thinks maybe he got mouthy and one of the robbers had a hair-trigger temper. Then I'll get into the number of robberies we've had this year. Four so far."

Peter looked up at Ben. "Ferris told me off the record that he thinks it's a well-organized gang. I can't quote Ferris, of course, but I got one of those guys on that new crime commission to say virtually the same thing."

Ben gave Peter's shoulder a quick pat. "Good job," he said as he left Peter's office. Peter pounded out the story and sent it to Ben for editing. He closed the file on his screen and stared at the empty monitor. Nancy's parting words rang in his head. One of the injured test engineers had delivered a message to her. From Michael. As he lay dying.

"Tell Groucho it was for Helen."

January 24, 1994: Sunnyvale, California

Peter rang the doorbell a second time. He'd ring it a third time, and a fourth and a fifth if he had to. He was convinced he could wear down the occupants. Although the curtains in the modest Sunnyvale home were drawn, he could see the outline of two female forms. One was young, slim and graceful. The other was plump and walked with a stiff, cautious step. He waited a few minutes and pushed the glowing button again. He'd gotten lucky with Michael Lee. The Lees, Kim and Michael, were listed in the first directory he checked, with their complete address. Most people weren't that considerate these days.

The door creaked open. A stout, gray-haired woman blocked the passage. "What do you want?" she asked, not bothering to hide her annoyance.

"I'd like to speak with Mrs. Lee. I'm Peter Ellis, with the *Valley Tribune.*" Peter pulled a business card from his pocket.

The woman ignored the card. "She doesn't want to talk to anyone right now. She's had a terrible loss. I'd think you people would understand," she said, glaring at him as if she thought her stare would frighten him away.

"I do understand, but a murder has been committed. We have to try to find out the facts," Peter insisted.

"That's a matter for the police."

"But I just want to ask her a couple of questions. I've learned something that might be—"

"No," she said, slamming the door in Peter's face.

Peter focused on the closed door, trying to collect his thoughts. It had been a long time since a woman, any woman, had slammed a door in his face. Reluctantly, he climbed back into his car and headed for the office.

Tell Groucho it was for Helen.

What's that supposed to mean? he wondered as he pulled into the *Trib's* parking lot. He collected his messages from Tina without a word, and headed into his office. He hadn't expected Kim Lee to know what the phrase meant, but he hoped that she might know who Groucho was, or maybe Helen. All he needed was a place to start.

Picking up the phone, he called Nancy Dobson at AMD. "Nancy, it's Peter Ellis from the *Valley Tribune*. Got a minute?"

"Yes." She sounded a little stronger than she had the day before, but not much.

"I'm still looking into yesterday's shooting and I'm trying to get some background on Michael Lee. Do you happen to know where he worked before AMD?" Peter asked.

"No. I'm afraid I don't."

"Do you know if he played any computer games?"

"Of course. Doesn't everyone?"

"Around here, I guess so," Peter agreed. "Do you know what kind?"

"Well, all the regular ones, *Mortal Kombat*. Stuff like that."

"Anything he called puzzle games or riddles?" Peter asked.

"Mm." She paused. Peter waited through the silence.

"I'm not sure. No, I don't think so," she said.

"Thanks," Peter said, disconnecting as one of the kids from copy edit knocked on the door. Peter waved him inside.

"Ben wanted you to look at this obit on Michael Lee before we ran it, in case you found out anything new."

"So far it's a no-go."

The kid handed him three sheets of copy. Peter scanned the pages. *Bingo*, he thought.

"Looks fine to me."

Peter watched the kid retreat, closing the door behind him. Then he picked up the phone.

"Hi, Nancy. It's Peter Ellis. I'm sorry to bother you again, but I just have one more quick question. Do you know if Michael was friends with a guy named Brian Tucker? They worked at HP around the same time."

"Brian? Of course I know Brian," she replied, chuckling. "He's such a nut."

She paused. Peter heard scratches as she covered the mouthpiece and whispered to someone nearby.

"Excuse me, Peter. I've got an urgent call on another line. Can I call you back?"

"Yeah, sure."

Peter flipped his cell closed and opened the drawer where he tossed his used notebooks, searching for the one he'd taken to CES in January. Something Brian's friend Joe had said was floating at the edge of his consciousness. He rummaged through his drawer, tossing the notebooks on the floor like New Year's confetti, hunting for the one he needed.

"What was it?" he muttered, dropping the notebook on his desk and flipping the pages. His office phone buzzed.

"Sorry for the interruption," Nancy said when he answered. "Where were we?"

"You were talking about what a joker Brian Tucker is," Peter reminded her.

"Oh, yeah." Warmth coated her tone. "Michael was the serious type, but when Brian was around they were always doing these old-time comedy routines."

Peter's hands stopped in mid-search as the connection sank in. "Like the Marx Brothers?" he asked.

"One of their favorites."

"Thanks again, Nancy," Peter said, with relief.

He clicked open his email folder and sent Tim an urgent one-line message: *Got Brian Tucker's handle. It's Groucho.*

Then he grabbed his keys and headed out the door. He'd finally secured an interview with Jake Mullens, and he couldn't afford to be late.

January 24, 1994: Cupertino, California

Draco Communications' Cupertino headquarters was built for power and prestige. From the twelve-foot sculpture of the dragon-inspired Draco logo at the building entrance to the expensive, original modern art lining the lobby walls, Draco's opulence and Win Davis's looming presence were meant to simultaneously bolster customer confidence and minimize adversaries.

Standing at the reception desk, a visitor's badge dangling from his lapel, Peter had no doubt where he stood on that continuum, especially when it came to Alex Kavanagh. Kavanagh was running late, a subtle but clear signal of the continuing battle between them.

Peter had just started to pull his cell phone from his pocket to check messages when he saw Kavanagh walking briskly in his direction, smile fixed, hand outstretched. The mandatory handshake accomplished, the gloves came off.

"I apologize, Peter," Alex said with all the sincerity of a carnival barker. "Jake Mullens is unavailable today. We'll have to reschedule the interview."

Peter glared at Alex. There were some things even a company like Draco couldn't get away with and this was one of them. He turned to take off his visitor's badge.

Alex blinked and continued in a smooth, consoling tone. "But I was able to set up an interview for you with Devon O'Reilly. I hope that will make your trip down here worthwhile," he said, walking toward the elevators and inviting Peter to follow.

Peter could hardly protest. The interview with O'Reilly was plum, but it came at a price. Alex had offered Peter an exclusive interview with O'Reilly, a prime get—and virtually guaranteed that he wouldn't be ready for it. Peter appreciated the political sleight of hand while his mind scrambled to prepare his questions.

Alex escorted him into the conference room where Devon O'Reilly stood waiting. As Peter entered, O'Reilly took a step forward, beefy hand outstretched, a glint of mischief in his lively green eyes belying the strength of ego that lurked just below the surface. He settled into the chair opposite Peter. Alex took a seat next to O'Reilly.

"Well, Peter. Where would you like to start?" O'Reilly asked.

Alex stepped in before Peter could open his mouth. "We do have one bit of news to share," he said. "Devon has just agreed to join the Horizon team as lead software developer."

"Really?" Peter fixed Alex with a steely-eyed look. "When did this happen?"

You bastard, he thought, reliving the humiliating retraction he'd been forced to write less than two weeks ago. Alex's face was impassive. As if he could feel the heat of the energy between them, O'Reilly looked uneasily from one man to the other.

"On Friday," O'Reilly replied.

"We'll be issuing a press release this afternoon," Alex added, letting Peter know he wasn't getting an exclusive on it. It would be part of the daily news cycle.

Alex's pager buzzed. He glanced at it and stood. "I need to take this," he said, exiting the room.

O'Reilly turned back to Peter. "Now that he's gone, what do you really want to talk about?"

Peter hesitated. An open and honest conversation was likely to be O'Reilly's style, but it was just as likely that Alex was using O'Reilly to bait him or send him on some wild goose chase. Peter decided to trust the twinkle in O'Reilly's eyes and edged toward frankness.

"Just out of curiosity, when did the conversations about you joining the team start?"

"Two, maybe three weeks ago," O'Reilly replied, confirming that Peter's original story had been accurate if not official. Alex had two points on him. Peter intended to use this private interview with O'Reilly to even the score.

"How does it feel to be competing against your ex-partner?"

O'Reilly settled into his chair and considered the question. "David and I have been on separate tracks for years now. I wish him all the best."

"The buzz is that Sapphire has it all over Horizon for technical innovation."

O'Reilly frowned and shook his head. "David has a good box, I'll grant you that, but the key to these boxes is the software and that's where David always struggles. Horizon has a better user interface, applications and security. At least it will when I get done tweaking the code," O'Reilly added proudly.

Peter smiled. "So Horizon beats Sapphire hands down on the technology?"

"No question."

"What about the video algorithm? I've heard you had some big problems with it and you might even have to push back the launch date."

O'Reilly's expression turned to granite. "Where'd you hear that?"

Peter met his gaze. "Around."

O'Reilly shook his head. "Someone's blowing you smoke. We about done here? I've got a meeting in a few minutes."

Peter changed tactics. "Just a couple more questions. I understand security is the biggest issue on the Internet right now?"

"You bet it is," O'Reilly agreed, relaxing again. "It's like the Wild West out there. To any halfway decent hacker it's like being a kid in a candy store. We're starting to nail down the standards and protocols, but we've got a long way to go. I'd like to see a lot more programmers focusing on Internet security."

Peter parsed the information. The connection was vague, but he figured he would give it a shot. "What about puzzle games? Would that be a good way to find security experts?" he asked.

"You mean crypto-riddles?"

"Yes." Peter jotted down the new term.

"Sure," O'Reilly said, looking at Peter with new respect. "It's one of the fastest ways to see who's really got the chops and who's giving you a line."

"Do you play them?"

"Play 'em?" O'Reilly replied with a short laugh. "Hell, yes. But mostly I write 'em. Give the kids a real run for their money."

"How do you play them?"

"On the Net. Open up a chat room. Invite a few players in. Of course, back in the pre-Internet days, we'd just post the riddles to a secure server onsite and let the kids have a go at them."

"What about sending disks directly to players?" Peter asked.

O'Reilly looked surprised. "You mean mailing floppies around?" Peter nodded.

"I can't imagine anyone doing that," O'Reilly replied, looking confused. He paused, narrowed his eyes, and added slowly, "unless the information was so top secret and hot that you couldn't risk exposure at any cost." He looked at Peter. "But then, if it was that important, it wouldn't be a game, would it?"

The door swung open and Alex reentered the room. "Devon, we have an engineering team meeting in two minutes."

Peter and Devon stood and shook hands. "Thank you for your time," Peter said.

"I'll walk you out," Alex motioned Peter to the door.

• • • •

Toby was making notes on a series of computer printouts as Devon and Alex entered the conference room.

"How'd it go?" Toby asked Devon, without looking up. Avoiding eye contact with Devon whenever possible was part of his strategy.

"Typical. He wanted all the dirt on Horizon versus Sapphire."

"He get anything?"

Devon shook his head. "He did ask one odd thing though." Devon's tone turned thoughtful. "He asked about crypto-riddles, you know, puzzle games. He asked who played them. How they were played."

Toby's eyes darted in Devon's direction before returning to the schematic before him. His shoulders tensed. "Really?"

"Yeah, I said we used them to test who had the chops in Internet security."

"True enough." Toby grunted.

"And that's when he asked the weirdest question of all. He asked about mailing floppy disks around. You ever heard of that?"

Toby froze. His fingers, clenching the pen, turned white at the knuckles. He forced himself to relax, smiled and turned to Devon with a shake of his head. "That's a new one. What did you tell him?"

Devon shrugged. "That it didn't sound like my kind of game."

Toby held the pen out to Devon. "Why don't you check these? See if there's something I missed."

Devon moved over to the worktable and Toby stepped away. He stood watching his engineering team file into the room for their weekly meeting, his mind in hyper-drive, trying to decide how to handle the reporter he could no longer consider just a nuisance.

January 24, 1994: Los Altos Hills, California

Peter parked his Porsche next to Jordan's Mercedes and surveyed the cottage. It was classic Cape Cod, white with dark green trim, almost a miniature of the house his parents owned on the Vineyard. As he stepped onto the porch, Jordan opened the door to greet him.

"Welcome." She wore jeans, a cashmere sweater and diamond studs in her ears. Her feet were bare. He offered her a gift bag. "Since I didn't know what we were having, I brought some choices."

She peeked in the bag and withdrew a 1992 Cakebread Chardonnay and a 1985 Silver Oak Cabernet. "Oh, lovely," she said, giving him a peck on the cheek. She took his jacket and hung it on a coat rack by the front door, then turned and smiled softly at him with lips too inviting to resist. He leaned toward her and planted a kiss on them. She let the kiss linger for a long moment before stepping back.

"My place," she said, with a wave of her hand.

Looking around the oversized living room, he appreciated the warmth and comfort of the décor. The walls were a robin's egg blue, the crown molding around the ceiling and doors bright white. Lacy curtains in a scallop design framed the wooden blinds. A white linen sofa was fronted by an oval teakwood coffee table. Two blue and white-striped accent chairs sat on either side of a brass-rimmed fireplace. The fire burned brightly. Peter, still chilled from the damp fog, moved closer to the heat.

"Great place," he said, noticing that her taste in artwork, land and seascapes, mirrored his own.

"Thanks. I like it." She handed him the Cakebread. "Would you open the wine? I'll get the glasses."

As she passed him, she seemed to startle at the envelope resting on the edge of the table. She picked it up and furtively tucked in the pocket of her jeans. Peter caught a quick glimpse of the corner and noticed the writing was not in English. French, maybe?

Jordan returned quickly with the glasses, a wine opener and a small plate of California rolls. As she sat down beside him, Peter uncorked the wine and poured her a glass of Chardonnay. "You do know your wines," she said, taking a sip.

"I belong to a couple of clubs. Silver Oak has a winemaker's dinner coming up in a couple of weeks if you'd like to go."

"What day is that?" she asked.

"Saturday."

"Can't do Saturdays." Jordan rested her glass on the coffee table, turned toward him. Her expression was guarded.

"Any Saturday?"

"Not right now. But Fridays are good," she said, biting into the last California roll. "Ready for more?" she asked.

Peter watched as she rose and headed back toward the kitchen. *So I get Fridays*, he thought sourly, wondering where and with whom she spent her Saturday nights. Then he chided himself. She didn't owe him anything, and generally he preferred it that way. Jordan returned with a large plate of sushi delicacies. Without knowing it, she had chosen all of his favorites: *toro, ika, hamachi, uni, saba, unagi.* Even quail egg.

"Looks fantastic," he said.

"Dig in," she said, picking up the *hanachi,* and dropping it delicately into her mouth. Peter took a piece of *toro.*

"How about some music? What do you listen to?" she asked. He noticed a wall unit almost entirely filled with CDs and record albums.

"I like classical when I write. It helps me concentrate. Otherwise, whatever's on the radio." He paused and gave her a knowing look. "I know what you like, the techno-house music we heard the other night."

Jordan laughed. "Not really. That's just for blowing off some steam when I want to dance for fun. My serious passion is… well, here, let me show you," she said moving to a large audio cabinet. The rack was stacked with equipment. Peter only recognized half of it, the CD player, receiver and turntable. The three other boxes were a mystery. She selected several CDs and placed them on the changer.

"Jazz." She swung her hips to the music as smooth sounds filled the room. Peter found her swaying hypnotic. He longed to embrace her. As he started to rise, she stopped dancing and turned toward him.

"David Sanborn," Jordan said, rejoining him on the sofa. "What do you think?"

"Nice."

The disheartened look on her face surprised him. "Very nice." He tried again, but her expression didn't change.

"Why don't you play some more?" he asked, buying time to discern her mood.

"Really?" That seemed to cheer her up. At least he was heading in the right direction.

"Yeah."

"Okay, this is a classic." She pulled an old vinyl record from her shelf, put it on the turntable and turned toward him. "Tell me how it makes you feel."

Peter leaned back on the couch and closed his eyes. He had no idea why this exercise was so important to Jordan, only that it was; for the moment, that was enough for him. He focused on the sounds and let his mind do what it did best: parse and analyze the data his senses were collecting.

"I'm on a city street, urban, kids are throwing coins in a gutter. Somewhere where stuff should be happening, maybe in the past, but not now. Like Hollywood and Vine."

"Are you serious? You got that from this song?" Jordan sounded incredulous.

Peter opened his eyes. "Yeah, why?"

"Because that's actually what that song is about, it's Wes Montgomery's "Bumpin' on Sunset.""

Peter sat up, gave her a grin and took a sip of wine. "I like it. How did you get into jazz, anyway?"

Jordan rose and pulled out another old vinyl record. "My uncle loves jazz. He gave me this record when I was seven," she paused, studying the album cover. "Miles Davis, 'Round About Midnight.' I've loved jazz ever since."

"I'd like to hear it."

She put the album on the turntable, glancing at him over her shoulder. "I don't want to bore you."

"You're not."

She studied him intently for a few minutes. "Well, okay."

Jordan listened enraptured, her face dreamy and distant. Peter knew he wasn't hearing what she was. He never did. His concert-going friends accused him of having a tin ear. All he ever heard were high and low sounds, the rest indistinct and muddled. He did better when he really concentrated, so he worked at it. Now, Jordan took him on a tour of the jazz greats: she played Miles, Coltrane, Dave Brubeck, Charlie Parker and Dizzy Gillespie before circling back to her new smooth jazz favorites, David Sanborn, Dave Koz and Richard Elliot. They sat nibbling sushi, drinking the Chardonnay  and then half the Silver Oak, until it actually was around midnight.

Jordan glanced at her watch as the last notes of Kenny G's "By the Time This Night is Over" faded away. "I didn't realize it was so late," she said.

Peter took her hand. She turned toward him, the joy of the music still lighting her features. He embraced her, tasting moisture and heat in her kiss. She responded tentatively at first, her lips brushing his cheeks. As her mouth found his, she softly suckled his lower lip. His breathing quickening, he pressed his lips against hers, his fingers lightly caressing the hollow of her throat.

"I'd like to stay," he whispered, pulling back to study her face glistening in the firelight.

She took his hand and held it as she moved away from him, her eyes bright with longing. "Not tonight."

Peter sat up and inhaled, waiting for his heart rate to drop. "Okay," he said in a voice both tense and husky.

She reached out and touched his cheek. "It's not you. It's me. I have some things to sort out first."

"This about those Saturday nights?" he asked, reluctantly standing.

"That's part of it." She stood next to him, a little too close for comfort, giving him a long, searching look. "You are just so not what I expected."

12

A SPEEDING POLICE CAR, ITS SIREN WAILING, PASSED PETER AS HE turned onto Hamilton Avenue. Falling behind it, he followed its course and immediately recognized its destination.

"What the hell?" he mouthed.

The police car screeched to a halt outside the Trib's offices. Two young officers, one a large black man, the other a thin dark-haired female, exited the vehicle and started toward the stairs. Peter parked his car and sprinted after them.

"Hey! What happened?" he called as he pulled his press credentials out of his wallet and flashed them at the cops.

The two officers exchanged glances. "We won't know anything until we've secured the scene and investigated. You'll help us the most by staying right here out of the way," the female officer said.

"I need to get into that building," Peter said, moving forward.

"Not now," the black cop responded, blocking Peter's way.

People spilled out of the neighboring offices, gawking as several more police cars arrived at the scene. Sam came running up beside Peter. "What's going on?" he asked.

"Don't know yet," Peter replied.

As they watched, the officers methodically moved to the stairs, pulling yellow police tape across the railing to prevent the crowd from gaining access. Then they entered the elevator, secured it and disappeared from sight. The crowd watched for a while, then bored with the inactivity, started to disperse. Peter paced in front of the police tape, frustration mounting.

"This is bullshit," he snapped at Sam. "I'm not going to stand around out here like some rubbernecker. C'mon. Let's check the back door."

They rounded the corner and bounded up the back stairs, through an open door and into the production room just as the two officers entered from the other side of the room.

The female cop shot Peter a warning glare as Peter and Sam walked slowly through the chaos. The production department was a disaster. Every filing cabinet and desk drawer hung open, its contents exposed. Graphics, art boards and layout materials littered the floor. A vase of flowers on one woman's desk had tipped over. The vase, pushed by the wind sailing through the open door, rolled back and forth on the desk as water dripped soundlessly off the edge, pooling on the carpet beneath. The back door to the patio was propped open with a steel toolbox.

The production team was huddled mutely in the middle of the devastation. Peter looked up and saw Doug Alvarez, the staff photographer, slumped against the door of the photo lab and looking inconsolable.

"Hey, Doug. What happened?"

Doug turned. His mouth trembled as he spoke. "They got the cameras, Peter, all four of them. And the PowerBooks, including yours."

"Son of a bitch," Peter groaned. His life was in that computer. He had no idea how long it would take to recover from the loss. He traded a commiserating look with Doug just as his cell phone buzzed.

"Yeah," he said into the phone, walking back to his office.

"Hey, Peter. It's Tim. You Okay? You sound weird."

"The *Trib* got burgled last night." Peter slumped into his chair and kicked the office door closed.

"Are you serious?"

"Yeah. It looks like they got everything worth fencing, including my PowerBook."

"Wow!" Tim exclaimed. "That's bad. Really bad. You have any idea what somebody could do with that information? Your security codes? Your passwords?"

Peter felt a chill at the words, but he dismissed the feeling as paranoid. "C'mon. Tim. We're talking about thieves here, not hackers."

"Yeah, well, just to be on the safe side, I'm changing all your passwords and codes right now," Tim replied, keyboard clicking at top speed. "I'll send you some new ones, encoded, this afternoon."

"Thanks," Peter said. Even though he thought Tim was overreacting, he was grateful for the support and concern.

"You called me. Got anything from those Internet groups yet?"

"Nope. I posted an email to Groucho guaranteed to generate a response, but it's only been up a couple of days. Let's give it till the weekend. More people log on then."

"Okay," Peter said. "I was hoping we'd get something by now."

"Well."

"What is it, Tim?"

"I didn't want to say anything until after the weekend, but I think these guys are private. Not on the Net. Maybe it was just Tucker and Lee."

"You're forgetting about Henry. He sent out the original package as far as we know, and now we have a Helen, too."

"Yeah, and four's a good number for a group to play a circuit. It's the disk that gets me. Mailing disks all over the place? That's weird, dude. Really weird. Even for the security addicts in these groups."

"I see what you mean," Peter said. "Let's chat this weekend, okay?"

Tim paused. Peter heard a heavy sigh through the receiver.

"I dunno, Peter. I've got some thinking to do," Tim said.

"What's up?"

"I finally got my re-org assignment. Six months on a stupid-ass maintenance project and then, in the words of my manager, 'We'll see.'" Tim's voice dropped. Peter could hear the disillusionment in his tone.

"Jeez. That's cold. After seven years. When did you find that out?"

"This morning. Anyway I've got to go."

"Okay. Keep me posted," Peter said, disconnecting and pocketing his car keys. His source on Horizon had promised him some big news, and he needed it to make up for that empty interview with Devon O'Reilly.

• • • •

Tina handed him her message as soon as he walked back into the office: *Jordan called. Change of plans.* Peter's shoulders slumped. He hadn't realized how much he'd been counting on her spirited presence, tonight, to erase the remains of the dismal day.

"She said she tried your cell," Tina said.

Peter dug his hand into his pocket and came up empty. "Must have left it on my desk."

"It's been that kind of a day."

"It sure has." He started down the hallway, passing Sam on his way to his office.

"How we doing?" Peter asked him.

Sam nodded, smiling. "We got her done. Production just broke out the brew."

"They deserve it." Peter felt a surge of pride in the *Trib's* production team. In the fifty-two years it had been publishing, the paper had never missed a delivery date. Today would be no exception, even with the tremendous odds against it.

He retrieved his cell from his desk and returned Jordan's call. He couldn't help smiling when she answered. It was good to hear her voice. "What's the change of plans?"

"A few of us want to go to *The Thin Man* festival that's opening tonight at the Esquire. Want to come?"

"Sure," Peter said. He hadn't seen those old movies in years, and he needed a good laugh, he thought, after the day he'd had.

"Great," she said. "There's just one more thing. We're all going in vintage 1930s clothes." She laughed lightly, enjoying throwing him yet another curveball.

"Jordan. How am I supposed to find vintage clothes in a couple of hours?" He could picture that wicked grin of hers, her eyes shining in merriment, and smiled despite the aggravation this new twist would create.

"Be creative."

Be creative. Thanks, Jordan, Peter thought, shaking his head as he walked over to the front desk. If anyone could help him out of this predicament, it would be Tina.

"Hey, Tina. Got a favor to ask. Can you tell me where I can find a vintage clothes store right now?" Peter asked.

Tina, who was used to odd requests from the *Tribune* staffers, even on a day as bizarre as this one, barely paused to consider the question before replying.

"Sure. I know just the place."

January 27, 1994: Palo Alto, California

The Thin Man Film Festival was more than just a night at the movies. It was gala event, Peter concluded, as he struggled to find an empty parking place near the theater. Vintage cars lined Emerson Street. A classic car buff, Peter immediately recognized a 1930 Blackhawk, a 1935 Studebaker President Eight and a 1938 Rolls-Royce parked in front of the theater.

Most of the crowd milling in front of the theater was dressed as he was, in vintage 1930s attire. Many of the men wore striped, herringbone or brown cheviot tweed single or double-breasted suits. All of them wore fedoras. Peter's double-breasted navy pinstripe suit, with its long trousers, fit right in. He surveyed the crowd and saw Tina standing in line next to her boyfriend. She gave him the thumbs up. He was glad he had asked her to help him pick out the right look.

The theater doors opened and the back of the crowd surged forward, moving Peter with them. As he was propelled toward the side door, he noticed Jordan's friend Grace, wearing a silver sequined gown, waving frantically and trying to catch his eye. Jordan and three other people he didn't recognize were standing close by. He managed to extract himself from the moving mob and walk toward them just as they approached the ticket taker.

Even in the sea of vintage dresses, little pillbox hats, veils and gloves, Jordan stood out. Her height, almost six feet in heels, helped; and her dress of silky turquoise charmeuse was backless to the tight waist, with a low V-neckline and braided straps. The soft silk floated around her long legs as she stepped forward, and she wore black evening gloves and a black pillbox hat. Jordan pointed to Peter as she handed two tickets to the usher, and they glided into the crowded lobby past a throng noisily buying popcorn, candy and sodas.

"Sorry I'm late," he mumbled to Jordan. "The *Trib* got broken into last night."

Jordan reacted with predictable shock. "Oh no! Did you lose anything?"

"My PowerBook. My life is in that thing."

"Oh, that's terrible."

"I'm just glad to be here," he said, smiling into her dark brown eyes.

She turned and placed a gloved hand on his arm as they walked toward the doors leading into the main theater. The seats were filling up fast. Jordan had her eye on the center row halfway up the tiered seating.

"Let me do some quick introductions," she said as they stood in the aisle waiting to enter the row of seats.

"You know Grace, and this is KC, Taylor and Josh," she said, pointing in turn to a medium-sized Asian man with wire-rimmed glasses, a dainty-looking strawberry blonde, and broad-shouldered, long-limbed, deeply tanned man with a relaxed smile.

"You're gorgeous," Jordan whispered to Peter as they took their seats.

"You look so Jean Harlow," he whispered back, giving her hand a squeeze as the lights dimmed, *The Thin Man* credits rolled and the comedy began. The crowd erupted with hoots of laugher. Peter, who hadn't seen the films since his college days, relaxed; he forgot, for the moment, the burglary at the *Tribune*, his disquieting conversation with Devon O'Reilly, and the puzzle disk he could no longer consider a game.

• • • •

"Let's go to Le Jardin Des Cygnes," Josh suggested to the group as they exited the theater two hours later.

"Great idea," Jordan and Taylor responded in union.

"Don't think I know that one," Peter said.

It just opened a couple of weeks ago. It's in an alley off Paulsen. We can avoid the crowds," Josh replied, ambling west on Emerson with the rest of the troop in tow. Peter recognized Josh as the take-charge type. From the way he and Taylor mouthed the lines of the film together, Peter also assumed Josh was the film buff who had planned the event.

One in every crowd, Peter thought. Taking stock of the subtle nuances that defined the social interactions of Jordan's set, he guessed that Taylor, Josh and Jordan had been grade school friends, and that Grace and KC were latecomers who had recently gained admittance to the tight circle. Being Jordan's new date, he understood the ritual of this social order demanded that he get the third degree tonight. It was another reminder of why he typically avoided dating girls like Jordan. The social games they played were so tedious. Then Jordan slipped her arm in his. As he felt the heat of her body through silky fabric, he decided that, for tonight at least, the third degree was a small price to pay for her company.

The leisurely stroll through the streets of downtown Palo Alto turned the walk into a promenade, preserving the magic and mood of the evening. The ladies' dresses seemed to glide across the pavement. As they walked along, Jordan filled Peter in on her friends' backgrounds and relationships. After a few stares from the passersby, Josh, Peter and KC doffed their hats at startled couples— to the constant giggles of the girls—until they reached Le Jardin Des Cygnes.

The café décor was French country garden. A splendid mural of a lake with two swans swimming past a lush garden of lilies, irises and floribunda roses filled the wall behind a counter stocked with pastries, sandwiches and desserts. As Josh had predicted, the café was virtually empty. The half-dozen other patrons looked at the six of them with idle curiosity as they arranged themselves around the center table.

"Champagne, anyone?" Josh queried to murmured assents from the group. He went to the counter to place the order.

"So, Peter. Jordan tells us you're a reporter," Josh noted, returning to his seat. He gave Peter the kind of look reserved for 'the alien among us'.

Let the games begin, Peter thought with an inward sigh.

"That's right."

Taylor leaned forward, interested. "Like murder and mayhem?"

Peter laughed. "Nothing quite so macabre. I cover business and technology."

Taylor looked disappointed. After three hours with Nick and Nora, murder was still on all of their minds.

"Do you know anything about this Internet stuff?" KC asked.

"A little," Peter replied.

"So enlighten us," Josh suggested, his tone slightly mocking.

"Have you heard the term 'information highway'?" Peter asked.

Heads nodded around the table.

"Well, they call it that for a reason. The Internet is a network of digital roads just like the interstate highway system. When the interstates were built, they opened up land for development in Santa Clara and Danville, all around the Bay, right?"

Peter had their attention. Only Josh retained a skeptical air.

"The Internet will open up new places to shop, to be entertained, even—" here Peter looked directly at Josh, the banker "—do your banking from home, twenty-four hours a day, seven days a week."

Josh's laugh was more like a cackle. He turned to Jordan. "Your boy's got quite an imagination."

Jordan looked amused, enjoying the action as she would a good tennis match. Peter could defend himself. She wouldn't ride to the rescue. The arrival of the champagne let Peter off the hook. The waiter placed a bottle of Perrier-Jouët, six glasses and two large plates of tea sandwiches on the table.

"Food!" Taylor squealed. "Josh, you're brilliant," she said, elbowing him in the ribs, giving credence to Peter's assumption that they had been schoolmates before they married.

"Cheers," Jordan said, raising her glass to the table. Once everyone had toasted, sipped and grabbed a sandwich, Josh turned his attention back to Peter.

Jordan stepped in before Josh could resume his interrogation. "I thought the Internet was about email." she said.

"We have email. We just got AOL," Taylor added, pulling a sandwich off the plate.

"Yeah. We got this CD in the mail." Josh shrugged. "Taylor wanted to try it."

"But I don't have anyone to email," Taylor complained. "Jordan won't do it."

"I don't want it. Too annoying." Jordan looked pointedly at Peter, "You want to talk to me, you need to call."

"Or maybe I'll just whistle." Peter grinned.

"Wrong movie," Jordan said dryly.

"Seriously, though, you really think the Internet is going to be that big?" KC asked, resuming the discussion.

Peter nodded. "Especially in entertainment. I'm following two companies now that are developing what's called Internet streaming video, technology that will make it possible for you to watch movies and TV shows on your laptop computer and eventually even on your cell phone."

In his peripheral vision, Peter saw Josh reach into Taylor's purse and pull out his cell phone. The thing was a monster. One of those old car phone jobs, with a backlit green LED screen about an inch square. Josh placed the phone on the table in front of him, staring intensely at it.

"How is that possible?" KC asked.

"It's called an Internet set-top box. It converts TV signals to computer signals..." Peter's voice trailed off as everyone's focus shifted to Josh, still staring intently at his cell phone. He broke into a grin, then a laugh, seemingly oblivious to their stares.

Finally, Taylor could stand it no longer. "Hells, bells, Josh. What are you doing?"

Keeping his eyes on the tiny LED screen, Josh replied, "I'm watching Seinfeld on my phone."

The entire table erupted in laughter. Taylor guffawed, covering her mouth with her hand. Jordan, giggling, dabbed the corners of her eyes with the edge of a tissue. Laughing along with the rest of them, Peter threw his hands up in mock helplessness.

"I can't tell you when, but I can tell you it's coming. It's in the lab. I've seen it," he said, still chuckling.

"Oh, it's in the lab. Like Frankenstein." Josh rejoined, stretching out his hands and moving them robotically. He looked over at Peter with humor in his eyes. Jordan elbowed him in the ribs with a grin, the way Taylor had done with Josh. Oddly and unexpectedly, Peter felt relaxed and comfortable with all of them.

Jordan playfully put her hands over her ears. "No more geekspeak," she declared. "Anyone planning to go to the French Open this year?"

Talk around the table turned to tennis as the evening wound down. Josh tallied the bill the waiter presented and they split it among the couples.

"We should get going, Josh," Taylor said. They stood to leave. KC, Grace and Peter rose as well.

"I'd like to talk to you some more about this Internet stuff," Josh told Peter as they shook hands.

"Sure." Peter turned to Jordan, who had remained seated. "Ready?" he asked.

She shook her head. "Let's finish the champagne."

There were about two glasses left in their second bottle. Peter poured them each a glass and sat back down.

"Nice people," Peter said, relaxing with a sip of champagne. He was delighted that Jordan wanted to continue the conversation.

"I've known Josh and Taylor since kindergarten. Josh was my first kiss," she said.

"Ah," Peter said with a smile. "The one that got away."

"Hardly," Jordan sniffed. "Josh is staid, conservative, way too traditional. And, in case you didn't notice, more than a tad arrogant."

"I noticed."

"But Taylor and I were inseparable. You should have seen the hysterics I pulled when Daddy wouldn't send me to Foxcroft," Jordan said with a light laugh.

"You wanted to go to boarding school?" Peter asked. He recalled the feeling of abandonment he'd experienced being tossed on a plane like excess baggage and sent across the country to New Hampshire, a place he'd never even heard of, at the age of eight.

"Of course. If Taylor was going, I was going too. We were joined at the hip. She was the sister I never had."

Peter's stomach clenched at the word *sister.* "You won in the end," he said, taking a sip of the champagne.

"I begged, pleaded, cajoled, screamed and cried until eventually I wore Daddy down. I think after all that he was happy to let me go."

Peter imagined so. He felt a brief stab of pity for Sid Langley and anyone else who attempted to thwart Jordan's strong will.

"But when Taylor and Josh went on to Princeton, I came back here to Stanford. I didn't want to leave Daddy alone for another four years," Jordan continued.

"Daddy seems like the possessive type," Peter observed.

Jordan's eyes flashed. Peter realized immediately that he'd said the wrong thing.

"I apologize," he said. "That was out of line."

She studied her champagne glass and did not seem to hear him.

The bubbles were fading away. When she looked back up at him, he could see through the netted veil of her hat that her eyes were darker, moist. He'd touched a nerve.

"I'm the possessive one," she said quietly. "It's just Daddy and me. My mom died when I was five. Breast cancer. She fought it for years. In and out of hospitals and treatment. I never knew her healthy and happy."

"I understand," he said. Ancient grief, suddenly potent again, contorted her features. *Do you really?* her expression asked.

His first instinct was to make her laugh, ease her distress, and avoid extending the uncomfortable intimacy of the conversation. Then Peter took a long, appreciative look at the enchanting woman sitting across the table from him. The plunging neckline. The soft luster of the pearls at her throat. Sitting in this French café, wearing vintage clothes; it all felt so otherworldly, like they were strangers on a train, each of them sharing their deepest secrets with someone they knew they'd never see again. Without making a conscious choice, he opened up to her.

"My sister Megan died when I was eight," he explained. "It was so sudden. One day she was a vibrant, alive college student, just about to graduate from Berkeley, and the next day she was gone."

"What happened?" Jordan asked, compassion replacing grief on her face. That look compelled him to continue.

"She had a brain aneurysm. It burst and she died. Her roommate found her slumped over her desk, books open, studying for finals," Peter said, a lump in his throat. He hadn't thought of Megan for years. He'd buried that tragedy, like his other painful memories, as deeply as he could. It startled him to realize that he could still feel it.

Jordan reached over and gave his hand a squeeze. "How dreadful," she said. "At least we had time to be prepared. You didn't."

"It was a quite a shock," Peter agreed, remembering how his family had reacted, in typical fashion, by scattering. He stared into his glass as tiny bubbles rose from the bottom and burst. He could feel Jordan's eyes resting on him as he resumed speaking softly.

"My father took off for Japan. My mother took to her bed and my older sister Margaret took charge. In her first act as titular head of the family, she shipped me as far away from home as she possibly could—New Hampshire."

"Why would your sister do that to you?" Jordan asked. Her feelings as an only child showed on her face. It was hard enough for her to imagine one sister dying young. That the other sister would choose to banish him was beyond her comprehension.

Peter hesitated, picked up his glass, swirled the last of the liquid and downed it. Jordan was watching him intently, expectantly. He'd opened the door, he thought, now he'd have to walk through it.

"She hates me," he said finally. "She has from the moment I was born. You see, I stole her birthright." He tried for a smile but it died on his lips.

"The male heir," she replied. Unlike Jessica, Jordan didn't need an explanation of what that meant.

"Fifteen years after the fact," he added.

"A late, nasty surprise. No wonder. It's sad, though, to have a sister you're not friends with," Jordan said. Her eyes matched her words.

Forget friends. Try mortal enemies, Peter thought. TriCorp was just the latest in a lifelong series of injuries Margaret had inflicted.

"Yeah," he agreed with a shrug.

Jordan pushed her sandwich plate to the side. "It can't have been easy."

"What?"

"Letting go."

Her remark startled him. It hit so close to the truth and was uttered in such a quietly confidential tone that Peter wondered if she had already discovered what he had avoided telling her.

There was a longing in her eyes that he couldn't fathom. She continued to mystify and intrigue him. Tonight he saw Jordan as the consummate socialite, fully enmeshed in a world he despised and had renounced. A world he refused to be drawn back into. The girl he'd met for drinks presented herself as a free spirit. Then there was the fierce tennis competitor. Finally and most unnerving was the intuitive woman who seemed able to unlock his deepest secrets with ease. He had a vague, uneasy feeling that spending time with Jordan was going to cost him something, but he had no idea what it would be.

"Depends on what you have to gain," he replied.

"And what did you gain?"

"I think the only way to answer that question is to first tell you what I've lost."

Jordan leaned forward.

An older man approached the table. "I'm sorry, sir. But we are closing. It's midnight."

Peter glanced at his watch and back at the man. "So it is. Time to go," he said to Jordan.

"Thanks for the lovely evening," she said as they walked along now-deserted streets.

"My pleasure."

When they reached her car, she turned to him, hesitating. Her eyes crisscrossed his face. Folding her hands behind his neck, she reached for him. Her mouth feathered his with gentle caresses. He responded with a long, lingering, deep kiss, his fingers lightly stroking her naked back. She shivered and pulled him closer.

"We could go to my place," he whispered.

"I can't," she said, breaking the embrace. "It's nearly one o'clock in the morning. I'm meeting Daddy for breakfast at six and I can't go like this." She stepped back, running her fingers down the sides of her vintage dress from bodice to hips.

"Why not?" Peter asked with a devilish grin. "I would."

Jordan laughed. "I bet you would, too," she said, playfully pulling his fedora down over his face.

She stepped back in, melting against him, the soft puffs of her breath warming his cheek. He was so hot for her he couldn't move. She pushed his hat back up and looked directly into his deep blue eyes.

"How's Saturday for you?"

"Saturday? I thought that Saturdays were off limits?" he asked, puzzled.

"Just nights."

• • • •

Toby leaned against the wall of the old theater, now dark and deserted, watching them flirting, laughing; not a care in the world. She pulled his hat down over his eyes, kissing him. They looked so ridiculous in those silly costumes. Like foolish, vulnerable children.

Toby studied Peter as he open her car door, watch as she left and then start strolling down the street, his head held high, without even a glance around to see what dangers the night and shadows might contain.

Earl Junior was like that too, Toby thought with a snort. *Blissfully ignorant. Gilded children. They never see it coming.*

HORSEBACK RIDING WAS NOT ON PETER'S LIST OF FAVORITE THINGS. But it was on Jordan's. So, here he was driving down a country road in search of the adventure Jordan had planned for them. She had told him, during that first drink at the BBC, that she wanted action and adventure; and she had yet to disappoint him, though he was not looking forward to this one. He had a distant memory of a riding a horse at a long-ago summer camp and a vague feeling that it had not gone well.

He turned off Woodside Road toward Greenhaven Stables and headed down a long gravel driveway. A horse trailer passed him going in the opposite direction. The size of it on the small road almost forced him into a ditch. *Not a good omen*, he thought, driving up to the stables past a large arena where a group of giggling teenage girls practiced jumping drills. He noticed a girl washing a white pony, just as the pony shook himself vigorously and sent a splash of water down the front of his young owner's sweatshirt. She laughed and sprayed water from the hose back at him.

Parking next to Jordan's car, he got out and turned toward the barn, an oversized gray wood building split into three sections. The two outer sections held stalls and paddocks for about ten horses each. The horses, lazily chewing hay, tails actively swishing at flies, seemed innocent even to Peter's wary eye.

Next to the fence, Jordan stood talking to a young man holding the reins of a massive black horse. They were both dressed in typical riding attire: long, shiny black boots, beige breeches with leather pads at the knees, white stock-tied shirts. Instead of riding jackets, both wore dark wool sweaters. Strolling up to them, Peter felt uncomfortably out of place in his plaid jacket, old blue jeans and Nike running shoes.

He forgot about it as Jordan greeted him with a sunny smile. The young man swung easily atop his mount and trotted off in the other direction.

"Morning," she said. "Horses are saddled and ready."

As she said it, a groom walked over with two horses. One, a large bay with a shiny black mane and tail, was saddled English-style. The horse tossed his head and snorted when he saw Jordan. She took the reins from the groom and gave the horse an affectionate pat on the neck. He arched it against her hand. He looked big and high-spirited; this heightened Peter's concern about the adventure.

"This is Reggie. He's mine," she said. "And this one is yours." She pointed to a smaller, more placid-looking dappled gray mare, saddled Western-style.

"I thought you'd be more comfortable riding Western, but we can switch it to English if you want," Jordan told Peter.

Peter looked at the postage stamp-sized saddle on Reggie's broad back and the more solid-looking equipment on the gray. His saddle had a horn to hang onto and bulging saddle bags behind.

"Western's fine with me," Peter said. Even the gray looked too big. The thought that he was actually going to have to get on this animal filled him with trepidation.

"Her name is Sweet Pea. She's a school horse," Jordan explained. "We put all the beginners on her. She's fail-safe," Jordan added, noticing Peter's concerned look.

She swung up on Reggie's back. The groom held a stirrup out for Peter and he climbed atop his mount. Sweet Pea took a step and

Peter lurched forward.

"Sit back and settle into the saddle. Don't perch and don't tense up. Just relax and go with her rhythm," Jordan advised, watching him protectively.

He tried to follow her instructions as they started down the trail at an easy walking pace. The gentle clip-clop of the horses' hooves and warm sun filtering through the branches relaxed him. As they covered ground, moving under a line of live oak trees filled with the trill and call of birds, Peter began to enjoy the ride.

"Do you ride a lot?" he asked as they wandered along.

"Not as much as I used to. What with school and getting ready for my internship, Reggie here was getting ignored," Jordan said, giving the horse a soft pat. "I lease him out now so he gets worked. I was very competitive at Foxcroft. Taylor and I were both on the hunter circuit."

"Doesn't surprise me," Peter said, thinking of the competitive energy she brought to the tennis court.

"I like to win," Jordan said. "Besides, the love of my life at the time was training for the Olympics."

"Seriously? Did he make it?" Peter asked.

"Max Gunther, from Germany," she said, smiling fondly at the memory. "He was over here riding at the American Academy of Equestrian Sciences in Leesburg. We met on the jumper circuit and had quite a fling until he went back home. He rode in the 1992 Summer Olympics but he didn't medal. He's getting ready for '96 now."

"So was he the one that got away?" Peter asked.

"In some ways, maybe. He was my first real love, but we had, what I guess you'd call irreconcilable differences," Jordan said, giving him a sideways glance. "And you and love?"

"There were a couple of SOs, but it didn't work out," he replied with a perfunctory smile.

The longer-legged Reggie had pulled ahead on the trail. Jordan held him back so Peter and Sweet Pea could catch up. "You're going to have to do better than that," she said when he reached her side.

Peter considered his answer. He was adept at satisfying curiosity without revealing anything of substance. In his mind, Jordan had gotten far more out of him than he ever intended. She wasn't getting this.

"Well, you know about Mollie. I mean Adin." He gave her a sly look, and got an eye roll in return. "Then there was Jessica. She's also a reporter. We worked together at *Computer Industry News* before I joined the *Trib*."

"What happened with you and Jessica?"

"Work got in the way," Peter replied, with a casual shrug.

"Where is she now?" Jordan asked with evident interest. They had moved past casual dating to the place where old relationships could have consequences, Peter mused. Jordan wanted to know where things stood. It boded well for their future.

"She's heavily involved with some industry type. I expect they'll get married," Peter replied, realizing that finally, and he hoped forever, he simply didn't care.

"C'est la vie," Jordan said.

They approached a gate. Jordan dismounted and pulled a key from her pocket, opened the gate and waved him through. Once he was on the other side, she rode through and relocked it. "The trails are private here," she explained, "and this one leads to a meadow where I thought we could have a picnic."

"Don't picnics usually involve food?"

"Everything we need is in the saddlebags behind you," she said, giving him a knowing look. "When I plan a picnic I do it properly."

"I'd expect nothing less," Peter said, chuckling.

The meadow, alive with new spring flowers and soft grasses, surrounded a stand of small trees where Jordan was headed. They tethered the horses by the trees, and Peter watched in wonder as she pulled an amazing array of food and a blanket out of the saddlebags and set up their lunch. He sat down on the blanket and she handed him a bottle of water.

"I've got ham, turkey and roast beef sandwiches, potato salad, corn chips and chocolate chip cookies. Help yourself," she said, kicking off her riding boots.

Peter pulled the wrapper off a ham sandwich and took a bag of corn chips. Jordan chose the turkey.

"Great idea Jordan," Peter said watching as she sat nibbling on the sandwich, legs folded comfortably at her side.

"How are things going at the *Trib*?" Jordan asked.

"Starting to get back to normal, finally. We got the paper out every day," Peter said with pride. "I told Adam that in the computer industry, dedication like that was usually rewarded with a commemorative t-shirt." Peter thought that if Adam didn't take the hint, he might order the t-shirts himself.

"We may not be the biggest paper in town, but we have loyal readers and they count on us to bring them the news," he added. "We've just started an online edition. The first in California."

"That's impressive. So what are you working on now?" she asked, reaching over and grabbing a few corn chips out of his bag.

"No poaching," he said, playfully moving the bag out of her reach.

She stretched, took another chip from his bag, and nibbled it as slowly as possible, watching him with a gleam in her eye. He smiled back at her and tossed the bag between them.

"Remember that story I did on David Lockwood a couple of weeks ago?" he asked, stretching beside her.

She nodded.

"Well, I'm trying to confirm that he's going to do a deal with MediaBuilders with his new Sapphire Project," Peter said.

"Is that important?"

"Huge. MediaBuilders is locked in a battle with their archrival, Draco Communications. With Sapphire, MediaBuilders could shift the balance of power and dominate the Internet market. Billions are at stake. Breaking that story could be a real game changer for me."

This story, more than any other he'd written since the TriCorp debacle, had the potential to change his career trajectory. Peter was treading—albeit carefully—through a potential minefield with both Sam and Margaret to worry about; but it was too good a story to pass up. Sam hadn't gotten anywhere with his sources, Peter wasn't going to worry about Margaret unless he had to, and he wasn't going to Ben with the story until it was airtight.

"You really love what you do, don't you?" Jordan asked.

"I do."

"Did you always know you wanted to be a reporter, even when you were a little kid?"

"No. I was firmly on the Ellis family law school path until I got to Harvard. But I started getting restless back when I was at Exeter. Masses of people all headed in the same direction. You get the message from day one—you are the brightest and the best, and you had better prove it every day, in every way, for the rest of your life," he said, sitting back up and taking a final bite of his sandwich.

Jordan nodded. "Be perfect or go home. It's hardest when you can't meet your own expectations. Then all that's left is the self-flagellation."

She understood it perfectly, he thought. "You too?" he asked.

"Not me. I like disappointing people," she grinned at him, and reached for a chocolate chip cookie.

That's because you never have, he thought.

He could imagine her at Foxcroft, riding with the hounds in the late autumn sun. Adored daughter. Blissfully content. He was sitting in the reflection of that adoration and contentment now, and it offered a few precious moments of peace. He was glad Jordan had suggested this trail ride.

"You still haven't answered my question," she said, breaking into his thoughts. "Why a journalist?" Jordan had pulled a purple wildflower from the grass and was absentmindedly twirling it between her fingers. He watched her hands toy with the greenery for a moment before he continued.

"Serendipity. I met this girl at a party, she was a writer. She and her brother had just started a little off-campus paper. She invited me to join them, so I did. Honestly, it was a way to get next to her," Peter admitted.

"And did you?" Jordan asked, chuckling.

He looked up at her. "What do you think?"

Jordan laughed. "So what happened?" He took a cookie and settled near her. "Nothing much. She fell in love with someone else. And I fell in love with writing. Not just the writing but being paid to poke around, find stuff out, especially the stuff no one wants you to know, and then tell the story. I wouldn't trade it for the world, good thing because…" His voice trailed off and his face turned somber.

"Tell me." Her voice was soft but insistent. Peter studied the sky, crafting a careful response. He felt Jordan shift her position and put her arms around him from behind. "Tell me," she murmured in his ear.

He leaned against her, conscious of the soft cushion of her breasts against his back, and spoke. "When I refused to goose step my way into law school, my father flew to Boston in a rage and we had it out. He gave me the ultimatum. It was law school or nothing. I chose nothing."

Peter took a sip of his water to ease the dryness in his throat. "I said I needed to tell you what I lost. Money, power, position. That's what I lost."

He glanced back at her to gauge her reaction. She sat motionless, staring straight ahead.

A flock of crows passed noisily overhead. Reggie looked up and snorted at them before resuming his grazing. Peter watched the birds disappear over the hill. Jordan's silence was fraying his nerves.

"Not lost," she said finally, tightening her arms around him. "Gave up. Left behind to go your own way. That takes courage. The kind of courage most of us don't have."

She had that same wistful look he'd seen at the café the other night. His reporter's itch was beginning to needle him.

"Was it worth it, Peter? Letting it all go to follow your dream?"

"Every day. In every way," he replied with conviction.

Jordan was running her fingers lightly through his hair. It was getting distracting. He turned on his side and pulled her down beside him. His lips grazed the tip of her chin and gently moved along her jawline until they reached the soft velvet of her earlobe. She sighed. Her mouth parted and she turned toward him, pressing against him.

Her kiss reached deep within him. Neurons fired throughout his body, waking every nerve ending. She pulled back, tasted her index finger and traced the outline of his lips.

"You're awfully hard to resist," she whispered, moving away from him so their bodies were no longer touching.

"Why resist?" he asked, keeping his voice teasingly light, fighting the drumbeat of his heart in his ears, entreating her to choose the afternoon delight he knew they both imagined.

"I just need a little more time to settle some things," she said in a faint voice.

"Is there someone else?" Peter asked, guessing that maybe Jordan had a romantic hangover like the one he had for Jessica. She shook her head. Her hair swung across her face."What it is, Jordan?"

"I just need a little more time, okay?"

"Okay," he said gently.

"We'd better get back."

Jordan brushed crumbs from her clothes and started packing up the lunch. Peter handed her the containers and trash halfheartedly, increasingly frustrated by their unconsummated relationship. He knew women and their desires well enough to know that Jordan wanted him as much as he wanted her. She was deliberately putting up barriers.

She turned toward him as she swung into the saddle. "I am curious, though. The tennis club. The Porsche. That's not on a reporter's salary."

"My grandfather left me a small inheritance. I've tried to invest it wisely. I'll do fine as long as I'm not extravagant. Frankly, I don't need much."

"Except the freedom to do what you do."

Jordan nudged Reggie with her heels and they started across the field.

"Yes."

He was more comfortable in the saddle now, in synch and enjoying the steady movement of the horse beneath him. They passed through the meadow, took another trail, crossed a small brook and rode down a gully to another large meadow.

A muffled gunshot rang out somewhere in front of them. Reggie jumped sideways, spooked at the sound. Jordan moved with him and quickly got him settled. Peter was grateful that Sweet Pea seemed oblivious to Reggie's gyrations.

"Damn hunters," Jordan said, crossly. "They are not supposed to be in these hills."

"What could they be hunting this time of year?"

"They're probably kids, looking for rabbits," she replied, her face set. She was concentrating hard on her riding. Reggie still seemed tense, and had broken into a little jig. Jordan was trying to steady him as Sweet Pea plodded on unaffected by Reggie's nerves. Failsafe, Peter remembered Jordan saying. He reached down and patted the horse's neck. Another shot cut the air, quickly followed by a third immediately to Peter's left. Reggie reared and Sweet Pea bolted.

Peter pitched forward, and his weight shifted to his left as the horse broke into a mad gallop. His body bounced up and down, his feet freed from the stirrups dangling uselessly. He slipped further down the horse's side, and the ground was coming up to meet him at thirty miles an hour. Instinctively, he reached for the horn to stay on the horse, letting the reins slip from his hands.

Sweet Pea was heading straight for a stand of trees in front of a wooden rail fence, and Peter's heart thumped as wildly as the horse's hooves beating against the ground. Which would hurt less, his mind crackled, hitting the ground at thirty miles an hour or sure collision with the trees and fence? The fence was fifty yards away— now twenty—now ten. He heard Jordan's voice behind him. She was riding fast and shouting instructions like a drill sergeant.

"Grab those reins! Sit up straight! Lean back," she yelled.

He caught the reins and managed to sit back in the saddle. It didn't slow the horse down. The trunk of a large oak seemed to be barreling toward him as the panicked horse ran directly into its path.

"Grab the right rein and pull hard. Get it as short as you can. Hold steady with the left rein," Jordan shouted. She was almost even with him now. He did as she said and Sweet Pea turned in a large circle.

"Keep the pressure on. You're doing great."

Sweet Pea continued to circle. Her gallop dropped to a canter and then a trot, and finally to a halt. Both horse and rider were breathing hard. Peter's face felt frozen. The horse had stopped, but Peter's body still trembled from fear and exertion.

Jordan trotted up beside him. "Great riding, Peter," she said, smiling with relief.

"You didn't panic. I'm proud of you." Her tone was congratulatory and filled with respect.

Peter offered a wan smile in return, the color just beginning to return to his cheeks. He shifted in the saddle and a spike of pain hit his groin. He winced and shifted again to relieve the pressure.

"Sore?" Jordan asked.

"In all the wrong places," Peter admitted.

He looked at Jordan. Her eyes were bright and moist. She was biting her lower lip.

"Jordan Langley. After you got me on this loathsome beast, don't you dare—" Peter fumed.

That was all it took. Jordan burst into gales of laughter. Peter gave her an indignant look, which made her laugh even more. Her boisterous laughter was contagious; and soon Peter started laughing too, more from relief than anything else.

Jordan regained her composure. "Are you okay?" she asked, wiping her eyes with her tip of her fingers.

"I'll live," he grunted.

"Okay. Good." She gave Reggie a gentle nudge with her heels and they started back down the trail toward the barn.

"I guess I won't be getting you on a horse again anytime soon," Jordan said, as they plodded along.

"Try me in the next century."

They rode in silence for a while. Peter tried without much success to recapture the pleasure of the sound of songbirds, the feel of fresh air and sunshine. Jordan appeared deep in thought and he was in no mood for conversation. What he really wanted was a hot shower, a cool drink and a long pull on a cigarette.

"Where do think you'll be in the year 2000?" she asked at last.

"Don't know. Hopefully at the *Wall Street Journal*. Probably covering Y2K."

She looked over at him, puzzled. "Y2K? What's that?"

"The big computer disaster everyone is expecting at 12:01 a.m. on January 1, 2000. The doomsday scenario is that all the computers in the world will stop working at once. Prison doors will open. Planes will fall from the sky, and chaos will run rampant."

Jordan looked startled. "Planes will fall from the sky?" she asked, her voice small. "Is that possible?"

"Theoretically, yes. When programmers started writing software in the 1940s, they weren't thinking about the turn of the century and memory was precious. No one wanted to waste even a couple of digits of code, so all the clocks embedded in software and later on in microprocessors were written so only the last two digits change. So many programmers, like my buddy Tim, think the computer clocks will reset automatically to 1900 and stop working."

"But why would planes fall from the sky?" she asked, her tone nervous.

"Because they have microprocessors in them to control the wings, air speed, landing gear, instruments. If they stopped working all at once, they could fall."

Peter glanced at her. She genuinely looked scared.

"Don't worry, Jordan. That's not going to happen. Hundreds of brilliant programmers are working diligently to make sure that it doesn't. We've got six years to get it right."

Jordan still looked apprehensive. "What do you think will happen?"

"Doomsday will be avoided. Some technical glitches will occur, and everyone will blame Microsoft," he said with a breezy laugh.

"Don't ever torture me with that kind of tech talk again," she admonished him.

"Okay," he said, grinning. "How about I shower and change and take you out to dinner tonight instead?"

"Not tonight. I have plans, remember?" she replied, staring straight at the trail ahead. Peter was beginning to doubt her denial of another man. *What else could she be doing on a Saturday night?*

They were back at the stable. Jordan swung off Reggie's back. Peter did the same with Sweet Pea, grateful to be on solid ground again. His legs were rubbery, his groin was still sore and he looked forward to that shower and cigarette.

"Thanks for the near-death experience," he said, giving Sweet Pea an affectionate pat. Sweet Pea snorted gently in return. The groom took both horses and led them away. Peter stood next to Jordan as she sat in her car, removing her riding boots and putting on tennis shoes.

"You sure you have plans tonight?" he asked. He wasn't ready to say goodbye. She avoided his eyes as she tossed her boots in the back of her car. Then she looked up at him and smiled. "Yes, I do. But I don't have to be there until seven. Why don't you come back to my house now? We've got the rest of the afternoon."

January 29, 1994: Los Altos Hills, California

He showered at her place and changed into the spare sweatshirt and jeans he'd thrown in the trunk just in case. Jordan was sitting on the sofa reading a book and sipping tea when he entered the living room.

"I made tea if you'd like a cup."

"Soda?" he asked.

"In the fridge."

He retrieved a Coke and walked back into the living room. The music changed to a smooth saxophone solo he thought he recognized. "David Sanborn?"

"Dave Koz," she replied without looking up. "E for effort, though."

"More like D for Dave, or David as the case may be."

"Well, aren't you in rare form?" She looked up, eyes crinkled in amusement. "And looking like the cat that swallowed the canary. What's up?"

He placed an envelope in front of her on the coffee table. "Open it."

She picked it up, turned it over and slid her finger under the flap, pulling out two tickets. She stared at them for a frozen moment. "Oh, Peter. I don't know what to say."

"The jazz festival in Newport Beach next week. I know you can't go Saturday, but it's on Thursday and Friday too, so I thought..." His voice trailed off. She seemed not to hear him. Her only movement was to wipe the corner of her eye with her knuckle.

"Such a generous gift. I'm overwhelmed." Her eyes were riveted on the tickets. She didn't seem all that happy, and he felt a flush of embarrassment.

"Look, they're your tickets, Jordan. You don't have to go with me. You can take anybody you want. Even Mr. Saturday Night," he finished roughly.

Only then did she look up at him. "There is no Mr. Saturday Night. At least not in the way you think."

"What is it, then? Just tell me. I don't care if you're in a coven. I just gotta know."

That startled her. "You think I'm a witch?"

He sat down beside her, started to put his arm around her. "I know you've bewitched me."

She offered him a small smile, and another one of those searching looks he'd been getting lately. He felt scrutinized, as if he were struggling under the weight of a heavy appraisal or some test he was in danger of failing. Then, as quickly as it had come, her expression changed. She lit up with a merry smile and the eagerness of a young girl.

"Can I play you something?" she asked, standing and moving over to the CD player.

"Yeah, sure." Peter bit back his frustration. He wanted answers, not more music.

"It'll all make more sense once you hear this."

Placing a new CD on the changer, she turned up the volume as the sounds of a drum, guitar and sax rhythm began. Peter settled back on the couch, eyes closed, listening intently. The guitar and sax traded notes back and forth in syncopated rhythm as if they were meeting, mating, and intertwining. They reached a crescendo and then softly faded away. Peter opened his eyes.

As the song ended, Jordan turned to him, the power of the music still imprinted on her face.

"That's 'Lily Was Here,' by Candi Dulfer." Jordan held the CD cover toward him. Peter took it and studied the photo. "She's hot," he said. Jordan's lips curved upward as she nodded.

"Yes, she is. She's also the first woman saxophone player to break big on her own. That's what I want to be when I grow up," Jordan said, enunciating each word, watching him closely.

"You play jazz saxophone?" Peter was astonished. He tried to imagine her holding the large brass instrument but he couldn't conjure up the image, so he started to laugh.

Her face darkened. "Sure, go ahead and laugh. Why did I think you'd be any different?"

He jumped to his feet, reaching for her. "Hey. I wasn't laughing at you. I was just surprised. How long have you been playing?"

"Since I was nine. Two years ago I started playing with a jazz band. We play at Blue Note West in San Francisco every Saturday night."

She paused, her expression pensive. "Daddy hates it. He thinks it's unladylike. Taylor and Josh think it's bizarre. Josh is always ragging on me about hanging out with a bunch of stoners." Her eyes flashed as her voice hardened in defense of her passion and her friends. "They are not stoners. They are musicians. Great musicians."

Peter realized with a start that this was the secret she had been hiding, and that he was probably one of the few she had shared it with. The thought thrilled him.

"Wow! I think it's cool. Very cool."

Her smile contained both happiness and relief. "I was hoping you'd say that," she said, moving next to him.

"Would you play for me?"

Her eyes seesawed in panic. "Here? Just the two of us? No. I couldn't. It would sound too weird without the band."

And too vulnerable, Peter thought, deciding then that he had to have it from her. He wanted to experience her living out her dream, feel the energy that drove her, know her as completely as possible. He knew what it felt like to have a fire blazing within and be rejected for it. To realize Jordan had a passion as intense and personal as his own made her even more exciting.

"You practice, don't you?"

"Of course. All the time."

"Why don't you just practice and I'll listen."

She shook her head. "It wouldn't sound right."

"Okay, but can I see?"

Jordan went into her bedroom and came back with a rectangular black case. She opened it so Peter could see the shiny brass instrument. It was bigger than he had expected.

"Alto sax," she said, removing it from the case.

"I'd really like to hear you play."

She studied his face, indecision weighing heavily on her. "I've never done this before."

He watched her draw a breath, and touch her instrument lightly. She turned her back to him, and the sax slipped a bit in her hands as she started to replace it in its case.

"It would mean a lot to me," he said quietly, almost reverently, so she would hear in his tone that he understood how much it meant to her. She pulled the sax close to her body and turned to face him again. Her cheeks were pink with excitement or agitation. He couldn't tell which.

"What do you want to hear?" she asked, finally.

"How about the one you just played. The Lily song."

"Lily Was Here," she corrected him, giggling.

"Yes," Peter agreed. "That one. Please," he added for emphasis.

She pulled a tall stool out from the corner of the room, sat down on it and rested the sax between her knees. She wet her lips, lifted the reed to her mouth. Her cheeks puffed as she began to play. Peter studied her profile. Eyes closed, face glistening with energy, she played with heart and soul. He knew he was seeing the best of her. Hair swinging, her body moved to the rhythm of the beat. The sax wedged between her legs brushed against her thighs, swaying with her limbs as she pressed her lips to the mouthpiece. Her fingers stroked the keys slowly at first, then more rapidly as the sweet early notes of the tune deepened with strength and presence.

As she swayed with the music, the sight and sound of her made Peter restless. He shifted from one foot to the other to relieve the pressure, and moved closer to her. She finished and pushed the mouthpiece to the side of her face, resting the sax on her shoulder. Looking up at him, her eyes said everything that needed saying. *That's my secret self,* they proclaimed.

"Beautiful," he breathed, standing in front of her. He reached for the sax and she let him lift it out of her hands and put it down beside the chair.

"Careful," she said. "It's precious."

"I know."

••••

Peter woke first. Early evening light streamed through the bedroom window. He glanced at the clock. A little after five p.m. Jordan was sleeping facedown, right arm flung across his chest. Gingerly, he began to stroke her arm. She stirred, raised her head and looked at him.

"Hi there." Her voice was still groggy from sleep.

"Hi yourself," he said, smiling at her. She looked sensational even with her bedhead hair concealing half her face.

She pushed the hair away from her face. "Peter, there's something I need to tell you." Her face and voice were tense. She half-sat up, leaning on one elbow.

"I'm leaving for Germany at the end of March to do an internship in microfinance. I'll be gone six months, maybe a year. And I don't want any—" Jordan paused and chose her next words carefully. "Entanglements. No lingering looks back. No regrets. When I go,

I'm gone. I wanted to tell you about this before we got this far, but you swept me off my feet before I got the chance." She gave him a faint smile and a concerned look. "I just want to have a little fun and there's no one I'd rather play with than you, especially now."

She ran her hand across his chest and brushed his lips with her fingertips. Her eyes were soft, warm and hopeful. "I'm just being honest. We could have a great seven weeks. But when it's over, it's over. Understand?"

Peter wasn't sure he'd heard her right. Jordan—adventurous, challenging, sensual Jordan—was offering him the gift of intimacy without commitment. He couldn't believe his luck.

"Perfectly." He leaned over and kissed her mouth affectionately, possessively, hoping they could stay in bed a while longer.

"What time is it?" she asked, turning her head toward the bedside table.

"Around five."

"Oh, no! I need to be in the city by seven. I've got to get dressed."

She popped out of bed, giving Peter just the slightest glimpse of her sensuous naked body before she pulled on a power-blue silk robe. She wrapped the robe around her torso and turned toward him.

"Why don't you come tonight? Really see me play."

"Great. Can I invite Tim and Marie?"

Jordan thought for a moment. "Sure. Why not? I'll leave your names on the list."

They showered together, and then Peter went outside for a smoke. When he came back into the bedroom he found her standing topless at the mirror, wearing a tight pair of black satin pants and red stiletto heels and putting on her makeup. He sat down on the edge of the bed and watched with undisguised pleasure as she dusted off her face and snapped on a tiny black push-up bra. She put on a boxy red silk shirt with a deeply plunging neckline that exposed the contours of her breasts and finished with large gold hoop earrings.

Peter had a brief, uncomfortable image of her dressed like that, playing the sax onstage in a smoky jazz club crowded with half-drunk, horny males. He suddenly knew why Daddy didn't like the jazz scene. He didn't like that image too much either. But given the arrangement he'd just agreed to, he didn't get a vote. It must have shown on his face. As she turned around, her smile slid into a frown.

"This is what I wear when I play," she snapped. "If you don't like it, stay home."

January 29, 1994: San Francisco, California

At seven-thirty that Saturday night, Peter was racing down I-280 toward San Francisco, anticipating the evening ahead: hearing Jordan play jazz with her band and finally meeting Tim's elusive girlfriend Marie. He preferred the longer and less congested I-280 to the crawl and stall of 101 because of the opportunity it gave him to open up the Porsche and let the German-engineered car do what it did best—fly down the open highway at top speed. He stepped on the accelerator just as his cell phone rang. He flipped the phone open with a smile, anticipating Jordan's lyric contralto.

"What in the hell are you doing?" Margaret barked in his ear.

"Driving, right now," Peter said, holding the phone away from his ear. He'd long ago learned that bland responses worked best with Margaret's apoplectic rants.

"Don't get smart with me," she snapped.

"Wouldn't dream of it." Peter eased off the accelerator and edged the car into the slow lane.

"What is it, Margaret?" he asked, already battle weary in anticipation of her assault.

"MediaBuilders! Stop harassing Victor Henderson. Now!"

"I'm not harassing Henderson. I'm following up on the MediaBuilders press conference he held." Peter worked hard to keep his tone moderate, his anger in check. As always, his first instinct with Margaret was to dive deep and stay down.

Margaret paused and changed tactics. "Don't you care anything about this family, or our law firm and its clients?"

"You've never given me a reason to," he said, with uncharacteristic honesty.

He heard her sharp intake of breath. That was as close to insubordination as he'd ever come with her and it surprised them both. He braced himself for the firestorm his careless remark would ignite.

"I don't know what game you think you're playing, but you're way out of your league," she began, her voice scorching.

Peter hunched over the wheel, feeling himself shrink physically as Margaret raged on in his ear. It was this very confrontation Peter had sought to avoid by punting the MediaBuilders coverage to Sam in the first place.

But this isn't about MediaBuilders. It's about Lockwood, and Lockwood is mine. I own that coverage, he consoled himself, clinging to the thought as her battering splintered what little confidence he had left.

"I won't let your idiotic blundering and that worthless little rag you call a newspaper destroy a client relationship that took my father and me years to build," she continued undeterred by his silence. "Back off. Do you understand me?"

The words lay on his tongue, waiting to be uttered yet again: *Yes, Margaret. Whatever you say. Whatever will make you go away and leave me alone.*

She's right, he thought miserably. He had blundered his way into this mess. *This is my own fault. Just say yes and she'll be gone,* the voice in his head advised, growing more insistent as miles of asphalt slipped beneath his rotating tires. Margaret waited through the silence for the capitulation she anticipated. His head hurt. His mind was playing tricks.

Unbidden, he saw Jordan standing before him, brown eyes solemn, face riveted on his. *Was it worth it, Peter? To give it all up to follow your dream?*

Every day. In every way.

He knew in that moment what he had to do, regardless of the cost. "No," he told his sister, his tone solid and challenging. "You back off."

She gasped. He could imagine the shocked expression on her face. "What?" she shrieked.

"You heard me."

"You're making the biggest mistake of your life," she countered, banging the phone down.

Peter flipped his cell closed and tossed it on the floor of the car where he couldn't reach it if it rang again.

"Maybe so, but it's worth it," Peter muttered, slamming his foot on the accelerator.

••••

Blue Note West, a smaller, less sophisticated version of its famous New York counterpart, was located in a renovated warehouse off Mission and 6th Avenue. Peter saw Tim standing near the queue to enter the club, a queue that was growing longer by the minute.

"Where's Marie?" Peter asked, joining Tim as they entered the line. The doorman was checking names off the list and accepting cash only for the cover charge.

"Something came up," Tim said.

Peter gave Tim an amused look. "I'm beginning to think that Marie is like your little imaginary school friend. The one only you can see."

"Naw," Tim said with a rueful grin. "She had a church thing."

"Church?"

"She's really involved in her church," Tim said as they inched forward.

"Hmm. She Catholic?" Peter knew Tim was Catholic, although a very lapsed one, at least until Marie came along. Tim nodded. "But she goes to contemporary worship. I've been going with her."

Whatever that means, Peter thought. He felt itchy. He didn't like God talk in any shape or form. It bothered him to think that this thing with Marie might interfere with his friendship with Tim. Tim was the best friend he had. At least now Peter knew why Tim had been missing their regular Sunday morning tennis matches the last few weeks.

"The music's good," Tim added, as they reached the head of the queue.

"Name?" the bouncer asked. "Cover's twenty dollars each, cash only."

Peter gave his name and pulled out his wallet. Tim did the same. Between them they had sixteen dollars. He looked back at the bouncer, who was running his finger down The List.

Perfect. Just what I need, he thought, trying to remember if he'd seen a Bank of America with an ATM. He'd have to jump out of line and they would probably miss the start of the show.

"Peter Ellis?" the bouncer asked. Peter nodded.

"You're covered and you've got a table reserved. Enjoy the show," he said, handing them a pair of tickets.

Peter and Tim entered the club just as the warm-up band was finishing its set. The music faded and the crowd got up to get drinks, smoke and socialize

during the intermission. The space was tight and dimly lit, with small, henna-style lamps set on burnished brown tables. Ornate sconces lining the walls gave the room a distinctly Moorish feel, enhanced by the bluish smoke drifting through the room. Four rows of circular tables, each set with an ashtray and candle, filled the space between the

stage and the horseshoe bar at the back of the room. Large portraits of jazz greats like <u>Dave Brubeck</u>, <u>Miles Davis</u>, <u>Louis Armstrong</u> and dozens of others Peter didn't recognize covered all of the available wall space. Jordan was right about the women, Peter noted, as the lounge hostess showed them to a table just left of center stage. He only saw one on the wall

and wandered over to read her name. <u>Ella Fitzgerald</u>, the brass plaque read.

"Two-drink minimum. I ordered you Scotch," Tim said, when Peter returned to the table. The thin blue curtains fronting the stage fluttered. Peter could see several male silhouettes arranging the instruments. The club was filling fast with an older, more sophisticated group sitting near the stage and a younger, rowdier crowd clustered around the bar. A waitress returned to their table with two Scotches for Peter and two beers for Tim.

The stage lights dimmed as the curtains parted to reveal Jordan and her band. She stood center stage, sax in hand, wearing the tight black pants and revealing red satin shirt with the deeply-plunging neckline Peter had seen her in that afternoon.

Tim's eyes lit up. "Wow. She's hot, man."

"Watch it," Peter hissed, giving Tim a hard look.

"Just saying," Tim said, looking away. "Like every guy in here isn't thinking the same thing."

"This is San Francisco. At least half of them are gay."

"You wish."

Peter's quick glance around the room confirmed Tim's statement. There were plenty of salivating males in that club. The band's guitarist, a medium-sized man with blond ringlets and a wispy goatee, stepped up to the mic.

"Hello everyone. We're The EJs. We'd like to start off with a couple of classics and then play you some of our originals. This is our cover of 'Take Five,'" he said. Besides Jordan and the guitarist, the band was made up of a drummer, a keyboardist and a bass player.

Watching Jordan play with her band was different, Peter realized. She cascaded across the stage, hair swinging, flowing in rhythm with the music, the saxophone her dance partner. The expression on her face was pure joy. The band played a second tune and then a third.

"Great tits," a voice sprang out from the crowd just as the band launched into 'Chicago Song'.

"Nice ass, too. I want a piece a that," a second chimed in.

Peter shifted his head sideways and took in the pair. One, head shaved, muscles bulging, mouth twisted in a permanent sneer; the other thin, dark and hairy with interlocking tattoos lacing both forearms. They put their heads together and laughed, slugging back tequila shots in unison.

"Hey, baby, come here and blow me like that," Baldy said.

"Pussy. I wanna taste of pussy," Hairy chimed in, banging his shot glass down.

Peter had heard enough. He scraped his chair back. Tim grabbed his arm and held it against the table.

"Don't do it, man." Tim had a vise-like grip on Peter's wrist. "They're drunk as skunks. You'll start a fight."

"I'm not taking this shit," Peter said, trying to shake off Tim's hold.

"Think about the band, damn it. You start a fight and they could lose their gig. What's Jordan going to say about that?"

Peter paused. "She'd be pissed." He shifted in his seat, still tense. Tim relaxed his hold. Peter tossed back his Scotch and tried to refocus on the music. The thugs behind them quieted down as Jordan began playing the light rhythms of Kenny G's "Songbird."

"Gonna lay her down tonight. Spread her out. Knock 'er hard," Baldy snarled above the music.

"Yeah, I'd like to do a rusty trombone on that one," Hairy snickered.

"That's it!" Peter jumped up before Tim could stop him.

He turned and stood eyeball to eyeball with the club's bouncer. At six foot six, his arms bulging out of a Blue Note t-shirt, the bouncer looked like he could handle the situation. He nodded for Peter to take a seat as he placed a meaty hand on Baldy's collarbone.

"It's time to go, gentlemen," the bouncer said, pulling back Baldy's chair. Baldy got up and lurched toward him. A second bouncer stepped up behind him and caught him as he started to fall, grabbing Hairy with the other hand. Quickly and efficiently, the bouncers maneuvered the two men out the door.

Onstage, the guitarist said, "We'll take a short break and be back for our second set."

Peter sat back down. "Thanks, Tim," he said, taking a sip of his second Scotch. "You saved my butt."

Tim nodded.

"You ever hear anything from Groucho?" Peter asked as the crowd mingled around them, chatting, getting drinks and food.

"Nope. I think it's a dead end."

"Keep checking, okay?" Peter couldn't shake Devon O'Reilly's final words to him. *If it was that important, it wouldn't be a game.*

If Tucker had the disk, he could be in real danger. Peter hadn't shared Devon's warning with Tim. All he had were a few disconnected tidbits and half-formed ideas. It might not amount to anything. Why burden Tim until he knew more?

Tim stared into his beer, downcast. "I'm leaving Sun. There's nothing there for me now."

Peter studied his friend, sharing his despondency. "Know where you're going?"

Tim shook his head. "I'm going take some time and figure that out. Spend some more time with Marie and figure that out too," he added.

"Is it serious?"

"Heading in that direction. What about you?" he asked, inclining his head toward the stage. The band had just returned to begin their second set.

"The girl just wants to have fun." Peter filled Tim in on their arrangement as Jordan stepped up to the mic.

"We're starting this set with one of our favorites," she said, staring straight at Peter. "Lily Was Here.'"

She faced the guitarist as he strummed the first notes. Then she answered with her sax, the two instruments trading lines in a perfectly syncopated conversation. Peter shut out the noise of the crowd, ignored the guitarist and the rest of the band, mesmerized by Jordan as she played. He imagined that she was playing for him and him alone.

••••

A handful of regulars remained at the club, sitting around the bar finishing their drinks. After Tim left, Peter stood with them, waiting for Jordan. When she entered the room twenty minutes after the performance ended, she had changed into jeans and a white cashmere sweater.

"Well, how was I?" she asked, joining Peter and giving him a quick kiss.

"Amazing. Thrilling. Are you ready to go?" He'd shared her long enough; he needed to have Jordan all to himself again.

"I want you to meet the boys. We're having chicken and waffles. It's tradition." She took his arm and led him to a table for six set in the center of the club. The rest of the band arrived. Jordan provided hasty introductions, ending with the curly-haired guitarist, Eric Crowley. The bartender placed a range of drinks in front of them, Manhattans for the boys, Merlot for Jordan and Scotch for Peter. The band members, except for Eric, pulled out cigarettes and lit up. Peter joined them.

"Where did you get the name, The EJs?" Peter asked.

Eric eyeballed him. "Jordan and I started the band, together. E-J for Eric and Jordan."

Peter caught the emphasis on the word together, just as he had felt the chemistry when they were onstage.

Eric and the boys stood up. "We've got to do a final equipment check, "Eric said. "We'll be back in a few."

Peter looked over at Jordan when they were alone. "Eric and Jordan?"

She bought herself some time with a sip of Merlot. "It's been over for a year."

"What happened?"

"I suppose you want all the dreary details?" she asked wearily.

"Only if you want to tell me."

"Short version. Eric is possessive and territorial. Not about me," she added quickly, "about jazz. It's his life. He demanded it be my life too. Not just part of my life, all of it. He wanted me to quit school. He was even jealous of the time I spent with Taylor. It was all too much. I left the band for a while but in the end the music won out. We're friends and we play well together."

"I can see that." Peter leaned over and kissed her. She pressed her mouth to his, the taste slightly metallic, a hint of her sax still on her lips.

"We're not interrupting anything, are we?" Eric stood over them. Jordan broke the embrace, blushing as the waiter set down a large platter of fried chicken and waffles.

The band took their seats and dug into the chicken and waffles. Eric studied Peter with an insolent expression. Peter saw that despite Jordan's assurances, Eric viewed him as an opponent, here to steal her away from the music, or perhaps from Eric himself.

It didn't matter which. What did matter was, they were rivals, and Eric owned her Saturday nights.

March 21, 1994: Menlo Park, California

PETER CUT HIMSELF SHAVING. HE STARED AT HIS REFLECTION IN the bedroom mirror, dabbing at the blood oozing from the nick in his chin. It had been the best seven weeks of his life, personally and professionally, and it was all ending today.

Draco was introducing Horizon at Moscone Center this afternoon, and Jordan was leaving for Germany tonight. There was nothing he could do about either. Peter's source inside the Horizon development team was golden. The team couldn't make a move without Peter knowing and reporting on it, to the point that Ben jokingly started calling his source "Deep Throat." Reporters on the big dailies and the wires were taking cues from his stories. It was like TriCorp had never happened.

His biggest coup had come this morning, when Peter preannounced Horizon as the new Draco Universal, with all the product details. Kavanagh was going to get his ass kicked for that one, Peter thought happily, tossing the wet tissue in the basket. The blood had clotted to a pinpoint no bigger than a pimple.

Trouble was, he mused, pulling on his standard business garb of khaki pants and buttoning a dark blue cotton shirt, he had nothing to follow Horizon. He'd never gotten anything solid on Lockwood's deal with MediaBuilders. Even Charlie had given him the runaround. He'd never found Brian Tucker or solved the mystery of the puzzle games. His bag was empty. And Jordan was leaving.

Jordan, sensuous, alluring, incomprehensible Jordan, had altered the rhythms of his life. In the last seven weeks they had spent all their free time together. They played tennis, sailed the Bay with Taylor and Josh and discovered a shared interest in seascapes. The new Louise Kamp hanging above his fireplace was a gift from Jordan. Jordan had even coerced him into dinner with Daddy. In exchange, he'd confiscated one of her precious Saturday nights for a long weekend in Hawaii where she'd amazed him yet again, this time with her proficiency on a surfboard.

"College reunion?" Jordan stepped into the bedroom fresh from the shower. She had kept the cottage, but spent most nights at Peter's. Now she stood behind him in the powder-blue silk robe she'd worn their first night together, watching him in the mirror as he straightened the knot on his Harvard tie.

"Horizon product intro. This is just to remind a certain marketing guy exactly who he's dealing with."

"Alex Kavanagh," Jordan nodded knowingly. She'd taken a real interest in his reporting. Unconsciously, Peter began relying on her engaging questions and perceptive insights to sharpen his coverage. Even Adam had noticed the improved quality of his stories.

"Southie," Peter said, referring to South Boston, where Alex was from.

"Ah. Growing up in the shadow of Harvard and not invited to the club."

"Yes. Can you give me my class ring? Brown box, middle drawer."

She pulled out the box and opened it. "This is nice. Why don't you wear it more often?"

"I don't know. Seems a little pretentious."

"Except when you want to be," she chuckled.

"Yeah. I guess I'm being a bit much," he agreed with a rueful smile. "Forget it."

"No. Wear it. I wish I had one." Jordan took the ring from the box and held it up to the light.

"Why don't you?"

"Oh, it's stupid. Eric and I were hot then and he dissed the whole college thing. I told you he wanted me to quit school and play sax full-time." Peter nodded, watching her roll his class ring around in her palm.

"We were going to cut a record. Ha ha," she explained. "That never happened, but he made me feel silly about getting a class ring so I didn't."

"You could always get one now."

"Wouldn't be the same. I'm not a co-ed anymore. Besides, I'm leaving the country, and I'm not planning to be back anytime soon."

His stomach reeled with the finality of the statement. Goodbye, for real, was a few hours away. He wasn't ready for it.

"Here, give me your hand." He held it out toward her. She slipped the ring on his finger. "Good to go," she announced with a slight smile.

Peter turned to grab his keys. "See you tonight."

She stepped close to him, took his face in her hands and kissed him. "It's been wonderful, Peter. But let's say goodbye now. It's time."

"No. I'm taking you to the airport," he insisted, pulling back.

She shook her head. "Not a chance. The last thing I want is one of those dreary airport goodbye scenes. Besides, we had a deal, remember?"

"Our deal was for after you left. Not before. I'm taking you to the airport." He felt his face getting hot, heard his voice becoming agitated.

"My luggage won't even fit in your car." Jordan's moderate tone said "be reasonable." He couldn't hear the notes.

"I'll borrow Tim's or rent one. Look, Jordan. I've played by your rules since day one. You owe me this. I'm taking you to the airport and that's final!"

Peter caught a glimpse of his twisted, angry face in the bedroom mirror. He was shouting at her the way his father had always bellowed at him. She regarded him with the same mixture of puzzlement and mirth Peter himself had always employed to good effect. He'd never felt so exposed. Embarrassed and deflated, he turned his back on her.

"I'm sorry. I don't know where that came from," he mumbled, shoulders hunched, staring down at the carpet. "Do whatever you want."

He shoved his wallet in his back pocket and stepped over the threshold. Her voice touched the tips of his ears and floated down. "Pick me up at the cottage at seven, okay? Don't be late."

March 21, 1994: San Francisco, California

"Step it up. You got three minutes to wrap this up," Toby Eastman barked as his team of programmers hunched over keyboards, tapping frantically. Video on three oversized monitors gyrated, rastered out and disappeared.

"Fucking spaghetti code," Toby muttered as the programmer on Demo #3 rebooted his system for the fourth time.

Onstage at Moscone North, Devon O'Reilly, Alex Kavanagh and Win Davis's admin were finishing a sound check for the Horizon product introduction. Soon O'Reilly would be backstage to review the demos. Demos with blotchy picture quality, erratic lip-synch timing and, as Toby glanced over at Demo #3, a screen full of broadcast snow. The screen bounced as the programmer slammed his fist into the keyboard.

"Give it to me." Toby bumped the programmer off his station. As he took control, Toby heard footsteps tap across the hardwood floor.

"How's it going?" O'Reilly stepped up behind him.

"We had a code break." Toby focused on the numeric string. It only took one bad character to ruin the lot. Ignoring O'Reilly hovering over him, Toby located the bad sequence and tweaked the code. "Now it's fixed."

"Ambitious demos, Jake," O'Reilly said as they watched the monitor flicker.

"Marketing," he grunted. "Overpromise and expect us to deliver." Toby took a deep breath of relief as the video of last Friday's basketball playoff, NCAA Tournament Round 1, Indiana vs. Ohio, flooded the screen. Video on demand at its finest.

"Got that right." O'Reilly took a last look at the video as he turned back toward the stage.

Stepping behind his team for a final system check, Toby felt more like a magician than an engineering manager. The applications Kavanagh had chosen to demo were technically feasible but far from commercially viable. The sleight of hand required to produce the quality performance needed to wow the crowd was masterful, a tribute to the skill and cunning of a crack team under superior leadership. His leadership.

Toby knew he could rely on Draco's M-bone, a virtual Internet backbone, for multicast transmissions between Dallas, New York and San Francisco, for the access speed he needed up to Moscone Hall. It was inside the building, the last hundred feet, where everything could go wrong. They were still coding to enhance Horizon's capability to interpret and display video images. He needed more processing power than he had in the demo units. Pushing up the intro date might come back to bite him after all, he thought irritably.

Stepping over the thick black cable snaking through his studio, he viewed *Demo #1: Video Conferencing*. The planned live chat between O'Reilly onstage in San Francisco and Win Davis in Dallas required blazing speed provided by T1 lines to each workstation. Although T1 speed was commercially available, only the largest global corporations and governments could afford it. It would be years before the average consumer could access T1-level speed and the fluid video pictures that it offered.

Demo #2: Live Internet Streaming Video was the trickiest to pull off. Kavanagh wanted to broadcast the closing bell of the New York Stock Exchange precisely at one p.m.. There wasn't a nanosecond to spare, and they were still fighting erratic lip-synch timing. Toby wiped the sweat from his brow as he studied the final demo.

Demo #3: Video on Demand. The basketball playoff. Despite the adjustments he'd just made, maintaining the picture quality still worried him. Toby had set up a studio-quality command and control center behind the stage to avoid that sort of problem. His workstation had three active windows with override capability linked to the massive video screens onstage. He hoped he wouldn't need to use it.

Only Toby knew about the fourth window, with Telnet capability connected directly to David Lockwood's super-secret engineering lab. At the exact moment Lockwood's ex-partner Devon O'Reilly introduced Horizon, now officially named Draco Universal, Toby would launch a series of commands that would destroy the primary algorithm for Lockwood's Sapphire Internet set-top box. His triumph would be unparalleled.

"Ladies and gentlemen, please welcome Devon O'Reilly," the announcer's voice called out to thunderous applause. Devon was onstage. His programmers were concentrating on their demos. It was time. Toby's only regret was that he couldn't share the moment with Devon. Devon hated Lockwood almost as much as he did. Toby was sure Devon would appreciate what he was about to do.

Drawing a deep, calming breath, Toby moved behind his command post and invoked the Telnet command that gave him access to Lockwood's engineering lab. Lockwood had hidden his engineering team in his Woodside mansion, limiting their contact with the outside world.

"Won't save you this time, David," Toby chuckled softly.

Tapped into Lockwood's private network remotely, Toby watched the code sequences appear on his screen line by line as one of Lockwood's best programmers ran through a mandatory test sequence he used every day. Keystroke by keystroke, click by click, tap by tap, Toby saw the programmer's nimble fingers approaching the deadly command string. One string away. Toby licked his lips, salivating in anticipation.

The characters crossing the screen stilled. The programmer stopped. Toby held his breath. Typing resumed, a steady clickety-click. A final keystroke and the logic bomb exploded in the heart of Sapphire's code.

The initial blast disrupted the sequence, sending shards of

useless code across the screen. Lockwood's entire team converged on the injured workstation, engaged in the battle to protect the precious video compression-decompression algorithm. Toby watched gleefully as engineer after engineer logged on with a new command set. With each failed attempt, the bomb absorbed the codec string and spread the destruction deeper into the vital code.

Lockwood's team was making a heroic effort to save the algorithm, but the logic bomb had exploded in the computer's instructions set. Like a senile old man aimlessly waving his arms, the computer had reacted by flinging lines of code wildly in all directions while dispassionately displaying notices of its impending demise. PROCESS ABORTED and KILL DAEMON warnings littered the screen, coming faster and faster as the system reached overload. Toby savored that intoxicating moment, eighteen years in the making: the defining moment, when they knew it was hopeless.

SYSTEM SHUTDOWN. David's system ID gave the final command. Toby imagined hands reaching for ESC keys as, line by line, the screen before him went black. The heartbeat of the engineering lab stopped.

Toby the outcast, the pariah, judged unworthy to play on Lockwood's stellar Trxton development team, had avenged the past by condemning Lockwood's future. Score settled. Justice served. It was finished.

March 21, 1994: Palo Alto, California

"Lingerie?"

"Definitely not," Tim responded with an emphatic shake of his head.

"Perfume?"

"I dunno, man. Doesn't seem special enough."

Wandering around Nordstrom for a couple of hours while Tim sought the perfect gift for Marie's birthday was frustrating for both of them. Tim had no experience picking out gifts for girlfriends, and was counting on Peter for some flash of brilliance he had yet to offer.

"Jewelry. You can't go wrong with jewelry," Peter suggested. They wandered over to the jewelry department. A pert blonde with a ready smile offered to help.

"We need a great gift for a very special lady. His girlfriend," Peter told her inclining his head toward Tim.

"What does she wear?" She looked to Tim expectantly.

Tim shrugged. "I've never really thought about it." Tim paused, thoughtful. "She wears a silver cross necklace a lot."

"How about a bracelet to go with the necklace?" The salesgirl moved toward the display. Tim leaned over, studying the bangles and beads. He looked up at her with a brightening smile. "She has a charm bracelet," he said, as inspiration hit him.

"Great. We have lots of charms." She moved over to a second case containing dozens of tiny little boxes. Tim glanced at Peter. He nodded. "Good idea. Something that's special to her. Shows you've been paying attention to what she says."

"Do you have any religious ones?" Tim asked.

The salesgirl studied the case for a moment. "We have these three." She pulled out a cross, a tiny Bible and a pair of praying hands and lined them up in front of Tim.

"I'll take the praying hands." Tim looked relieved and pleased with his decision, taking a final look at the charm case.

"Peter, check it out." Tim nudged Peter with his elbow and pointed. Peter followed the line of Tim's finger and saw a miniature saxophone. "You have to get that for Jordan."

"She doesn't wear much silver."

"We have the same one in gold." The girl reached inside the case and pulled it out for Peter to inspect.

"She doesn't have a charm bracelet and I don't see her wearing one." He declined the purchase. Jordan didn't want emails or phone calls. He doubted she'd want a gift from him either. Their deal was to extinguish the flame and move on.

"We can put it on a necklace." The girl, working for the sale, pulled out a velvet display tray of gold chains. "Do you see one you like?"

The saxophone winked at him under the lights. It was Peter's turn for ambivalence. Would she see it as a token of affection or possessiveness? It would look so good on her neck, nestled in her cleavage, especially with the red silk shirt she liked to play in. He decided to take the chance.

"You choose." He offered the girl his brightest smile and enjoyed watching her eyelashes flutter, just because he knew he could. She selected a thin ribbon of gold, letting it slide delicately through her fingers. "We can have it ready in three days."

"She's leaving for Europe tonight."

"We'll have it ready when she comes back."

"She's not coming back." Peter saw her fingers falter. Her mouth formed a small 'o'. "Let me see what I can do."

She turned her back. Peter watched her wiggle her way down the store aisle.

"You ever think there might be more to life than chasing stories and a piece of ass?" Tim asked.

"I'll let you know when I find it." Peter kept his eyes on the salesgirl, using her cheery freshness as a balm to sooth the laceration of Jordan's impending departure.

"Jordan was good for you. You were good for each other. You should have tried harder."

Peter shrugged. "I knew the rules when we started."

"You ever going to get close enough to someone to really care about them? Or let them care about you?"

Peter sensed concern rather than accusation in Tim's question. It was this new, empathetic side of Tim that Peter was still struggling to come to terms with. Peter, staying on safe neutral ground, ignored the remark. "It's time to move on. There are plenty of fish in the sea."

Tim gave him a scrutinizing look. "Quit lying to yourself. A potted plant could see you're in love with that woman."

Peter laughed. "Don't confuse love with accommodation. Enjoyment does not eternity make. It was fun while it lasted." Peter liked the way the words sounded, light and easy, so at odds with the searing feeling in his gut.

"So, now that I've helped buy her a birthday gift, do I finally get to meet this mystery woman of yours?"

Tim stared down at the praying hands charm. "There's one thing you're going to have to understand about Marie. She's passionate about her faith. Just like Jordan's passionate about jazz and you are about chasing the story. Marie's going to want to know where you stand with the Lord."

A Bible thumper. Worse than I thought. No wonder Tim's been so secretive.

"What Lord?" Peter asked.

Tim was studying him, Peter saw, testing the question for sarcasm or honesty. *A little of both,* Peter admitted silently. *But what the hell could Tim see in a woman like that?*

"She's a really strong Christian and I've become one." Tim looked defensive, no doubt expecting some kind of cutting remark. Though it was tempting, Peter declined the invitation.

"I thought that's what you were." Peter stared past the clothing racks, willing the girl to come back and end the uncomfortable conversation.

"I was raised Catholic. It's all rules and rituals. This isn't about church. It's about a personal relationship with Jesus Christ as Lord and Savior." Tim was speaking rapidly, like he had to get it all out before his courage failed him.

"It's knowing that God loves me. The God of the universe cares about little me. Not for what I should be or I'm going to be, but for me right now. I've learned I don't have to do anything to please God. He knows all my faults and flaws and He's forgiven me. For a kid who grew up thinking God was all about punishment, it's— well, it's mind-blowing. It's changed me."

"I can see that." Peter had seen the change in Tim, the quiet confidence he now possessed even away from the keyboard, as if a burden had been lifted. Peter assumed it was the new girlfriend.

"I want you to meet Marie, but…" Tim's voice trailed off, then resumed. "She *will* ask you where you stand with the Lord. She asks everyone. She thinks it's the most important question anyone can answer."

Peter mulled the question, trying to think of a response that wouldn't offend or ridicule Tim. It was a heavy lift, and staring at the sparkling charms in the display case wasn't giving him any insights. "Honest answer—I don't know," he said, finally.

The salesgirl was back, and Peter was more than relieved. He was comforted by the normal, commerce-based exchange, rescued from participating any further in the ridiculous carnival sideshow Tim's declaration imposed on him.

She handed him a gift-wrapped box. The necklace with the dainty saxophone charm attached was inside, polished and gleaming. He hoped Jordan would be pleased.

• • • •

They parted company. Tim was off in Peter's Porsche to celebrate a birthday dinner with Marie. Peter leaned against Tim's Honda, borrowed for the trip to the airport, watching the bluish vapors from his cigarette drift upward. The conversation with Tim had disturbed him more than he was willing to admit. Marie and her God had already driven a deep wedge between them; Peter knew his friendship with Tim would never be the same. He stared intently at a small cluster of stars hanging off the horizon, thinking vehement, murderous thoughts.

Hey, you. If you're up there, listen to me. Don't you have enough people? Why'd you have to go and take my best friend?

March 21, 1994: Los Altos Hills, California

Everything Jordan needed for her new life was packed into four large bags, stuffed inside Tim's Honda. Placing the saxophone case on the floor of the passenger seat, she turned to Peter.

"Ready?"

"I'm going to do one more check just make sure we haven't forgotten anything." Peter walked into the now-vacant cottage and took a quick tour of the rooms. Satisfied with the room check, he stood with his hand poised on the switch, about to turn out the lights for the final time.

So many memories in such a short time. He recalled their first romantic dinner together, conjured up the vision of Jordan playing the sax, giving him a view into her secret self, the passionate lovemaking that followed. Muted strains of music diffused the thin air as he saw her caress the instrument and offer him its sweetest sounds.

The scent of her perfume drifted past him as she stepped up

behind him and nuzzled the base of his neck. A quick flick of her tongue in his ear instantly enlivened him. Her hands dropped to his waist and unzipped his jeans.

"I want you, right here, right now," Jordan whispered, fondling him. As he grew hot and hard in her palm, she ran her fingernail down his ridge. Neurons fired inside him, sending pulses of white heat to every nerve ending. He stepped out of his pants, turned and pulled her close. His kissed her greedily, opening her lips with his tongue, probing deeply into her mouth, as he fingered apart the buttons on her blouse and unsnapped her bra. She let them drop to floor. Her jeans and lacy black bikini landed in a heap beside them.

He drank in her nakedness, cupped his fingers around her breasts and began to massage them, lightly caressing her cherry-colored nipples. Jordan moaned and arched her back as the sensation ripped through her. He caught her, almost in a dance sway, and lowered her gently onto the carpet. He lay on top of her, burying his face between her breasts. Tenderly suckling each one in turn, his hands explored the curves and swells of her body.

His weight pinned her to the floor. He pulsed with the inescapable urge to hold her there. Captive. Locked together. Lost in time. No plane to catch. No space between them. His hands traveled lower. She spread her legs, his fingers nimbly fondling her sweet spot. She groaned with pleasure. He caressed her swollen lips with light feathery strokes, his rhythm increasing as he sensed her body responding. Her flesh twitched convulsively as she began to reach her peak. Her body, glistening in the setting sun streaming through the windows, was as taut as a drawn bow. For an instant he stopped stroking, holding her fate in that crucible where the desire for release verges on agony.

"Peter, yes, now," she moaned.

"Jordan," he whispered, entering her and matching his rhythm to hers. Her climax rocked them both. As she enveloped him, he wrapped his arms tightly around her giving himself up fully and completely hers.

March 21, 1994: San Francisco, California

"Now boarding United Flight 2735 to Munich." The official announcement, though expected, filled him with dread. He could not make time stand still. Jordan was leaving."Time to go." She rose from the seat she'd occupied for the last hour as they made idle small talk laden with long pauses. Picking up her purse, she turned back to him with a slight smile.

"Remember, no phone calls, no emails and tell Tim no hacking."

"No hacking," he agreed, standing beside her.

"Okay, then."

"Jordan, I got this for you." He pulled the gift box from his pocket and handed it to her. "It's just a token."

She slid the white ribbon off the silver box and opened the lid. Reaching for the necklace, she held it up. The tiny saxophone dangled before her eyes. "It's gorgeous. I love it." Leaning toward him, she brushed her lips against his cheek. She handed him the gold strand, then twirled around lifting her hair away from her neck. "Put it on, okay?"

He circled her neck with the chain and fastened the clasp. As she turned back to him, he saw the charm settle below her throat and between her breasts, just as he had imagined it would. It killed him to think he would never kiss those breasts again. Wrapping his arms around her and locking his hands behind her back, he pressed his forehead against hers.

"Whatever happens over there, do this for me. Find a way to play your music. Don't let anyone stop you. Live your passion." He touched her lips gently with his, then pressed harder to block the harsh static of the boarding call.

"Last call for United Flight 2735 to Munich."

Jordan broke his hold, slid her finger across his still moist lips. "I will never forget you," she murmured, picking up her saxophone case. She joined the trickle of passengers easing through the jetway.

Peter stood mute, immobile, staring straight ahead as the jetway doors closed and the ticketing crew locked up their station and left the gate. Even then, he found it impossible to walk away. Instead, he moved over to the plate glass, standing close enough that his breath fogged the window, and watched the plane's red taillights blink into the darkness. It may not have been Jordan's plane. They stack them up. But it didn't matter. She was gone.

He had never expected it to be this hard. He'd had so many women. *She is just one more,* he reminded himself. He gave what he could to each of them, loving them to the extent he was capable of, always careful to shield his inner being. Always determined to be the one to walk away, to reject before he could be rejected. Forever on the lookout for one more connection-less connection where he could rest for a while, disenfranchised and content.

But Jordan had tripped him up. She had taken his heart when he wasn't looking and exposed his deepest longings. And now? He stared inward at the emptiness he had created. It no longer mattered what he wanted. He would have to live with what he had, and he could fit it inside a thimble.

16

April 22, 1994: Palo Alto, California

IN THE FOUR WEEKS, FIVE DAYS, THIRTEEN HOURS AND TWENTY-four minutes Jordan had been gone, Peter remained adrift, unable to concentrate on anything for more than a few minutes. The words on the CRT screen in front of him faded in and out of focus as he tried to edit Sam's story on MediaBuilders' latest acquisition, an Internet applications company called HotHub. The startup was developing Web-based video conferencing software that combined PC desktop file sharing and real-time video for face-to-face meetings. MediaBuilders got caught in a bidding war with Draco on that one. Sam played up the clash of the Internet titans well. Peter clicked the *Send* button, leaned back in his chair and grabbed his cigarettes. There were four cigarettes left in the pack he'd opened that morning before breakfast. It was only ten a.m.

His cell phone buzzed. He answered with a vacant "Hello."

The voice that responded was stiff and strained with no trace of Charlie's customary heartiness. "I've got to talk to you, Peter. It's urgent."

"Sure. Name it."

Peter heard a heavy sigh. "Alpine Inn. Noon." The phone clicked.

The Alpine Inn was by no one's measure an inn and even the term restaurant was a stretch. It was a good, old-fashioned counter service hamburger joint and bar with a rough-hewn character that had become increasingly endearing as the surrounding towns of Woodside and Portola Valley grew in affluence and pretension.

Peter and Charlie walked through the front doors, past the well-stocked bar and into picnic-style seating section of large plank style tables and benches. The tables were scarred from the hundreds of knives that had carved initials into their wood.

"Get the drinks. I'll order the food. Whaddya want?" Charlie asked.

"Burger. No cheese."

They sat opposite each other, sipping Cokes and making irrelevant small talk while they waited for their food. The restaurant was empty except for a lone pinball wizard near the front door, and their order came up quickly. Charlie returned carrying a tray laden with burgers and fries. They ate in silence for a while. The quiet made Peter edgy.

"We going to talk or what?"

Charlie attacked his cheeseburger with vigor. "It's about MediaBuilders."

Peter hunched forward. "I'm listening."

"They're buying Lockwood's company."

"You mean licensing the technology," Peter corrected him.

"No. I mean buying the company. Not just the technology. The IP. Patents pending. The whole shebang."

Peter paused in mid-chew, almost forgetting to swallow. "What the hell? Why would MediaBuilders do a buyout instead of a straight licensing deal? Why would David Lockwood, the ultimate maverick, sell his baby to a global conglomerate?"

"Good questions."

"Got some answers?"

Charlie ignored him. Pushing aside the remains of his first cheeseburger, he started in on the second, spacing the bites with large handfuls of greasy red-capped fries. Peter studied Charlie's gastronomic binge while he considered the implications of Charlie's revelation.

"Wait a minute. This was your big score, wasn't it?" He grinned broadly in Charlie's direction. "That's why you were all over Horizon. You were using Horizon to pressure Lockwood to deal with Victor Henderson and MediaBuilders, weren't you? Explains why you were giving me the runaround."

Charlie nodded. "Client confidentiality."

"So something must've happened to queer the deal. If you were still in play, we wouldn't be sitting here now, would we?"

Charlie's face darkened. "The bastards screwed me." He shoved aside the debris of his lunch and stood, Coke glass in hand. "You want a refill?"

"Yeah, sure."

Charlie grabbed two more Cokes from the bar and set them down on the table. He didn't flinch when Peter pulled his notebook and pen from the back pocket of his jeans. He was finally willing to tell his story.

"Henderson hired me around the beginning of December. He'd just started this new acquisition team for the company. Meant to position MediaBuilders for the global infobahn. You know everybody wants in on that one," Charlie said, hands moving in characteristic pantomime.

"He had four companies at the top of his list. Three of 'em, Delta Software, PointNClick and HotHub, are done deals. I did great work there. Worked with Margaret on 'em. She's a good lawyer." Charlie stopped talking, eyeballing Peter, waiting for his reaction.

Peter nodded. "She is."

Charlie took a sip of Coke and continued. "The real prize was Sapphire. We looked around but none of the other boxes we vetted even came close to Sapphire, so we went in looking for a nice technology-licensing deal. Nothing complicated. You know Lockwood is the devil to deal with, so it was a long, slow dance.

Eventually, between Margaret and me, we got him to the table about a month ago, right before the Horizon intro. Even Blaylock was there."

Peter glanced up from his notes and whistled. "Blaylock was there?"

"Yeah, it made it that much worse." Charlie's smile faded as he relived the event.

Peter could feel his pain. If Charlie had invited MediaBuilders' Chairman and CEO Jonathan Blaylock to sit in, Charlie must have assumed he had the deal in the bag. *But that means Margaret is embarrassed too,* Peter thought, suppressing a smile as he refocused on Charlie's tale.

"The gang was all there. Lockwood and couple of his people. Blaylock, Henderson, Margaret and me on our side. Then, just before we started collecting signatures to nail the thing shut nice and tight, Blaylock and Henderson boot everyone outta the room so they can talk to Lockwood in private. Ten minutes, later Blaylock and Henderson are sprinting down the hall with their dicks hanging out. The deal is stone cold dead. Margaret is as shocked as I am," Charlie said gruffly.

"Next day I get this call from Henderson. 'Very sorry, old boy,' he says in that snobby British way of his. 'Appreciate your hard work, but your services are no longer required,' and all that shit."

"But you're saying the deal went down anyway, right?"

"Yeah, this morning I got a call from my source inside who says the deal is back on. Bigger and better. Lockwood is selling out to MediaBuilders. So MediaBuilders gets Sapphire and I get the proverbial shaft."

Charlie wadded up his napkin, threw it onto his ketchup-ribboned plate and gave the plate an exasperated shove. As the plate slid to the corner of the table, Charlie met Peter's gaze. The depth of his disappointment was palpable.

"You talk to Margaret?"

"Tried. She said she couldn't do anything for me."

Typical Margaret, Peter thought in disgust. "So what's your

next move?"

"She can't help me. But you can." Charlie grinned, a conspiratorial glint in his eye. He looked like he had when they played pranks together in college.

"It's a big story and nobody's got it yet. You get the scoop. I get to see these bastards squirm a little in the process."

The pleased look on Charlie's face told Peter that Charlie was seeing the headlines pre-announcing the Lockwood buyout—surprising MediaBuilders and Victor Henderson in the same way Peter's Horizon coverage had ambushed Alex Kavanagh. Embarrassing Margaret was just a bonus for both of them. Charlie, like most of his friends, saw the gulf between Peter and Margaret as typical sibling rivalry. He figured Peter would welcome the chance to pull his sister's chain.

Peter ran his finger along the rim of his empty plate. Charlie wasn't just offering him a blockbuster exclusive; he was begging Peter to help him get even. As far as Peter was concerned, Charlie had pulled in his marker and Peter owed his old college friend more than a few. It was time to admit the truth. He'd been circling around MediaBuilders for months, using Sam for cover, hoping the kid would protect him from a direct confrontation with Margaret. Charlie's request exposed his cowardice. It both galled him and propelled him forward. He wanted the story all right, the whole story.

"What's wrong with Sapphire?" Peter leaned forward, eyes locked on Charlie's face.

His gaze met confusion. "Whaddya mean?" Charlie asked, brow furrowed.

"Lockwood would never sell Sapphire unless there was something wrong. Something so wrong he couldn't fix it himself. If he's selling out to MediaBuilders it's either because he needs the funding or he wants to shed another failed product. Which is it? That's the real story."

The restaurant had filled almost to capacity, the hubbub of conversation now in marked contrast to Charlie's silence as he pondered the question. "I don't know," Charlie said finally.

"Can I talk to your source?"

Charlie shook his head. "No can do. He's nervous. He'd never talk to a reporter."

"Off the record. Deep background only." Peter ignored Ben's voice in his head demanding he formally source all his stories. He'd deal with Ben when he had the story in the bag. "How badly do you want to get these guys?"

Badly, Charlie's face told him. Charlie lumbered up from the bench, strolled over to the corner of the restaurant, out of earshot, and pulled out his cell. Peter watched as his expression changed from cautious to hopeful. When Charlie returned to the table, his ruddy features were bright with delight. "He'll talk to you. Tomorrow. Saturday morning. It's your only shot. After that, he's on vacation for two weeks."

Charlie scrawled out the name and number. "He's one of my best sources, Peter. Treat him with kid gloves. Kid gloves, Okay?"

Peter took the paper Charlie held out. "Yeah, sure. Who is this guy?"

"David Lockwood's money man."

April 23, 1994: Hayward, California

The lawn in front of the science building at Cal State Hayward looked as if the circus had come to town. Dozens of blue, green and red pop-up tents dotted the lawn, arranged in a semicircle around large, fenced-off squares of what looked like playground equipment. Peter walked toward the steep cement staircase leading down to the lawn. He paused and took in the scene from above. The closer he got, the more it looked like doggie Disneyland. He saw dogs jumping through tires, barreling through plastic tunnels, racing up and over ramps and, the only word Peter could think of, was *weaving* through a line of white poles while people ran behind, alongside and around them. It sounded, from the shouts, screams, claps and non-stop barking, like they were all having fun.

Peter trotted down the stairs and walked toward a tall, angular-looking woman with short black hair. Its shade nearly matched the deep charcoal of the dog crouched in front of her. As Peter approached, the dog turned its head and fixed Peter with an unrelentingly manic stare. Peter kept a wary eye on the dog as he addressed the woman.

"Excuse me. Do you happen to know Frank Landau?"

The woman turned and the dog spun around her leg to her side. Both of them gave Peter the once-over. "Frank runs a golden. He's probably by the gamblers ring. Our group is up next." She pointed in the general direction of the rings.

Peter must have looked as confused as he felt. Her face softened into a smile. "New to agility?" she asked.

He nodded. "Completely. I've never met Frank and I don't know what a golden is," he confessed.

"Golden retriever," she chuckled. He imagined that the eyes behind the dark sunglasses held an amused glint. She pulsed with a competitive energy Peter found achingly familiar. He saw Jordan in nearly every woman he met, now. Sometimes he felt as if he were living inside a pinball machine, bounced around by the routine of daily life, taking a new bruising at each brief encounter with a woman.

"Give me a minute to warm Carson up and I'll walk you over." When she turned the dog spun with her as if he were attached to her leg. She sent the dog out over a jump and back several times in a figure eight formation without a word, using just her lithe body and shoulders. To Peter it looked like a series of dance moves. She leashed Carson and they started toward the rings, Peter on one side, Carson on the other.

"There's Frank." She pointed to a medium-sized man in navy shorts and a white t-shirt with reddish hair and a small moustache, standing directly in front of the entrance to the ring. "Looks like he's up. You'll have to wait till he finishes his run," she added, starting to walk on.

"Thank you," Peter said.

Peter turned and watched as Frank and his golden entered the ring. As the dog ran a pattern through a tunnel, over a bridge and over a series of jumps, another man in the middle called out numbers in sequence. Without warning, a whistle shrieked. Frank ran toward the middle of the ring and came to a dead stop. "Perry out," Frank yelled. "Over. Out chute. Weave."

Frank stood in place while the dog raced forward and over a jump, then into a white barrel with a long cloth attached. Perry twisted through the white poles, leaping onto the table to finish. The crowd cheered as Frank and Perry exited the ring. Peter eased his way through a knot of spectators and introduced himself.

"Hi, Frank. I'm Peter Ellis, from the *Valley Tribune*."

"Appreciate you coming all the way out here." Both Frank and his dog looked winded. Frank wiped his hand across a sweating brow and against his shorts. Perry stood beside him, tail wagging, eyes bright, pink tongue lolling out of one side of his mouth.

"Looks like fun."

"It is. We're addicted, Aren't we, Perry?" Frank looked down at his companion with a smile. The dog seemed to smile back up at him.

"My setup's this way," he said, turning. "Oh, Kit's up. Let's watch her run and then we can talk."

The tall woman who helped him earlier was at the starting line. "Her name is Kit and her dog is Carson?" Peter asked, grinning, as they lined up beside the ring.

"Lady's got a sense of humor," Frank chuckled. "But she's serious about agility. She's one of our best handlers. She and Carson won the USDAA nationals last year."

"What type of dog is that?"

"Border collie."

Kit walked out past the first two jumps, while Carson crouched at the line waiting to spring into action. "Want me to walk you through it?" Frank asked.

"Please."

"This is Master's gamblers. Each of the obstacles has a point value. You get thirty seconds to collect as many points as possible. Then, when the whistle blows, you have to complete the gamble in fifteen seconds to Q. The gamble here is jump to chute to weaves to table. The handler has to stay behind the line and send the dog." Frank pointed to a thin pink ribbon stretched across the grass.

"Q?"

"Qualify. It means, successfully complete the class. Those two people are the timer and scribe," Frank pointed to two people sitting under the canopy by the start line. "The timer has a stopwatch to record the dog's time on course and the scribe writes down the points and records mistakes called by the judge. Best time and points wins."

The timer yelled go. Kit dropped her arm and Carson flew off the line, taking obstacles at lightning speed while the judge called out the numbers: 1-1-3-3-5-3-5-1-7.

"The sequence is 'Jump, jump, tire, tunnel, A-Frame, tunnel, teeter, jump, dog walk'." Frank explained.

As Carson dashed up the dog walk and across the narrow blue plank, his foot slipped. His body twisted. The crowd gasped at what looked to be a certain fall. Pitching forward, Carson held onto the plank with his front paws and pulled his feet back underneath him, almost into a sit, as he slid to a stop at the yellow bottom of the dog walk. His front feet stretched out, touching the grass at the end of the plank. Carson's ears were pricked forward, his eyes locked on Kit.

"Nice contact," someone called as the whistle blew.

"Let's go!" Kit yelled. Carson arrowed over the jump and into the chute, snaked through the weave poles so low it looked like his belly was on the ground before leaping onto the table with seconds to spare.

"Nice run," Frank called as Kit exited the ring. She gave him a sunny smile and pointed to Carson. "He always saves my butt," she called back. Peter watched her saunter down the row of canopies until she disappeared from sight. Then he turned back to Frank.

"Gay. Just in case you were curious," Frank said, with a sideways glance.

"Good to know."

"Let's walk." With Perry tugging hard on the leash, Frank led them to a smaller lawn on the other side of the science building. There he let the dog off the leash to sniff, pee and play.

"Charlie said this was off the record." Frank kept his eyes on his dog. "I can't even be quoted as an anonymous source. Deep background only."

"Understood."

"Okay. Shoot."

"Why sell the company? Why not just license the technology?" Peter asked, as they walked across the lawn.

"It's a long road between concept and commercialization, and even David's resources are not inexhaustible." Frank sighed. "It's been a heavy lift."

"The Valley of Death."

Frank nodded.

"What about an equity deal?" Another dog handler team appeared and Peter watched as Perry trotted over to greet the new dog.

"We started there. We set up a meeting a few weeks ago for what I thought was a nice, safe fifteen to twenty percent equity buy-in. But when Henderson and Blaylock got to the meeting, it was clear they wanted control. Henderson played a switch and wouldn't come in for less than fifty-one percent. David went ballistic. He stormed out, pissed, determined to do Sapphire on his own."

"Then what happened?"

"Short answer. He couldn't. The Sapphire code is tricky. It's very unstable. After all, nothing like this has ever been done before. David's team has been taking two steps forward and one step back for months. Glitch after glitch."

Frank watched a hawk glide across the field in search of prey. "David's got some bright kids working for him. Very bright. They come to him because of Trxton. He had his greatest success in 1977, when he was twenty-two, and he's been living off it ever since. But what David refuses to acknowledge, even today, is that he didn't do it alone. He had a partner for Trxton that he didn't have for Falcon and doesn't have for Sapphire."

"Devon O'Reilly."

Frank nodded. "After the Horizon, I mean, the Draco Universal, intro last month, even David realized we were running out of time and money. He came to me privately and told me he would agree to give up control if that's what it would take to get Sapphire done."

"What about the code problems?"

"Solvable, David says, with time, money and a bigger team." Frank paused, whistled for his dog. "The truth is, we need MediaBuilders as much as they need us."

Frank whistled again. Perry ran back to join them. Frank leashed him up and they started back toward the rings. "Got what you needed?"

"Just one more question. Why talk to me? Why leak the story before the deal's done? Why not stay under the radar?"

Frank paused in mid-stride, turning toward Peter. Their eyes met briefly. "Fair question. My job is to protect David's interests, to get the best deal I can and make it stick. With a company as big and powerful as MediaBuilders, I need leverage. You're it."

April 23, 1994: Palo Alto, California

MediaBuilders Acquires Lockwood's Sapphire Project
By Peter Ellis, Tribune *staff*

In a bold move guaranteed to change the balance of power in the Internet Wars, MediaBuilders USA has acquired all rights to the development and distribution of David Lockwood's Sapphire Project for $1.2 billion in cash and securities.

The acquisition, currently an agreement in principle, is expected to be confirmed by MediaBuilders' Board of Directors at their quarterly meeting next month. With the acquisition of Sapphire, MediaBuilders has control of

every critical piece of the information highway: Internet
access box, programming content for the Web, ecommerce
applications, and with their recent partnership with AT&T,
global communications capability.

Goodbye Draco, Peter thought with relish, rereading his lead
for the fourth time while punching up Alex Kavanagh's direct
line.

"Hi Alex. It's Peter Ellis."

"Hello, Peter." Alex's voice was curt. It sounded like only his
duty to the media kept him from banging the phone down in
Peter's ear. "What can I do for you?"

Peter provided Alex with the details on MediaBuilders'
purchase of Sapphire and was rewarded with the stunned silence
he had anticipated.

"When are you planning to run this?" Alex asked.

"Tomorrow morning. Sunday business section."

"That doesn't give us much time to respond."

"We're a daily paper, Alex," Peter reminded him, unable to
resist the sarcasm. "It's three now. If you can get me a comment by
five, I can get it in."

"I'll do my best," Alex replied, and disconnected.

Peter left a message with Victor Henderson's admin. Reaching
David Lockwood would require more creativity. After the initial
flurry of media coverage, Lockwood had dived back into obscurity.
Now Peter understood why. Peter typed a message for Lockwood
including the same collection of facts he'd left for the others, and
sent the email with no expectation that Lockwood would respond,
even if he got the message.

He had one last call to make. Hands trembling, willing his
voice not to quiver when she answered, he picked up the phone
and dialed the New York offices of Ellis, Blackwell and Barnes.

• • • •

"I thought I'd find you here, you son of a bitch."

Peter, enjoying a celebratory cigarette after filing the MediaBuilders takeover story, swiveled his head in the direction of the voice. Sam stood on the sidewalk, leaning over the wrought iron gate that separated the patio from the street. For a second, Peter thought he would jump over the fence. Instead, he pulled the gate, stomped onto the patio and stood just inches from Peter's face.

"What is it, Sam?" Peter asked wearily.

"You know damn well what it is. MediaBuilders. I brought you in, asshole. I gave you a chance to prove you weren't the douchebag everyone says you are. Well, you showed me, didn't you?"

"That was as much a Lockwood story as it was MediaBuilders. I got it from the Lockwood side. With my sources. It's mine."

"Bullshit. You should've brought me in and you know it."

"Like you would have?"

"Sure."

"Yeah, right." Peter laughed. He took a last pull on his cigarette, threw the butt on the concrete and ground it into the pavement with the toe of his shoe.

Facing Sam squarely, he said: "Quit whining. You've been on MediaBuilders for weeks. Rewriting press releases. You had as much chance to break this thing open as I did. Get off your ass and do some investigative reporting for once. Maybe you'll learn something everybody doesn't already know."

Sam's face turned red. His fists clenched. "You owe me half that by-line," he claimed, taking a step toward Peter.

Peter held his ground. Sam seemed determined to start a fight. Too many TV westerns, Peter thought, as the absurdity of the situation hit him. He struggled to keep a straight face. "Grow up," he retorted. Peter's direct refusal seemed to enrage Sam. He took another step forward, eyes narrowed, fists tight, mouth set in an angry line.

"You really want to fight?" Peter asked, feeling his muscles tense. Sam was two inches taller and had a long reach. Peter stepped back just out of range, cocked back on his heels, ready as with a tennis serve to move in any direction, watching Sam for a twitch or eye roll that would signal his first move. He figured Sam for a quick left uppercut. They circled each other slowly, warily.

"Peter!" He looked toward the voice from the balcony above and felt a crack as Sam's fist slammed into the side of his jaw. His head snapped back.

"Shit," Sam yelped, jumping back and flinging his left hand in the air. Sam seemed as surprised as Peter that the punch had connected.

"Peter, Ben wants to see you now." Tina's voice was wobbly, shock at the display she'd just witnessed evident in her expression.

Peter nodded, his eyes fixed on Sam like the blue flame from a welder's torch. "We done here?"

Sam, wiggling fingers still numb from the punch, looked away. "Guess so."

Peter turned and headed up the stairs. Tina greeted him with a sad shake of her head. "Juvenile," she said. "Yeah," Peter agreed, rubbing the side of his jaw to lessen the sting.

Ben met him outside Adam's office and they walked in together. Adam held a finger to his lips and pressed the intercom button.

"My managing editor, Ben Carter, has just joined us. I'd like him to hear what you have to say. Please continue."

"Hello, Ben." Margaret's voice filled the office. Peter stared at the phone, eyes glazed. His joints, still tense from the encounter with Sam, felt locked, making movement painful. Ben shot a sideways glance at him before speaking.

"Hello, Margaret."

"As I was telling Adam. Victor Henderson has been keeping an eye on The *Tribune* for the last few months, and he likes what he sees. He thinks your paper would be a strong addition to our media news group. MediaBuilders has the resources you need to compete more effectively with the larger dailies in your market, like the *San Jose Mercury News* and *San Francisco Chronicle*. In short, we want to purchase the *Valley Tribune*. We're prepared to make you a very attractive offer."

Peter's shoulders slumped. His sore jaw throbbed as blood rushed to his face. He looked from Ben to Adam. Ben's face registered shock. Adam's was impassive. He picked up a pen, scribbled a note and passed it to Ben.

"How attractive?" Adam asked.

"Ten million dollars."

Peter's mouth dropped open. It was twice what the *Tribune* was worth. Adam, who struggled every month to bring in enough advertising to make payroll, would be a fool to turn it down. Adam leaned back in his chair, feigning relaxation. He refused to look in Peter's direction.

"That's quite a generous offer."

"You have a great paper, Adam. You took a small inconsequential throwaway and turned it into a strong voice in the business community. That's a major achievement. We're especially impressed with the new online edition. But there's strength in numbers, for advertising, operations." Here Margaret paused briefly and delicately. "Even editorial strength. MediaBuilders can offer all of that."

"What about my people? The Web edition was Peter's idea." Ben broke in.

"We'll do our best to keep everyone on the editorial side, Ben, if we can," Margaret continued smoothly. "If for some reason we can't keep them at the *Tribune*, we'll try to find a role for them somewhere else in the company."

Adam glanced uneasily at Peter. "You've given us a lot to think about, Margaret. Ben and I will discuss it and get back to you in the next day or two."

"I'll fax a preliminary agreement for your review within the hour. There's just one small favor we'd like to ask: while you're considering joining our organization, hold the story about our deal with David Lockwood. Just for a day or two. As a show of good faith."

Adam looked at Ben. Ben shook his head. Adam sighed.

"Yes," he told her. "We'll hold it for forty-eight hours."

"I look forward to hearing from you," she said, and disconnected.

Peter stood frozen, breathing arrested, as Adam glanced at his watch and Ben gathered up his paperwork. Visions of TriCorp played in his head, almost robbed him of his courage. Almost—but not quite.

Stepping forward, he leaned over Adam's desk. "This is a setup. Victor Henderson doesn't want the *Trib*. He just wants to bury the story. Call her back. Tell her to go to hell. She doesn't control the news, we do."

Adam's eyes narrowed. "You're crazy. Nobody would pay ten million just to bury a story."

"Ten million's a rounding error to Henderson. He wants Sapphire and he wants it bad. He lost it once and he's going to make damn sure he doesn't lose it again," Peter insisted.

Concern flickered across Adam's face. He massaged his chin with the heel of his hand. When he turned back to Peter, his features had hardened to obstinacy. "I'm the publisher of this paper. Besides, what the hell do you care? You don't really don't like working here anyway, do you?"

April 23, 1994: San Francisco, California

Peter glanced around Blue Note West, packed as usual on a Saturday night. The jazz greats, Brubeck, Coltrane, even Ella, smiled benignly down at him. He'd managed to grab the last table at the back ten minutes before The EJs were set to play. It was standing room only. Around him, the waiting crowd pulsed with energy. Smoke from dozens of cigarettes, including his own, curled toward the stage. Peter had not been back to the club since that first time he'd seen Jordan play, but he had discovered that he genuinely enjoyed her music. He listened to KKSF, even started a small jazz CD collection. He told himself that he was curious to see who the new sax player was. Taking a quick sip of the Scotch the waitress set down, he waited for the band to begin.

"Hello, would you mind sharing a table?" a female voice asked.

Peter looked up and was greeted by the wide smile of a petite Asian woman whose lean athletic build instantly reminded him of Jordan's friend Grace. But her black tube-top jumpsuit, white mesh scarf and red beret asserted a flair for the dramatic the quiet, conventional Grace lacked. She held a glass of red wine in her hand. "If you're waiting for someone?" Her question held more invitation than curiosity.

"Not at all. Please join me." Peter stood automatically and pulled out her chair.

"I'm Toni," she said, placing her wine glass on the table as she took the seat. He noticed a spicy cinnamon scent as she drew her arm past him. "And you are?"

"Peter."

"Do you follow the band, Peter?"

Peter gave her a quizzical look. "Not sure what you mean."

"I follow them. Meaning I come hear them every chance I get. They've got a unique sound. I usually come with a couple of friends but they couldn't make it tonight. Can I bum a cigarette?"

"Sure." Peter offered her the pack. She pulled one out and waited for him to light it for her. "Too bad they lost the girl, though. She was talented," Toni said, inhaling and tapping the ashes into the green molded ashtray.

Her innocent remark hit him like a cold spike between the ribs. "Yes. She was," Peter agreed.

The curtains opened, the crowd roared and Peter got his first glimpse of the sax player who had replaced Jordan: young, black, with a shaved head and large diamond studs in his ears. Eric stepped up to the mic and introduced the band, just as he had before.

"Hello, we're The EJs and we'd like to start with a classic…"

You can't really be The EJs without the J, Peter thought sourly, as the new sax man blew out the notes to "Take Five." He played with a raw power that Jordan didn't possess, but he lacked her subtlety and warmth.

Beside Peter, Toni let the music carry her away. Body swaying, hands fluid, she seemed memorized by his performance. "He's great," she whispered to Peter.

Peter nodded. He'd come to the club to forget the day, to feel close to Jordan, and to block out the harrowing implications of the impending sale of the *Tribune*. Instead, he felt disembodied, his mind, heart and body contorted. Entering the club, his senses had eagerly consumed the crush of the crowd, the smell of sweat, smoke and booze. His body had hungrily absorbed the echoes of cheers and clapping that greeted the band, which played with its smooth, artful blending of sax, guitar, keyboard and bass.

Yet in his desperation to reclaim the past, Peter's desolate heart clung to phantom images of Jordan onstage, her hair flying, body melded to her instrument. Briefly, he relived the joy of that golden moment when she looked right at him smiling, raised the sax to her lips and puffed out the notes to "Lily Was Here." Then the memory, like the lady herself, simply disappeared.

Now, his back pressed against the chair, sipping Scotch, he watched Eric and the band play familiar tunes with an unfamiliar man on sax as he sat next to a girl he'd just met, pretending to enjoy her company. He put it on autopilot, half-listening to her chatter, making her laugh, flirting with ease, practicing a gentle seduction that nurtured the blossoming desire in her eyes. It fed his ego but did nothing to calm the turbulence in his soul.

"What's your favorite tune?" Toni asked.

"Lily Was Here," he said, immediately wishing he could reclaim the words. That song was Jordan's gift to him. It felt like a betrayal.

"That's her signature song. I doubt they'll play it since she's gone."

"Jordan. She has a name. It's Jordan," Peter blurted. Toni looked over at him, startled. "I thought you didn't follow the band."

Onstage, Eric closed the first set and the houselights rose.

"Can I get you another glass of wine?" he asked, standing, covering his slip with a boyish grin, his blue eyes stroking her face. She nodded and he felt her gaze follow him as he sauntered over to the bar.

The band's second set was easier to handle than the first. Peter allowed the music, the Scotch and Toni's charms to succor his spirit. As Eric and the band took their final bows, Toni placed her hand on Peter's arm. "I could use some company tonight, how about you?"

He caught another whiff of her spicy cinnamon scent. Her voice, like her skin, was warm and silky. He gave her athletic body a long lingering appraisal, liking what he saw. It had been awhile and, hell, he could use the exercise. She leaned closer, her breasts moving in rhythm with her quick breaths as she began to softly stroke his arm. His chest muscles tightened in response. Favoring her with an affectionate smile, he removed her hand from his arm and gave it a squeeze. "Tempting. But not tonight."

The curtain fell, chairs scraped across the thin carpet, the crowd began to disperse.

Why don't I give you my card?" Toni said, standing, and pulling a white square from her purse, holding it out to him.

He shook his head. "I'm glad we met, but I'm not on the market right now."

He tried to soften the statement with another pleasant smile. Toni shrugged as if to say, "your loss," picked up her purse and walked away.

Peter couldn't bring himself to leave. His townhouse was sterile and cold. On Monday Adam's decision could mean the loss of his job. He was already beginning to regret his quick refusal of Toni's company. Jordan had severed their ties. He owed her nothing. Still, he couldn't imagine being with anyone else. He wandered over to the bar, joining the regulars who hung out after every performance. Tonight they'd be discussing the new sax man. Sipping his third Scotch, he listened to the hum of conversation.

"She's gone, you know." Eric's voice was acrid and rough behind him.

"Yeah, I know," Peter replied, turning to face him. Eric's face was moist, his blond ringlets plastered against his forehead.

"She's not coming back."

"I know that too."

"Then what are you doing here?"

"I came to hear the music."

"You like the music?" Eric sounded surprised, then mocking. "I thought all you were interested in were the fringe benefits."

Peter sighed. He'd begun the day in a fistfight with Sam. He didn't want to end it fighting with Eric. "How about I buy you a drink?"

Eric gave him a hard stare that ended in a shrug. At Eric's nod, the bartender laid out a shot of tequila with lime, Dos Equis on the side. Eric tossed back the tequila, mouthed the lime and took a sip of the beer. "What do ya think of the new sax man?"

"He's not Jordan."

"No one is."

The regulars had cleared out. They were alone except for the bartender mopping up the other end of the bar. "You going to change your name?"

"We got too much invested in our brand." Eric leaned an elbow on the bar, studying the ceiling of the aging, converted warehouse. "We were gonna cut a record," he said, twirling the empty shot glass.

"She told me."

"I couldn't come up with the dough."

"Jordan's dad," Peter suggested.

"Gowns, jewelry, parties, but not a penny for her music. Not ladylike." Eric's breath held the fetid odor of dead dreams. The bartender slid over another shot. Eric tossed it back and took a hard pull on the Dos Equis. He stared past Peter at the empty stage, his body limp, his expression funereal. Peter felt the room contract.

Eric took a final pull on the beer. "We've been playing here for two years. I guess it's time to move on. Find a new place to play."

IT IS NEARLY IMPOSSIBLE TO KEEP A SECRET IN A NEWSROOM. BY Monday morning everyone had heard about MediaBuilders' offer to buy the *Tribune*. The news cheered the ambitious, frightened the deadwood, and angered the traditionalists. Only Adam, Ben and Peter himself knew what the change would mean for Peter.

"I'm covering the buyout," Sam called jovially to Peter as he passed him in the hallway. Sam was among those who saw the opportunity. Peter ignored him as he headed toward production.

"Peter, can I see you a minute?" Ben called as he passed.

Peter stopped and swerved into Ben's office. "Any word from Adam?" Peter asked.

"Not yet and the Lockwood story stays spiked." The weariness in Ben's voice suggested a long heated battle with Adam without resolution. Peter felt a surge of gratitude and fierce loyalty toward his editor. No one had ever fought for him the way Ben had. He caught Ben's eye with a look of appreciation. Ben nodded and closed the door.

"I've got an assignment for you," he said with a grimace.

"What is it?" Peter asked, quelling the anxiety that arose at Ben's grim expression.

"The Palo Alto City Council meeting tonight."

"You can't be serious."

Ben studied him, face impassive. "Sam asked for the night off. I figured you were the best one to handle it."

"You sidelining me, Ben?" Peter asked incredulously.

"I don't have a choice. We have to tread carefully here. MediaBuilders. Your sister. Your father's law firm. The *Trib*'s editorial integrity. It's all on the line. Adam and I agreed that until this is settled, you're benched."

"Dammit Ben!" Peter exploded in frustration as the irony of the vise Margaret had managed to put him in hit with full force. He couldn't do his job until the *Tribune* was sold; and when it was sold, he wouldn't have one.

"Who broke the Sapphire story in the first place? Whose stories on Horizon hit the wires, day after day? Mine! Adam didn't turn the *Tribune* into a voice in the business community, you did. If the *Trib*'s worth millions to MediaBuilders, it's thanks to us, you and me." Peter stopped shouting and gasped for breath. Ben stood by, giving Peter time to regain his equilibrium before he spoke.

"You may be right, Peter. But it doesn't change the mess we're in," Ben said quietly, holding out the City Council agenda.

Peter took the agenda and turned to leave the office just as Sam burst through the door without knocking. His breathing was ragged, as if he'd just come from a hard run.

"This just came off the wire," he gasped, waving the thin paper in front of them.

The headline was enough to coat the back of Peter's collar with sweat. *MediaBuilders to Acquire Sapphire.*

Ben grabbed the press release, scanned it and jumped out of his chair. "Show of good faith," he snorted, giving Peter a penetrating look. "You two stay here. I'll be right back," he said, slamming the door behind him.

• • • •

"Adam's livid," Ben said, when he returned to his office a few minutes later. "We've got carte blanche. I want both of you on this. Peter, take the lead, talk to your sources and get to Lockwood. Find out why the hell Lockwood is so eager to sell Sapphire. Is it really the key to the information highway or is it another dog like Falcon? Sam, get the MediaBuilders story. Make sure you get to Henderson. Let's break this thing wide open, boys."

They took off in different directions. Peter went to his office and placed calls to Charlie, Tim and the PR rep listed for David Lockwood. He scanned his email. Still no word from Lockwood. Frank, his best bet, was on a Caribbean cruise. Peter crossed his fingers and called Frank's cell. Even if Frank had his cell phone with him on vacation, the chances he had cell coverage were almost nil. Cellular coverage outside major cities was spotty at best.

Sam stepped into Peter's office, wearing a smug smile. "I just got off the phone with Henderson's people. You got the facts wrong. The price for Sapphire is 2.2 billion dollars, not the 1.2 billion you reported."

"Seriously? Why wasn't that in the release?"

Sam shrugged. "Don't know. But I got it. You didn't."

"Hell of a lot of money for one unproven application."

Sam's face darkened. "Not for the best Internet access box available. Not for the chance to muscle out Draco and win the Internet War. You said that yourself." Sam's voice and posture were defensive.

"Not arguing with the reporting, Sam. Just the business logic. My source was one of the deal makers. More than double the price? That's got to mean something. What?"

"Lockwood played hard to get."

"Yeah, maybe. Do me a favor, Okay?" Peter faced him. Sam regarded him warily.

"Get someone, anyone, to talk about the timeline. Facts. Analysis. Speculation. I don't care. Find someone who'll go on the record and say when this product will see the light of day."

"Yeah, sure," Sam responded, his expression puzzled.

"I've got a theory," was all Peter would tell him.

Peter's cell buzzed. He nodded Sam out of his office and took the call.

"Where the hell is our story?" Charlie thundered into Peter's ear.

"Spiked."

"What!" Charlie exploded. "Ya had Frank. Ya had me. What more do ya need? Bells and bows?"

"Adam wanted more details. I did warn you. I've been working it. But now that MediaBuilders has gone public, we have to be a little more creative," Peter's tone was measured, pushing down his own frustration.

"Whaddya mean, gone public?"

"MediaBuilders issued a press release this morning saying that they're acquiring Sapphire." Peter glanced at the updated release Tina had placed on his desk. It had the correct buyout numbers that the first one lacked. Peter was still struggling to get his head around the exorbitant price tag, even considering the competitive pressure of the Internet gold rush. "To the tune of 2.2 billion."

"What! That's insane."

"I'll fax you the release. Then see if you can get to Frank. I really need your help on this one."

"You got it."

• • • •

"Okay, what do you two have?" Ben had called a four o'clock check-in meeting, an hour before the *Tribune's* five p.m. front page copy deadline. Peter felt on top of his game. The adrenaline rush keyed him up. He felt like he did when he played a hard-fought tennis match against a worthy opponent. *This is what it feels like to be in the big leagues*, he thought, seeing himself working for Ben not at the *Tribune*, but at the *Post*.

Sam spoke first. "I talked to Henderson. He confirmed that MediaBuilders is buying Sapphire for 2.2 billion, and that he sees

Sapphire as the cornerstone of their information highway strategy. The board of directors is set to approve the sale at their next meeting. And," Sam paused, looking Peter with a triumphant smile, "they're on schedule with development and distribution. They expect the first set-top boxes to be available within four to six months."

Ben turned his gaze to Peter. He shook his head.

"Then Sapphire's a dog. Just like Falcon. The video compression-decompression algorithm is corrupt. That's the heart and soul of these Internet set-top boxes. Without it there's no Internet-to-TV compatibility. No Internet streaming video," Peter explained.

"It will take Lockwood's team six to nine months just to get it rebuilt and running again. They're a year behind Draco. Victor Henderson just paid 2.2 billion dollars for the Internet's biggest white elephant."

Peter pushed the memos Charlie had gotten from Frank across the table.

The memos told the story of the persistent codec problems; and with Frank's name blacked out, Peter had protected his source. Sam looked crestfallen. Scooping Sam didn't feel so good to Peter now. The kid had tried hard.

Peter turned to him. "Good job getting confirmation on the timeline, Sam."

"Yeah, right," Sam replied, taking the comment as sarcasm.

"The timeline was critical. You proved my theory."

"What theory?" Ben asked.

"Simple. If Henderson's development timeline was short, he didn't know about the codec problems. If it was long, say 12-18 months, he did. Sam's intel proves he didn't know. His due diligence sucked."

And you, dear sister, royally screwed up, Peter thought with enormous satisfaction.

• • • •

At five p.m., standing behind the *Trib's* production team, Peter admired the headline as the story went to press: *Sapphire Not Ready for Prime Time.*

They'd led with the production problems, implied that Lockwood had tricked MediaBuilders into paying a fortune for worthless technology and buried the details of the impending purchase that Peter was sure the big dailies and broadcast media would lead with. It was another big score for Peter, and a career boost for Sam. Peter grabbed his briefcase, shoving the Palo Alto City Council agenda inside. Even that silly assignment, which Ben insisted he keep, couldn't chill his feeling of jubilation. He wished he could see Margaret's face when she read his story.

"Hey Peter," Sam called as he headed out the door. "I've got something for you."

Peter turned as Sam walked up, fax in hand. "Weren't you looking for some guy named Brian Tucker a few weeks ago?"

Peter nodded. "Yeah, programmer for Delta Software. But it didn't pan out."

"Think you might want to take another look. He's dead."

THE PALO ALTO CITY COUNCIL CHAMBERS WERE ALMOST EMPTY when Peter entered; the council members had yet to arrive. Like most rooms of its ilk, it was functional and practical. At the front of the room, the council members' table was flanked by an American flag on one side and the California Bear on the other.

Peter stuffed himself into a miniature classroom seat, trying not to bruise his knees on the folding desktop. He pulled out the police blotter fax copy on Tucker's death and reread it while he waited for the meeting to begin.

MEDIA ADVISORY/PRESS RELEASE
For Immediate Release No. 20140322-028
Monday, April 25, 1994

Homicide

On April 25, 1994, at 2:25 a.m., police responded to a call from a passing motorist on Alviso-Milpitas Road regarding a wounded man in a yellow Volkswagen Beetle. Upon arrival, police discovered the victim slumped over the steering wheel with a single fatal gunshot wound to his head from a small caliber gun. The victim has been identified as Brian Tucker, 28, a resident of Palo Alto.

The San Jose Police Department's Homicide Unit and Crime Scene Investigations Unit responded to investigate. Based on information obtained during the ongoing investigation, witnesses reported seeing a medium-sized man in a dark-colored ski mask flee the scene. Gang Detectives also responded, and are rapidly following up with any possible leads. Carjacking is being considered as a potential motive in the shooting.

The nearby neighborhood of Alviso had more than its share of gang-related activity. Sam, Peter knew, had filed stories on a couple of other carjackings in the area. *It's a plausible scenario,* Peter thought, *only if you ignore the fact that both Michael and Brian died violent deaths.* And Lee had left a message meant for Brian alone: *Tell Groucho it was for Helen.* Maybe the deaths were unrelated. Peter decided he would accept coincidence only when he'd ruled out the alternative.

The sound of the gavel interrupted his musings. The council had entered the chambers. As they ran through the usual opening duties, minutes accepted, motioned and seconded, Peter pulled out the agenda packet and scanned it. The issues were too minor for even a paragraph in the *Trib.* Good, he thought, relieved. He started to stand, ready for a quick exit, when a vaguely familiar voice stopped him cold.

"I believe it's less an issue of funding than of moral obligation," the speaker said firmly.

Peter's head jerked upward. He didn't recognize the face, but the speaker's head, with its frizzy, almost albino-white hair, caught his eye. It took him a minute to remember where he'd seen it before. Then he had it: the Consumer Electronics Show in January. Jimmy Fuzzyhead was a Palo Alto City Council member. Formal name—according to the plaque in front of him—James Wheaton. Peter jotted it down, recollecting. Jimmy and his friend chatting in the Tymelink suite. Jimmy's concern about the package for Brian

Tucker from the still-mysterious Henry, a package that might have contained an encrypted computer disk.

Peter was on Jimmy's tail the minute the meeting ended. As the council members filed out of the chambers, Peter kept his eye trained on the frizzy white head bobbing and weaving its way through the crowd.

"Jimmy? Do you have a second?" Peter asked falling into step with Jimmy as he left the building.

Jimmy half-turned. He looked tired and aggravated and in no mood to talk. It didn't help Peter that none of the issues Jimmy championed had made it past a cursory discussion.

"It's awfully late. Any chance we could do this tomorrow?" Jimmy asked, no break in his stride.

"I only need a few minutes." Peter stuck out his hand. "I'm Peter Ellis, from the *Valley Tribune.*"

Peter had counted on Jimmy to be the polite type who would feel guilty about dismissing him. He was right. Reluctantly, Jimmy stopped walking and returned the handshake. They were standing just outside the old courthouse. The few hardy souls who had lasted the entire meeting were spilling out around them. Several waved as they left, one or two casting Jimmy a sympathetic eye.

"What can I do for you?" Jimmy asked, his tone implying he wanted Peter to be quick.

"Actually, it's not about the meeting. It's about Brian Tucker. He's a friend of yours, isn't he?"

"Brian. Yes, we worked together at HP. He's quite a character, Brian is. Never know what he'll think up next." Jimmy smiled slightly, his eyes focused on a crack in the sidewalk, his mind hinged on some apparently pleasant memory.

Peter hated his next line. Although he'd delivered grim sometimes gruesome news on occasion, he'd never gotten comfortable with the role.

"I'm sorry to be the one to tell you this, but Brian is dead. I'm following up on the police report," he said quietly.

Jimmy reacted to the news with predictable stunned distress. His body stiffened. He struggled for control.

"What happened to him?" he mouthed, each word an effort.

"I don't have all the details, but it appears he was the victim of a carjacking."

"My God!" Jimmy turned pale, overwhelmed by shock.

"Look," Peter continued, "it's damn cold out here. How about if I buy you a drink and I'll tell you everything I know."

"I think I could use one," he agreed.

They walked several blocks before Jimmy spoke again. "I haven't seen you at the meetings before. You new?"

"No, subbing. Regular guy couldn't make it."

"I've talked to him. Tall thin kid with fiery eyes. Real earnest."

"Sam Parker."

"Yeah, that's it. What's your regular beat?"

"Business and technology."

Peter understood what Jimmy was doing. Compartmentalizing to avoid the pain. He'd been doing plenty of that himself lately. They rounded the corner and entered Raphael's, a fussily urban and pretentious café with art deco walls and black chrome tables and chairs. Jimmy ordered a Merlot from the list of nearly a dozen red wines written in pink on the spotless black lacquered display board. Peter stuck with his customary Dewar's."Tell me again what happened," Jimmy said. He stared at Peter, leaving the wine untouched.

"I don't have much. They found Tucker inside his car, a yellow VW, on 237 between Alviso and Hilton Ave. He'd been shot once in the head."

"That old yellow bug. Bry'd never give it up. Even when he had plenty of money," Jimmy said with a sad shake of his head. "Crazy just like him."

Jimmy fell silent and sucked on his wine, fingers locked around the stem of his glass. "Lord," Jimmy whispered. "That's all three of them. They're all dead."

"Three of who?"

"The guys from my old team at HP. First Henry, then Michael, and now Brian. What is this?" Jimmy stopped talking, looking at Peter as if he had just become reacquainted with his presence. *Why should I trust you?* His expression queried.

Peter knew that look and just how to handle it. He caught the waitress's attention and ordered another round.

"Look, your friends are dead. There might be a connection."

"It could be a coincidence," Jimmy said woodenly. "We live in awfully violent times."

It was not coincidence, Peter thought, sipping his Scotch. All three of them, Henry, Michael and Brian, played the puzzle games. A circuit Tim had called it. Round and round until someone got a puzzle he couldn't break.

Tell Groucho it was for Helen.

Michael's last words reverberated in his brain. He had to find that disk and he had to find Helen. Jimmy was his only lifeline. Peter glanced across the table. Jimmy was slouched down, staring into his empty glass. Peter felt the connection he'd established slipping away.

"I'm sorry," he said quietly. "I know it hurts. But talking to me couldn't make it any worse, could it? And if there is a connection, we need to find it or someone else, someone we don't know about yet, may be next."

Jimmy glanced up quickly, fear in his eyes. Peter saw Jimmy was the type who would never forgive himself for remaining silent if it might endanger someone else. The waitress replaced their empty glasses with full ones. Jimmy allowed himself a small sip. Then he began speaking.

"Henry was the first. He was killed in December. Stabbed to death at home. No one knows why. Didn't make sense. There was no forced entry. Nobody took anything. Police still have it listed as 'unsolved.' It got to all of us. The old HP team got together and put out a reward for information about Henry's death on the Internet. We even ran ads in the paper."

"What was Henry's last name?"

"Rhodes," Jimmy replied.

"Spelled?"

"R-H-O-D-E-S." Jimmy paused again, his face caught between pain and pleasant memories.

"Henry was such a great guy," he continued softly. "Give you the shirt off his back. He really liked the kids. He was kind of a mentor to them, half-father confessor and half-professor. Brian and Mike were two of his favorites. Always pushed them to the limit, but kept the safety net there in case they got into trouble. Great guy. Really great," Jimmy repeated, swirling the wine in his glass.

"Mike who?" Peter prompted for confirmation.

"Michael Lee."

"With AMD? Killed during a computer chip robbery?"

"Yeah. Now it's Brian. So hard to believe that—" Jimmy drew a sharp breath. "You don't think this is a coincidence, do you?" he asked, looking up.

"No. I don't."

"What do you think it is?"

Peter scrutinized Jimmy's face and considered his answer. Some people asked questions to reaffirm their already-immutable opinions, some because they wanted reassurance. Jimmy looked like he wanted the truth.

"I've been trying to find out about Brian and Henry since January. I know they were crypto-analysts, specialists in breaking encrypted computer code. I later found out Michael was too. They called it solving puzzles."

Jimmy nodded slowly. "I knew about the puzzles, but they were games. Just for fun."

"Remember CES?" Peter asked. "You got a package for Brian by mistake, didn't you?"

"Yes." Jimmy looked surprised. "How did you know?"

"I overheard you talking at the Tymelink party. That's how I recognized you tonight. That package you got by mistake held a computer disk. But I think it has more than a puzzle on it. It has information that someone is willing to kill for. Three people are already dead and there may be a fourth person in danger if she got a copy of the disk. A woman named Helen. I don't know if that's her real name or a code name. Does that name mean anything to you?"

Jimmy struggled to absorb the information. Finally, he shook his head. "No, I don't know anyone named Helen."

"What happened to the package?"

"A couple weeks after the show, I got an email from Brian. He told me to send the package to a P.O. box in Palo Alto. I did, and I didn't think any more about it."

Jimmy pushed his empty wine glass to the end of the table. It teetered on the edge.

"You think Henry was murdered because of what's on this disk?"

"Yes."

"What about Brian and Michael?" Jimmy asked.

"I can't prove it, but I believe it's all connected."

"My God," he whispered.

"Is there anything that they all had in common besides working for HP and the puzzle games?" Peter asked.

"Not that I know of."

"A programmers' association? Social clubs? A comedy club, maybe? Brian and Michael liked to do old-style comedy routines."

Jimmy pursed his lips, tented his hands. Finally he shook his head. "I just knew them from HP. Saw them at the reunions and then the talk was all work-related."

"What about a work connection then? After HP, Michael went the chip route, did graphic chip design first for Intel then AMD. Brian wrote gaming software at Electronic Arts, then Delta. After Delta Brian dropped off the map," Peter continued. "I scoured the Valley and couldn't find a trace..." Peter saw Jimmy flinch and avert his eyes.

"Do you know where Brian went after he left Delta?" Peter asked with deliberate calm, watching intently for Jimmy's reaction.

"I can't say." Jimmy's mouth formed a stubborn line.

"Can't or won't?" Peter tensed, leaning in. "Jim, if we can't find the disk, if we don't find Helen, then—"

Jimmy thrust his palm toward Peter. "Enough. I've heard enough."

"Please. You're my only lead." Peter heard the frantic edge in his own voice. He took a sip of Scotch to quell his nerves and waited through Jimmy's silence.

"I guess it doesn't matter, now they're both dead," Jimmy mumbled darkly into his glass. He sat silent for a moment, a period of mourning and reconstruction. When he resumed speaking, his voice was low but calm. "The only connection I can think of is Sapphire."

"Brian Tucker was working for David Lockwood?" Peter asked. His heart thumped wildly at the new information.

Jimmy nodded. "And Michael was going to start the week he was killed. They were in stealth mode. Holed up in Lockwood's house."

Peter's hand shook as he jotted down the details. "And Henry?" he asked, working to keep his voice calm.

"No, it doesn't have anything to do with Henry. I really have to get going," Jimmy added, glancing at his watch. "It's late, my wife will be worried."

Peter pulled a business card from his pocket. "If you think of anything else, will you give me a call?"

Taking the card, Jimmy nodded. "I hope you find some answers. God knows we need them."

• • • •

Peter lit a cigarette on the way back to his car and mulled Jimmy's disclosures. He was too keyed up to go home. The office, deserted and dark except for regulation security lights, would accommodate the kind of methodical digging necessary now.

He drove to the *Trib* offices, trotted up the stairs to the third floor and opened the door, shutting off the new burglar alarm just in time.

His first stop was the small galley kitchen near the production room, where he could brew a pot of coffee while mentally preparing his plan of attack. Then, Peter grabbed the stories that fit his timeline from the *Trib*'s morgue files and returned to his office, stopping for a cup of coffee on the way. Once there, he lit a cigarette in his office after hesitating less than a second. Blowing the smoke lazily out of his nostrils, he enjoyed the unaccustomed luxury of smoking in his office and using a *Trib* coffee mug as an ashtray. Someone would notice tomorrow and complain, but it was worth it.

The brief, one-column article on Henry Rhodes's death added nothing to his store of facts. Luckily, Sam had written the story. He'd have a copy of the police report. Peter rose and cautiously entered Sam's office. A reporter's files, like his sources, were his most private and personal possession. Even when reporters were on good terms, asking to borrow a file or a source was sticky. Taking one without asking was unconscionable. Sam could rightfully claim Peter's head if he ever found out.

Peter flipped on the light and glanced around the office. The only likely candidate was a four-drawer file cabinet near the window. He tugged hard on the first drawer and realized he could have saved his conscience the lecture. It was locked. Quickly, he searched Sam's desk drawers for the key and came up, disappointingly, empty. He had no alternative but to return to his office. Though his mind refused to rest, there was nothing more he could do tonight.

He tidied up the kitchen as questions mounted in his mind. Henry, Brian and Michael were dead. What was on that disk they had shared that was worth killing for? What did Sapphire have to do with it? The video compression-decompression algorithm was corrupt—was it bad engineering or, as he was beginning to suspect, sabotage? And finally, who was Helen? Could he find her and the disk before it was too late?

Yawning broadly, Peter finished the menial chores, returned to his office and grabbed his briefcase. Rapidly, he turned off the lights, reset the alarm and headed to his car.

The night was cold, sterile and eerily quiet. As Peter unlocked his car, he felt a whoosh of cold wind sweep by him. He started to turn. The sharp crack of a heavy weight connected with the back of his skull. His legs crumpled. The scenery gyrated wildly before him, turning yellow, then black as he fell against the car door and slid to the ground. Another blow landed heavily across his shoulders and he felt nothing more.

PETER AWOKE SHAKING WITH COLD, GRUDGINGLY RETURNING TO consciousness. His mind struggled for clues to his surroundings. He was lying in deep grass fresh and moist from recent rains. The roar of engines engulfed his ears. He heard cars traveling at high speed. He judged he was somewhere near the freeway.

The wind was frigid and bitter and stung his body. He realized, almost as an afterthought, that he was naked. His hands were cuffed behind his back. His head and shoulders ached from the blows that his unseen assailant had so effectively delivered. A moan escaped his lips as he wiggled to relieve the pressure on his wrists.

The long, green grasses spawned during the rainy season itched as they brushed against him. He longed to scratch every part of his body all at once. The grasses behind him rustled faintly. The hair rose on the back of his neck. Instinct rather than conscious thought told him that he was not alone. He heard the crunch of heavy steps approaching. The steel toe of a work boot prodded him.

"Come around, have you? I thought you'd be awake before now. You're not as hardheaded as I've been led to believe."

Peter forced himself to listen closely though the pounding in his temples. The voice was deep and well-modulated, the register somewhere between a baritone and a bass. Educated. He lifted his head toward the sound and felt the heavy pressure of a boot on his neck.

"Keep your face in the dirt," the voice commanded.

Peter pressed his face into the grass. Keeping his body still took effort. His every nerve ending was on fire.

"Who are you? What do you want? Money?"

His assailant laughed a throaty, wickedly amused laugh. "You think this is about money? If I wanted money, I'd go straight for the mother lode, your dear old dad, Peter Andrew Ellis, Junior."

Kidnapping? Is that it? Peter wondered. Horror filled him. He saw images of himself abandoned, buried alive in one of those little coffins with a battery-powered fan, waiting for rescue. Death would not come easy. He swallowed, a reflex that brought no relief to his parched throat. The man continued speaking. Peter could hear the sneer coating his tone.

"You're nothing. A pimple on someone's ass. A little tin soldier. Playing at games you don't understand. You listen to me. Forget about Michael Lee."

A savage kick thumped Peter's rib cage and he yelped in pain.

"Good. I've got your attention. Now forget about Brian Tucker."

Thwack. Peter's body bounced as a second bone-cracking blow landed between his ribs. Sucking for air, he bit his lip almost in half to quell the scream of agony that rose in his throat as his assailant's boot stomped down a third time on his shoulders. The taste of his own blood was strangely relaxing. It enabled him to hold fast to his sanity.

"Forget about that computer disk. It's none of your fucking business. You understand, preppie?"

The heavy boots moved around Peter like a predator circling downed prey. Then the motion stopped. Peter felt the cold barrel of a gun pressed against the back of his neck. With sudden clarity, he recalled that bullets had killed both Lee and Tucker. Now it was his turn. He couldn't stop shaking as he waited for the click of the chamber and the explosion that would end his life. Moments passed.

He found his tongue.

"Go ahead. Kill me. You can't stop me any other way."

His declaration was rewarded with another amused laugh. He felt the barrel of the gun pressed deeper into his flesh. Then, leaning over Peter's bare back, the man slowly withdrew the weapon. Peter felt hot puffs of acrid breath sting his naked skin.

"I'm not going to kill you, you rich little fucker. But by the time I'm done with you, you'll wish I had."

BLOOD. DRIPPING FROM HIS NOSTRILS. BLOOD. OOZING FROM HIS
split lip, trickling down his chin. Blood. Streaking between his legs.

The dampness of the dew-soaked grass revived him. His nose
itched. As his fingers instinctively twitched toward it, Peter was filled
with an almost palpable sense of relief. He was alive and unfettered.
The handcuffs had been removed. His assailant was gone.

Peter licked his lips seeking moisture, tasted iron and salt.
Pressing his palms into the grass, he raised his head slowly, fighting
the pangs of white hot pain shooting through his shoulders. His
forearms trembled against the exertion and collapsed. His head
landed on the soft earth. His mind floated, disembodied. So easy to
lay prone in the wet grass, and let the darkness take him.

He pressed his hands against the ground and forced himself to
try again. And again. As he sat up at last, a wave of nausea engulfed
him. Clenching his teeth, he stood awkwardly, his legs as wobbly as
a newborn foal's. He shuffled forward, placing one foot in front of
the other by sheer force of will. He wandered a few paces and was
startled to stumble over his own clothes, tossed in a heap by a large
rock. As he picked up the soiled white shirt, his mind erupted in
murky, semiconscious images of the fabric being ripped violently
from his body. The tear on the side of the shirt and the broken

zipper on his tan slacks attested to the reality of the half-formed memories. He dressed slowly, pain shooting from every nerve ending. He spotted a two-lane road ahead and began to walk.

As he shuffled along slowly placing one foot in front of the other, his mind struggled with disjointed images of his ordeal. He fought for lucidity with the only weapon he had. He knows me. He knows me. The mantra drummed into his brain as he plodded along the roadbed. *If you know me, I must know you,* he thought dimly. The revelation intensified his revulsion at the attack. He stared straight ahead, walking with as much determination as he could muster.

A set of high beams swung around a curve and flashed in his face, momentarily stunning him. The pickup truck passed him and then suddenly jerked to a stop. A short, stout woman in her mid-fifties jumped from the driver's seat. She walked rapidly toward him, carrying a large flashlight.

"Hey! You! What do you think you're doing?" She raised her arm, the flashlight ready for battle.

"I'm lost." Peter called, throwing his bruised hands up protectively. He'd suffered too many random blows that night not to be prepared for yet one more. She scanned him with the light. It hit his retinas with a jolt that intensified his throbbing head. Compassion flooded her features. "What in God's name happened to you?" she asked.

Peter's heart thumped. Panic threaded his breathing. His mouth formed words he struggled to utter. "I was robbed," he replied finally, his voice strained. "I was just hoping to find a phone and call a friend."

"You're pretty far up the hill. You'd probably have to walk about an hour to find a phone, and from the looks of you I doubt you'd make it," she replied sympathetically. "You get hit on the head?" she asked, stepping toward him for a closer look at his bloodied face.

Peter drew back, adrenaline pumping through his muscles, the tension increasing the throbbing pain.

"Are you dizzy? Nauseous?"

"Yes," he whispered.

"You can't stay out here. You could go into shock."

The bitter wind cut through his shirt. He started to tremble with cold and fear. "Are you a doctor?"

"Vet," she responded. "We need to get you warmed up. My house is just ten minutes up the road. Come with me. You can use the phone there."

She spoke gently, as if to a child. He felt his rapid breathing slow.

"I don't know how to thank you," he said quietly.

"I'm Carol Bleeker, by the way. What do I call you?"

"Peter. Peter Ellis."

"Can you walk okay?"

He nodded. She turned and headed for the truck, with Peter limping behind. He climbed into the cab slowly. He felt a hundred years old.

"You know, Peter, you're lucky I was even out here this time of night. If I hadn't had a colicky mare to deal with, I would've been in dreamland like everyone else around here, and you wouldn't have seen a car till six o'clock. Maybe later," Carol said, giving him a consoling look as she started the truck's engine.

A few minutes later she pulled into the driveway of a large tri-level redwood house, popped out of the truck and turned the lock in the front door. The door swung open unleashing a motley crew of canines, tails wagging, joyously barking welcome. The pack greeted Carol with unbridled enthusiasm and headed toward Peter. They swarmed around his legs, sniffing protectively as he cautiously stepped down and closed the cab's door.

"Come on in. The phone's in the kitchen."

Peter shuffled through the door, noting the comforting disarray of the surroundings. The family room was littered with books, papers and magazines about horses and horse showing. The dark mahogany mantel was laden with silver trophies and multicolored horse show ribbons. Each piece of furniture, from the well-worn brown sofa to the two plain, green and brown chairs, called out to his sore muscles, inviting him to sink into deep cushions.

He fought the impulse and followed Carol through the family

room to the kitchen. It was equally warm and inviting, with colorful braided rugs on the hardwood floor and shiny cooper pots on the walls. He picked up the phone and dialed Tim's number. He had no one else to call.

"Be there. Please," he urged, through multiple rings. He was about to give up when he heard Tim answer in the groggy, half-unconscious grunt common to those jarred from deep slumber.

"Tim. It's Peter."

"Peter, are you nuts? It's…" He paused. "It's after four. Are you drunk?" Tim's voice increased in volume as he woke.

"No," Peter replied, woodenly. "Listen, Tim. I'm in trouble. I really need your help."

"What's wrong?" Tim asked, concern shaking off the last vestiges of sleep.

"Tell you when you get here."

"Yeah, okay. Where are you?"

Peter gave him the address on Old Page Mill Road, replaced the receiver and walked back into the family room.

"He said twenty minutes," Peter replied to Carol's questioning glance. "Can I use the bathroom?"

"Sure. It's around the corner." She gestured toward a small room off the living room.

Peter disappeared into the closet-like facilities and relieved himself, attempting without success to zip his broken fly. The room was small and dingy, its fixtures gray with the residue of multiple washings. Reddish-brown and white animal hairs clung to the sides of the basin of the sink where Carol, Peter imagined, undoubtedly cleaned up after energetic days spent in the earthy company of dogs and horses. Peter stared hollow-eyed at his reflection in the mirror and tried to remember what it felt like to be clean.

Moving deliberately, he turned on the faucet and picked up a gray-tinged chunk of soap. He held the chunk under the water, watching it turn a sparkling white as gray streaks of dirt slid down the drain. He wished that he could send a part of himself down with it. For the first time in his life, he wasn't sure what to do next.

"Peter, are you okay?" Carol called through the door, breaking the debilitating spell.

"Yes." Peter rinsed quickly, dried his hands and walked back into the living room. Carol sat in one of the cozy plaid armchairs. She shooed a dozing dog off the other and waved Peter toward it. "I made you a cup of tea," she said. "How is your head?"

"Better." He settled gratefully into the chair and took a thirsty gulp of the hot tea, feeling the liquid warm and renew him. He wished he had a cigarette to go along with it.

"I don't know how to thank you. I don't know what I would have done without your help," he said, his voice strained and dull.

"Don't mention it." She paused and smiled faintly. "Too few helping hands in the world today, if you ask me. Didn't used to be that way, especially around here."

The doorbell rang, invoking multiple canine alarms. They both stood up, and dogs swirled around their legs. Carol went to open the door and returned with Tim at her side.

"Peter. Oh, man." The shock showed on Tim's face and in his voice.

"Not a pretty sight, eh, Tim?"

"I'm taking you to the hospital."

"Okay."

Peter turned toward Carol and worked up as pleasant a smile as his bruised face would allow. "Thank you for everything."

She nodded, hovering with maternal concern at the door while Peter and Tim climbed into Tim's Honda Accord and backed out of the driveway.

"What the hell happened to you?" Tim asked.

"I'm sorry to drag you into this." Peter's voice was barely above a whisper.

"What happened? Tell me," Tim demanded.

"It's about the disk, Tim. The one we've been looking for. The guy who attacked me knew personal stuff. My name. Called me a preppie, the fucker."

"What the hell?"

"The guy must have been tailing me. He must have seen me with Jimmy."

"Jimmy who?"

"James Wheaton. He was one of the guys I overheard at the trade show in January. He was the one who got Brian's package by mistake. I was covering the council meeting for Sam and I recognized his voice. He's a council member. We had a drink and he told me he worked at HP with Henry, Michael and Brian."

Tim fingers went white on the steering wheel. Peter saw his jaw drop open. "What else did he tell you?"

"He told me Henry worked with lots of young engineers at HP. Brian and Michael were two of his protégés. I'll bet Helen was too, and if she got a copy of that disk she's in trouble. One thing is for damn sure: whatever is on that disk is worth killing for. The three of them are dead, and someone just used me to practice for a shot at the heavyweight title. He warned me off, Tim. He told me to forget about the computer disk. I'm going to find that bastard, Tim, and when I do, I'm going to make him pay for this, all of it," he insisted flatly.

This expenditure of energy drained the last of Peter's resources. His head dropped against the car seat. Moisture coated his face. He heard Tim's question through the buzzing in his ears.

"Hurt a lot?" Tim asked.

"Like hell." He paused, swallowing to reduce the chalkiness in his throat. When he spoke again his voice was thin and raspy. "I think the disk has something to do with Sapphire. I found out tonight that Brian was working for Lockwood, and that Michael Lee was just about to join the team."

"Brian Tucker was working on Sapphire?"

Peter heard the surprise and anxiety in his voice. "Tim, what is it?"

Tim slowed the car as a stoplight flashed from yellow to red. Then he turned to Peter, body tense. "I just started working for Lockwood."

"You what?" Peter's stomach twisted. He fought the urge to vomit.

"I got a personal invitation to join the project. I couldn't turn it down. Lockwood's adding people to the team to speed up development because of the logic bomb."

"What logic bomb?"

"The team was just about to go to first code freeze on the video algorithm when most of the code was destroyed by a logic bomb. It completely destroyed the algorithm, and wiped out about nine months of work. We're just now ready to start coding again," Tim said, accelerating as the light changed.

"Quit, okay? Cash in your Sun stock and take a long vacation," Peter urged, with an intensity of feeling he didn't know he still possessed.

Tim shook his head. "I can't do that. Especially now."

"Somebody's killing people, Tim, and he'll keep killing people until he gets what he wants. One of the things he wants to do is stop Lockwood. Feel like going through this?" he asked, touching his bruised face for emphasis.

Tim glanced at him. "That gonna stop you?"

"Hell, no."

"Me either." Tim's jaw was set as granite.

Peter's body convulsed with the realization that the menace threatening him now could and likely would target his best friend as well. The pounding in his temples increased. He was losing the battle to stay alert. Eyes dimming, he looked over at Tim. Tim's lips were moving rapidly.

"What are you saying?" he asked.

Tim's voice echoed dimly through the pain. "I'm praying for you, Peter."

"I think it's a little too late for prayers."

"It's never too late for prayer," Tim whispered.

April 27, 1994: Menlo Park, California

The well's sides were moist and slippery as smooth stones in a running brook. Peter was amazed that he was able to stay vertical as he traversed the sheer walls. It was almost as if he had suction cups on his hands and feet. He pressed his naked flesh against the side of the well, eyes focused on his goal, a spot at the top emitting a sliver of rosy light. Ordinarily, he would be too large to pass through such a minuscule opening; but now, as he climbed, he was shrinking. By the time he reached the top he would be as transparent as a puff of smoke, able to float easily through the tiny crack to freedom.

He could succeed only if he didn't look down. If he looked down, he would plummet to the bottom of the well. He would feel that weight on top of him again. That thrusting deep inside his body ripping him apart. And he would die. A bell rang, deep in the distance, rattling him. The jangling became louder, more insistent. It broke his concentration. As he turned his head toward the sound, he lost his grip on the side of the well and began his free-fall...

Peter awoke with a groan, his head on fire. His body was drenched with sweat. The bed sheets, clammy with moisture, bound him. He reached clumsily for the phone, knocking it off the nightstand.

Through the speaker, a man's voice called:

"Peter. It's Ben."

He stretched woodenly across the bed and grabbed the phone from the floor. "Hullo," he said, his voice groggy.

"Are you okay? I got a call from your friend Tim. He said you'd been in some kind of an accident."

"I got mugged Monday night. They got my briefcase, all my notes, everything. I've got a bad headache and a couple of cracked ribs." Peter had his cover story down now.

"Good Lord!" Ben exclaimed.

"I need a few days off. But I still have a couple of stories I want to pursue."

"Of course. If you need help, just let us know."

Peter paused, struggling for coherent thought. "I'd like Sam to call me. Give me about an hour or so to pull myself together."

"Sure. Take care of yourself. Keep me posted."

"Will do," he said, and disconnected. He checked the clock. It was eight-thirty a.m. He'd slept eighteen hours straight and it was an effort not to drift back to sleep for another nine. He flopped against the feather pillows, trying to gather the strength to rise. Every muscle in his body strained against the exertion. He lifted a bottle of pills from the nightstand and blinked at the prescription: "Take every six hours for pain as needed," it read. The pills brought on the grogginess and the dreams, and he couldn't afford either one.

Tossing the bottle aside, he walked into the bathroom and turned on the shower. When the water was as hot as he could tolerate, he entered the stall and began scrubbing every inch of his body, over and over. His head throbbed from the concussion.

The visit to the hospital had only extended the nightmare of his assault. The doctor had examined his cracked ribs and bruises, and scrawled out the prescription. He warned Peter about dizzy spells and about something else. Something that Peter could not bear to think about. A final, ominous pronouncement: that he should have an AIDS test. Every six months. For the next three years. Despite the heat and the steam, he started to tremble. He opened up the hot water faucet further. As he felt the rush of water, he wished he could stand under the showerhead forever as layer after layer of his skin melted away. Maybe then he could feel clean again.

His thoughts swirled. He had never fully comprehended the impulse to murder before, despite dozens of visits to crime scenes and interviews with suspects. He had heard the motives and the rationalizations, but he never understood the basic urge. He did now. He reached up, turned off the water and gingerly patted down his sore muscles with a cotton towel. Then he pulled on his cleanest sweatsuit and headed downstairs.

In the kitchen, he brewed a pot of coffee and filled a large glass with orange juice, downing the refreshing liquid in two gulps. After spooning some cereal into a fluttery stomach still bouncing from the previous night, he lit a cigarette. A single query held his mind captive. *Why am I alive? Why didn't you kill me like you did the others? You wanted to. Badly. I could feel it.*

You'd be dead already if your fucking family wasn't so influential.

"Yeah, maybe," Peter grunted. He could see the drama unfolding: his father's righteous rage; his mother's stoic silence; his sister's calculating solace. They'd turn up the heat on his murder if only to conceal their shame at his life, his career and the ignominy of his death. That spotlight alone could threaten his assailant.

Beyond that was the deeper, more ominous reason for his rape.

"I'm not going to kill you, you rich little fucker. But by the time I'm done with you, you'll wish I had."

Peter heard it first from the wire service guys. What happened behind enemy lines in the Gulf War. The death of a journalist was a story in its own right. The Fourth Estate had its own band of brothers, and a dead journalist created a trail other journalists would follow, exposing and—with luck—aiding in the capture of the perpetrators.

Rape was the great silencer. It happened far more often than people knew or would admit. Journalists, women and men, hid rape from their editors to avoid reassignment, carried on if they could, or, if they suffered too long or too deeply, changed their post or their line of inquiry. Either way, their assailants won and the stories died.

A determined few went aggressively on the offense, knowing the next step in the battle could—and often did—lead to death. That he'd been raped in Palo Alto, not Iraq, didn't alter the stakes. His next moves would determine if he lived or died. Henry, Michael, and Brian were all dead. All of them part of the puzzle club. Two of them connected to Lockwood and Sapphire. That he could be next only sharped his resolve.

Stubbing out his cigarette, he poured another cup of coffee and walked into the bonus room off the kitchen he had turned into an office. Normal movements, like retrieving paper and a pen, now required intense effort. He jotted a few notes, and stopped. A sense of futility hovered at the edge of his consciousness. He tossed the pen aside, lit another cigarette and wandered into the living room. Flopping down on the couch, he powered on the TV and randomly punched buttons on the remote.

He settled on a nature program with a screen full of bouncing baby lion cubs. They batted, chased and rolled over each other in such uninhibited play that Peter couldn't help but smile at their antics. He felt the shadows of the night before start to recede. Then the camera shifted and zoomed in on an amorous male lion, sniffing expectantly around his mate. The lioness craned her neck toward him. The male placed his shaggy paw on her head, a demand for submission, and mounted the lioness, his body engaged in that natural mammalian sway.

Peter felt a sickening jolt as a wave of nausea engulfed him. He jumped up and dashed for the bathroom, heaving the contents of his stomach into the toilet just in time. When his retching ended, he lay prone on the cold tile, too drained to move.

My God, he thought. *What is happening to me?*

The telephone clamored for attention, but Peter had no energy to retrieve the call. The beep and the sound of a male voice roused him. He got up shakily, awkwardly, and tried to wash the vomit off his face. His scrubbing lit the nerves in his chin, sending shooting pains from his jaw to his neck. He leaned against the counter and allowed the burning to subside, taking breath after breath before he found the strength to move again. The light on the answering machine was blinking, seemingly indignant, when he padded into the office. He collected Sam's message and called the *Trib*.

"Hi Tina. It's Peter." She responded with an outpouring of heartfelt sympathy that touched him deeply. He offered his thanks and she connected him to Sam.

"Ben told me. How are you feeling?"

"Better. I need a favor, Sam."

"Yeah? What?" Sam sounded cool and wary. Despite the teamwork on Sapphire, Sam apparently hadn't forgotten or forgiven Peter for working around him in the first place.

Peter ignored the warning. "You remember a murder you covered in December, a guy named Henry Rhodes?"

"I cover a lot of murders, and that one doesn't sound vaguely familiar."

"Well, could you dig into it? Get everything you can on the guy. All I know is that he died around the middle of December and that he was a veteran at HP."

Sam was silent. Peter heard steady breathing and the sounds of office chatter through the line. At least Sam hadn't hung up on him.

"What's in it for me?"

"Joint byline on everything we do. Just like we did on Sapphire. I need you, Sam. I can't do this alone," Peter said. "I'll put it in writing, copy you and Ben. Even Adam if you want."

"Send me the email and I'll think about it. Gotta go."

Peter placed the phone in its cradle just as the front doorbell rang. He walked over and swung open the door.

"Oh my God," she said, her eyes widening in horror.

He saw his reflection in the mirror of her gaze: ashen complexion, bloodshot eyes, chin black and blue where he'd nearly bitten his lip in two and now laced with overnight stubble. She stood before him, hand covering her mouth. He tried for that sterling smile he could always count on, but he couldn't quite pull it off. Her name caught in his throat.

"Jordan," he breathed. "Jordan."

"Tim called. He said you were in trouble and needed help. I couldn't stay over there wondering what was happening to you. Wondering if you were okay. But you're not okay." She looked frightened by the sight of him.

"I'm a hell of a lot better now than I was five minutes ago."

Her face broke into a wide smile as she reached for him. He could see a hug coming, feel the jolt of the impact as her body pressed against his cracked ribs. He caught her hands before they touched his torso. "It's so good to see you," he murmured.

Kissing her palms, he drew her inside the doorway and pressed her hands gently to his face before letting them go. As she entered the room, Peter stopped, cringing at the mess. Newspapers littered the coffee table and floor. The bitter smell of overheated coffee and old cigarettes choked the air. The ashtray was overflowing with butts. He stepped ahead of her, trying to tidy it up. She put her arm out to stop him.

"What happened to you, Peter?"

He turned back and faced her. The word "mugged" sat at the base of his tongue, waiting to be uttered. One word and done with her questions. People got mugged all the time. But he couldn't feed that to Jordan. He couldn't lie to her.

"It's a long story."

"I've come a long way to hear it."

"How about some coffee?" He picked the ashtray off the table and took it into the kitchen to dump it.

"I could use some," she replied, joining him in the kitchen. Moving around the kitchen with practiced ease, she poured out the sour coffee and made a fresh pot. He stood beside her as the coffee brewed, gaining strength from her presence.

"Let's go sit down," she said, handing him a fresh cup.

Peter eased himself on the couch. Watching his clumsy, robotic movements, the fear returned to her face. "Talk to me," she pleaded.

He avoided her eyes. Jordan couldn't handle pain; it was watching her mother fight the losing battle against cancer when she'd been only five years old. All Jordan knew of her mother's life was sickness and death. She'd run from pain ever since. Her face now was pale, clammy, shadowed with fear sliding toward panic. If he didn't act quickly, she would leave him again.

"Don't worry." He smiled, patted her knee. Some of the color returned to her cheeks. He chose his words carefully. "Do you remember Brian Tucker, that programmer I was chasing a couple of months ago, the one with the puzzle disk?"

She nodded.

"Well, I found him, murdered. Then the guy who probably killed him found me. He grabbed me at outside the office and…"

Peter's voice faltered. The buzzing in his head was intolerable, blocking out conscious thought. The images came at him unbidden, fast and hard. He was back in the hills. His assailant stood over him. A wicked laugh filled his ears. *Are you ready for me?* Peter's throat constricted, oxygen diminished. His heart pounded. A low moan escaped his lips. "I can't."

Cool hands touched him, pulling him back from the brink. Jordan wiped the moisture from his brow. "He tortured you, didn't he?"

Peter didn't trust himself to speak. His jaws felt as though they'd need to be oiled to work again. With a slight nod, he opened his eyes. Tears were streaming down her face. Her mouth wobbled. "I don't want to hear any more. I can't take it. I'm no good at this."

Peter put his arm around her, pulled her close. "It'll be okay."

"I came to help, but I'm no good at all."

He lifted her chin with his hand and traced her tears with his finger. "No one's ever cried over me before. Not in my entire life. Those tears are very special."

She studied him for a long interval and gave him a small smile. "I'm going to wash my face."

When she sat back down beside him again, he saw the gold saxophone charm wink at him from between her breasts.

"You're wearing it."

"I never take it off. Even in the shower." She leaned close to him. He tucked his arm around her.

"Will it hurt if I kiss you?"

"Probably, but it'll be worth it."

She sprinkled his mouth and nose with kisses, carefully avoiding his bruised chin. It was a sugary dusting of affection and comfort that left him hungry for more.

"You know, when you gave me this…" she paused, touching the sax charm. "And told me always to find a way to play my music, it took everything I had to walk away."

"It took every bit of willpower I had not to buy a ticket and jump on that plane beside you."

She scooted closer, leaning against him. Her lips brushed his ear. "You know why I had to come back."

"You missed me?" He took a deep breath to capture and hold her scent inside his lungs. She smiled, her familiar crooked grin.

"More than that. You didn't make me choose. All Josh and Max wanted was the party girl. Eric only had time for the sax player. You…" She paused, searching his face, then continued. "You let me be me, you wanted the whole me, not just one part. I couldn't forget that about you no matter how hard I tried. And I did try."

He leaned over and stroked her face. "I will never ask you to give up any part of yourself or your dreams for me, Jordan. Never."

"I have an idea," she said, resting her head against his shoulder. "Come back to Germany with me."

"I can't. I have a job to do here."

Jordan sat up abruptly. "You're not thinking of chasing this story, are you?"

"I have to. I know about the disk and about someone named Helen that Michael Lee died trying to warn. I know the disk is connected to Sapphire and David Lockwood. Tim's working for Lockwood now. He's my best friend. What would you have me do?" His face held an honest question.

"Go to the police. Tell them what you have. Let them handle it."

Peter shook his head. "I don't have anything. All I have are bits and pieces. A half-baked theory and a thin web of lies. I need to find the truth."

"You need to protect yourself first. It's not safe here. Come back with me. You can cover the international business beat. You'd love that." She took his hands, her face a plea a statue couldn't refuse. "And we can find out how well we fit together."

Peter kissed her fingertips one by one, delaying his answer. "I can't run away, Jordan. If I do, he wins and my life isn't worth squat no matter where I am."

"You're scaring me." Her face was white. The panicked look was back.

"It scares me too. But I've got to finish this thing."

"No!" she declared, eyes and voice stormy. "If you insist on sacrificing yourself to this quixotic crusade, you're on your own. I want no part of it."

She stood up and moved toward the door. He got up to follow her. The room tilted. His stomach lurched. The loss of equilibrium forced him back on to the couch.

"Jordan." Her back stiffened as her hand clutched the doorknob. "Please. Don't make me choose between you and what I know I need to do."

• • • •

"I don't like this," Tim said, eyeing Peter warily as he opened and loaded the chambers of the revolver.

"Not asking you to." Peter swung the cylinder closed.

"You know half the people who have guns for protection get killed with their own weapons."

"That means half don't." Peter's fingers encircled the butt of the gun. The feel of the cold metal in his palm gave him confidence and quelled the fear he felt at the memories of his attack. It wasn't going to happen again.

"Let's talk about Sapphire, Tim." Peter slid the gun into its holster and shoved it aside. He pulled out his notes and charts and placed them on the kitchen table. Tim leaned in for a closer look.

"The way it looks to me now is, everything points to Sapphire.

Destroying Sapphire was the goal. The disk was a means to that end."

"That looks like the connection," Tim agreed.

"The central question is why? Who wins if Sapphire is destroyed?"

"Draco."

"Yeah, that's what I think. It's the only thread that makes sense. Not only does Draco eliminate competition from Lockwood, they get to stick it to MediaBuilders. That's a pretty powerful incentive. But we don't know who, within Draco. It could be Kavanagh, or the engineering VP, Jake Mullens, or even Win Davis himself."

Tim furrowed his brow. "You think Win Davis is involved?"

Peter shrugged. "I don't know. All I'm doing is throwing out the possibility. But whoever it is, that computer disk must be damn incriminating. The thing is like a voodoo curse. Everyone who touches it turns up dead."

Peter paused, looked over at Tim. "He warned me off it, too. He was very persuasive. Just not persuasive enough."

Tim glanced at Peter, at the gun and nodded.

"I figure we have two options for finding that disk. Either one of the people we know about, Michael, Brian or Henry, kept a copy; or there's someone else, maybe Helen, who has it and we haven't found them yet. Have you looked through Brian's files?"

"I have. I've checked every member of the team for something unusual, and so far, nada."

Peter felt a tug of anxiety. "You haven't given up, have you?"

"No way. I'm planning to comb the server again today."

"Then I'll let you take care of Brian. Sam is digging up background on Henry. I've left a dozen messages for Kim Lee and we still have nothing on Helen. I figure Jimmy Wheaton is worth another try to find her."

"Sounds like a plan."

The steadiness of Tim's tone frustrated him. "We've got to find that disk, damn it!" Peter threw his pen across the table, pulled a cigarette from his pack and lit it.

"I know." Tim said. "I'm in this too, you know."

"Sorry, Tim. Guess I'm a little tense. Jordan came by yesterday."

"She did? From Germany?"

"Yeah," Peter replied with a bitter half-smile. "What did you do hack her credit cards?"

"Nope," Tim replied with a smug smile. "I called Daddy and asked him to get a message to her. I thought she'd call."

"She came back instead." Peter reflectively thumbed his Harvard class ring, the one she'd placed on his finger the day she left, the one he'd yet to take off.

"Wow. So where is she now?" Tim was looking around like he expected to see her come walking down the stairs at any minute.

"Probably on a plane back to Germany."

"Why? What happened?"

Staring down at his notes, Peter wished that it wasn't ten a.m. If it were later in the day, he would pour a Scotch. Maybe, if Tim weren't here, he would pour one anyway.

"I disappointed her. Big surprise. She wanted more from me than I could give her. Story of my life. You'd think I would have learned my lesson by now."

Peter rose, walked to the patio doors and stared out. He pulled on his cigarette until he could feel the nicotine scar his lungs. Turning, he tossed the butt in a dirty coffee cup by the door and faced Tim.

"Don't be so hard on yourself. None of us know what women really want," Tim said.

"You and Marie seem like you've got it figured out."

"For now, but I'm just holding my breath. C'mon, man. Focus."

Peter grabbed a fresh cup of coffee from the kitchen. "Want some?"

"Yeah. With milk."

"I think I know who was responsible for trying to destroy Sapphire." Peter placed the steaming cup in front of Tim and sat down across from him.

Tim arched an eyebrow. "Really?"

"The person who planted the logic bomb. The bomb exploded at precisely the right time to cause the most damage. Your first code freeze, the first complete version of the software, right?

"The execution was flawless," Tim agreed.

Peter started tapping a pen against his lips as if the rhythm would help his concentration. "Are you sure no one on the team is responsible?"

"Absolutely. We found a security breach, though," Tim added, frowning. "There's a small chance that someone could have gotten in through the Internet, but they would have to know exactly what they were doing."

Peter tossed the pen on the table. A jaunty grin lit his features. "That's my point. And that person is Devon O'Reilly."

"What?"

Peter leaned toward him. "Think about it. Who else has the skill, the motivation and the opportunity?"

Tim shook his head. "No. You've got it wrong."

"I know you admire the guy, dude. But listen." Peter ticked off the fingers of his right hand. "One, we know he has the skill. Couldn't he plant a logic bomb like that?"

"Yeah, but."

"Two, he's hated Lockwood for eighteen years. Everyone in the computer industry knows about that feud. I'd call that motivation and then some. Three, he's working for Draco. We've already established that Draco benefits most from Sapphire's demise. It's O'Reilly, all right."

"Lots of programmers could have planted that bomb. Including me," Tim protested.

"But they didn't, did they? I know O'Reilly's one of your demigods, but facts are facts."

"Devon is not involved in this."

There was too much conviction in his tone for Peter to dismiss the objection as mere loyalty. "What do you know that I don't?"

"Nothing. I just know Devon, that's all."

"You've got to give me more than that."

Tim hunched over his coffee cup. Seconds ticked by. Peter lit another cigarette and tapped his pen on his chart, looking at

O'Reilly's name. "Time's up," he said.

Tim looked up. His face was strained. "You can't write about this."

"Okay. Deep background only."

"I gave my word."

"I'll protect you. I always have, haven't I?"

"This is different. Lives are at stake."

"Yes," Peter agreed. "They are."

Tim gave Peter's bruised face a long, appraising stare. Then he rose and walked away from the table. He stood with his back to Peter for a moment. "Devon O'Reilly is working with Lockwood again," he said finally, turning to face Peter.

"He personally asked me to join the team. Now we're fixing the code. He's waiting for me at the lab right now."

"What?"

Tim nodded. Peter tossed his cigarette in the ashtray. He took a step toward Tim.

"You're telling me that O'Reilly and Lockwood are working together again. After all these years? O'Reilly and Lockwood kiss and make up and life goes on. No explanations. I don't buy that."

"I don't really know the whole story, but you have to understand Devon." Peter heard the defensiveness in his tone and figured Tim knew more than he was telling. Peter chose not to press him.

"Will he talk to me?"

Tim's eyes narrowed.

"Look, I accept the fact he's not involved, but he might have some idea who is."

Tim shrugged. "I'll ask. That's all I can do. I've got to get back to the lab. You okay? Want me to come back and spend the night?"

"No. I'll be fine."

"The doc said you should have someone around for the first forty-eight hours, just in case. What if you have a seizure?"

"I'll be okay, really."

Tim started toward the door.

"Tim. Thanks. You're a real friend."

"Yeah, I know. Who else would put up with you?" Tim called back with a loud laugh.

With Tim gone, the townhouse was too quiet. Peter wandered around the living room, picking up newspapers and tossing them back down again.

Something had broken inside him in the last two days, letting long-buried emotions escape like steam heat. He had to regain control before they consumed him. Yet for a moment, staring at the seascape Jordan had given him, he allowed himself to wish that his mother, not a faceless string of nannies, had patched his scraped knees. That he'd grown up at home instead of at boarding schools, shuffled among relatives and friends on school breaks and holidays at Margaret's whim.

He had been proud of the way he'd adapted, stepping casually through an ever-changing circle of friends, sucking what he could from each encounter and leaving nothing tangible behind when it ended. Now he saw it as pathetic. He longed for the closeness Jordan had with her father and Tim had with Marie. He just had no idea how to get there. But he felt compelled to do something. Picking up his cell, he pulled up Jordan's number and summoned the courage to call. He left a message at the sound of the beep.

"Jordan, it's Peter. You... we've come too far for things to end like this. Call me. Please... I need to hear from you."

Flipping the phone closed, he returned to his chart and forced himself to focus. He moved O'Reilly's name from the Draco team to Lockwood's. That was a real game changer, Peter mused. O'Reilly could easily make up the ground that Lockwood had lost to the logic bomb. He might be the only one who could. The mystery surrounding O'Reilly's sudden change of allegiance added to his storehouse of questions. It was time to resume the hunt for the answers.

Peter placed his first call to Alex Kavanagh.

"Hello, Peter." Alex's voice was cool, but cordial.

"I've got a couple of follow-up questions on the new Draco Universal."

"Okay, what do you need?"

"I understand that Devon O'Reilly has left Draco, care to

comment?"

Peter heard a sharp intake of breath and a few seconds of silence before Alex responded. "What makes you think Devon has left Draco?"

"If he's available, I'd like to interview him."

Alex sighed, a long, painful, defeated sound that confirmed Tim's story. "O'Reilly is on an extended leave of absence for the next several weeks."

"The translation being, he's gone and we're trying to get him back," Peter asserted.

"No comment."

"Thank you, Alex. You've been helpful." Too bad I can't use any of that, Peter thought, wondering how Draco would react to his inquiry. He left yet another message on Kim Lee's answering machine, lit a cigarette, then punched up Jimmy Wheaton's home number. It was the only lead he had left.

"Jimmy, it's Peter Ellis, from the *Valley Tribune*. We met at the council meeting on Monday."

"How could I forget?" The voice through the receiver was clearly still strained by recent revelations.

"Yes." Peter paused respectfully and continued. "I'm still looking into Rhodes's death. I remember you saying that Michael and Brian were two of his favorites. Did he have any other real favorites, besides those two?"

"Not that I can think of. But I wasn't with the company all that long."

"Know anybody else I could check with?"

"No, not really." Jimmy's voice faded, as if he were starting to hang up.

"C'mon, Jim. You're my last lead. It's for Henry and Brian. Help me out."

In the ponderous silence that ensued, Peter could picture Jimmy sitting across from him at Raphael's, cloaked in reluctance, in his quest for anonymity and distance. Peter waited through Jimmy's uneven breathing until he found the words.

"You should probably talk to Noel Connors. He's a fixture at the company. Started the same time Henry did. He's a bigwig now though, VP of engineering for the workstation division."

"Got a number?"

"You can try him at the office." Jimmy paused. "Here's his direct line. Go easy. He's a bit on the caustic side," he warned as he rattled off the number.

"I won't mention your name."

"No, you'll need to. Be sure and stress it's about Henry. They were close. Noel was the one who put up the money for the reward for information."

"Thanks." Peter disconnected and punched up the number Jimmy had given him.

"Noel Connors, please."

"Speaking," a deep bass voice replied.

"Mr. Connors, my name is Peter Ellis, from the *Valley Tribune.* I'm—"

"I don't talk to reporters. Ever. Call our PR department," he snapped.

"It's about Henry Rhodes's death," Peter said quickly, listening for a click to signal that Connors had hung up.

"Henry died four months ago. Where were all you hotshot reporters then? Man gives three decades of his life to this Valley and his community and what does he get? Spit. He's not glamorous, like some whiny-ass twenty-two-year-old rock star who ODs. No glamour. No news." He paused for a deep, wheezing breath. "How did you get this number, anyway?"

"From Jim Wheaton. I'm looking—"

"Jimmy knows better than to give my private number out to a reporter. He's going to catch fucking hell from me. You can bet on that."

Great, Peter thought. *A bit caustic didn't begin to cover it.*

"I've come across some new information, sir." Peter pulled out his best prep school manners. "That's why Jimmy thought I should talk to you. If I could have ten minutes of your time—"

"Who'd you say you were with?"

"The *Valley Tribune*."

"Never heard of it."

"We're local. Mr. Connors, you put out a reward for information on Henry's death. You must want some answers. So do I."

Noel Connors didn't respond. Peter felt his last lead slipping away. Connors was playing a classical CD, a Debussy nocturne Peter recognized. The movement ended. Connors cleared his throat. "I can give you twenty minutes tomorrow evening. Take it or leave it."

"I'll take it." Connors rambled through some complicated directions to a street in Saratoga before he slammed down the phone.

Peter took a drag on his cigarette. His energy was ebbing. His head throbbed. He felt like he was chasing the story through a mountain of cotton candy, feeling sicker by the minute and getting nowhere fast. He stubbed out the cigarette and flopped down on the couch to rest his eyes for a few minutes.

• • • •

The chime of the doorbell wrenched him from slumber. He opened his eyes and raised his wrist to check his watch. It was after six p.m. He'd slept away the entire afternoon. Sitting up, giving his head a chance to clear, his stiff joints settled into place so he could walk without losing his balance. The doorbell rang again, more insistent this time. He put his hand on the knob and twisted. A whiff of the alluring, classic fragrance of exotic florals and vanilla she often wore floated into the room as he cracked the door. He threw it open.

Jordan stood still in the doorway, looking small, her face a mixture of regret and apology. She glanced up at him, tentative. "Sometimes, I can be a royal pain in the ass."

"Actually, I've always liked your ass." He grinned so widely, it cracked open his lip. He tasted the blood with the tip of his tongue, and didn't care. She held a plain brown bag out toward him.

"I've come to join the crusade. I brought Kung Pao Chicken. Are you hungry?"

His eyes drifted over every inch of her, from her snug green t-shirt and painted-on jeans to her brown loafers. "Famished."

"Can I come in?"

"Please." He stepped back.

She handed him the takeout bag, walked into the living room and turned toward him. "Nick and Nora," she said. A small smile tugged at the corners of her mouth. "I kept thinking how awfully good you look in a fedora."

He dropped the takeout bag on the coffee table and moved toward her. She saw the blood oozing from the split in his lip.

"Oh, no. You're bleeding." Taking a tissue from her purse, she gently dabbed at his face.

"It's okay." He took the wadded tissue from her hand and tossed it on the floor. "You're here."

He surrounded her with his limbs, ignoring the mule-kick in his ribs, hugged her hard enough to hear her gasp. His hands moved shakily, wanting to touch every part of her at once. She lifted her lips to kiss him. He stepped back, turned his head away. She looked startled at his abrupt move away from her. She started to speak, an unwanted question in her eyes. His cell buzzed.

"I'd better get that. I've got a lot of calls out," he said.

"Oh. Hello Jess. What a surprise," he replied to her greeting. Out of the corner of his eye he saw Jordan's head jerk up in his direction.

"Peter, I need to talk to you. It's important. Can I come by tonight?"

"I'm kind of busy right now. What is it?"

"I really don't want to talk on the phone. Can we have breakfast tomorrow? I really need your help."

"Yeah, well, okay."

"Meet me at Hobee's at seven?"

"Okay." Peter cradled the phone. Jordan busied herself with the takeout. With the Kung Pao Chicken, she'd brought egg rolls, Buddha's Delight and white rice. She laid all this out on the dinette table. Peter noticed that she'd stacked his notebooks and charts on the kitchen counter.

"That was Jessica," he said. "She wants to meet me for breakfast tomorrow."

"Do you two talk often?"

"No. I haven't seen or heard from her in weeks."

"So why now?" Jordan handed him a plate.

"She said she needs to talk to me." Peter sat down and filled the plate with food. The aroma enticed him the way nothing had in the last two days. He dug a fork into the chicken and rice with relish, consuming half the food on the plate in a few bites.

"And you can't resist rescuing a damsel in distress. I never figured you for the type."

"I'm not. Besides, you know how I feel about getting on a horse, white or otherwise."

He was glad to see that got a chuckle out of her. He reached over and gave her hand a squeeze. Slowly, she withdrew it and studied him. He felt the weight of her gaze, and, as hard as it was to do, returned it.

He hesitated, then forced out the words, one syllable at a time. "The thing is, two days ago I was in distress and this lady Carol and Tim rescued me. I don't know where I'd be if they hadn't." He studied his plate of food, appetite gone.

"What if this was Eric? What would you do if he needed help?" Peter gave her a inquiring look.

Jordan was preoccupied with her chicken and rice. She pushed it around the plate several times without taking a bite. Then she laid down her fork and found her voice.

"Eric did call. The sax guy they hired quit. Said he'd found a better gig. Eric asked me to play with them on Saturday night."

"And I'm having breakfast with Jessica."

April 28, 1994: Palo Alto, California

"Peter! What happened to you?" Jessica exclaimed as he walked toward her.

"Accident," he replied, with a light smile.

"What kind of accident? You're not drinking again, are you?" she asked, her expression sliding from surprise to maternal concern.

"Nope. Slipped on the court." He shrugged. "Let's get a table, okay?"

Peter barely recognized the woman sitting across from him at Hobee's. Jessica had cut her hair super short. The tapered green paisley jumpsuit she had on, with its oversized shoulder pads and loose-fitting, pleated blouse, was trendy in a way that defied her Midwestern values. It wasn't a look the Jessica he'd dated would have chosen for herself, and she couldn't quite carry it off. But it was the disheartened look in her eyes that really got to him. He blamed Alex Kavanagh for all of it.

"Like the new look," he said as they perused the menus.

"Blueberry coffeecake," she told the young waiter.

"Florentine scramble," Peter said. The waiter refilled their coffee cups before he left.

"So? You said it was important."

Jessica watched him cautiously. "I need a favor. A big favor. One I have no right to ask, but I have to." She spoke in a voice barely audible in the crowded eatery.

Peter leaned forward, face taut. "What is it, Jess?"

She took a sip of her coffee. Looking over his head at the brightly decorated walls, she said, "It's about Devon O'Reilly leaving Draco. I'm asking you to hold the story for a few days."

"You know I can't do that. I've got an exclusive. Unless you're writing it."

"I don't cover Draco. For obvious reasons. You're the only one who knows. And I assume you got it from Tim."

Peter felt a spike of anger. "Alex send you here? He hiding behind your skirts?"

She shook her head. "I came here alone. I know it's a big ask."

Her eyes crackled. The first real energy he'd seen from her. Peter took a deep breath and forced a controlled tone.

"Not big. Impossible. Your boyfriend came after me. Embarrassed me in front of Ben, and forced me to write a retraction on a story that he knew was true. A story, coincidentally, about Devon O'Reilly."

Jessica looked down. Her tone softened. "I know. I warned him. I told him it was stupid. That he was underestimating you." Her face held respect, the kind of admiration he used to get from her. It no longer moved him.

"That horrible Jake Mullens was putting so much pressure on Alex, he had to do something. He never really knew you before TriCorp, so he didn't know how good you are."

"Guess he knows now."

The waiter appeared, put their plates in front of them, and hurried away as if he could feel the heat of their unease and anger. Peter glanced at the dish, one of his favorites, and felt his stomach twist.

Jessica poked the coffeecake apart with her fork. It turned into a crumbly mound on the plate.

She met his eyes, that frank gaze he knew so well. "I love him, Peter. He asked me to marry him. His family's in Denver and we want to move there, but his career is in tatters, thanks to your unrelenting

Horizon coverage. If you break this story now, Win Davis will fire him and he won't get another job in the industry. All our dreams will go up in smoke. That's why I'm asking."

Her tone was pleading, her expression an urgent appeal. "It's in your hands," she added, as if to confirm that he held the key to her happiness.

Peter frowned. "Don't do this to me, Jess. I'm not responsible for you or"—he finished with grunt—"him."

"I know. I thought maybe, just maybe, you'd be willing to consider it for what we once had together. I guess I'm asking too much."

Peter took a few bites of the egg dish to give himself some time to think. He watched the film cover her eyes. Saw her blink it away. She loved Alex enough to come to him, to risk his indignation and sarcasm, knowing she'd probably walk away empty-handed. That was a love he'd never known and never expected to know. But he experienced things differently now. Physically and emotionally raw since his attack, he struggled daily to cap the torrent of emotions cascading through him. His intellect was no longer a reliable shield from the pain of others.

"How much time do you need?" he asked gently.

"A week to get a press release out and for Alex to resign on his terms." She paused. "I know you'll lose your exclusive. But it's just one story." She stabbed the crumbed mass on her plate with her fork to avoid his eyes.

The mixture of desperation and hope in her voice reminded Peter of the day he stood before Ben after they'd learned about TriCorp. Legs rubbery, heart thumping, he waited for Ben to pronounce his fate; it could have gone either way for him. Now he held that same power over her. He'd be lying to himself if he said he didn't want to stick it to Kavanagh. But, he decided then, not at Jessica's expense.

"Okay. I'll hold it." He watched as her rigid face softened with relief, and realized with a start that it felt good to protect her. "I'm glad you found the right man, Jess, and that he makes you happy."

She gave him a sunny smile and started in on her crumbled mound of blueberry coffeecake.

"Don't eat that. Can we have another one of these, please?" Peter asked, handing the waiter the plate of crumbs.

"What about you? Are you seeing anyone?" Jessica asked.

"You know me. I get around."

"Oh, I know." She paused. "I also know that playboy act you put on isn't the real you. You're sweet and you have a really big heart. It's too bad nobody ever gets to see it." Jessica studied him over the rim of her coffee cup. In that moment she reminded him of his sister Megan, the only one in his family who had ever cared for him. It touched him, lingered inside, and warmed him. He hesitated then plunged in, leaving detachment behind. "Actually, there is someone I've been seeing a lot of."

Jessica leaned toward him, her expression delighted. "Tell me. Who is she? Where did you meet her?" The kid was quick. He set down a fresh slice of coffeecake and she took a bite.

"Her name is Jordan Langley. I met her at the tennis club."

Jessica peppered him with questions and he answered every one of them, allowing himself to enjoy the newfound camaraderie and the opportunity to talk about Jordan.

"She plays the saxophone in a jazz band," he said, finally. He was running out of things to say.

"Really? That's a new one." A soft smile played at the corners of Jessica's mouth.

"Yeah, and she likes to go clubbing," Peter added.

Jessica's eyebrows arched upward. "You on a dance floor? Oh, I'd pay to see that one." She started laughing and Peter joined in.

"It's pretty scary, actually. But it makes Jordan happy and I pretty much do what Jordan tells me."

Jessica's eyes brightened with sudden awareness. "You love her."

Peter's chin prickled as his nerve endings lit up. He rubbed it to stop the itching. "No. It's not that serious. We're just having fun."

"C'mon Peter. I know you better than that."

Peter studied her. Jessica was looking at him the way she did when she could see right through him. He'd almost forgotten how well she understood him. He took a final sip of sip of coffee and responded, "I don't know if it's love. All I know is that when Jordan is with me, the world feels lighter. You gave me so much, Jess. I never told you. You were my rock. You gave me stability. But Jordan gives me wings."

He needed a smoke. The check was waiting. He tossed a few bills on top of it and started to get up. "Ready to go?"

"Oh, no you don't," Jessica said, staring straight at him. "You really do love her. There's a light in your eyes I've never seen before. Have you told her?"

Peter shook his head.

"No, of course you haven't. What are you waiting for?"

"I dunno," he said, standing. "Handwriting on the wall?"

Jessica laughed. "You always could make me laugh, more than anyone," she said, taking his arm as they left the restaurant. Once they were outside, she turned toward him and gave him a quick hug.

"Tell her," she whispered in his ear. "Don't wait until it's too late."

April 28, 1994: Menlo Park, California

"How'd it go?" Jordan asked, when he returned to the townhouse later that morning. She was in the kitchen, unpacking groceries. He took a quick look around. The townhouse sparkled. Every surface, including the kitchen floor, was spotless. She must have cleaned for hours.

"She asked me to hold the story on Devon O'Reilly." He took a can of tomato soup from her hand and put in on the top shelf of the pantry.

"Weren't you going to hold that story anyway, for Tim?"

"Yeah, but only for a couple of days. She wants me to wait until after they issue a press release."

Jordan flatted a grocery bag and stuck it in the bottom of the pantry. "Won't that kill your exclusive?"

"It's just one story." He grabbed a cup of coffee from the fresh pot she'd made and took a sip. "Your coffee's better than mine."

Jordan stopped unpacking and looked at him, frowning. "You're giving up an exclusive for her?"

He walked over, gave her a quick kiss, and murmured in her ear. "She's marrying Alex. They're moving to Denver in a week. All she wanted was for me to give Alex the time to leave on his own terms. I said yes. It was my goodbye gift."

He pulled her closer and kissed her until her face softened into a smile. "She's not a threat to us, Jordan. Nothing is."

She hugged him back. "I got you some more Advil." She handed him the bottle. He took a couple and downed them with the rest of his coffee. His headaches were so persistent he'd begun to ignore them most of time.

"You look a little tired. Go sit down. I'll finish up here."

He took her advice and wandered over to the couch. He noticed the sax case was back in its former spot by the fireplace. *She isn't just visiting,* he thought with a contented sigh. *She's home.* Pulling out his cigarettes, he glanced around for his lighter and ashtray, but they had disappeared. "The place looks great, amazingly great."

Jordan picked up a piece of paper from the kitchen counter and walked over to him. "In case you get too impressed with my skills as a domestic diva." He saw it was a receipt from The Molly Maids.

"Smart."

"They charge extra for smokers. New house rule. Smoking outside only. Or my personal preference, not at all."

"Yes. Ma'am." Peter got up, intending to go out to the patio. His eye fell on his chart and notes. He felt a stab of fear. He was lying to her and to himself. Until he figured out who was chasing them and why, none of them—Tim, Jordan, himself, maybe even Devon O'Reilly and David Lockwood—were truly safe.

"I've got to find a way to talk to her."

"Talk to who?" Jordan asked, stepping up beside him.

"Michael Lee's wife, Kim. I left her dozens of messages, but she's never returned one of them. She's my best lead for finding a copy of that disk. If there is one."

Jordan looked apprehensive. He watched her shrug it off just as he had done. "Do you have her number handy?" she asked.

"Yeah. Why? What are you thinking?"

"I could call her. She might talk to another woman more easily than to a man."

"I don't think that's such a good idea."

"Well, I do." Peter shrugged and handed Jordan his cell phone, open to his contacts. Jordan scrawled the number on a post-it note and held it up. She looked at him the way she did when she was about to ace a serve. "Nick and Nora, remember?"

April 28, 1994: Sunnyvale, California

A little after one o'clock that afternoon, Peter and Jordan pulled up in front of a row of single-family homes on a busy, car-lined street in Sunnyvale.

Kim Lee had been waiting for them. She opened the door almost before they rang the bell. A petite, softly curvy woman, she greeted them with an expression that was equal parts sorrow and determination. She had been wounded, her demeanor indicated, but she would survive.

Inside, the furnishings, though sturdy and practical, were cushioned in quiet pastels that made the brown leather La-Z-boy recliner in the center of the room seem all the more incongruous. Kim slid her hand over the recliner as she passed it in what looked to Peter to be a familiar ritual of mourning.

"That was Michael's joke," she said, gesturing to Peter and Jordan to take a seat on the sofa. Kim sat down in an overstuffed armchair that seemed to further diminish her small frame.

"Michael's father had one, and none of the kids was allowed in it—ever. So that was one of the first things he bought when he was out on his own. I thought it was horrible. Still do, but now I couldn't possibly get rid of it."

She was staring at the carpet, lost in private grief. Then, as if she'd just remembered her company, she turned toward them. "I don't know what I can tell you about Michael's murder that I haven't already told the police."

"We're following up a different angle from the police," Peter explained, leaning forward, notebook ready. "I was wondering if you knew Brian Tucker?"

"Sure," she broke in almost cheerfully. "He and Mike were like brothers. They worked at HP together. He got Mike his new job. Or he would have if—" Her voice dipped and her chin trembled as she strained against the tears.

"I'm sorry. I thought I was getting past this," Kim said.

"It takes time," Jordan said.

Kim leaned back against the chair and pulled her knees up to her chin, turning herself into a ball as she wrapped her arms around her legs.

"It's so crazy," she whispered. "The last two weeks before he was killed we were fighting all the time. I was furious at him for spending so much time away from me. If he wasn't at the lab, he was in front of that damn computer playing those stupid games he and Brian dreamed up."

"Did he play with anyone else?"

Kim nodded. "They were in some kind of club. I think there were four or five of them."

"Anyone named Helen?"

"I don't know. The only two I met were Brian and Henry. He was at our wedding. Henry had dinner here often. Henry was like a father figure to Michael." She stared past Peter and Jordan, eyelashes tinged with moisture.

Peter followed her gaze and saw her focused on a photo on the mantel: Michael with an older man in a policeman's uniform.

"Michael's dad?"

Kim nodded. "He was a cop in San Francisco."

Peter studied the faces, father and son, arms entwined, smiling broadly. He felt a sharp pang, hurriedly buried, at the look of pride on the elder Lee's face. "Did Michael get a package from Henry around mid-December? It might have been a computer disk?" he asked.

"Yes, he did. That started the biggest fight of all. Here I was, just married, and I felt like I was living alone. I was such a bitch. I gave him hell about all the time he spent with those silly puzzles. Now I really am alone." Soft drops glistened on her cheeks. Jordan pulled a tissue from her purse and handed it to her. Kim blotted the tears and collected herself, turning back to Peter.

"Do you happen to know what he did with the disk?" he asked gently.

"I'm sure he logged it into the computer. He kept a record of everything he got."

"Did he log the puzzle games?"

"Yes. They had time limits attached to them, Michael said. Once he got one he only had so many days to solve it and get it back to whoever sent it. Keeping track of them was critical. That's one of the things we argued about. When he got one he'd barricade himself in the office until it was solved or time ran out."

"Any chance I could look at his computer?" Peter asked, trying to contain his excitement.

Kim led them down a short hallway to a bedroom overflowing with computer equipment and pointed inside. Michael had set up a mini-lab with two monitors linked to a tower server, hard disk backup unit and several high-speed modems. Peter flipped on the nearest monitor and waited for it to boot up.

"What are you looking for?" Jordan asked.

"It's a Linux server. I'm checking the log files. We're looking for the activity log or a database log. As a last resort I'll search for puzzle*, crypt* or encrypt*."

"It sounds complicated," she said.

"It can be." Peter checked the activity log. "Nothing! Wiped clean. Damn."

Jordan stood behind him as he ran through the same sequences on the database log as he had on the activity log. "I'm glad you know what you're doing." She put her hand on his shoulder and gave him a squeeze. Her way of asking for a miracle, he supposed.

"This one's empty too," he told her, moving on to the keyword search. "Shit. There's nothing on these drives."

He felt Jordan's hand tap his shoulder. "You know, Henry

couldn't have known those disks were dangerous. Not the way Kim described him. He would never have sent them if he did. He would have protected his boys."

"You're right. I should have thought of that," Peter said.

"He must have gotten the disk from someone he completely trusted," Jordan suggested.

"Like Helen. When we find her, maybe we'll find some answers." Peter powered off the workstation.

Their eyes met. Jordan's face reflected his own growing tension and fear.

"Find anything?" Kim asked from the safety of the armchair when they returned to the living room. She looked from Peter to Jordan expectantly, her expression shifting from hope to frustration as Peter slowly shook his head.

"I'm sorry," he said, despising the inadequacy of both the words and his efforts on her behalf. "We'll keep looking."

She walked them to the door, giving Peter one last look at her grieving face as she closed the door and went back inside.

"Fucking worthless waste of time," he grumbled, shoving his hands into his pockets.

Jordan touched his arm. "You did the best you could."

"For all the good it did her. Or any of us. He's still out there, and we don't have any clue about who he—or they—are."

April 28, 1994: Saratoga, California

It was starting to sprinkle—a surprise late, cold April rain shower— when Peter pulled into the circular driveway of a large ranch house in an exclusive Saratoga neighborhood.

Peter rang the bell, listening to the insistent tapping of the rain on the roof as the storm picked up steam. He lifted his hand to give the bell another ring just as a middle-aged man opened the door.

"Noel Connors?" Peter asked.

Peering suspiciously at Peter, he gave a brief nod. "You the reporter?"

Noel looked to be in his early sixties with the kind of protruding midsection that makes a man susceptible to heart attacks. The few strands of oily gray hair that remained on his head were combed over his crown in an unsuccessful attempt to hide his bald spot.

"Peter Ellis," he replied, offering his hand.

"What the hell happened to you?" Noel said, peering at Peter's bruised face.

Peter's mind shuffled through the list of explanations he'd concocted since his attack and offered Noel the only one that he thought might buy him anything.

"I got a cease-and-desist message from the same friendly folks that murdered Henry Rhodes."

Noel studied him, heavy lips pursed. "My God," he said.

"Trouble is, I'm a bit on the reckless side. I tend to run through those kinds of red lights. All they did was make me more determined to find the answers."

Noel wagged his head from side to side. Peter wasn't sure if Noel was reacting to the news of his attack or his unwillingness to give up his pursuit in the face of it.

"Thought we'd talk in the den. It's where I usually am this time of day." He led Peter through a maze of expensively decorated rooms to the back of the house.

"Lovely home," Peter said, breaking the silence.

"We just remodeled the whole place. Cost a fortune. The wife's at her sisters or she'd insist on giving you the grand tour, showing off every doodad."

Noel ushered Peter into his den, a square, wood-paneled room with a large picture window facing a backyard garden. The room and its contents, a dull-brown leather sofa and two matching chairs, smelled of stale cigar smoke. The room felt oddly familiar to Peter; he recalled that his father had a space like this, with rows of leather-bound law books and a huge marble fireplace. It was a singular male retreat, unsullied by the feminine touches that dominated the rest of their home. In his youth, Peter had entertained the secret fantasy that at some point his father would invite him in there for a few drinks and an evening of serious conversation. It would be a signal to them both that he had come of age in some consequential way. It had never happened; until now, Peter had forgotten he ever thought it would.

Noel lowered his round body into a chair and waited for Peter to do the same before unwrapping a cigar. "I smoke and I don't apologize for it," he said. "I also drink alcohol and eat as much red meat as I please." He puffed on the cigar, tapping the ashes into an already overburdened receptacle.

"You won't get an argument from me," Peter said, reaching into his pocket for his Camels. Noel looked satisfied at the gesture. As Peter lit a cigarette, he could tell that with a simple flick of his wrist he had opened a communication channel that might otherwise have remained closed.

"Let's get down to business," Noel said, leaning forward.

"I'm following up on Henry Rhodes and his kids. I understand he was a tutor and a father figure to many of them." Peter pulled out his notebook and pen. Noel's face turned wary.

"This is just to help my memory. We're on deep background here. No attribution."

Noel seemed to take Peter at his word. "Yes, he was."

"Did have any favorites?"

"He worked on being impartial, but like everybody else there were a few that really got to him. An inner circle you might say."

"I heard that Michael Lee and Brian Tucker were part of the inner circle. Were there any others? A woman named Helen, perhaps?"

Noel paused. Leaning back in his chair, he let the cigar rest in the ashtray, studied the ceiling. "I can't believe all three of them are dead. Henry. Two of his boys. This world's gone mad."

"Yes, it has," Peter commiserated, trying not to let Noel's melancholy discourage him. "That's why your help is so important."

Noel searched Peter's face again. "It's been five months and the police haven't done anything," Noel said almost to himself. He shifted in his chair.

"Henry coached a few young women. Not too many. The only one I recall is Anne Siegel," Noel said, after a few moments of silence. He took a distracted puff on his cigar.

Peter felt a rush of excitement as he jotted down her name. "Do you have a number for her?"

"Anne's in Japan, setting up a new technical support center. I can give you a number but you're likely to get a faster response with email." Noel scrawled out the address and handed it to Peter.

"Anyone else you can think of?"

Noel shook his head. "No one recently. Just a couple from the old days. One of them was Devon O'Reilly. He wasn't one of the college recruits, but he and Henry hit it off. Henry, God bless him, was one of the few that could exercise some control over that demented Irishman."

"I didn't know Devon worked for HP."

Noel fixed him with a cold stare. "That's where he and David Lockwood met. They were on my engineering team. Together. That's when I took up martinis."

"I think I understand. I've interviewed both of them." Peter gave him a knowing nod of the head.

"You don't know the half of it," Noel countered. "They're both crazy. David's obsessive about everything, and Devon's obsessive about nothing and making sure everyone knows it. You haven't lived until you've spent six hours out of an eighteen-hour day cleaning up after a Devon O'Reilly practical joke. I wished 'em well, believe me, but I can't say I was too crushed when they left the company."

"Did Devon and Henry socialize much? Confide in each other, maybe?"

Noel rubbed his hand over his chin. "I wouldn't say so, no. They got along, but if you're looking for someone Henry would confide in, I doubt it would be Devon.

"Henry was a bachelor, you know. No family to speak of. Got a battle-axe of a sister up in Sacramento, name's Mabel or Mary, something like that. Anyway, if he had a favorite son, it'd have to be

Toby Eastman. Worked for the company around the same time as O'Reilly and Lockwood. Around 1976."

Noel lit another cigar. "Anything I can get you? Water, coffee?"

Peter shook his head. He could have used the water, but the memories were flowing freely now and Peter didn't want to break the spell.

"You know in a way it was Toby that got Henry's program started," Noel continued. "He was a Vietnam veteran. Good-looking, personable when he bothered to make the effort, but he was the quiet, loner type. Not unusual for some of those boys that saw the heavy action. I heard he was at Tet," Noel confided.

"That was one of the biggest actions of the war, wasn't it?"

"It was a wholesale slaughter," Noel snorted, stabbing the air with his cigar.

"How did he end up working with Henry?" Peter asked, trying to hold the line between letting his source ramble and getting the details he needed.

"As I said, Toby came in a little on the soured side, but Henry took him under his wing and it turned out to be exactly what Toby needed. You couldn't help but be pleased with the results. Toby became a real team player, started showing the kind of initiative that managers like, even leadership potential. We had our eye on him, I'll say that. Henry showed he had a real talent for mentoring the youngsters so we encouraged him to do more of it."

"Do you know if Henry and Toby played games together, computer games—they might have called them puzzles or riddles?"

Noel ruminated, pulling on his lower lip. Then he shook his head. "Not that I know of."

Peter scanned his notes and flipped his notebook shut. "Would you have a phone number or email address for Toby Eastman, by any chance?"

"I've got a P.O. box in Garden City, New York. I sent Toby a card when I heard about Henry. Thought he, of all people, would want to know. Kind of surprised I never heard back from him, but maybe he's moved on. That's one thing you'll learn about Toby Eastman.

No roots. Doesn't like to stay in one place for too long. Henry always complained about it."

Noel rose and rummaged around in his desk. He jotted the address on a scrap of paper. Peter added it to the one he'd already collected for Anne Siegel.

"I appreciate your help," he said, standing.

Noel nodded thoughtfully, eyes resting on Peter's bruised face. "I hope you know what you're doing."

THE LIGHTS OF THE TOWNHOUSE BECKONED WITH A LUMINOUS golden glow as Peter parked the car and strolled up to his front door in the lingering drizzle. He twisted the key in the lock. As he entered he sniffed the tantalizing aroma of sautéed garlic and herbs. The smooth sounds of sax man Dave Koz filled the air. His empty stomach growled, reminding him that, as usual, he'd eaten little that day.

Jordan sauntered up to him with an air of innocence and a crafty smile. She leaned in to kiss him and immediately pulled back, wrinkling her nose.

"Ewww! Where have you been?"

"The proverbial smoke-filled room. My source was heavy-duty cigar smoker." Peter pulled off his raincoat and hung it in the closet near the door.

"Who catered?" he asked.

She offered him another glimpse of her familiar wicked grin before saying, "I'm cooking."

"Jordan, you don't cook."

"Except when I do. Men always seem to want a home-cooked meal. This is one of my two. Poached salmon with Mediterranean vegetables."

"Sounds wonderful." He stepped toward her.

She put her hand on his chest. "Please go take a shower before I have to get the place fumigated." She turned and headed back into the kitchen.

"Okay. Just need to make a couple of calls." He retreated into his office and placed a call to the New York operator in search of Toby Eastman. Then he booted up his laptop and sent an urgent email to Anne Siegel, asking about Henry, puzzle games, and "Helen." He closed the window with a whispered invocation: *Please be Helen.*

••••

The hot shower and his first shave in three days revived him. Jordan was bent over the cutting board slicing a tomato when he returned to the kitchen. She handed him salad plates and he took them to the table.

"Open the wine, would you?" she asked, handing him a bottle of Zinfandel.

He took that to the table too. She followed with the salmon and vegetables. He watched as she lit the candles with quick, practiced movements. They sat opposite each other. *So natural,* he thought. A flash of anxiety cut through him. *But how long will it last?* The reflex, like a tap on the kneecap, reminded him of the consequences of counting on anything too much, especially now.

Jordan's silky voice broke in to his thoughts as they ate. "Tim called. He wants you to meet him and Devon at the lab tonight at one a.m."

"One a.m.?" Peter stifled a groan.

"He said it was the only time you all could have a private conversation."

"Okay."

"So, what did Mr. Smokestack have to say? Fill me in."

"He gave me two more leads and about twenty more questions.

Everything's jumbled up. It's all connected and disconnected at the same time."

He raised his hand and ticked off facts. "I've got the encryption club, connected to Lockwood, at least Michael Lee and Brian Tucker are. MediaBuilders is trying to buy out Lockwood to gain traction in the information highway war against Draco. Lockwood's former partner, Devon O'Reilly, joins Draco to build Horizon, directly aimed at Lockwood's Sapphire, and then quits and joins Lockwood again."

"It sounds like it's all connected to Lockwood, doesn't it?"

"Except that Michael Lee was killed before he could join Lockwood's team, and his warning was for Helen, also unconnected. Henry has nothing to do with any of it except the encryption club. It's like a giant spider web. And every time I look at it, it spins in a different direction."

Peter paused, pushed his salad plate aside and dug into the salmon. "Delicious. You never cease to amaze me." He offered her a droll look. She met it with a coy smile. "I intend to keep it that way."

Jordan returned to her dinner, finishing most of it before she spoke again, slowly, thoughtfully.

"Not a spider web so much as a vortex. Beginning with one person and drawing everyone else in, forcing them to deal with the impact."

Peter's fork stalled in midair. "You've got my attention."

Jordan hunched forward, her body taut, her expression intense. "What is the one central fact in all of this? The most important thing?"

Peter spun the facts in his head, shuffling them like cards. They all seemed important: Henry, his boys, the puzzles, Lockwood, O'Reilly, MediaBuilders, Draco. The central fact could be any one of them. Then he felt the hair on the back of his neck rise as a malevolent voice echoed in his brain.

Forget about that computer disk. It's none of your fucking business.

"The disk." Peter told her.

"I think so too," Jordan agreed. "And I'm wondering why Michael would have erased all the information in his log files. I admit I don't know anything about computers, but I've watched you and Tim. Kim called it logging, didn't she? You guys log everything. You're obsessive. Like Kim said, Michael was too. Why would he erase his log files?"

"I don't think he did," Peter countered. "Our logic bomber did. He could hack into Michael's server."

"But why would he? He was looking for a disk."

Peter considered this in a way he hadn't before. "You're right. Michael must have erased his own files, which probably means he broke the code. And the message he sent to Brian was to tell him that he broke that code. Why didn't I think of that? Brilliant."

Jordan flashed him a victorious smile. It disappeared as quickly as it had come. "Which means he erased the files because he knew how dangerous they were. To him, his friends and his wife," she added softly, her face darkening.

Peter smelled her fear, absorbed her anxiety. "If Michael cracked the code and he erased his files to cover his tracks, he would have kept a copy of that disk somewhere, maybe in some secret hiding place. But where? We have to find that damn disk!"

Peter flung his hands out in frustration. The back of his wrist connected with the salad plate, sending it flying off the table to land upside down on the freshly cleaned beige carpet.

"Aw, crap," he said, jumping up and picking up the wet lettuce, tomato and cucumber piece by piece from the floor. Jordan pushed her chair back, grabbed her napkin and leaned down to dab the oily spot oozing into the carpet.

"It's my mess. I'll clean it up," he said, taking the napkin from her hand to rub at the spot.

"Let me help." Jordan faced him, eyes latched to his. "Get me a wet paper towel, will you?"

Peter went into the kitchen, retrieved the paper towel, and handed it to her. He stood by watching her dab the carpet until the spot disappeared.

"Gone," she said, turning toward him with a warm smile. He

took her hands and pulled her toward him. They stood face to face, a breath away. "What are your plans? How long are you staying?" he asked.

"Until you don't need me anymore." Her eyelashes fluttered.

"What about your internship?"

"I told them to give it to someone else. I can always reapply if I want to."

She stared down his bruised chin, gently fingered his still-swollen lip. His mouth sought hers in a rough, needy kiss of long-suppressed desire. She responded eagerly, pressing her mouth against his, parting her lips. He felt the rise and fall of her breasts against his chest.

"Let's go upstairs." he whispered.

He needed her tonight, to feel her envelop him, loving him, restoring everything that had been ripped from him so violently that night. In a gentle embrace, entwined in caresses fondly remembered, they entered his bedroom. She toyed with his shirt buttons, teasingly undoing each one until she pushed off the cloth to expose his chest and back.

"My god. Oh my god." She gasped.

Her face was chalky. He was so used to seeing his battered body in the mirror he'd forgotten how it actually looked. He saw it fully revealed again in her anguished expression: boot mark across his neck and shoulders where his assailant had stomped his face into the dirt; the elongated black and blue marks running down his sides from the repeated kicks of the steel-toed boots against his ribs.

"Oh, Peter," she cried. "You look so horrible."

He heard the panic in her voice, sensed she would run again. He reached out and trapped her in his arms, letting the searing protest from his ribs rip through him. He couldn't let her go.

"It'll be okay," he said. "I'll heal."

She pressed her head into his shoulder while he stroked her hair and felt her body begin to relax. Her breathing slowed, gentle puffs against his chest. After a few minutes, she stepped back, surveyed him with red, moist eyes.

Noticing the bottle of pain pills on the nightstand still full, she held it out to him. "How much pain are you in? Tell me," she implored. He studied her for a long moment before replying.

"A lot," he admitted. "I'm trying to ignore it. I didn't want to worry you."

"Well, I am worried. You're injured, badly injured, and exhausted. You need to rest. I'm going to call Tim and cancel that meeting."

"No." It was Peter's turn to panic. "I have to see Devon. I need to know what he knows. Time is running out."

The fear was back in her eyes. He chided himself for reminding her of the dangerous game he was playing.

"We should leave, Peter. Get away. Let someone else deal with this." Her tone was defiant. She stood, backing toward the doorway.

He stepped toward her. "Who?"

"Anyone but you." She stared up at him. "I need you."

Such wonderful healing words, he thought. At any other time, in any other place, he would have booked a flight to anywhere she wanted to go, taken her there, made her happy, and allowed himself the luxury of a few moments of peace. But now was not that time or place. He reached out and took her hands, walked her back inside the bedroom.

"There's no hiding in cyberspace. These people we're dealing with, they're building the Internet. They control the data and the access and they know how to use it as a weapon." His voice was firm, his face determined. He had to make her understand.

"Say we did run, to Australia or the Caymans, wherever. All it would take is one careless email, one poorly encrypted wire transfer, and boom, they'd find us and we'd be gone. I have to stop them Jordan, for your sake, for mine. Stop them for good."

His energy evaporated. He eased himself down on the bed, hands hanging limp between his legs. "Leave if you have to. Go ahead. I'm used to it," he said, staring straight ahead.

She sat down beside him and cradled his right hand, running her fingers along his like she had when they first met, when she was trying to figure out what he did for a living. She pressed her finger into the indent in his index finger. "I'm not leaving. You can send me away, but I'm not leaving. Nick and Nora, remember?"

"Yeah, I remember." He smiled and kissed her forehead. "Call Kim Lee. Ask her if Michael had any secret hiding places, a safe or something, anything."

She nodded. "Get some sleep."

April 29, 1994: Mountain View, California

The blue and yellow glare of streetlights exploded off his wet windshield like tiny firecrackers as Peter drove through deserted streets to the site of Lockwood's new lab on Marine Way in Mountain View. The rain and the flashing lights, on top of his lack of sleep, slowed his pace to a crawl. He had the radio tuned to KKSF. "Good morning, folks it's one a.m. Keeping it smooth, here's Wes Montgomery and "Bumpin' on Sunset.""

The buzzing in his ears started as a low hum, like an electrical charge from a live wire. It intensified, drowning out the radio. Peter pulled the car to the side of the road as the images hit him like a convulsion: his assailant's boot pressed against his neck as he lay naked on the ground. Gagging on the rough bourbon poured down his throat. The pounding of raw flesh deep inside his body.

Dizzy, seasick, Peter tugged at the car door handle. Throwing the door open, he leaned over the asphalt and vomited. A second wave hit and then a third. Head hanging, he watched the vomit puddle and pool in the wet like tapioca pudding. Then, as suddenly as they had come, the images ceased tormenting him. He pulled himself back into the driver's seat and mashed his forehead against wheel.

His cell buzzed. Flipping it open, he heard Tim's voice cut through the pounding in his temples, and free his frozen limbs. "Peter, where are you? Are you okay? We're starting to get concerned here."

Peter glanced at the dash. The clock read 1:20. Had it been only four days ago, at this very hour, that he'd been grabbed and taken up into those hills? Four days. A few hours after midnight. Yet his life would never be the same.

"Sorry, Tim. Got a little lost," he mumbled. "I'll be there in five minutes."

"Okay."

Peter tossed the cell on the passenger seat. Looking into the rearview mirror, he recalled the ski-masked visage of his assailant. The image bobbed before his eyes. "You tried to destroy me. Instead you gave me back the two people who matter most, Tim and Jordan. Now we're coming after you," he proclaimed, reigniting the engine and pulling away from the curb.

Tim met Peter at the door of the lab. He removed a security key card from his pocket and slid it into the box by the lab door. The door clicked. Tim shoved it open and Peter got his first look at the genesis of Sapphire. It reminded Peter of the photos he'd seen of the original Trxton Lab. The hardware had been updated, of course, from dumb terminals to high performance Unix workstations. The programming method was now object-oriented rather than text-based. But the rest was vintage Lockwood. The racks of test equipment shone as if polished by a careful hand. The long worktables were free of clutter, software manuals meticulously arranged. Still, there was one chaotic corner of the lab, Peter observed, seemingly held in deliberate disarray. In the middle of that corner stood Devon O'Reilly.

Devon came forward, hand outstretched. "I remember you. You broke all those stories on Horizon. Nearly gave poor Alex a heart attack."

Peter smiled. Devon squeezed his fingers tight. "Sure would like to know where you got your information," he added, maintaining his grip.

"Not me," Tim volunteered.

"I protect my sources. That goes for you, too." Peter said. Devon pursed his mouth and nodded. He pointed and they took seats on high stools at one of the worktables. Tim grabbed Cokes and bottled water for the table. Peter opened his water and drank deeply, grateful for the cool moisture on his scratched and soured throat.

Devon scanned his face, taking in the damage. "They really did a number on you didn't they?" he asked.

"It's turned out to be a powerful incentive," Peter replied neutrally.

"So, what do you need from me?" Devon's tone held a measure of wariness and skepticism. Despite Tim's assurances, Devon seemed a reluctant source. Peter kept his summary short and to the point.

"I believe there are at least three people involved, including your software bomber. One is the mastermind, the architect who profits, handsomely, from Sapphire's destruction. Two is a programmer, maybe a hacker for hire, or a disgruntled engineer who has a personal beef with Lockwood. The third is a professional killer. Somebody killed three people and made the deaths look unconnected. I believe they are, because of the trail of the encrypted disk. That disk has some kind of evidence or information on it that implicates the mastermind or the others."

Peter paused for a sip of water. Devon nodded, rubbing his hand across his chin. "And Tim tells me that you suspect someone at Draco."

"Draco is the only company that profits here. With Sapphire out of the way, the Draco Universal wins the Internet set-top box war, worth billions. And MediaBuilders is left holding the bag. It's Draco, all right."

"I agree, and we have proof." Devon turned to Tim. "Tell him what we found."

Tim leaned forward, elbows on the table. "Remember I told you we found a security breach?" Peter nodded, pulling out his notebook and pen. "Go on," he said.

"We traced it to Brian Tucker's workstation. He pulled a testing tool off the Internet and the logic bomb was embedded in the program."

"Did he know?"

"I doubt it. It was a standard upgrade to a bug-tracking tool we were already using. But there are dozens of bug trackers. Someone had to know how David Lockwood works, the tools he likes to use, to pull it off."

"Sounds like a disgruntled engineer, maybe someone from the Falcon Project, angry about losing the opportunity to join the millionaire's club," Peter suggested.

"Could be," Tim said, "except that we traced the bomb back to its source." Tim paused, glancing at Devon. Devon nodded. "Tell him the rest."

"Someone on the Draco development team remotely triggered the bomb. We found the command sequence. It was set to go off during the Horizon product intro." Tim grabbed his Coke, took a swig and continued. "We think we know who it was."

Tim started drumming his fingers on the table, refusing to meet Peter's eyes. In the silence of the lab, a workstation whirled to life. Tim, looking relieved at the intrusion, went to check on it.

"Who?" Peter called after him.

"Rather than start with who we think it might be, let me tell you who we've ruled out," Devon interjected. "Davis, Kavanagh and Mullens."

"Why?"

"Simple. Kavanagh doesn't have the skill or the balls. Davis is too good a strategist not to see the potential blowback for Draco if this was traced back to them. As it was. Same for Mullens. He'd recognize the risk and he is fiercely loyal to Win Davis. So that leaves the rest of the team, twenty-one people in all. I got to know most of them. But there was one who seemed to have an agenda beyond the team."

Peter felt his frustration rise. Devon and Tim seemed to be talking in circles and taking him nowhere. "Who?" he asked again, struggling for patience.

"The same one that had no problem leaking every detail of the Horizon project to the press. Your source." Devon's eyes hardened like green cut glass. "We want to know who that was."

Peter met Devon's stare with an equally uncompromising one of his own. "Not a chance."

Peter saw that Tim was hiding in the corner, focused on the

workstation monitor, pretending he wasn't hearing the conversation.

Devon glanced Tim's way. "When I found the trigger for the logic bomb, I quit the team that same day and I left something behind, a worm in the central server. Now, digitally, we see what they see, every keystroke on every monitor. They can't make a move, anywhere in Draco's corporate empire, without us knowing about it."

He turned his attention back to Peter. "Your source is our most likely suspect. Clearly, someone with no scruples."

Peter ignored the barb. "I've never sold out a source and I'm not starting now."

"We think he's a paid hacker whose plan was to destroy Lockwood and use Draco as cover. Leaking the product details created confusion. Mullens put the team in overdrive. Easier for the hacker to trigger the bomb undetected and get away or lie low." Devon's voice grew cold. "Either way, he's protected because you're protecting him."

Peter felt the heat of his anger. Devon's beefy hands clenched. He seemed to want to wrap his hands around Peter's throat. Peter pushed back from the table, got up and moved away from Devon. "No. I'm not betraying a source for some idle theory you've concocted."

He looked over at Tim and spoke directly to him. "Remember TriCorp? That was a trumped-up job. I just about lost my job and my career. If I were going to give up a source I could've done it then and saved my own skin. But I took it. The laughs, the shunning, the humiliation. I took all of it, Tim. You know I did."

Tim walked back to the table. "Yeah, I know. But this is different. This guy didn't just destroy a product; he destroyed the dream of all of us here."

Tim scanned the cavernous, empty lab, his eyes resting on each workstation in turn. Peter counted seventeen seats, each of them belonging to someone who had given everything to make Sapphire a reality and who had stood by helplessly as one man—possibly his source—had shattered that dream.

"Do you want to see what it looked like?" Tim asked. Without waiting for Peter to respond, he headed over to another workstation. Pulled by morbid curiosity, the kind that causes people to stop for fatal car crashes, Peter joined Tim in front of the monitor.

"The initial blast disrupted the sequence and tore the code apart," Tim explained. "You can see the command lines as everybody logged onto Tucker's workstation. They tried hard, but the way this thing was written, the bomb absorbed each command string and spread the malware deeper into the code. Brilliant and deadly." Tim voice faltered as he clicked through the screens, each one more devastating than the last.

"The logic bomb exploded in the computer's instructions set. It vaporized the codec algorithm immediately. Sapphire was dead on impact."

Even Peter, who didn't know a line of code, recognized the death knell as he studied the sequences displayed on the monitor.

"Peter, you really want to protect this guy? Who knows, he might even be involved in murder."

"Tim, don't ask me. Please don't ask me."

"Well, I'm asking." Tim looked straight at him, choosing this time and place to pull in the dozens of favors Peter owed him, including rescuing him four nights ago. Peter's shoulders slumped, and the bongo drum in his head intensified. He leaned against the workbench to steady his mind and body.

"It's the right thing to do. I know it doesn't feel like it, but it is," Tim said.

Peter sighed, tore a piece of paper from his notebook and wrote down the name: *Ravi Gavaskar.* Tim took it and handed it to Devon.

"Figures. He quit the team same time I did. Wonder why? Tim, IRC him, will you? Privately. Something nice and friendly."

"IRC?" Peter asked.

"Internet Relay Chat. It's a form of instant messaging."

Devon turned back to Peter with a hollow smile. "When we find him—and we will find him—maybe we'll get some real answers. The ones we all want."

"Maybe you could start with answering some of my questions."

The exchange had left a sour taste in Peter's mouth. The statement came out rough, almost belligerent. Devon seemed to understand. He went over to a small refrigerator and pulled out three beers. Sitting back down at the worktable, he waved Tim over.

"Floor's yours." Devon said, opening his beer, taking a deep gulp.

Peter took a sip of the beer. He was still working off the disgust he felt about giving up his source. It would haunt him, even if Ravi turned out to be guilty. If he wasn't... Peter immediately shoved the thought away. "What I care most about is the disk. And that trail starts with Henry Rhodes, our first victim."

Devon's face darkened. He slapped the table with a force that made the bottles jump. "Pisses me off about Henry. If there was a man who didn't deserve to die, it was Henry. He gave his life to the company and his boys. Too bad you never met him," he said, turning to Tim. "Salt of the earth, he was."

Peter watched as Devon struggled to pull himself together with another long pull on his beer. When he refocused on Peter, his face was stoic. "Help you any way I can."

"I'm trying to find anyone Henry might have trusted enough to send a copy of the disk. I'm convinced Henry thought it was just a harmless puzzle. He might have sent it out to anyone in his encryption club. We know Brian and Michael got copies. Then yesterday I learned about two more: Anne Siegel and Toby Eastman. Are either of those names familiar?"

"I don't know Anne, but who could forget Toby? He was on my first programming team. Brilliant programmer, but a real renegade. Liked to break the rules. Now if that isn't the pot calling the kettle black," Devon chuckled, looking at Tim and receiving a knowing smirk in return.

"But Toby was reckless," Devon continued. "Cut too many corners. Didn't know how to run a proper test suite and didn't give a fuck about it either. And he was wily. Got himself into trouble, but he could usually wiggle himself out. Couple of times, though, he got stuck in his own muck and Henry had to step in.

Yep, Henry sure had a soft spot for Toby."

"Did Toby hang around with anyone? Anyone who might have kept in touch with him all these years?" Peter asked.

"Not really. Toby was the private type. Really didn't attach himself to any of the herds. He intimidated a lot of the younger guys. He had this way of looking at you. More like looking through you."

Devon stared at a misty set of faces in his own memory. "No, the only one I know he got close to was Henry. But Toby was something, I'll say that. We had some good times together. I guess we shared the same philosophy: work hard, play hard." He offered Peter and Tim a broad, mischievous grin.

"That's one of the reasons I wanted him on the Trxton team. Figured his style would be a relief from David's obsessiveness. But he and David had a run-in and that was that."

Peter stopped scribbling and stared at Devon. "What kind of run-in?" he asked slowly, while his mind shifted Toby Eastman from potential victim to suspect.

"I am a fool," Devon said, as he, too, recognized the connection. "I'd forgotten all about that, forgotten about Toby, in fact, until you started asking. After all, it has been eighteen years," he added almost sheepishly, as if to excuse the memory lapse.

"What happened between David and Toby?" Tim asked.

Devon frowned in concentration. "Toby and I went out for drinks one night, and I mentioned our idea for a true personal computer. He didn't laugh, which surprised me. That was March 1976. Before the Apple 1, even. There were a few hobbyist kits out then, but nothing that could make a market. David and I were handpicking the team and some of the engineers we approached laughed so hard they almost fell over. Toby was enthusiastic and came back with some good ideas of his own. Naturally, David was furious I'd talked to someone without clearing it with him first. He was paranoid about security."

He turned to Tim. "You think he's bad now, you should have seen him in those days. But Toby impressed him, and eventually

David came around."

"So Toby was on the team?"

"For about a week."

"Then what?" Peter asked, scribbling furiously.

"We were all working like demons to finish this very sensitive government project. David and I wanted to see it through before we left HP."

Devon paused, eyeing Peter and Tim in turn, then continued. "Everybody was cutting a corner here and there to meet the deadline, Toby no more than anyone else. But when we ran the final test suite, the application broke and the problem was traced to Toby's part of the code.

"We missed the deadline and suffered contractual penalties. Hell boiled over from HP management. David and I planned to leave HP as conquering heroes and this fiasco sent us out the door with our dicks dangling. So David kicked Toby off the Trxton team. I thought he overreacted, but I couldn't talk him out of it. Self-righteous to the core, David is, when he decides to be," Devon muttered, seeming to disappear inside himself.

"Toby could be our disgruntled hacker, then," Peter suggested.

"It's possible." Devon shrugged. "But last I heard Toby was in South America."

"Well, telnet works from South America, doesn't it?"

"Yes. But according to Henry, he was doing damn good down there. Struck it rich in some kind of import/export business. Why now, after eighteen years?"

"Hate does funny things to people."

Devon nodded and fell silent once more. Peter wondered how many of Devon's inner musings were about his own relationship with David Lockwood. It made Peter even more determined to learn what had made Devon leave Lockwood; and, more importantly, what had caused him to return.

"Don't forget," Tim's voice interrupted his thoughts, "that logic bomb was triggered from the Horizon product introduction in real time, which still makes Ravi our most likely suspect."

Devon nodded. "Besides, I was there. If Toby Eastman was anywhere near that event, I would have recognized him. And there's one more thing wrong with your theory," Devon added, his voice flat and firm. "We know the logic bomber is tied somehow to the disk and to the murders. Even if Toby held a grudge against David, he would never, ever do anything that would hurt Henry. I'd stake my life on that one."

Tim's screen lit up. "Got a message from Ravi."

"Ask him why he left the team in such a hurry," Devon said.

Tim typed, waited, and then responded: "He went back to India because his mother was ill, but she's doing better now."

Devon leaned forward. "He know anything about the logic bomb?"

Tim shook his head. "Total shock. But he said everyone on the team had access to the demos. Anyone could have done it."

"One more question, Tim." Devon glowered in Peter's direction. "Ask him why he gave confidential product information to a reporter."

24

April 30, 1994: Menlo Park, California

SATURDAY MORNING DAWNED CLEAR AND SUNNY. PETER STOOD idly by as Jordan grabbed her tennis racket and sports bag, off to play tennis with Grace and then to the city to rehearse for her return engagement with The EJs.

"Don't pout," Jordan said, tweaking his cheek. "You'll be back on the court in no time. Besides if you get really bored, you can always watch Seinfeld on your phone," she giggled.

"Ha ha. Very funny," Peter replied. He leaned over and collected a quick kiss before she sauntered out the door.

Just as he started to close the door, he caught sight of Sam walking up the path.

"Hey, Sam," he called.

Sam jerked his head toward Peter's voice, his wary half-smile tumbling into shock as he caught sight of Peter's face.

"Wow! Ben said they beat you up. But man oh man! How do you feel?"

"Better." He ushered Sam inside and sank into the couch. "Want some coffee?"

Sam shook his head and took the chair opposite Peter.

"So, what have you got?" Peter took a sip of coffee.

"Do you want to start with the murder or the background?"

"Murder."

Sam pulled out his notebook, shuffled the pages and began. "It's still unsolved. Rhodes was killed on the eighteenth of December, sometime between eleven-thirty p.m. and two a.m. They think he either knew or was expecting his killer, because there was no sign of forced entry. He was awake, though. There was an open bottle of Napoleon brandy and one glass found near the body. Detective thinks it was a professional or trained killer because there was one small knife wound, made by a stiletto-type knife, from kidney to heart."

"No one heard anything?"

"Nope. And the houses are close together in that part of Palo Alto, too," Sam replied.

"Nothing missing?"

Sam shook his head. "Want background?"

"Yeah, go ahead."

Sam flipped a few pages. "He worked for HP from 1970 until last June, when he retired. He started out as a software programmer but he evolved into this role of supervising the new college recruits as they came on board."

Sam shifted in his chair. He looked edgy, which meant he was holding something back. Peter had little patience for it, but managed to adopt a casual tone. "There's more?"

Sam nodded slowly, focused on Peter's face. "When Henry Rhodes retired a few months ago, he started a consulting practice. His one and only client was MediaBuilders USA."

Peter sat upright. "Rhodes was working for MediaBuilders?"

"System security. He was helping them revamp their network strategy. They were building an intranet and a handful of Web sites, and they'd had some hacker problems."

This was the missing link, Peter realized. He knew MediaBuilders was tied into this conundrum, but the only connection he'd had was the fact that MediaBuilders was trying to buy out Lockwood, a perfectly reasonable acquisition play in their bid to own the information highway market. Now he had a direct link between MediaBuilders and the encryption club—and the disk that could expose the mastermind and murderer. He glanced toward the kitchen table, eager to return to his notes.

"There's one more thing I was going to check out, but you'll have to handle it yourself. I've got plans tonight. Rhodes has a sister. She got all his stuff when he died."

"Yeah, I heard. Sacramento?"

"No. She was, but she moved in with her daughter in the city a few months ago. Here's the address. I'll let you know if I find anything else," Sam called as he stepped outside.

Closing the door, Peter got the sense that he actually meant it.

April 30, 1994: San Francisco, California

An hour later, Peter circled the rim of Golden Gate Park, scouting for the ever-elusive parking place. Finally, he spotted a tight slot about twelve blocks from the address Sam had given him and pulled in, whispering a word of thanks to whatever parking gods had arranged the favor.

The old Victorian Mary McPhearson shared with her daughter and son-in-law sat among the Painted Ladies lining 19th Avenue. The gingerbread structure, like most of the others on the block, was painstakingly preserved. A cherry tree blossomed in the tiny square plot claimed from the concrete surrounding the residences.

Peter's knock at the door was greeted by a tall, large-boned woman, dressed for a trip to the gym. Her head was covered with a bright, patterned silk scarf. Long gold corkscrews dangled from her earlobes.

"Mrs. McPhearson? I called. I'm Peter Ellis, from the *Valley Tribune*."

"Oh yes," she said, stepping back quickly. "Come in. We've stored Henry's stuff in the back," she explained, striding down the long hallway.

"Remind me again why you want to go through all this." She waved him into a small bedroom, overflowing with cardboard boxes.

"I'm trying to get a lead on some of the young engineers that worked with Henry at HP. Does the name Toby Eastman mean anything to you?"

"Good lord, no. But I'll admit I never paid much attention to what Henry was doing. We weren't that close. I have no idea what we're going to do with all this stuff. I would have stored most of it, but Sandra—that's my daughter—was fond of her uncle, and she keeps promising to go through it." She shook her head, waving her hand distractedly at the clutter.

"I'm sure you'll find something in here. He was always prattling on about his 'boys.' I guess it's because he didn't have any children of his own. I, on the other hand, have two," she continued with obvious pride.

"Sandra is in securities here in the city. My boy's a doctor up in Seattle. Think you can go through this in about an hour? I've got a yoga class."

"Sure. No problem."

"All yours," she said, closing the door.

Peter started digging. The first several boxes contained classical literature that spanned the centuries. Two others were filled with computer manuals. Peter pulled out one on coding secure software and leafed through it as if he could absorb some message that would lead him to the missing disk.

Eventually he tossed it aside and focused on the personal mementos. He lifted out a set of photographs. As he shuffled through them, a disquieting sense of his own mortality cloaked him. Held timeless in the shiny press of film, Henry Rhodes, Michael Lee and Brian Tucker horsed around against a backdrop of autumn colors. The camera caught Brian waving from behind a large maple tree, Michael scattering leaves and all three of them standing beside an outcropping of rocks, Henry with his arms around the two boys, smiling broadly. Peter stared at the photos, acutely aware of how close he had come to sharing their fate.

Just as he started to close the box, Peter spotted an envelope tucked into a corner so tightly that it was almost folded in half. He tugged it out. The return address was a P.O. box in Garden City, New York. The address Noel Connors had given for Toby Eastman. He shook the one-page letter from the envelope and scanned it.

Setting the letter aside, Peter shoved his arm deep into the box, snaking his hand through the mountain of cards and letters, looking for more of Toby's strikingly irregular handwriting. He spotted his quarry, a thick stack of letters bound by a stiff rubber band stretched to the limit. As he claimed the stack, the rubber band broke and snapped his hand.

"Ouch. Damn it," he said. The freed letters were now scattered about the room.

Mary pushed open the door. "Are you going to be much longer? I need to get going."

"No. I found what I was looking for. Would you mind if I borrowed these for a couple of days?" he asked, pointing to the photos and letters littering the floor.

She shook her head, tapping her foot impatiently while Peter scooped up his cache.

"I'll show you out," she said.

April 30, 1994: Menlo Park, California

The approaching dusk cast shadows on the walls of his empty townhouse as Peter unlocked the door. Entering his office, he glanced at the silent answering machine and flipped on his PC to check his email. He'd gotten a reply from Japan.

Fingers flicking over the keys, he called up the message:

Peter, would like to help you find Henry's killer. I still miss him. But I don't know anyone using Groucho or Helen as handles. Suggest that you try Toby Eastman. He knew Henry better than anyone. Good luck, Anne.

May 1, 1994: San Francisco, California

Toby sped through the deserted streets of San Francisco just after two a.m. in search of a payphone. Spotting his quarry outside a smoke shop on the corner of Mission and 18th, he pulled up beside it and jumped from the car. He grabbed the receiver, tossed a handful of coins into the slot and called up Carl's emergency beeper number in West Palm Beach. Foot tapping, distractedly scanning the urban scrawl littering the booth, he waited for the phone to ring. It was answered on the first *brring*.

"Only five people in the world know this number. Which one are you?" a woman asked. Her voice echoed through the receiver, taut with anxiety.

"Where's Carl?"

"Answer my question first," she demanded. "Who are you?"

"Toby. Toby Eastman."

"He said to ask you for some identification that only you and he would know," she said. "Her name."

Toby clutched the receiver. They had worked out this code years ago, hoping never to use it. He forced himself to sound calm.

"You're Rita, right?" he asked, recalling Carl's wife, a slight Puerto Rican woman with a fiery temper and an iron will.

"Yes. Tell me her name."

"Myong. I called her Mae."

"You're Toby." She sounded relieved. "He left a message for you."

Toby heard the rustle of papers, the sound of an envelope being ripped open, and she was back on the line. "It's just two words," she said, mystified.

"Cut loose."

"Yes. How did you know?"

The message was a signal telling him time was running out and to save himself while he still could. Toby felt as if unseen hands clasped his throat, cutting off the flow of oxygen. He drew a ragged breath.

"Where is he, Rita?"

Rita was silent. He could almost hear the rapid beating of her heart, feel her fighting to keep her balance. "He told me I could count on you," she said finally. "The FBI picked up him for questioning yesterday afternoon."

Toby tensed, feeling the noose around his neck tighten another notch. "Carl will be fine. He knows how to handle those guys."

"Even if he doesn't, I prefer it to the alternative," she replied woodenly, hanging up before he could reply.

As he slowly replaced the receiver, Toby fought unsuccessfully to keep his mind from considering the alternative. He'd never know what they did to Eddie, and never forget what they did to Arno.

May 1, 1994: Menlo Park, California

HIS BACK BURNED. HIS RIBS ACHED. THE MURKY BLACK LIQUID IN his cup, hardly recognizable as coffee, was stone cold. One more cigarette butt would cause the ashtray to overflow onto the table.

Peter shifted to relieve the pressure on his back and lit yet another cigarette. The two dozen letters from Toby Eastman that Henry Rhodes had carefully preserved were spread out before him, photographs from several generations of Henry's boys scattered nearby. In the past seven hours, as Saturday night yielded to dawn, Peter had become intimately familiar with Toby's stilted, formal prose sandwiched between his customary salutation, "My Dear Friend," and closure, "Stay Vigilant, Toby."

The return addresses on the letters spanned the globe. They were filled with exacting descriptions of the sights and sounds of the desert, the jungle, cities, wherever Toby happened to be. Through it all, the affection between the two men was readily apparent. But there was no mention of Lockwood, puzzle games or an encrypted computer disk. As morning broke, Peter felt shackled, ensnared in a carefully crafted web of lies from which he could neither escape nor find the truth.

The phone clamored for his attention. Peter glanced at the clock as he picked up the receiver.

"Is this Peter Ellis?" a female voice boomed. Peter moved the phone a few inches from his ear.

"Yes."

"I'm Sandy Bertrand. You spoke to my mother yesterday about my Uncle Henry."

"Yes, I did."

"Mother said you took some letters and photos. She shouldn't have let you do that. They're personal. I really must have them back."

Her tone was accusatory and imperious. Peter scowled at the phone and tried to filter the irritation from his voice. "I'm trying to look into your uncle's murder, Mrs. Bertrand."

"Really? Isn't that a matter for the police?"

"Yes, but . . ."

"I'd like to pick them up this morning," she interjected. "Could you give me your address, please?"

Peter sighed and gave her the information she requested.

"I'll be there in thirty minutes," she said, and disconnected.

Peter sorted through the pile and picked out a couple of photos he hoped she wouldn't miss. He also made copies of the letters before he rearranged everything exactly the way he had received it. He figured Sandy for the type who would notice anything out of place.

• • • •

She was definitely Henry Rhodes's niece, Peter noted, opening the door percisely thirty minutes later. Although she dressed in the same high-fashion, extroverted colors her mother favored, Sandy had the round bespectacled face and doughy body of her uncle. On her, the size and weight were used to communicate authority.

"Come in." Peter stepped back as she swept into the room.

"I can only stay for a minute. I'm having brunch with clients in fifteen minutes." She thrust her wrist toward her eyes. "Let's have those photos," she demanded in a foghorn of a voice.

Peter declined to reply as he passed three neat bundles into her hands. As he had anticipated, she opened the photos and spun through them, stopping for a moment to gaze at a picture of her uncle standing beside an attractive man with turbulent black eyes and an immutable jawline. When she refocused her attention on Peter, her face had an absent, dreaming look.

"I imagine you must think I'm a little huffy, but my mother has no interest in these mementos of Uncle Henry's and they're very important to me," she explained, her voice and manner softening as she caressed the photos.

"I'm sorry for your loss. These last few months must have been very difficult for you."

"Yes. He was a special man." She opened her purse, placed the bundles in it and closed it with a definite snap, as if she resented the fact that Peter had ever touched her uncle's papers.

"If I were going to let his things go, it certainly wouldn't be to a reporter." She spat the word out. "I'd give them to that other young man. At least he was a friend," she said, her voice returning to its normal stridency.

"What other young man?"

"Michael Lee. He called about a month after Uncle Henry died, and wanted to see his things just like you did. But he never came by."

"I am very sorry to tell you this, but he's dead."

"But I just talked to him," she insisted, trying to stave off the unwelcome news. "He was one of Uncle's favorites. What happened?"

"His company was robbed. Michael was shot. The police think it's a simple case of wrong place, wrong time. I think the robbery attempt was set-up to camouflage an execution."

She stiffened at the words and then, as if to dismiss them, asked: "What makes you think you know more than the police?"

"I have more at stake. The answers are important to me. Personally."

She stared at him, reevaluating his motives, appearing to notice the bruise on his face for the first time. *Buy, sell or hold?* Peter wondered which choice the securities dealer standing before him would make.

She glanced at her watch. Caught between curiosity and an ever-present ticking of the clock, she granted herself permission to remain a few more minutes. *Hold*, at least for now. She looked at him expectantly. Peter held her gaze for a moment and continued.

"I started asking questions about your uncle's death and Michael's, and I ended up with a concussion and a couple of cracked ribs. I'm still asking questions. Now at least, I have a few answers."

She looked impatiently curious. "What answers?"

"I know that your uncle received something he shouldn't have, something lethal that was encoded on a computer disk. Without realizing it, he passed the information on to some of his boys."

He spoke rapidly, now as conscious as she was of the ticking clock. "That's why I wanted letters and photos. To find out who else might have gotten a copy of the disk. Anyone who got a copy is in danger."

"Michael got a copy?"

"Yes. Another boy, Brian Tucker, got one too." Peter decided he wouldn't tell her about Tucker unless he had to. "Your uncle sent them packages in the mail."

For the first time since she entered the townhouse, Sandy Bertrand looked uncertain. It was clearly not a comfortable or familiar feeling for her. "What would those packages look like?" she asked.

"Probably brown envelopes, about six inches square."

Uncertainty shifted to concern. "I must have mailed those packages," she said, frowning. "Uncle Henry and I had lunch a couple of days before he died and he had three packages with him. He wanted to stop at the post office and I said no. We were running late."

Automatically, she glanced at her watch. This time, it seemed to Peter, she failed to see the hands moving. "I offered to mail them for him."

"How did he act when you said that?"

She shrugged. "Not worried, if that's what you mean, except he said that I should mail them that day, because those boys would need all the time they could get. Then he laughed. Like it was a joke. A joke," she repeated vacantly.

"Who was the third package addressed to? Do you remember?" he asked, fighting the anxiety building inside him.

"A fellow named Steve Marshall. But it was never sent. I tried twice, but it came back."

Peter felt beads of sweat form on his forehead. His pulse quickened. "Where is that package now?"

She stepped toward the door. "In my trunk. I didn't know what to do with it after Uncle Henry died. But I do now. It's going straight to the police."

Her hand encircled the door knob. Peter stepped forward, putting his hand on her arm.

"Mrs. Bertrand. Sandy. The police won't be able to do anything with the disk as it is. It's encrypted with a special computer code that makes it impossible to read. A specialist, a cryptologist, needs to look at it. I have a friend who is one. If you give me the disk, I know he can retrieve the information, and I promise you we will give it to the police."

She looked from the door to his face and hesitated. Peter could tell that she really didn't want the added responsibility that suddenly had been thrust upon her.

"If we can save the police time and effort, they can solve the murders faster. Otherwise, they might give up. How much have they done so far?"

The question grabbed her. *Buy*, he begged silently.

She opened her purse and pulled out a photo, one of her uncle with Brian and Michael. She turned it over and read her uncle's scribble on the back marking the time and date. Then she dropped the photo back into her purse again.

"All right," she said.

As he followed her out to her car, Peter felt himself start to breathe normally again. She opened the trunk, handed him the package and glanced at her watch. The dismay of those bound by time spread across her features. "Oh, Lord. I'm so late. I'll have to call my clients immediately."

She opened the car door and grabbed her car phone as she slid inside. Peter held the door to keep it from closing. "I apologize for keeping you, but could I ask you one more thing?"

She held up one finger as she spoke into the car phone. Then she replaced the receiver and looked back at him with a relieved smile. "It appears my clients are running late too."

"I really appreciate your time. I know how valuable it is," he said, politely. "Do you happen to know Toby Eastman?"

"Of course." She smiled with genuine pleasure. "Darling man. Spent holidays with us occasionally."

"He must be in the photos. Would you mind pointing him out?"

She pulled the pictures from her purse and spun through them once again.

"That's Toby there," she said, resting her bejeweled index finger on the photo of the attractive man with the stark black eyes that had captured her attention earlier.

As she studied the image, her mouth curved upward in memory, Peter suspected that in a past not completely buried Sandy had had more than a casual interest in Toby Eastman.

"You know, that was taken about ten years ago. We didn't see much of Toby after that. Maybe it had something to do with that woman."

"What woman?"

"There was this woman who kept calling Uncle Henry looking for Toby. For a while she was absolutely frantic, calling constantly, at all hours of the day and night. She'd ask after Toby, give her name and hang up. Got on Uncle Henry's nerves. She kept it up for about three months. Then, all of sudden, she stopped."

"Do you remember the woman's name?"

"Of course I remember. She recited it like a litany every time she called. 'This is Jennette Harris, from Plano.' Plano, Texas is Toby's hometown."

"Thank you so much." Peter swung her door closed.

He shredded the brown envelope as soon as he was back inside the house and lifted the blue, three-and-a-half-inch floppy with the tips of his fingers. Placing it by the phone, he dialed Lockwood's lab.

"Tim, get your ass over here." he yelled when Tim finally answered. "I've got the disk."

• • • •

Peter leaned over Tim's shoulder as Tim ran yet another code sequence. Tim had been working the puzzle for the last two hours. Peter was trying to keep anxiety at bay. Anxiety was winning. The frustrated expression on Tim's face wasn't helping.

"Look, Tim, where are we here?" The monitor displayed what looked like hieroglyphics.

Tim tapped the keyboard. "Not close."

"What's the problem?"

"This guy, whoever he is, wrote his own encryption scheme."

"So, I thought that's what you all did."

Tim looked up at him. "Not really. Most encryption patterns are standardized either on the RSA algorithm or the DES government approach. This is unique. It doesn't fit any of the patterns I know, and I know most of them."

"What does that mean?"

"It means it's going to be harder to crack." Tim turned back to the computer and resumed typing. "You better get this place cleaned up before Jordan gets back from San Francisco, or your ass is grass."

"Yeah." Peter looked around. It had taken him less than a day to let everything deteriorate. Jordan was sure to notice how completely he had disregarded her "no smoking in the house" rule when she got back from the city later that afternoon. He stopped worrying about Tim's progress and focused on cleaning, beginning with dumping his overflowing ashtray.

"Son of a bitch!" Tim yelled.

Peter hurried back into his office and surveyed the scene. Tim was staring hollow-eyed at the computer monitor, his fists clenched, looking as if he wanted to put both the computer and himself out of their respective miseries.

"What's wrong?" Peter tapped Tim on the shoulder to break the pall.

"Nothing's working. Nothing." He slammed his fist on the keyboard. The characters gyrated up and down, then stilled. Sliding out of the chair, Tim stood rigid, muscles taut, his body as tight as a spring. Tim's normally calm and unruffled exterior had been sorely tested. Peter had never seen him so close to unraveling. Peter pulled a chair up to the desk and gestured for Tim to sit back down. He declined with a rough shake of his head. Peter studied the back of his neck.

"I'm no tech wizard, but walk me through it step by step," Peter suggested. "Maybe we can figure out what's missing."

Tim stared at the wall, muttering words indistinguishable to Peter's ears.

"Look, it can't hurt," Peter insisted.

The request seemed to reenergize Tim. He sat down, cleared the screen and tapped out a series of keystrokes.

"You remember that the basis of encryption is substitution, right? Pre-computer, it was alphanumeric, combinations of letters and numbers. Now it's digital and the pattern of substitution is based on computer code." Tim looked over at Peter to confirm the point.

Peter nodded, with an inward smile at Tim's air of authority. Tell mode, Peter had called it privately the first time Tim had launched into the series of lectures on technology that Peter had convinced him to provide. The meeting that had ultimately led to their friendship had been prompted, oddly enough, by a letter to the editor in which Tim had launched a scathing attack on Peter's lack of technical acumen.

Tim was a reluctant tutor. Only Peter's persistence and willingness to pay the bar tab kept Tim coming back to the Tide House to impart his knowledge. The verbosity of Tim's lectures increased with the quantity of Guinness he consumed. Now Peter needed to listen to Tim more closely than ever, if it meant that together they could solve the riddle.

"What we're looking for is a pattern," Tim explained. "Once we see a consistent pattern, we can look for the irregularities. I expected to find a remnant of it in Brian's code-cracker. Good thing Devon found it when we were restoring the Sapphire code or we'd be dead meat."

"Why?"

"Generally, these guys, the real cryptologists, keep copies of puzzles they've solved in a database. When they get a new puzzle, they run the code-cracker, looking for patterns. Even matching one or two sequences can give a good cryptologist the right start."

"But you didn't find any matches?"

"No, and I should have. People who write code, encrypted or not, don't change their styles that much. They tend to use a similar set of sequences and just switch them around."

"The software equivalent of Chex party mix," Peter said, grinning.

Tim glowered, not yet ready to leave the professorial lectern.

Peter raised his hands in mock apology. "Okay. I'll behave."

Tim pecked at the keyboard. Peter leaned forward, watching a new set of data accumulate on the monitor, thankful that Tim's earlier, immobilizing frustration had vanished.

"I've reset the code-cracker. Let's take another look."

Tim tapped out a sequence and restarted the code-cracker. The strings scrolled across the screen. Peter leaned in for a better look just as the words "NO MATCH IDENTIFIED" flashed on the screen. Tim slumped back in his chair and templed his hands, eyes closed. Peter wondered if Tim was praying for help. If so, God didn't seem to be answering. After a moment of silence, Tim turned to him, his expression glum.

"Sorry, Peter. I can't do this one. It's too complex." Tim's deflated, defeated tone caught Peter by surprise. Wrapped in his own concerns, Peter had forgotten how much Tim had invested as well. Tim wanted to crack the code by himself to prove something to Peter and, most likely, to Devon. Peter understood the motive and need well.

"You did good, Tim. You did your best and that's what counts."

Tim responded with a sardonic smile. "Mind if I take this back to lab and play around with it some more?"

"Go for it." Peter responded with a pat on Tim's shoulder. Tim shut down the computer and stood, encrypted disk in hand. "Call you as soon as I get something."

Peter wandered out to the patio and lit a cigarette, hoping Jordan would get back soon. He didn't like the empty feeling that now came with the solitude he used to cherish.

Returning to his office, he picked up the telephone. He had his own portion of the mystery to solve, and it was leading back to Plano, Texas. He waited while the operator retrieved the number for Jennette Harris.

"It's been changed," she said, after a pause. "The new number is in Dallas."

He got voicemail. He left his name, number and a message: he was hoping to locate a friend or colleague of hers, Toby Eastman. Glancing at the clock, he saw it was nearly three. His stomach rumbled. He'd been running on coffee and cigarettes since dawn. Though he had little appetite, he fixed himself a sandwich and a glass of milk. The buzz of the telephone interrupted his first bite.

"Hey, sweetie. It's me." Nothing sounded better than Jordan's silky voice cooing in his ear.

"Hi, hon. Be home soon?"

"I'm still with Taylor. We've been shopping and we want to try Picardo's tonight. It's sooo hot. Come join us."

"That new Italian bistro?" Peter stifled a groan. The last thing he wanted tonight was a noisy, crowded evening at the hottest new restaurant in San Francisco. And he wanted to stay close in case Tim called.

"Yes. It'll be lots of fun. Around six, okay?"

"I better not."

"Still hurting?" She sounded disappointed, but resigned.

"Yeah."

"Okay. Don't wait up. I'll be back late."

"Stay with Taylor and Josh tonight if you want. I'll be fine."

"Okay. See you in the morning."

The phone rang as soon as he re-cradled the receiver.

"Hello?" a female voice queried cautiously. Then, stronger, "I'm trying to reach Peter Ellis."

"Speaking."

"This is Jennette Harris. You left a message about Toby Eastman. Would that be Tobias Jonah Eastman from Plano, Texas?"

Peter grabbed a pen and jotted down the name. "Yes. Do you know him?"

"He's my cousin."

Family relations, Peter knew, were notoriously unhelpful in situations like this. He phrased his next words with great care.

"Er, I'm trying to locate him for a story I'm doing. Just a few simple questions, really. Would you have any idea where he is today?"

"If it were up to me, he'd be rotting in prison." She drew a deep breath and continued in a caustic voice. "Or better yet, in hell."

"Pardon?"

"Toby Eastman murdered my brother."

May 1, 1994: San Francisco, California

JENNETTE HARRIS, AS FORTUNE WOULD HAVE IT, WAS STAYING AT the Nikko Hotel in downtown San Francisco, negotiating the opening of a new sales office. Peter considered this a good omen. He fervently hoped the good luck would spill over to Tim's code-cracking efforts.

She was waiting in the lobby, a petite blonde wearing the beige wool pantsuit and bowler hat she had described to him over the phone. What she'd failed to mention, he noticed as he strolled up to her, was her attractive heart-shaped face, high cheekbones and slim, athletic build. She greeted him with a firm handshake and took his measure with a pair of shrewd gray eyes. About the only family resemblance Peter could see between Jennette and the picture he'd seen of her cousin Toby was a hard line to the jaw. Jennette Harris would be no pushover in business or in bed. He motioned toward the lobby bar. She shook her head.

"I've been inside all day. It's still nice out. Mind if we walk?"

Outside the hotel, the late afternoon sun bathed the buildings in an orange hue. They turned a couple of corners and headed up Market Street. They walked side by side for a few blocks. Then Jennette paused and looked at him with an expression he couldn't decipher.

"After all these years." Her tone held a sense of awe, of a long-held wish about to be fulfilled. Her expectations for the conversation were clearly as high as his. He had no idea whether either of them would get what they wanted.

Jennette stopped walking and peered into a t-shirt shop. Peter doubted she was intrigued by the fluorescent black and orange portrayal of the Golden Gate Bridge the shopkeeper obviously thought would attract tourists. Her eyes fixed on the t-shirt, she began to speak in a low measured tone.

"For years, I beat my fists on every door that I thought might open and no one would listen to my side of the story. Now it seems everyone wants to talk about T.J. Maybe now he'll get the justice he deserves."

Peter heard the bitterness in her voice, watched her swallow it with a sigh. Her manner, when she resumed speaking, was brisk, more like a business executive discussing a deal than a woman still struggling to comprehend her brother's murder.

"What's your interest in T.J.?" she asked, facing him. "We always called him T.J., at home."

Peter provided her with a broad sketch of the details of Sapphire, the logic bomb and the encrypted computer disk, leaving out, for the moment at least, the three murders.

"Where does T.J. fit in to all this?"

"I'm not really sure. But I think he may have created the logic bomb that destroyed Sapphire. He seems to have a grudge against David Lockwood. He's an accomplished software programmer, certainly skilled enough to wreak this kind of electronic havoc."

"So, he's added sabotage to his long list of sins," she replied. "It's criminal, no doubt, but hardly in the same category as murder."

"You're convinced he murdered your brother?" Peter pulled out his notebook and pen as they walked along.

"It was no accident. Even though he made it look that way."

"Could you give me the details?"

"I'm not sure it will make sense unless I explain the family situation."

"Start anywhere you want."

"Our family is quite influential in Texas. We control three of the largest regional banks. One of which was founded by my great-grandfather."

She stated it as a fact, without arrogance or pride. Peter admired her style.

"My grandfather had three children," she explained. "I never knew my uncle Drew. He was killed during World War II. My father, Earl, was the middle child, but when Drew died he assumed the responsibilities and privileges of the oldest son. The youngest was Silvia, T.J.'s mother. She was a beautiful girl, blonde, blue-eyed and petite. Like a living doll, my grandfather always said. He doted on her, fulfilled her every whim, so naturally she was headstrong and spoiled. Her temper tantrums were legendary."

She looked faintly amused. Peter studied her, wondering whether the family resemblance extended to temperament. In Jennette, though, he saw strength and resolve; the ballast that enabled her to continue her quest.

"When Silvia was nineteen she met and fell in love with Jack Eastman. He was ruggedly handsome, with jet-black hair and dark eyes. T.J. looks a lot like him. Jack was also a gambler and something of a cad, according to family gossip." She paused and watched as Peter scribbled down her life story.

"The first time I saw *Gone with the Wind*, I thought of Uncle Jack. He was a regular Rhett Butler. He'd never talk about his past, only his future—which was a real shock to a family that can trace its roots proudly to dozens of Texas pioneers."

"I know what you mean. I'm a fifth-generation Californian."

"Really?" She sounded surprised, and then grinned at him as if they'd struck a bond she hadn't expected.

"I don't have to tell you the rest, do I? It's almost a cliché." She chuckled.

"Clichés become clichés because they have some truth behind them."

She nodded. As they paused at a street corner, waiting for the light to turn, she looked up at the skyline. Her welcoming gaze seemed to drink in the lights, the city's entire panorama. Peter felt she was gaining a small measure of peace simply from being invited to tell her story.

The light changed, and she refocused her attention on her narrative as they walked. "My grandfather forbid the marriage, so naturally they eloped with no money and no prospects. Uncle Jack was a wildcatter." She turned toward him. "Do you know what that is?"

"An independent contractor for oil companies?"

"Yes. Someone who looks for new oil deposits in an unexplored area. It's either boom or bust."

"That would appeal to a gambler."

"It did. They lived like gypsies. Always moving. Always looking for his next big score. But my grandfather had a soft spot for Silvia. About a year after the marriage, he gave her a lavish dowry; but at my father's insistence, he didn't settle any capital on her, just presents: jewelry, gowns, furs. Everything Silvia loved from her old life. Daddy believed that Jack, irresponsible gambler that he was, would eventually try to get money from the family. Silvia wouldn't care about the money, but if she had to watch Jack sell off her cherished possessions one by one, she would come to her senses and leave him."

"And did he?"

"Naturally." She treated him to an enigmatic smile.

"And did she?" He smiled in return.

Jennette shook her head.

"No. But once T.J. was born and they'd been shuffling all over Texas, Oklahoma and a few other states for years, I believe Jack's charm began to wear thin. To Silvia's credit, she stuck by him, though I don't think it would have lasted if he hadn't been killed in a rig blast when T.J. was nine."

"So they came home?"

Jennette nodded. "They had no money. Daddy offered to take them in but Silvia was stubborn. She'd already thumbed her nose at the family once and she didn't back down, despite her wretched situation."

Peter heard a mixture of admiration and despair in Jennette's tone. Admiration, woman to woman, for her aunt's strength. Despair, Peter surmised, because her aunt's decisions had contributed to her brother's death. The wind picked up as the fog drifted across the city. Glancing over at Jennette, Peter saw her shiver.

"How about a cappuccino?" he asked.

"Sounds great."

They dipped inside a tiny shop. Jennette seemed to need the warmth and comforting smell of the freshly-brewed beverage as more than just a refuge from the cold. The toughest part of her story was yet to come.

"How did they live?" Peter asked, as he retrieved two cappuccinos and a plate of biscotti. He placed them before Jennette, who was sitting at a small table near the window.

"Simply. But they still needed some money. Finally, Silvia asked Daddy for a loan. He refused. Daddy could be stubborn too," she added, with a shake of her head at the folly of her elders.

"Eventually he gave her the loan, but he forced her to use her dowry as collateral. He was a banker, after all. It's in the blood. He also wanted to force her back into the family for her own good and T.J.'s."

Her tone had become defensive. It seemed she understood the unflattering picture she was painting of her father and wished it were different.

"She didn't go back?"

Jennette shook her head. "He misjudged her. He only saw the spoiled little girl, not the woman she'd become. She sold just about everything back to him before…" Her voice trailed off. She dunked a piece of biscotti in her coffee and bit it, chewing and swallowing absentmindedly.

"Before Earl Junior's death," she said, finding her voice again. "When Daddy lost Earl he didn't care about anything anymore. He kept going, but he was dead inside."

"How did it happen?"

"It was the Fourth of July. Everyone came to our house for the big barbecue. T.J. and Earl Junior were playing in the backyard." She took a sip of coffee.

"But didn't you say that your father and Silvia snubbed each other?"

She offered him a faint smile utterly void of amusement. "That was the best part. Daddy would invite them to the big house to show Silvia everything she had lost and remind them that they were poor relations. Silvia would show up to prove that she and T.J. were doing just fine, thank you, without the Harris family. The digs were polite, not so subtle, and very effective."

"Sounds familiar," Peter murmured.

She stared at him. He hadn't realized he'd spoken aloud.

"We do have some things in common," he said, with a quick smile. She looked ready to pose a question. He jumped in with one of his own. "So you saw a lot of T.J.?"

She held his gaze for a moment. "Most of the big holidays, when tensions run the highest and all the nasties come out. Earl Junior. and T.J. were the same age, so they usually played together. If you could call it that."

She stared into her cup, suddenly out of words, haunted by the memories.

"Tell me the rest," he coaxed.

She sat hunched forward, folded in on herself. "Earl wasn't a bully, really. Children can be so cruel, especially little boys, don't you think?" She raised her eyes to meet his.

Peter nodded. "Especially when they overhear the adults."

She traced the rim of her cup with her finger, caught herself, stopped the motion and continued.

"Earl taunted T.J. constantly. T.J. was a small child. Earl called him "P&P," for puny and poor. When Earl got a new toy, he'd shove it in T.J.'s face and lord it over him because T.J. had so few things. Or he'd goad T.J. into a fight and beat the tar out of him. But boys do these things. That's no reason to—" she stopped, looking up at him as if he weren't there, seeing the memories, watching her brother die. Peter reached over and squeezed her hand to give her the courage to continue.

She rewarded him with a grateful smile. "Over the years, as T.J. got bigger and stronger and could hold his own in a fight, it seemed like they got along better. That summer, they'd both turned fifteen. We were all inside the house when we heard the shot from the backyard. I got there first," she added softly. "Earl was lying on the ground with a huge hole in his chest, spurting blood. I started screaming. T.J. looked over at me. He was still holding the gun. It was just a brief glance, but I'll never forget the look on his face. He was—the only word I can think of is—gloating. Like he'd done something he was very proud of."

She took a deep breath and continued speaking so quietly Peter had to strain to hear her. "He should have been frightened. He should have been horrified. But he was gloating," she repeated. "When the adults came out and the real shouting started, he looked frightened; but I always thought he was more afraid of getting caught than of the fact that he had killed Earl."

"What happened to him?"

"Nothing, really. The boys had gotten into Daddy's gun collection. They had a pair of pearl-handled dueling pistols. The police and the family investigated and decided it was a tragic accident. But only T.J.'s gun was loaded. Earl's was empty. And I'll never forget that look."

Peter picked up his notebook, jotted a few notes as he finished the last of his cappuccino, and studied her. A feeling she had, even the unbalanced pistols, wouldn't be enough to convince anyone— especially him—that Toby Eastman was a murderer.

"Do you have any proof?" he asked.

"I have this." She reached inside her handbag and pulled out an envelope. She dropped its contents, a rabbit's foot and a handwritten note, both yellow with age, on the table. Peter recognized the childish scrawl as Toby's. The note was a terse, six-word statement: *I did it for you, Ma.*

"The rabbit's foot was Earl Junior's. He always had it with him, but it wasn't in his pocket the day he died. I found this envelope in the bottom of a bureau drawer that belonged to Silvia."

Jennette paused. Her lower lip wobbled. She took a deep breath, and continued: "Now, I carry it so I'll never forget what T.J. did."

Peter stared at it. It was hardly proof.

"You don't believe me, do you?" The disappointment in her voice matched the feeling in his gut.

"I'd like to, but this is supposition, not fact."

Jennette's hand brushed the rabbit's foot. "There were other incidents."

"Such as?"

She pulled out a well-thumbed notebook from her purse and placed it on the table. "I waited until Daddy passed on. I didn't want to cause him any more pain, but I couldn't let it go. For the last few years, I've been tracking T.J. I imagine I know more about Tobias Jonah Eastman than he knows about himself."

Opening her notebook, she slid her index finger along the meticulously recorded entries. "After he killed Earl Junior, the family sent him to a military academy in Virginia," she said briskly. The vulnerability Peter had seen earlier had vanished.

"It was a reform school, really, with military trimmings. His second year there an upperclassman died of a broken neck. Three of them had been drinking late one night in T.J.'s room. T.J. and another boy claimed that the boy fell from the fourth-floor dorm window. Just like with Earl Junior, they investigated and called it an accident. T.J. and the other boy were suspended briefly for drinking and that was the end of it."

"But you believe T.J. caused the fall?"

"I found the other boy in a veteran's hospital in Atlanta. His name is Rick Summerhill. He and T.J. joined the Marines together." She flipped a few pages.

"They were in the same unit in Vietnam for two years, from 1968 to 1970. At first he didn't want to say anything. I knew it was because of T.J. Finally I managed to convince him that T.J. was dead." Her mouth tweaked upward. She was pleased with her artifice, and the facts it had allowed her to gather.

"You'd make a good reporter," he told her.

"The pay's too low." She chuckled.

"True," he agreed. "But your boy Rick talked after all, I take it."

She nodded. "He told me that the boy who died and T.J. were fighting and T.J. shoved him out the window. Maybe it was an accident, he told me, but that boy didn't fall on his own. Once Rick got started, he didn't want to quit. Maybe the priests are right, confession really is good for the soul." She offered him a small smile.

"What else did he say?"

"Rick told me that just before he, T.J. and a bunch of others were due to ship out, back to the States, their commander, a Lieutenant James, was killed mysteriously in a Saigon whorehouse. He'd gone there to party, but when the party turned sour, apparently, he took it out on the girl he was with. She ran into the main card room naked, bleeding and screaming. The owner and some of the American servicemen who were there, including Rick, went back to the room and found Lieutenant James lying there in a pool of blood. His throat was slit. They never found out who did it."

"Same question. Why T.J.?"

She consulted her notebook. "He was twenty minutes late for his watch. Very unusual behavior according to those who knew him, and Rick said the girl, Myong, was Toby's favorite. He was protective of her. Gave her lavish presents. Things he couldn't afford."

"What about an inquest? The Marines don't take these things lightly."

"Inconclusive. No one was ever charged with anything." She sighed.

"But you still think it was T.J."

Jennette sat up straighter. Her gaze was direct and unflinching. "I know my cousin. He was always obsessively possessive about anything he considered his. He'd kill a man for hurting her," she insisted. "But that wasn't his only motive. Rick said that earlier that week, Lieutenant James had started asking questions about T.J. in conjunction with drug trafficking at the base."

"What kind of drug trafficking?"

"Rick didn't know. It was just rumors. He'd heard that T.J. and two other bush pilots, Eddie LeRoy and Arnold Tollie, had organized this profitable little drug enterprise."

Peter shrugged. "From what I've heard about Vietnam, that kind of stuff was pretty common. Could you give me Rick's number? I'd like to follow up with him."

"He's dead. Natural causes," she added, to Peter's raised eyebrow. "Heart attack."

• • • •

"Can you do anything with this?" she asked, as they stood outside the café later.

Peter hesitated. She read his expression and he felt her energy dissipate, taking his with it. She was at the end of a long road, and he wasn't helping her find the answers she sought. He felt drained, bone-weary of the chase and the endless string of questions.

"I'll find him," he told her, with more confidence then he felt. Her face drawn, she nodded. Turning toward him as they parted, she spoke quietly, her tone a mixture of warning and fear.

"If you believe nothing else, believe this: he likes hurting people. I saw it in his eyes the day he killed my brother. For T.J., causing pain is power, and pleasure."

May 1, 1994: Menlo Park, California

Peter's mind spun as he entered his townhouse. He still didn't have any real proof, but he couldn't deny the similarities between her story and the three deaths he knew about: a gun, a knife, a clever cover-up. Then and now. Familiar patterns repeated.

The silence in the townhouse was oppressive, weighing him down physically. He sank into the sofa, flat on his back, and lit a cigarette.

He watched the smoke curl upward, regretting his insistence that Jordan spend the night with Taylor and Josh. He needed the comfort of her presence, the soft touch of her fingers on his skin, her astute understanding of the conundrum facing them. He wanted to run the new information by her, get her take. He considered picking up the phone just to hear her voice, but they'd be in the middle of dinner in a noisy bistro by now and it was no place to talk.

The urge for company, even just noise, was too compelling to ignore. He turned on the CD player and let Tim's favorite classic rock blare. Wandering into the kitchen, he lifted a bottle of Scotch from a lower cupboard and poured two fingers. He took a drink and felt the amber liquid coat his throat. Returning to the living room, glass in one hand, bottle in the other, Peter placed the half-full bottle on the coffee table. Shields tenuously in place, he sat down and considered the reality of his adversary.

His assailant had a name, a face and an identity. If Toby Eastman was capable of the cold-blooded murder of a man who had loved him as a son, and for whom he had professed love in return—Peter was becoming increasingly convinced that he was—by contrast Peter's rape had been mere sport, a tidbit tossed to a soul grown corpulent from its own blood-lust, never satisfied with its own capacity for evil. He hoped Tim could break that code. And soon.

Toby killed for expediency and, as Jennette had warned him, for pleasure. Toby was the operative, the black-hearted puppeteer pulling strings in a hundred different directions and never in the same location twice. But was he also the mastermind? Sucking on his cigarette, Peter thought not. The taunts he had hammered at Peter suggested a more subservient role.

"If your fucking family wasn't so influential, you'd be dead already."

Given the choice, Peter was sure Toby would have taken his life. Toby was taking orders. From someone who didn't want Peter killed. The question now was, who? Who was running Toby? Who was he listening to? And why did they want Peter alive? Peter downed his first Scotch and poured another in a vain attempt to shut out that maddening voice of ridicule.

"I'm not going to kill you, you rich little fucker. But by the time I'm done with you, you'll wish I had."

Only now did Peter realize how prophetic those words had become. *What do I do now?* he wondered, sipping his Scotch, waiting for his mind to numb. His insides were hollow, his emotions dry as an autumn leaf. He rose and studied his reflection in the mirror by the couch. The bruises on his cheek and chin had turned from black and blue to a sickly yellow. They would be gone in a few days. How long before the internal abrasions healed? He had promised Jordan he would protect her. Promised Jennette that he would find Toby and the answers she sought. Raising his glass toward the mirror in a toast, he practiced a confident smile. The eyes that stared back at him were stark, the smile brittle. There was no antidote for the poison invading his soul. He had lost all faith in himself.

Drowsy from the Scotch and lack of sleep, he stretched out on the couch and let unconsciousness take command of his senses while he drifted gratefully into the kind of deep sleep he used to take for granted.

May 2, 1994: Menlo Park, California

PETER AWOKE SUDDENLY WITH THE SICKENING REALIZATION THAT he was not alone. He froze, his skin wet with sudden perspiration, and curled possum-like, wedged against the couch, feeling his heart thump in his throat. He thought about his gun, upstairs, out of reach in the nightstand. He should have kept it with him. A tall, dark figure walked silently around the room holding something. Peter saw a glint of metal, too large for a handgun, a rifle maybe?

The dark form moved a step closer to the couch. Then another. Stealthily, Peter reached out to retrieve the Lladro statuette from the lamp stand and held it ready. With the other hand, he flipped on the light. In the flash, he saw her standing over him.

"Jordan. What are you doing here?" he asked, voice trembling, trying to catch his breath.

"Trying not to wake you," she replied coldly. "I'm leaving you, Peter. There's a note." She jerked her head toward the dinette. The sax case in her hand glittered in the light. He'd mistaken the latches for a gun.

"Why? What's the matter?" He sat up and placed the statuette on the coffee table next to his empty glass, shaking the remnants of sleep and the residue of the booze from his head.

She narrowed her eyes. Her face darkened. The words poured out of her. "I saw you, you bastard. We all did, you two-timing son of a bitch. You said, 'I'm too tired to drive to the city.'" Her mocking, sarcastic tone, so reminiscent of Margaret's, pummeled him. He stared at her, speechless.

"Then, an hour later, I see you sitting in some coffee shop with this cute little blonde."

"She was a source, damn it," Peter snapped, finding his tongue.

"You hold hands with all your sources?" she jeered. "We saw you! Then, I had to endure a dinner full of 'I told you sos' from Josh and Taylor, who never wanted me to date you in the first place because they, like everybody else I talked to, knew your reputation. Knew that you used women like paper towels."

"You set the rules. You were the one who wanted a fling." He spoke neutrally to coat her anger, put out the fire in her eyes.

"You want to know why I wanted a fling? Because I didn't trust you. I didn't want to get hurt. I figured at least you'd be good in bed." Her mouth curled into a sneer. She gripped the sax case, her knuckles turning white.

Peter stared at her, biting his lip, feeling his anger build. If it was anyone else standing there, he would have turned his back and let her go. He'd done it a hundred times. But Jordan was his world. If she walked away, there was nothing left to fight for. So he stood there and took it; he let her rage at him until he could feel her anger waning. When she was out of breath, still berating him with her eyes, he spoke.

"You played for me, Jordan. You trusted me enough to offer me that part of yourself. It was special and I treasured it," he said softly. He wanted to reach for her, but it was too soon. She wasn't ready. The connection, if they still had one, was as fragile as a bubble about to pop.

"And you came back. I didn't come after you, you came back to me. If I'm the asshole you say I am, then why did you come back?"

Her face was frozen. She wasn't giving an inch. "I don't know. But now I'm sorry I did."

The jab sunk deep as a fishhook in his flesh. His half-smile ended as a grimace.

"You told me it was because I didn't make you choose between me and your music, and I never will," he paused and studied her face. Her eyes met his briefly. She was starting to listen. "Yes, I have been with a lot of women. But no one like you. And no one since I met you."

Her eyes flashed with renewed anger. "You're lying. Eric saw you with a girl at the club a couple of weeks ago. He told me on Saturday, and then, last night, after you told me you were staying home, I saw you with another woman. You really are a bastard." She turned to leave. He stood, moved quickly and blocked the door. She glared at him.

"At the club? We were just sharing a table. That place is always crowded. Eric knows I didn't go home with her. We had a drink afterward."

Jordan looked baffled and uncertain. "He didn't tell me that."

"I'm not surprised."

She stared past him, clutching the sax case, shifting her weight from one foot to the other. She'd be out the door any minute. He talked faster, to hold her in place.

"And Jennette Harris, the woman in San Francisco, is a source. She called me right after you did, and what she had to say was important enough that I had to meet her right away. I don't remember holding her hand. I might have. She was telling me how her cousin had murdered her brother. It was a hard story to tell and to hear. She told me all about Toby Eastman."

Jordan stood still. "Who's Toby Eastman?"

"The man who murdered Henry, Brian and Michael, and assaulted me."

Jordan's eyes widened. Her jaw dropped and her fingers opened. As the sax case landed with a thud at her feet, Peter's cell phone buzzed. Without removing his eyes from her face, he picked it up and answered. Tim's excited voice exploded in his ear. "Peter, how fast can you get to the lab? We've broken the code."

"On my way." He flipped the phone closed. "That was Tim. I've got to get over to the lab."

She gave him an almost imperceptible nod. He picked up his keys. "Will you be here when I get back?"

"I don't know."

May 2, 1994: Mountain View, California

Tim met him at the door of the lab, made a quick appraisal of Peter's stubbled chin and the rumpled clothes he'd slept in. "You look like hell, man."

"It's been a long night."

"This ought to cheer you up. We've got something big to show you."

They walked past a row of unoccupied workstations to the work tables in the center of the room. As Devon joined them at a table, Peter was reminded of his last visit, when Devon and Tim coerced him into giving up his Draco source. It still rankled, especially since Ravi had added nothing to their quest.

"Sure is quiet in here. I thought everyone would be in a mad rush to meet the deadline." In the hush of the lab, Peter's voice sounded harsh and raspy in his ears.

"David gave the team a few days off while we reconstructed the damaged code. They're all due back here tomorrow night," Devon said.

"Why do you guys do all your work at night? You vampires? Afraid of sunrise?" Peter asked, chuckling.

"No interruptions." Devon grinned back. "The marketing and sales guys are in the bar. The executive types are on a plane somewhere, and all the nosy reporters are tucked nighty-night in their beds."

"Okay, I get it." Peter smiled. "Can we talk about the disk?"

"You know about Trojan horse programs?" Devon asked.

Peter nodded. "Yeah. It's a fake program put into a computer system by an unauthorized user who wants to gain access to the network, a hacker usually. The Trojan horse pretends to be part of a valid login sequence so that when a user with a legitimate password logs on, the Trojan horse fakes them out, collects the password and, bingo, the hacker gets into the system."

"That's part of it. The key is the copy process. The Trojan horse picks up critical information and passes it on—"

"Wait a minute," Peter interjected. "Enough Technology 101, will you please tell me what was on that damn disk." His adrenaline running, he was drumming his fingers restlessly on the table.

"A Trojan horse with a pathway directly into a Unix server in San Francisco," Tim said. "A doorway right into MediaBuilders's Unix network as a Superuser, with full system access."

"The same MediaBuilders who hired Henry Rhodes as a security consultant," Peter noted.

"You got it," Tim confirmed.

"It's one of the most sophisticated Trojan horse programs I've ever seen," Devon added.

Peter nodded. "That's the connection we've been looking for, then. It ties all of them—Henry, Michael and Brian, and the disk— directly to Lockwood and Sapphire."

"Yeah. Everyone except Helen," Tim reminded him.

"She's the missing link, all right. Let's see if this Trojan horse can help us find her." Peter turned toward the monitor as Tim called up the program.

Tell Groucho it was for Helen. The phrase spun in Peter's head. "Tim, I know who Helen is."

Tim looked up from the keyboard. "Who?"

"Helen of Troy. I mean, that's why you call it a Trojan horse, right?"

Tim's face was bright with understanding. "Michael cracked the code, found the Trojan horse and tried to tell Brian what he'd found—cryptically, just like they did everything else."

"That's part of it. But Michael's message was bigger than that." Peter began pacing in a circle around the lab, tapping his pen against his lips.

"Well, this is a real bad-ass program, dude. Really bad."

"I'm sure it is, Tim. But think about it. Michael was dying. He knew Henry had been killed. Using his last breath, he didn't say, 'Tell my wife I love her,' he said, 'Tell Groucho it was for Helen.' That's got to mean something big, right?"

"Yes, but what?" Tim asked.

"Betrayal," Peter asserted, glancing at Devon, hoping he wouldn't have to smack Devon with the connection. When Devon didn't respond, he continued.

"The Trojan horse was the ultimate betrayal: a weapon of war masquerading as a gift of peace. Michael didn't just find the Trojan horse, he figured out who wrote it. He knew who betrayed Henry. Betrayed them all. And so do I."

"Who?" Tim and Devon asked in unison.

"Toby Eastman," Peter replied, watching Devon closely. "Toby Eastman isn't just a hacker. He's a killer."

"Not possible." Devon slapped his hand against the side of the monitor. "I can believe a lot of weird shit about Toby. But he would never hurt Henry. Not in a million years."

Devon turned toward Peter, expecting confirmation. His features sagged when all he read in Peter's face was denial. "Do you know what, in God's name, you're saying?"

Devon's agony rippled through him. Still reeling from his fight with Jordan and the emotional ripcord of the last few days, Peter took a moment to respond. "I'm sorry, Devon," he said, forcing himself to meet Devon's anguished eyes. "But I spent the afternoon with Toby's cousin. He's a killer all right. He started at fifteen."

Devon looked down at the floor and wiped a moist hand over his face. "Holy Mother," he whispered. "Why? In God's name, why?"

"He wrote the logic bomb because he wanted to destroy David Lockwood, a man he's hated for eighteen years. Remember, all of this started when David returned from exile right before CES and set out to be the conquering hero again," Peter explained.

"Also, we know the only company that benefits here is Draco. Toby must be working with someone at Draco, and he used the

Trojan horse to keep tabs on the competition so he'd know exactly when to set off the logic bomb. Without Sapphire, MediaBuilders is no threat to Draco. Toby gets paid to take revenge on Lockwood. It doesn't get much sweeter than that."

"But why send the disk to Henry and let him know about it?" Tim asked.

"I don't think he did," Peter said, slowly, brow furrowed in concentration. "What if Toby had a contact inside MediaBuilders who was supposed to get the disk—another Draco plant, maybe even someone on Henderson's acquisition team—and it came to Henry by mistake because he was head of security?"

Peter felt another piece of the jigsaw puzzle fall into place. "From Henry's perspective, it was just another game. Think about it. Henry gets a puzzle from Toby, his brightest and best. He sends the copies to the other boys to test their creativity. No wonder Henry's niece said he was laughing when he mailed those packages. But Toby doesn't know this at first. When he finds out he's exposed, he goes nuts and he starts killing to protect himself and whoever he's working for. First Henry, then Michael and Brian."

"I don't believe it. I knew him. Worked beside him for years," Devon said, shaking his head, but there was little confidence in his tone.

"It's the truth," Peter insisted. "He's already come after me once, and now he's got a good reason to come after the two of you. The proof is somewhere in this mass of data he's been killing to protect."

Peter looked at Devon, who seemed to be ignoring him in favor of concentrating on the monitor that held the markers of the Trojan horse. Tim stepped up beside Devon and studied the screen. The two men exchanged glances, coming to grips with their personal peril. When Devon turned to face Peter, his mouth was a thin, hard line. "Let's go get the son of a bitch."

Tim nodded his ascent, and Peter felt a surge of fraternal pride in the courage of his friend. Tim sat back down at the workstation, fingers poised over the keyboard. "Where do you want to start?"

"At the beginning. When Henry Rhodes became head of security."

Peter stepped up behind Tim. "I'm betting that the mastermind is Win Davis. Let's see what this Trojan horse can tell us."

"It's clever. The program is set up for disk mirroring, which means that all the information that passed through MediaBuilders' corporate communications network was recorded in a duplicate, locked file, a separate server for Eastman, or whoever, to peruse at will," Tim explained, pointing to the screen. "We've downloaded emails, contracts, even copies of the weekly video links between London and San Francisco. The file's huge, six gigs of data so far, the equivalent of a small library, and we're just getting started."

"You should know that we only broke the first part of the code. There's a whole lot more we still don't have a handle on," Devon said.

"Really?" Peter's shoulders slumped. *One step forward, two steps back*, he thought. Devon shot him a commiserating look. "You two start on this. I'll dive into the rest of the code."

Tim fiddled with the keyboard while Peter studied the screen. The more he looked, the less he saw. "Where's the pattern, Tim? There's got to be a pattern."

Tim shrugged. "With code it's usually where the data's the most complex.""Where's that here?"

"Around the acquisitions."

"Of course." Peter's face lit up with sudden clarity. *It's so obvious. Why haven't I seen it before?* "Tim, can you get me everything that the MediaBuilders acquisition committee has done since December first and print it?"

"You sure, Peter? That's gonna take hours."

"You get me the haystack. I think I know where to find the needle."

28

May 2, 1994: Menlo Park, California

THE FIRST PLACE PETER LOOKED WHEN HE ENTERED THE townhouse was in the corner by the fireplace. Her sax case was gone. As he stood staring at the empty corner, the tears he'd been barricading for so long broke loose and traversed his cheeks. The first light of morning streamed under the blinds turning the living room from night to day. He drew a deep breath to relieve the pressure in his chest, compose himself and allow the tears to recede. Rubbing his hand across his damp face, he dropped Tim's printouts on the dinette and trudged upstairs to get some sleep.

In the bedroom doorway, he tripped over an errant shoe and kicked it out of the way. It was one of her high heels. Her note had said she'd send someone for her stuff. He tossed his shirt over a chair. As he flipped on the lamp, he saw her lying facedown on the bed, her minty-green floral sheath dress bunched up around her hips, arms flung out in opposite directions. She was so still that he bent down to feel for a pulse. As he brushed her cheek, she gave a small sigh. Relief sidelined him. He sat down beside her and stroked her arm.

"Jordan."

She lifted her head, shaking tangled strands of hair from her face as she turned toward him. "I wanted to wait up, but I guess I fell asleep. Are you okay?" she asked, sitting up, taking in his haggard, tear-streaked face.

"I am now." He grinned, brushing the back of his hand against his face. "You stayed."

"There was more to say."

"Yes, there is." He placed his hands on her shoulders. "I thought I lost you tonight. And I realized I can lose everything else in the world, but what I can't lose is you."

"What are you saying?" she asked, her body tense beneath the tips of his fingers.

He swallowed hard and gave his tongue time to find the words. "I lo... lo…" He stuttered and gained confidence: "I love you. I need you. I can't imagine my world without you in it."

"Do you mean that? Or is this just more words? You're awfully good with words, Peter. That much I do know."

"I mean it." He reached for her, the urge to hold her overpowering.

Jordan moved away, burying her face in her hands. "Since I came back, I've been so frightened. Frightened for you. For me. For us. I told myself to believe in you. To trust you. Then, when I saw you with that woman yesterday, holding hands, I felt like such a fool. Like I was just another trinket you could wear around. Like this."

She clutched the saxophone necklace at her throat and pulled. A red mark started to form on her neck from the pressure. He took her hands, felt the tremor in her fingers. She was hunched over, breathing rapidly. He put his arm around her and hugged her tight. "I never cheated on you, Jordan, and I never will."

"Don't make promises you can't keep."

"I'm not. If you want to run, Jordan, then we'll run. We'll go anywhere you say. We can leave tonight."

She gave him a long look, scrutinizing every muscle in his face. He felt her trying to strip away the layers, really see him, to convince herself that she could trust him. He'd put his fate in her hands and all he could do was wait for her judgment. Across the room, his cell phone buzzed in his jacket pocket. He tightened his hold on her waist.

"You said, 'You can't hide in cyberspace.' Do you really believe that?" she asked.

"Yes. I do."

"Then we have to stay, don't we? Stay and fight." She offered him a tiny, unsteady smile.

"I love you." He planted a kiss on her forehead. Her smile brightened.

"I don't think I'll ever get tired of hearing you say that." She leaned back against the pillows and brought him with her.

"Good," he whispered nestling next to her. "Because I'm not going to stop saying it."

May 2, 1994: Los Gatos, California

At six o'clock that evening, Peter swung into Charlie Sheffield's driveway, parked and rang the bell. Charlie opened the door with his customary jocularity. Peter entered cautiously, bracing himself for the welcoming chaos of Charlie's wife, three kids and two German shepherds. The quiet that greeted him was eerie.

"Where's the gang?" he asked.

"Family's at the movies. Dogs are in the back. I pulled everything on the acquisitions I did for MediaBuilders," Charlie explained as they walked into his masculine hideaway.

A dedicated Anglophile, Charlie had striven for the look and feel of a nineteenth-century men's club. To Peter the dark wood paneling, black leather sofa and chairs, and deep-piled red carpet were stifling, more oppressive than inviting.

"How ya feeling?" Charlie asked, pouring them each a sherry.

"Coming along. I'll be even better when we nail these guys." Peter eased himself into one chair while Charlie settled back behind his desk.

"Same here. Let's get down to it." Charlie took a sip of sherry and pushed the glass aside.

Peter dumped the contents of a large paper bag on the desk.

"Officially, I know nothing about this." Charlie eyed Peter.

"Even unofficially."

Charlie turned on his computer and started shifting through the paperwork. "What's your theory?"

"MediaBuilders, or I should say Victor Henderson, had a very specific list of acquisition targets, companies that would set up MediaBuilders for a big payoff on the information highway."

"That much I know," Charlie snorted. "I did those deals, remember?"

"I remember. Let's start with Sapphire. The original price tag, according to what I got from Frank, was 1.2 billion dollars. But when the deal was announced, it was worth 2.2 billion—nearly double the price. Granted, we think Lockwood hid the code problems from them. Still, does that make any sense to you?"

"Not much. But you know how it goes. A couple captains of industry get together and tap class rings on the table-top and decide to do a deal. They shake hands and the architects move it. People like Frank and me, we frame the deal. The tangibles—real estate, capital equipment, furniture—they're a no-brainer. The fun starts with the intangibles. How do you price R&D? A customer base? Can the new company retain it? Maybe? Maybe not. Realistically, it's all a SWAG."

"Sweet wild-ass guess," Peter agreed.

"It's a crapshoot in any business. But with this new Internet technology, it's nearly impossible. The vision of the entrepreneur, the skill of the engineering team, can make you or break you. Is it the next big thing or a fart in the wind? Knowing the difference, that's the magic."

Charlie picked up a sheet of paper and waved it at Peter. "You take this Delta Software acquisition. That was easy pickings. The executives were hungrier than hell to deal and I got a great price. But it looks like I didn't have the whole story there. They were holding out." Charlie shrugged. "Hell, it happens. Even to me. Not often, but it does."

"What, tell me."

"See for yourself. Attached to the contract is a memo from

Henderson explaining that the company has the hottest multimedia game on the market today and another blockbuster on the way from the same team, led by this boy genius Brian Tucker. So it just goes to show—"

"Hold it. Time out. Did you say Brian Tucker?" Peter felt his stomach twist. "What's the date on that memo?"

"January twentieth."

"No way, Charlie. I was chasing Tucker. You asked me to check him out, remember? He'd left the company by that time. They issued a press release."

"It's weird," Charlie agreed, massaging his chin. "But everybody gets caught with their pants down once in a while. The heavy action starts, it's auction fever. You remember that famous pissing match between Davis and Blaylock when they both put their dicks in play, and Blaylock ends up with a studio that costs him, what? About six hundred million more than it should have."

"Something like that. What about the other companies? Any other surprises?"

"I gotta take a closer look."

Peter finished the last of the sherry and stood. He'd held the urge for a cigarette at bay as long as he could. "I'm going to grab a smoke."

"Yeah, okay," Charlie mumbled, concentrating on the computer screen.

Peter stood on the brick patio, pulled a cigarette from his pack and lit it. Puffing lightly, blowing the smoke through flared nostrils, he focused on Victor Henderson. He'd seen too much of the shrewd, savvy Henderson to believe that he was being routinely hoodwinked into paying too much for these tiny Internet companies, no matter how much he wanted to be king of the inforoad. Then there was Margaret. It was her job to vet these companies. Perform the due diligence. Validate the purchase. Even if Henderson was drinking the Kool-aid, Peter was damn sure Margaret wasn't.

What is going on here? he asked himself for the hundredth time. He extinguished the cigarette and headed back inside looking for answers. "Find anything?"

"Not yet," Charlie grunted.

"Maybe I can help. This thing have a modem on it?" Peter pointed to the computer.

"Of course."

Peter sat down and began typing the series of commands that Tim had given him to invoke the Trojan horse program. The computer whirred and coughed up a query menu. Peter typed another sequence.

"What are you doing?"

"Don't ask."

"I want to know."

Peter pursed his lips, finished the sequence and sat back, satisfied. "I just requested all of Henderson's confidential emails. That ought to tell us something."

"I don't think I like this." Charlie stepped back as if to disassociate himself from Peter's inquiry, but curiosity got the better of him as the correspondence list blinked onto the screen. Peter and Charlie hunched forward and started reading emails. At the top of the list were the deals Henderson had done with the information highway acquisitions team.

"Let's dig a little deeper." Peter typed another series of commands. "Follow the money."

"Whaddya got?" Charlie barked, as the screen filled with numbers.

"Henderson was sure moving a hell of a lot of money around. Look at all these wire transfers."

"We needed a big war chest. We had a lot of balls in the air," Charlie explained.

"Yeah," Peter muttered, scanning the deal flow. "Like Delta Software, the company that had lost its star programmer; and HotHub, months behind in development. What about PointNClick? Sure, the ecommerce software seems to be working, but the customers they were claiming are phantom. Then there's Sapphire. The key algorithm destroyed on the eve of the big purchase."

"What is this?" Charlie scowled in Peter's direction.

Peter turned toward him. "Look, all the companies Henderson bought had one thing in common. They were all fatally flawed. And to top it off, he overpaid for them. All these valuations were bloated to justify incredibly high prices."

Peter and Charlie stared at the screen. Every one of the valuations had the same signature: Margaret Ellis, corporate counsel, Ellis, Blackwell and Barnes. Charlie sent an uneasy glance in Peter's direction.

Peter ignored Charlie's unspoken question as they watched the system cough up another set of archived emails. "Hey, what's this one? No recipient, no subject line. Let's take a look."

Peter clicked and the email flickered in their faces. For a moment, neither man breathed.

May 2, 1994: Menlo Park, California

"Did you find the needle?" Jordan asked as he entered the bedroom. She put her book aside, and looked up him. He undressed and lay down beside her.

"We did. Victor Henderson. He was working for Win Davis."

Jordan sat upright. "Seriously?"

"Yeah. He was bleeding MediaBuilders dry with bad acquisitions bought at stratospheric prices. Driving MediaBuilders straight into bankruptcy. It was clever, though; it could have taken years to unravel, and by that time Henderson would have disappeared."

"Why? I thought he was Blaylock's heir apparent."

"Greed, I'm guessing. We found several offshore bank accounts, each one with millions in it. Looks like, either Davis was paying Henderson handsomely for his work, or he was taking a cut off the top. Maybe both. He was moving money around like he was playing Three-card Monte."

Peter shrugged. "Either way, he set up Blaylock and used Charlie as a patsy. You should have seen the look on Charlie's face when he realized how badly Henderson screwed him. I could nail Henderson for that alone."

"What about Toby Eastman?"

"He was the hacker Henderson hired to help him set up the acquisitions for Draco, we know that from the Trojan horse. But my gut tells me his real focus was getting Lockwood. He nursed that grudge for eighteen years, and when he saw his chance, he took it. MediaBuilders and Draco were just the means to an end."

Jordan settled back down beside him. "But why kill Henry and his boys and come after you?" Her fingers lightly brushed the bruises on his side. He offered her a confident smile. He was healing, healing faster because she was there.

He took her fingers and kissed them. "The Trojan horse on the disk would expose him, and we got in the way. Devon's working on breaking the rest of the code. We'll have more answers soon."

She settled deeper into the pillows. Her blue silk robe flowed out around her. She was naked underneath. To his chagrin, Peter realized he wasn't feeling it. Jordan lay beside him, watching him.

"What about Margaret?" she asked finally.

It would come down to Margaret. He wore blinkers when it came to Margaret. Self-protection, whether through obeying or avoiding her, was his lifelong survival strategy. Whenever he'd shown the slightest backbone with her, she retaliated with an aggressiveness meant to emasculate; invariably, she had succeeded. So far, he had refused to look at her role in the conspiracy and betrayal. Now that Jordan had laid it out there, he had no choice.

He sighed and turned toward her. "That's the big question. Did she know? And if so, how much?"

"She had to know. It was her job to validate the shareholder value and profitability of those companies, right? M&A validations and contracts is the firm's specialty, isn't it?" Jordan asked. Peter nodded.

"Then how could she not know? Unless she sucks at due diligence?" Jordan's voice held frustration. At him, he supposed, for being so obtuse.

"No. She's brilliant at it."

"Well, then?"

He couldn't argue with Jordan's logic. Henderson could fool

Charlie. He was just the scout. But Margaret would have had all the contracts, all the details. He'd seen her signature on all the bloated valuations. She would have done independent verifications of the valuations with her accountants. It was her fiduciary responsibility. Jordan was right, he thought with painful clarity.

"She had to be in on it," he admitted.

"But why? Money?"

"Money doesn't drive her. She stands to inherit plenty from the family. Not money," he repeated. "Power."

It hit him hard, like one of the slaps Margaret was so fond of delivering. "She'll never be managing partner," he said, as the implication sunk in.

Jordan understood immediately. "The line of succession."

"The managing partner has always been an Ellis—we own the controlling shares—and always a man. I could have been managing partner, but she couldn't."

"But they could change the rules, couldn't they? I would think your father would want that."

"He would. But changing that rule would require a unanimous vote of the partners, and that's not going to happen."

"Why?"

He turned on his side, balanced himself on one elbow. "Barnes would go along. His children aren't lawyers. But Blackwell has two sons in the firm. With Margaret ruled out, one of his sons is next in line."

Oh God, he thought. Given that reality, Margaret was capable of anything, even destroying the family firm. Head flopping down on the pillows, his joints tightened. He tasted acid as the moisture in his mouth evaporated.

Jordan scanned his face as if she could feel his fear. "What are you going to do?"

He slipped away from her then. Slipped back in time, to when he got his first real taste of Margaret's venomous hatred.

The bathroom floor was cold under his bare bottom. He sat doubled over, his spine pressed against the porcelain tub, trying not to cry, trying not to pee even though he felt like he was ready to explode. The water sloshed inside his empty stomach. It hurt to move. She'd forced him to drink a full pitcher of water and ordered him to hold it until she came back. eyes fixed on the bathroom door, he ached for release. He didn't know how long she'd been gone. What does a four-year-old know about time?

Her hand felt so hot on his clammy flesh that he was certain it would leave an imprint. "Peter, where are you?"

It took him a minute to move, to shake off the nightmare memory and lubricate his jaws enough to speak. "I'm okay."

Jordan's face was ashen. She wet her lips as if she too was struggling to speak. "What did she do to you?"

He looked away from her. "Nothing."

"I don't believe that."

"It's not important." He tried for a smile, couldn't quite pull it off. "Sibling rivalry, typical family stuff."

"I don't know who you're trying to fool, me or yourself. But it's not working. Peter, you asked me to trust you. You need to trust me too."

He pulled her close. "Why does this matter so much to you? We have a future, why worry about the past? Especially the ancient past?"

She laid her head on his shoulder, ran her hands across his chest. "Because those memories and experiences are what make you you, and to really know you…" She paused. "Don't hide from me. I love you. I need to know who you are."

Her eyes drifted over him, her energy caring, warm and comforting. It set off alarms inside him. The urge for secrecy battled his need for her, the voice in his head growing more insistent as the seconds ticked by, telling him that he was making the same mistake with Jordan that he had made with Jessica, and that he would find the cost of this wrong choice not just irreparable but fatal.

He snuggled against her and spoke in a low, soft voice, directly into her ear. "When I was four, I was playing ball inside the house and I broke a vase, a very expensive vase. Margaret caught me, and she really laid into me. She yelled at me all the time, but this time was different. She was in such a rage. She slapped me hard. I started to cry and she slapped me again and..." He paused. The pounding in his chest made it difficult to hear or speak. "I peed in my pants."

"Little boys do that," Jordan said softly.

"I know. But she went ballistic. She dragged me upstairs and yanked all my clothes off and threw me in the bathroom and told me I would stay there till I learned to use the toilet properly. Then she locked the door and left."

"Where were your parents?"

"On a trip. Megan was at summer camp. It was just me and Margaret."

Peter slipped away again. He heard his own voice as an echo of his mind, talking aloud, telling her things he didn't want her to know.

There was nothing to do in the bathroom but wait for her. He was afraid to touch anything. She was already so angry. He sat in the corner, used the toilet when he had to. He knew what to do. He would show her when she came back. Light faded. His tummy ached. He was hungry. It should be time for dinner. She'd come soon. It was so dark out. The nightlight gave off a faint glow. He was still hungry. Now he was sleepy, too. He pulled the towels off the rack, made a bundle, lay down on them and fell asleep. The next morning he heard footsteps in the hall. She unlocked the door and walked in. She stood over him, pulled him up by his ears and scowled into his face.

"Have you learned your lesson yet? Show me." Her words spat at him. She took him by the shoulders and turned him around to face the toilet. "You better do it right."

He started to shake, felt the warm urine run down his leg.

"You're disgusting." She shoved him away. He slipped on the wet floor and fell. She dragged him across the floor. "Sit in it," she said, and he did.

Picking up the towels, she walked out again, locking the door behind her. He cried until the tears refused to come. Then he curled up on the bathroom rug and fell asleep. It was night when she came back. Flipping on the light, she walked into the room and shook him awake.

Pulling him to his feet, she pointed him at the toilet again. "Do it now."

He had to go. His bladder was bursting, but when he tried to go, nothing came. She stood over him, frowning, foot tapping. He couldn't do it with her watching. She grabbed his little pecker and pulled. "This isn't much use to you, is it?"

At her touch, he let loose. The spray hit her face, her clothes. She screamed and clutched him in a viselike grip. His body stiffened. She lowered the toilet lid and pressed his face against it, and, taking the shower brush, she spanked him until his bottom turned scarlet and welts began to rise. And then she was gone again.

He didn't cry this time. He'd learned it wouldn't help. He sat back on the floor and leaned against the tub. The cool tiles felt good on his raw bottom. He rubbed his sore tummy. So hungry. He picked up a bar of soap and licked it, but it tasted terrible. She told him she would let him out if he did it right. So he practiced. Drank water—it filled his empty tummy—and practiced some more.

She was back in the morning. "I'm giving you one more chance," she said. She held out a large pitcher of water and a glass. "Drink this. All of it."

Every time he finished a glass, she handed him another one until the pitcher was empty.

"Hold it till I come back and then I'm going to give you a test. If one drop goes where it shouldn't, you'll be in here a long time."

"Oh, baby." Jordan was stroking his moist face. The heat of her body against his thawed him. He felt less like a cadaver. "What happened?" she asked.

"I passed her test." He looked at her, saw the compassion in her eyes.

"What did she do then?"

"Stormed out. But she left the door open. I went into my room and put some clothes on, and went down to the kitchen. Annie, our housekeeper, was there. She asked me if I was hungry and I said yes. She sat me on a chair and gave me some butcher paper and crayons to play with. Then she fixed me tomato soup and grilled cheese. It's still my favorite comfort food." He gave her a wan smile.

"Where was this Annie when all this was going on?"

"Annie didn't live in. I don't know what Margaret told her, but it didn't matter. Nobody crosses Margaret. Especially the help."

"She's a monster," Jordan declared. "I want to drive a stake through her heart."

"My warrior princess." Peter chuckled, running his fingers through her hair.

"Or maybe I'll put a silver bullet through her brain. She's evil."

Peter kissed her ear, drawing strength from her vitality and courage. "I know, that's why I've always just tried to stay out of her way."

"That won't work this time, will it?"

"No. It won't." A spasm jolted his body. His skin prickled. That one spoken memory unlocked so many others he couldn't bear to voice. Jordan's nails pierced his arm. "Stay with me."

"I'm trying to," he murmured, fighting for lucidity.

Jordan pressed the length of her body against his side. Her toes stroked the inside of his calf. "Let me take care of you."

"You are, sweetheart."

"Let me take care of you now." She kissed his torso, her lips soft and fresh against his tight skin.

"I don't know if I can—"

She filled his mouth with hers. Reaching down, she fondled him. His body responded faster than he thought was possible. Smiling, she slipped herself around him. Drawing him inside, she stretched her body taut above him so he could enjoy the fullness of her breasts, the hollow suppleness of her stomach. She was so beautiful. His hands shook as he touched her nipples, and came to rest on her hips. He couldn't take his eyes off of her. She rocked him, gently at first, then faster, sucking him more fully within her folds. He dove deep inside her, felt her shudder. Heard her soft cry. And in his own release, he found restoration.

29

May 3, 1994: Mountain View, California

ACTIVITY IN THE LAB WAS FRANTIC WHEN PETER ARRIVED Tuesday evening. Every workstation was humming, the keyboards clicking in a syncopated rhythm. It reminded Peter of the *Tribune's* production room an hour before deadline. Tim and a young Asian woman were studying a monitor intensely. David Lockwood and Alok Gupta, his engineering manager, stood in the far corner, backs bent over the printouts from a preliminary test run. Only Devon saw Peter cross the room. He looked up from his printouts as Peter walked up beside him.

"You're not going to like it. Victor Henderson was secretly working for Draco. He was Eastman's inside contact. He wanted to get control of Sapphire so he could kill it."

"Fucking hell," Devon exploded. He turned to the center of the lab. "David, Tim. Join us, please."

Tim stopped his conversation with his colleague and hurried over. Lockwood held up his hand and turned back to Alok.

"It gets better." Peter pulled a coil of papers from his pocket. "This just came off the business wire."

Tomorrow. Everything Changes.
*MediaBuilders Invites You to Join Us as We Re-Route the
Information Highway.*
  Enjoy the Ride at the Empire Hotel, New York City

"Press conference," Peter responded to Devon's quizzical look. "Impromptu, hastily-scheduled press conference tomorrow at ten a.m."

Peter tossed the fax on the worktable. "That always means big news."

"What news?" Tim asked.

"Nobody knows for sure. But word on the street is it's to seal the deal on Sapphire." Peter paused and chuckled. "The big photo op: David and Victor, gripping and grinning for the camera."

"When hell freezes over." David Lockwood stepped into their tight circle.

"David, this is Peter Ellis. The reporter I told you about," Devon said.

"We've met." David Lockwood's intense brown eyes focused on Peter like high beams. They stood for a moment, locked eye to eye. Then Lockwood stuck out his hand. Turning to Devon, he added, "He got the holograms. Nobody else did."

"Doesn't surprise me." Devon gave Peter a respectful nod.

"Since we know what they aren't doing, can we find out what they are announcing?" Peter turned to Devon, one eyebrow raised.

Devon smiled. "Through the looking glass. One more time." Turning back to the keyboard, he invoked the Trojan horse. "What are we looking for?"

"Media kit. Press release. Agenda, that sort of thing."

Peter felt Lockwood's eyes on him as the monitor offered up document after document filled with minutiae. Devon stroked the keys like a virtuoso until he hit the right note.

For Immediate Release
MediaBuilders to License Draco Universal
May 4, 1994, New York City — MediaBuilders and Draco Communications Join Forces to Make Information Highway Dream a Reality. In a technology licensing partnership that will change the face...

"What?" Devon reacted first, throwing his hands in the air. "Not possible. All I heard at Draco was 'get MediaBuilders. If you do nothing else, get MediaBuilders.'"

Peter ignored Devon and scanned the release. It read like a typical joint venture. No blood dripping off the page. *Devon was right,* he thought, *it doesn't make sense, unless...*

"It's brilliant," Peter said. "Henderson and Davis do a legit deal and they can cover everything else up. MediaBuilders is still bleeding red ink from the bad buys, and a year from now, when the company can't meet its information highway promises, Win Davis flies in like Superman and saves the day. Blaylock and the board will be forced to sell. Davis will protect Henderson. Absolutely brilliant."

"What about Sapphire?" Tim asked.

Peter grinned. "That's the sixty-four thousand-dollar question, Tim. The one every reporter in that room will be asking. And there's only one answer that Henderson can give that will satisfy the media and protect him and Davis."

"Which is?" Lockwood asked, his tone flinty.

Peter glanced his way. Lockwood's face was impassive. No doubt he knew where this was going. Peter might as well spell it out.

"Sapphire was a doomed product. If Henderson couldn't kill Sapphire in reality, he can in perception and—"

"No need to finish that sentence," Devon interjected.

"What do we do now?" Tim asked.

"Show them what Sapphire can really do. Expose Henderson for the traitor he is, in New York, before the media and the world." Peter looked at each of them in turn.

"David." Peter looked him straight in the eye. "We have to go to

New York, and we have to take Sapphire with us. Without Sapphire, Henderson can tell the press any story he wants and they'll believe him."

David glanced at Devon, who said, "I don't know, David. That only gives us three hours to compile and compress everything. The code's still unstable. I'm not sure—"

David brushed his hand across Devon's shoulder. "C'mon, Devon. You're the one that likes to push the envelope. Never needed it more than we do now."

Devon's eyes lit up with merriment. "We always did it in the old days. About time we did it again."

He turned to Peter. "Debbie's over here." Devon pointed toward the far end of the room, where the young Asian woman Peter had noticed earlier sat looking intently at her screen. Her good luck charm, a Roger Rabbit puppet, greeted them from the top of the monitor.

Devon tapped her on the shoulder. "Debbie, this is Peter Ellis. He needs to put together a demo and David volunteered you."

Debbie stopped typing. She leaned forward her short bangs falling into her eyes. "Hi," she said to Peter with a friendly smile. "Grab a chair and tell me what you need."

"We're putting together a dog and pony for a big New York hotshot who's looking to make an investment in Sapphire."

"Marketing demo. No problem. I've done tons of them."

"Great. How fast can you do this?" Peter asked.

"That depends. The video compression-decompression sequence is the most complicated. We need to convert video signals to data, then shrink the files so they fit on the memory card."

She tapped at her keyboard, glanced at the clock and said: "With everything you want included, this will take about three hours to complete."

Tim walked over. "David's admin just booked us on United Flight 493. It leaves SFO at 11:35 p.m."

Peter checked his watch: eight o'clock. They had to be at the airport by ten-thirty or risk missing the flight. "We got two," he said, turning back to Debbie.

She gave him an exasperated look. "I can't rush this process. I have to complete the whole cycle correctly, step by step, or we could lose everything and have to start over."

"So what do we have to do to get it done?"

"First we convert the video frequencies to data the computer can understand. Second, we reduce the size of the data files. Finally, we reverse the entire process so the video appears fresh and clean on the computer monitor. I'll give you the video first, then we'll lay down the audio, okay?"

"Yeah. Just so it works."

She looked up at him. "This isn't true Internet streaming, you understand. It's all self-contained on the memory card. But it's safer this way. Most networks aren't ready to handle what Sapphire can really do yet."

"But this will get it done, right?"

She nodded, pushing her bangs off her forehead with a quick, habitual movement. "Yes. Sapphire's algorithm is the best I've ever seen. If any system can meet your deadline, it's Sapphire."

She returned to the keyboard, her typing accelerated. The screen flicked rapidly from one picture to the next. Peter forced himself to trust her confidence and hoped that it was based on something more than loyalty to David Lockwood.

Debbie was about to finalize the video sequence when Alok stepped up behind them. "How are you coming on the video, Debbie?"

"Not so good."

"What's the problem?"

"It's the DCT. It's not converting the image to the correct frequencies. All I get is haze." She looked up at Alok. "I can't even see the outline of the pictures."

"Shit." Alok leaned over, peering at her screen.

"What's wrong?" Peter took a quick peek at the clock. One hour. They only had one hour.

"The picture's muddy as hell. The conversion is off." Alok stared at the screen.

Adrenaline kicked in, a useless surge of energy. All Peter could do was stand by and watch the clock while Alok and Debbie tried to solve the problem. Its hands seemed to be moving faster with every revolution.

"Go up a step. Read everything into the Q-tables. Then reverse," Alok said.

"Not working. No change."

"Damn. Start over. Rescale the image."

"Okay," she said, fingers flying over the keyboard. "Got the image rescaled."

"Recompute the transformations."

Standing behind them, Peter shuffled from one foot to the other. *Hurry, please hurry.* Debbie punched a few more keys and a crisp, clear video image of Henderson appeared before them. Peter breathed a sigh of relief. Debbie looked up at him with a smile. Alok gave her a pat on the back.

Then her screen went black.

"It's gone."

Alok grabbed the keyboard, trying different sequences. Debbie stood up, her face desolate as she turned to Peter.

"Devon, we've got a problem," Alok called out.

Devon, David and Tim converged on the workstation. Devon bumped Alok off the keyboard and took control. He pulled up the algorithm and studied each code string. Two minutes later, he gave them the bad news.

"It's the quantization matrix." David, Tim and Alok exchanged grim looks.

"What does that mean?" Peter looked from one discouraged face to the next.

"That's the part of the code that decides what video elements are most important. It makes the code faster and easier to compress. When it goes bad it distorts the picture. Or, as in this case, it completely eliminates the information in some frequency components of the picture," Devon explained. "It'll take hours to fix it."

"We don't have hours. We only have forty-five minutes to get on that plane," Peter said.

"You'll have to go without video," Alok replied.

"We can't. That's our whole case. Without video—"

"Sapphire's a laughingstock," David said tersely. "That's not going to happen."

"So what do we do now?" Peter asked, deflated.

"Simple." David turned and faced the group. "We fix the code tonight and we stream the video from here tomorrow morning. Real-time video over the Internet. Sapphire unfiltered. Doing what only Sapphire can do."

"At the press conference in New York? Live?" Tim asked cautiously.

"With a preproduction unit," Alok added.

"And inherently unstable code," Devon affirmed.

David took them all in with one penetrating sweep of his eyes. Peter felt the full force of his energy.

"Anyone here have a problem with that?" David asked.

May 3, 1994: San Francisco, California

THE UNITED AIRLINES 767 JET TAXIED DOWN THE RUNWAY AND lifted gracefully into the air, leaving land and San Francisco International Airport behind. Peter relaxed against the wide leather seats in the first class cabin, stretched and took a taste of the Scotch the flight attendant placed in front of him. Three rows ahead of Peter, in the first row of first class, David Lockwood sipped a club soda and tapped restlessly on his laptop.

"Have a drink, Tim. You look like you need it," Peter advised Tim, seated to his left.

Tim nodded. He accepted a glass of champagne from the flight attendant. The Sapphire set-top box was tucked securely under his seat.

"Is this Internet streaming video thing going to work?"

"Devon's the best there is. If anyone can do it, he can."

Peter chose to ignore Tim's non-answer. The truth was, they wouldn't know if it was going to work until they were live in front of the international press corps—and they'd only get one shot. He could feel Tim's tension in the edgy way he leafed through the airline magazine without stopping to read a line. Peter took another small sip of Scotch and surveyed the cabin. A cute blonde stewardess was bending over, handing a drink to a young Wall Street stud in an Armani suit. Peter's eyes studied her form, drifting lazily up from her well-toned calves to her muscled thighs and her firm, pear-shaped ass. She stood up and caught his eye with a smile; and in that smile he saw a hint of the kind of invitation he no longer wanted to receive. *You idiot*, he chided himself, looking away.

"Tim, is it cheating if you look?"

Tim stopped reading and studied him. "That's an odd question for you to be asking."

Peter shrugged. "Just curious. Is it?"

"Depends."

"On what?"

"What you're planning to do about it."

Peter glanced in the stew's direction again. "Absolutely nothing."

Tim tossed aside the magazine. "What's up with you, man?"

"I'm thinking about asking Jordan to marry me."

"Wise decision."

"You really think so?" Peter's voice was rocky. It was a step he never imagined he would take with anyone.

"I said that before she left for Germany."

The stewardess stopped by his seat and picked up his empty Scotch glass. "Want another?"

He shook his head. She turned and headed back up the aisle. He watched her leave. "How do you make it last, really last?"

Tim shrugged. "You commit. And then you work it day by day."

Peter looked over Tim's head and out at the night sky. "My father's unfaithful. He's always had at least one mistress, maybe more. Who knows? He has offices all over the world."

"You're not your father."

"I've got his genes, don't I? I've always treated women like... like father, like son, right?" Peter's voice shrank. "All he ever wanted was a mirror to show his greatness to the world. Maybe, if I'd been willing to be a toady..."

"That's not who you are."

"I couldn't make him happy, no matter how hard I tried. What if I can't make her happy either?" Peter looked at Tim in earnest appeal. "What's the secret Tim? You and Marie seem to have it."

Tim studied his face. "Honestly? I'd have to say: Love. Trust. Faith."

"In each other."

"In more than each other."

Peter sighed. "Is this going to be a God talk?"

"It doesn't have to be. But if you want me to say that Marie and I could make it without God in the center holding us together, I'd be lying to you."

"This is about Marie, isn't it? Making her happy? I get that. We all do that."

Tim shrugged. "It started that way, I guess. Marie had a confidence about herself and her place in the world that I didn't have, and that I wanted. So, I went to church with her. The music was good, but the rest of it seemed pretty silly: All these people around me with their hands in the air and these weird looks on their faces."

Peter chuckled. Tim nodded, smiling. His face turned serious. "But then, Peter, I started listening. Not to the preacher. To the people around me. I started seeing the way they treated each other with love and respect, and a deep well of caring." Tim paused. "And my life was in crisis."

"Crisis? You?" Peter laughed.

Tim's brow furrowed. "Yeah, me. I'd just left Sun and I thought I'd retire from there. Here I was in a committed relationship for the first time in my life, and I had no idea how to handle that one. But, like you, I knew I wanted it to work. I just wasn't sure how. I was pretty scared."

Peter leaned forward.

"So, I started meeting with our Pastor Mark. I asked him the same question you asked me. I knew I was falling in love with Marie, but would it last?"

"What did he say?"

"He said, 'You can't fully love until you know how fully you are loved."'"

"What's that supposed to mean?"

"He asked me if I knew how much God loved me. He pointed me to John 3:16, and what Jesus, himself, said: 'For God so loved the world, that He gave His only begotten Son, so that whoever believes in Him shall not perish, but have eternal life.' God the Father sent his Son to die for us. For me."

"For some fathers, that wouldn't be such a sacrifice." Peter murmured into his Scotch glass.

Tim's back rested against the window frame. Behind him the night sky looked frigid and harsh. Tim's face held such deep compassion and understanding that Peter dropped his eyes. A white thread on the carpet held him entranced. The plane bounced; the fasten seat belt coming on. Peter automatically tightened the strap across his waist.

"The love and support you never got from your earthly father you can get from your heavenly one," Tim said gently.

"My father banished me, not just financially but completely. That night, when he disinherited me, he told me I was the biggest mistake of his life." Peter swirled the Scotch watching the tawny liquid run down the sides of the glass. He put it down on the tray and pushed it away.

"God can heal you, Peter, of everything you've been through. If you let him." Tim paused, drew a deep breath, and continued in a flat voice.

"I don't know what really happened to you that night in the hills. Knowing you, I doubt you'll ever tell me or anyone else. What I do know is this. You faced down pure evil that night. I've seen you mad as hell, I've seen you blind drunk, but I've never seen you look like you did that night. Those dead eyes. Whatever else Eastman did, he took a piece of your soul. Jesus is the only one who can restore it. As bad as it was, Jesus was there, protecting you. Otherwise I'm sure you'd be dead."

Peter closed his eyes and leaned against the seat for reassurance, remembering his last words as he lost consciousness that night. He had called out for God. It was a cultural reflex, he told himself. There wasn't anyone there who was really listening, was there?

He opened his eyes and looked over at Tim. Tim had put on his headset. The movie credits were rolling. He could put a headset on too, and escape this conversation. He knew where Tim stood. What more was there to say?

Peter took a few nuts out of the white bowl on the tray beside him, caught the stew's eye and ordered a refill on his Scotch. The stew placed a second glass of Scotch down. Peter took a grateful sip, and then tapped Tim on the shoulder. Tim removed the headset and turned toward him.

"Talk to me, Tim. I'm willing to listen."

Tim studied Peter for a minute and leaned toward him, hands folded on his lap. Peter got the feeling Tim had been waiting for a chance like this and didn't want to waste it. "The more time I spent with Marie, the more time I realized what Pastor Mark meant: that I could only love Marie if I knew how much I was loved first."

Tim reached in his bag and pulled out a small Bible, flipped the pages. "I wanted to learn more so I started reading the Bible."

"Oh, great. My best friend is now a Jesus freak." Peter chuckled.

Tim shook his head and reached for the movie headset. "I'll talk when you're ready to listen." He turned back toward Peter, his face tight. "I will say this, though, if there is anybody I know who needs healing it's you. I've watched you struggle with your demons for years."

Peter shifted uncomfortably and rested his head against the seat. "I have Jordan in my life now."

"You bring everything you're carrying into your relationship with Jordan you're both going to get crushed under the weight," Tim observed.

Peter felt a flash of anxiety at the truth of Tim's words, a realization that, despite her assurances, the more he opened up to Jordan the more likely it was that she would reject him. His life had always been that way. Why should it be different now, just because he wanted it to be?

"I want this thing with Jordan to work. Maybe I do need to make some changes," he said quietly.

Tim looked back at him with a skeptical air. "Call me a Jesus freak if you want, but knowing Jesus has changed me. And it's made what I have with Marie stronger and deeper."

Peter considered his friend. He's seen the changes in Tim. Remembered how Tim had been there when Peter needed him the most. How Tim had shouldered the burden of the peril they were now facing and would face again if things went badly in New York. He shuddered.

"I don't know, Tim. I guess my question is, Why Jesus? There are plenty of spiritual leaders out there. Many paths to God. What's so special about Jesus?"

"I agree other spiritual leaders can offer us good advice on how to have a better life, even to feel closer to God. But Jesus didn't say he could show us the way as other spiritual leaders do. He said he IS the WAY. In John 14.6, he didn't say he could show us the truth. He said he IS the TRUTH. And he didn't say he could show us how to have a more spiritual life. He said he IS the LIFE."

Peter shrugged. "What's the difference? It sounds like semantics to me."

Tim shook his head. "Jesus is the only one who can take away our sin."

"Well, that's something else I don't get. Sin. What is sin, really? And what's the big deal?"

Tim considered his answer. "I don't have a big fancy answer. Just what I believe: that God created us, and because of that he has the right to make the rules. Like the Ten Commandments. From the beginning, the very first people on earth said, we don't like your rules and we aren't going to follow them. That's sin. It's not just what we do, it's in our very nature. People always want to do what they want to do, not what someone tells them to do, right?"

"Pretty much." Peter suppressed a snicker. He wouldn't trade his independence for anything. Tim wasn't going to convince him otherwise.

"So, you like it that way," Tim added, knowingly. "Most people do. And God said, 'Okay, you are dead to me. Eternally. Not just in this life but forever.' We all know we can't escape death. We take it for granted. But the worst part is how we have to live. When our relationship with God was broken, so was every other relationship we have: parents and children, siblings, couples. None of our relationships is free of pain and hurt and guilt." Tim turned to Peter. "Is it?"

The remark hit home. "No," Peter replied quietly. "Not for me."

"We can try to change it ourselves, but we still screw it up. Only God can repair our broken relationships. Teach us what it really is to love and be loved—through death of his Son, for us."

"But lots of spiritual leaders have died for their followers, Tim."

Tim had the Bible open on his knees, staring at it, looking uncomfortable.

"Look, we don't have to talk about this. I was just curious." Peter hoped that Tim would take the hint and close the conversation. Instead, Tim turned to him with a renewed energy.

"On balance, would you say you're a good person?" Tim asked.

Peter nodded. "Yeah, I'm a good person."

"How good? On a scale of 1 to 10, how would you rate yourself?"

Peter looked askance. "Tim, what are you talking about?"

"Hang with me for a minute. What number would you give yourself?"

Peter shrugged. "I dunno. A seven, maybe."

"See, Peter, what you're counting on, what everybody counts on, is that God judges on a sliding scale just like we humans do. That he'll look at your seven and say, good enough, come on in. But what if he doesn't judge on a sliding scale? What if his scale is binary? Just 1s and 0s: one life; zero death?"

"I don't believe that." Peter took a sip of Scotch.

"Then you're fine. I'm fine. We're all fine as long as we do the best we can, right?"

"Yeah. That's what I think."

"Okay, but what if you're wrong? Jesus said we had to be perfect.

Matt 5:48 'But you are to be perfect, even as you Father in heaven is perfect.'"

"That's ridiculous, Tim. Nobody's perfect."

"That's the problem. God is telling us to be something we can't possibility be. So, either he has to put his law aside and ignore it. Something we humans do every day. Or, someone else has to do for us what we could not do for ourselves."

Tim opened his palm to Peter. "God is just. His law is absolute. The penalty is death. Only Jesus who is God, and who became man, the only perfect, immortal man since Adam, could cover our imperfection with his perfection.

"Jesus didn't just die for us. He died instead of us. He took our punishment for sin in that death; and then to prove he wasn't just another man dying for his followers, on the third day, he rose again." Tim faced Peter. The expression on his face was as intent and earnest as Peter had ever seen.

"He died and rose so that when you stand before God—and you will—that on his binary scale, God doesn't see your zero. With Jesus, the One, standing beside you, God sees you as a perfect 10."

Peter's head was spinning. He wasn't sure what to think now. He looked over at Tim. "Wow. That's a lot to process."

"Yeah, I know." Tim closed his Bible and put it back in his travel bag. "God loves you, Peter. He can heal you. Now and for eternity. All you have to do is ask."

May 4, 1994: New York City

The taxi driver inched his way toward the entrance to the Empire Hotel. With a gut-wrenching twist to the steering wheel, he gunned the car into an opening in the traffic and started to make his move into the drivers' circle.

"Could you take us around back instead?" Peter asked, leaning forward.

The driver peered suspiciously through his rearview mirror. "Around back?"

David removed his baseball cap and sunglasses, catching the driver's eye. "If you wouldn't mind. We're trying to avoid the media circus."

The cabbie's eyes widened in recognition. "Sure thing, Mr. Lockwood."

Swinging out of the taxi line, the cabbie circled the block and pulled up to a side entrance.

"Thanks for that," Peter said, as they entered through the side door off the back alley. David laughed, sounding almost gleeful. David Lockwood was here to take Victor Henderson down and he was going to enjoy every minute of it.

"What's the plan?" Peter picked up his pace as David marched them through the underbelly of the grand hotel with determination. Tim broke into a trot to keep up.

"Let's check the maintenance room and see what we find," David replied, turning left to face a set of gray swinging doors.

Peter was prepared for challenge, accusation and confrontation as David pushed through the doors. The cavernous room was empty. David checked his watch.

"It's twenty minutes before final sound check. All hands on deck." Strolling past the audio/visual carts and projectors lining the walls, stepping between the tool chests and piles of spare uniforms, David walked directly to an oversized locker in the corner. He pulled open the locker door in mid-stride and, reaching deep inside, he pulled out three blue maintenance shirts. Each had a sound wave logo on its breast pocket.

"Sound and light crew. Union. We'll blend." David handed each of them a shirt.

"How did you manage this?" Peter reached for the shirt.

"My admin is very resourceful," David replied with a crooked grin, swinging the locker door shut and pocketing the key.

"You've done this before, haven't you?" Peter asked, giving David an appraising look as he pulled on the work shirt and replaced his cap and sunglasses.

David's smug smile in response told Peter all he needed to know.

• • • •

Tim maneuvered the audio/visual cart to the left corner of the stage while David and Peter leaned casually against the back wall, staying clear of the hubbub. The stage crews were putting the finishing touches on the set: podium in place, demo stations humming. The Draco programming team was running through a final test sequence. It looked like they were going to do the same three demos today they had done at the Draco Universal product introduction.

"Hey, you!" Peter's head swiveled at the sound of the voice. A burly guy with a clipboard was motioning at them. Peter cocked his head.

"No, not you. Him." The guy pointed directly at David. "Get over here and fix that crooked spotlight."

David nodded, whispered to Peter, "Hey, why not?"

Sure, why not, Peter thought, suppressing a smile. *You'll be standing in it soon—if all goes to plan.*

Sauntering over to center stage, David climbed up the ladder and adjusted the light, tweaking it right and then left until the guy with the clipboard grunted and walked away. David rejoined Peter against the back wall as the two Draco programmers stood up and stretched. They stepped away from their stations. Three black-suited executives walked across the stage with the burly guy they'd seen earlier. They pointed. He wrote.

"Henderson's advance team," Peter murmured as they passed by and disappeared. The stage was finally empty.

"Let's get to work." David quickly moved to one of the demo workstations and booted it up. As the screen came alive, he tapped in a series of commands and produced a set of log files.

"Borrow your notebook?" he asked Peter, who handed him paper and pen.

"Can't let them see a file transfer," David explained to Peter's blank look.

"What about the log files? They'll see that you logged in."

"No. I used Devon's back door." David chuckled.

Turning back to Tim, he handed him the slip of paper. "Get this to Devon. He'll know what to do with it."

Tim responded with a smirk. David moved over to center stage, shaking his head in mock amazement as he stepped around the coils of black cable.

"Devon told me about this crap," he snorted to Peter. "And they're calling Sapphire smoke and mirrors. Unbelievable!"

"Enlighten me," Peter requested following behind as David walked the cable line, intent on finding something Peter couldn't quite decipher.

"They're not streaming media. They're just doing a digital download from a remote server and then running it off the local hard drive."

"It looked good when they did at Moscone."

"I'm sure it did," David scoffed. He'd followed the cable line to a banquet table against the wall, next to Tim's A/V cart. "Server's probably back there."

He turned to Tim. "You know how to splice a cable?"

Tim shook his head.

"You keyboard jockeys. Where would you be without the hardware?"

Peter saw Tim wince. David put his hand on Tim's shoulder. "No offense. Hand me those wire cutters and that splitter there."

David pointed and Tim complied. David took them and shimmed under the banquet table until only the lower half of his legs stuck out. Peter kept a watchful eye on the stage door. "What are you doing?" he asked.

"I'm borrowing Draco's M-bone," came David's muffled reply. "They've got multicast across the Internet, between San Francisco, Dallas and here in New York. We've got it in Mountain View. We piggyback on it and we can stream video real time from the lab."

"Hurry." Peter heard voices in the hallway and coming from the front of the room. The press arriving. Henderson, Mullens, maybe Davis himself could walk through these doors at any minute.

"Got it." David slid back from under the table. A jaunty grin lit his features as he stood and brushed the dust from his jeans. "I haven't had this much fun since my blue box days," he said.

David glanced over at Tim. "Ready?"

"Ready," Tim replied, standing.

"Let's get out of here." Slipping through the backstage doors and into the hallway, David stopped abruptly and turned to face Peter. "Join me," he said.

Tim's jaw dropped. His astonishment mirrored Peter's own. No one had ever joined David Lockwood onstage. Ever. David watched his reaction with amusement.

"You earned it," he said lightly.

Peter allowed himself a moment to savor the image: walking onstage beside Lockwood; the looks on Henderson's and Margaret's faces; standing there in front of the international press corps. Peter hesitated, then shook his head.

"You make the news, David. I just report it."

CLAD ONCE MORE IN HIS GRAY BUSINESS SUIT, PETER MINGLED WITH the reporters waiting for the press conference to begin. It was fifteen minutes past the hour and the crowd was getting antsy.

A young woman appeared onstage. "We'll be starting in fifteen minutes. Thanks for your patience," she said and quickly disappeared.

"That's what they said fifteen minutes ago," the reporter next to Peter grumbled.

"Yeah," Peter replied. He'd waited too long for a cigarette, so he headed out the double doors and into the lobby for a quick one. He pulled a cigarette from his pack, feeling inside his pocket for his lighter.

"What the hell are you doing here?" Margaret stomped up to him, standing inches from his face.

"It's a press conference. I'm press." Peter tapped the badge clipped to his lapel.

"This is New York."

"I'm aware of that," Peter replied blandly.

"I said, what are you doing here?" She tapped her foot, frowning, blinking rapidly. He was familiar with all of Margaret's gestures and how to read them. She was angry all right, but she was also uncertain. She was spooked by seeing him here. It spoke to her guilt. Peter put his cigarette to his lips, pulled out his lighter and lit up. He studied her impassively as the smoke curled above her head. His silence made her more uncertain.

"Answer me," she demanded.

Peter took a leisurely pull on his cigarette. "I'm going to stop you, Margaret."

She threw back her head and laughed. "Stop me. How?"

"I know what you did." He nodded his head toward the conference room filled with international media. "Soon, they'll know too."

She glared at him. "You don't know anything. You never do."

"I know it all. All about the bad deals. The bloated valuations. The secret bank accounts. The plan to bleed MediaBuilders dry. Give the assets to Win Davis and crown him King of the info road."

She looked at him like he was an alien. "For a reporter, you sure can't get your facts straight. But then that's no surprise, is it?"

She spoke again, slowly, as if he needed help comprehending the way a doddering old man needed a walker. "This is a strategic partnership. We are doing a licensing deal with Draco because David Lockwood tricked us into believing he had a product when he didn't. I'm protecting MediaBuilders' interests as their corporate counsel."

"Yeah, you're protecting Henderson's interests all right. What did he promise you, Margaret, to get you to betray everything you ever stood for?"

She stepped closer. They stood nose to nose. Unflinching, Peter absorbed the fury in her eyes. "I'm taking you down," he said through clenched teeth.

"You and what army?"

Peter snorted. "I don't need an army. Never did."

"You haven't got the—"

"Proof? Oh, I've got plenty of proof. I have irrefutable proof that Victor Henderson is working with Win Davis. He's guilty of collusion, conspiracy, fraud, who knows what else. And so are you."

Margaret stared at him, her face drawn, body rigid. "You're

crazy. You've been a problem since the day you were born, but this is insane. Get out of here before I have you thrown out."

"I'm not going anywhere. Look, I don't really care what happens to you. But I have discovered, I do care about what happens to the family firm," he said, taking another deep pull on his cigarette, staring intently at her. "After all, my name is on that door."

"What the hell has gotten into you?" Margaret snapped.

"Well, sister dear, it looks like I finally grew a pair."

Her mouth dropped open. Peter had never seen his sister speechless. He used it to his advantage. Leaning toward her, he whispered, "I said I had irrefutable proof. I meant it. Don't you want to know what it is?"

He could see her thinking. If she stormed away, she'd never know what kind of evidence he had, the kind of case he could make. He'd flown all the way from California. Even Peter wouldn't make these wild accusations without some proof. In spite of everything, he was an Ellis. It was in the blood. She opted for discovery.

"What is this evidence you think you have?" Her voice, though less confident now, still held a challenge.

Inside the hall, applause broke out. The press conference was beginning.

"Looks like you'll have to see it with the rest of world," Peter said, gripping her elbow and steering her inside the ballroom. They stood in the back of the room as Victor Henderson stepped out from behind the blue curtains that hid the demos from view.

"Thank you all for coming. We have some exciting news to share that, as promised, will supercharge the information highway and give all of you a reason to jump on the Internet bandwagon if you haven't already."

Henderson hesitated as if waiting for applause. He didn't get it. With a slight grimace, he moved on. Peter figured that whoever wrote those opening lines would be looking for a new job tomorrow.

"Today," he paused dramatically as both Win Davis and Jonathan Blaylock walked onstage, this time to brief applause, "we are announcing a partnership with Draco Communications to license the Draco Universal as our connection point to all the movies, TV shows, sports and entertainment events you want to enjoy along the information highway."

Henderson turned toward the curtains. The audience waited in anticipation. Peter released Margaret's arm and stepped into the aisle. "What about Sapphire?" he shouted into the silence.

"Yeah," another voice chimed in. "What about Sapphire?

A third reporter asked, "Weren't you buying that for 2.2 billion dollars a week ago? What changed?"

Blaylock and Davis looked to Henderson. He stepped forward and addressed the crowd. "It pains me to say it, as David Lockwood is, we all know, a legend in our industry. But Sapphire was a pipe dream. Now it's time to show you reality."

Henderson lifted his hand. The curtains parted and the audience gasped. David Lockwood stood center stage in his standard garb of blue jeans and navy blue turtleneck. He held his laptop, just as he had at CES, the thin wire connecting it to the Sapphire system barely visible under the harsh stage lights. He looked down at Henderson.

"You did say you wanted to see reality, Victor. Though this may be more reality than you're prepared for. This is Sapphire streaming video over the Internet from California to New York City."

The screen behind Lockwood lit up.

"The deals are done. MediaBuilders will be bleeding red ink by the third quarter." Victor Henderson's voice and face filled the screen.

"Excellent." Win Davis appeared in an inset screen. "What about Sapphire?"

"Crippled. It won't be available anytime soon," Henderson replied with a scornful laugh.

"The loose ends? The lawyer? That reporter?" Davis asked.

"Handled."

Peter's jaw clenched. Even though he knew it was coming, seeing and hearing Henderson on the giant screen infuriated him.

"What is this?" Margaret hissed in his ear.

Peter didn't have time to answer. The video cut to Jake Mullens.

Glancing at Davis with a triumphant smile, he raised his glass and began a toast.

Sound rose like a cacophony in Peter's ears as the video rolled and an all-too-familiar voice burst from the speakers. Peter felt the room tilt. His knees went weak and his stomach churned, sending a wash of acid over the back of his throat. He heard the voices surrounding him as if through a wind tunnel.

"Toby Eastman," he murmured.

"What?" Margaret asked, her face contorted.

Peter's neck was stiff with tension, his face moist. Adrenaline was pumping through his system as if it had been delivered by a hypodermic needle. The hum in his ears and the images invading his mind, made it impossible for him to respond. *Not now*, he pleaded silently, *please God, not now*. He drew a deep breath, held tight to the oxygen, willing the images to fade. Exhaling, he spoke through parched lips. "Jake Mullens is Toby Eastman."

Turning toward his sister, Peter was met with a look of total bewilderment. The scene around them had erupted into chaos: reporters jumping up, shouting questions; Blaylock, head down, rushing at Henderson like a mad bull; MediaBuilders' security team grabbing Henderson and Davis, roughly yanking them from the stage.

• • • •

As the commotion died down, David Lockwood motioned for silence and took control of the press conference. The press corps slowly resumed their seats, allowing David to showcase the power of Sapphire, damning Henderson and Davis further with every new email and video link. As the images flickered on the big screen, Margaret appeared to shrink, her face so chalky white her lips looked blue by comparison.

"He said he was protecting MediaBuilders," she mumbled. "He said that Jonathan didn't get the new ecommerce. He convinced me that a Draco-MediaBuilders partnership would strengthen both companies. That this was the only way to convince Jonathan to play ball."

She gave him a sideways glance. Her eyes were wet. Although no tears fell, it was as close to crying as he'd ever seen Margaret come. "Victor said that outside valuations would slow us down, and we'd lose our advantage. He's been my client for ten years. I thought I could trust him." In a voice barely above a whisper, she added: "He lied to me. I trusted him, and he betrayed me."

"He set you up, and now you're going down for it."

She averted her eyes and slumped into a vacant seat. Peter studied her impassively as she hunched over, rocking, mouthing words he couldn't hear. The press conference was over, and New York's media elite streamed by them both without a sideways glance.

Peter stepped into her space and towered over her as she sat curled inward on herself, just as she had so often done to him. "Tell me, Margaret," he asked coldly. "How does it feel?"

Victor Henderson Arrested!

*MediaBuilders' VP Charged with Corporate Collusion,
Conspiracy and Securities Fraud*

By Peter Ellis, Tribune *staff*

Victor Henderson, vice president of MediaBuilders USA,
was arrested yesterday in connection with a plot to drive
MediaBuilders into bankruptcy to protect and secure the
interests of Draco Communications' bid to dominate the
information highway.

Henderson has been charged with multiple counts of
corporate collusion, conspiracy, securities fraud and insider
trading. Winfield Davis, CEO and Chairman of the Board of
Draco Communications, has been questioned but not charged
in the case. A formal investigation is currently underway and
may result in additional charges, said New York State Attorney
General G. Oliver Koppell.

Like murder? Peter thought sourly, rereading the copy he'd filed
hours ago, just before hopping the five o'clock flight back to San
Francisco. Maybe Davis hadn't ordered the hit, maybe Henderson

hadn't pulled the trigger, but they were guilty. It was their greed and betrayal that had killed Henry, Michael and Brian. Peter wished he had some way to prove it.

With a heavy sigh, he stuffed the advance copy of tomorrow's *Tribune* article back into his jacket pocket, grabbed his carry-on, and followed Tim down the jetway. Marie met them at the gate. Peter watched Tim and Marie walk off, arm in arm.

David had stayed behind to chat with Blaylock. It looked as though MediaBuilders would get access to Sapphire after all. Between them, David and Peter had convinced Blaylock to consider retaining Peter's family's firm, though Margaret, charged as an accessory, was certain to lose her license even if she escaped jail time.

Peter wondered with idle curiosity how his father would handle the power shift in the firm his great-great grandfather had founded, but all Peter really cared about now was reaching Jordan. He'd been calling her non-stop since he'd left the hotel in New York, and all he'd gotten was voicemail. His frustration had reached a boiling point. He yanked his cell from his pocket to call her again as he headed outside the terminal. When he flipped it open, he heard O'Reilly's voice bark through the speaker: "Peter! How fast can you get to the lab? I've broken the rest of the code."

May 4, 1994: Mountain View, California

The lab was dark, with only the glare from a single computer monitor to cut the murk. Peter entered, treading carefully across unfamiliar territory. A brief nod from Devon, eyes secured to the monitor, was the only acknowledgement of Peter's transcontinental journey.

"We alone?" Peter pulled a chair over next to Devon.

Devon nodded and flipped on a single light for the room.

"What about the code?" Peter hunched closer to the monitor.

Devon's fingers flicked rapidly over the keyboard. Peter watched the sequence appear on the screen.

"Looks like a list to me." Peter smiled, relief flooding through him.

"It is, but not the one you're looking for. This is a series of pointers to servers all over the Internet."

"What do you mean pointers?"

"Another blind, Peter. Toby's too smart to keep sensitive information in one file. He scattered pieces of data all over the world and figured that nobody but him would figure out how to collect it. Each of these pointers is a path name to a different server. Funny, I recognize a couple as general-interest bulletin boards on the Web that everyone visits. Seems a bit risky."

Hide in plain sight, Peter mused. *Obscurity via the obvious. An Eastman trademark.*

"Let's check it out."

Devon nodded and hit a few keys. The screen changed colors. Modems on two continents snarled, buzzed and eventually shook hands in an electronic peace accord. The screen filled with a new set of characters that resembled Sanskrit.

"Damn it!" Devon shoved his bulky body off the chair.

"What it is? More encryption?"

"It's garbage, that's what it is." Still standing, Devon typed in another code string, watched the screen change and shook his head. "Garbage," he repeated, slapping the table for emphasis.

"What's garbage?"

Devon glanced at him, shook his head and spoke. "The code's disintegrated. Must have been timed code, set to deactivate by a certain date. Whatever he had there is gone."

Peter stared at the screen, his limbs beginning to numb. *This can't be happening,* he thought.

"Is it all like that?"

"We won't know until we try. I've checked the first two. Let's keep going." Devon typed resolutely, expression grim. The constant churlish sound of the modems connecting filled their ears.

Devon leaned forward. "Got something here. Look."

Standing behind Devon, Peter started reading. Devon clicked the download icon. The screen flickered, blue to green. Icons bobbed as if tossed from moorings and then stopped, frozen in place. Devon's fingers, gently stroking the keys, altered nothing. He reached for the mouse, moving it slowly in widening circles. The pointer refused to budge. The electronic connection severed.

"System's hung. I'll have to reboot." Devon performed the restart sequence while Peter paced around the lab, a futile waste of energy.

"Got anything?" Peter asked as the revitalized system whirred back online.

"More of the same." Devon stepped away from the monitor and allowed Peter to view the erratic movement of the characters strewn about the screen. They twitched like a corpse in its death throes, already decaying. They revealed nothing of substance.

"Try another."

"Waste of time. We're missing the key." Devon threw his hands upward in frustration.

"I thought we had it."

"So did I." Devon stared at the monitor. He looked stumped. Peter felt a sudden chill.

"He must have used a dual key system. One key encrypted the code and the other is required to invoke the download sequence. Download without it and the data disintegrates. Clever bastard."

"There must be some way—"

"There isn't. "It's impenetrable." Devon shut off the workstation with a heavy sigh. "Might as well get the team back. We have a project to complete."

Peter felt dizzy. His body swayed under the weight of the failure. Toby's scornful laugh filled his ears. He watched Devon as he moved to the telephone. The team's return meant an end to their quest. Devon glanced back at him, as if he also wanted to postpone the inevitable. Then he turned and picked up the phone.

"No, wait. What about the Trojan horse?"

"What about it?" Devon asked, turning.

"It's Toby's, right? He used it to throw us off track."

"Yeah."

"So, everything he's done fits the same pattern. Hide in plain sight. That Trojan horse, designed for data collection, is the most obvious place to leave the other key, isn't it?

Devon eyed him suspiciously.

"It was just a thought." Peter tapped his pen against the table.

"And a damn good one at that." Powering up the workstation, Devon resettled himself in front of the monitor. He invoked a series of commands for the Trojan horse. Stepping forward, Peter studied the monitor and waited impatiently for the digital pot to boil.

"Well, I'll be damned." Devon smiled, pointing. Peter leaned in and watched Devon trace the lines of text the program sent with his finger, as if he were reading a map. "It's headed for an old archival server at HP. Nobody's used that server in years."

"Since you, Toby and David all worked together?"

"Could be." Devon nodded. "The program is invoking an automatic download."

He sounded relieved. The screen changed, sparked, went black. Peter tensed. Devon's fingers poised over the keyboard, ready to invoke a fail-safe sequence. The screen changed again. Light from the monitor bathed their faces in an orange glow. Peter blinked. A face appeared in full-motion video. A young, determined face. Michael Lee's face.

"Greetings," he said solemnly. "And congratulations for getting this far. I hope when you have seen what you are about to see, that you will contact the authorities. Because your arrival here also means that I am unable to do that myself."

Peter felt a sharp pang as he recalled the image of Michael frolicking with his friends in the autumn leaves.

"The download will take about ninety minutes," Michael continued. "When it is complete, you will have all the evidence you need to arrest Toby Eastman for the murder of Henry Rhodes and other crimes too numerous to mention."

Peter and Devon exchanged shocked looks.

"That's one hell of smart kid. He must have tracked Toby just like we did, only he found the second key. I knew that Trojan horse program was altered; I just figured it was Toby trying another blind. But it was Michael who changed the program and used it to collect

Toby's markers and store them where nobody would think to look."
Devon tapped the keys to begin the download. Computer code
marched across the screen.

"How does it look?" Peter asked.

Devon sampled the data. "Intact," he pronounced, a grin forming
on his face. Peter hoped that Michael Lee, the policeman's son, had
been thorough in his task.

"This is going to take a while. How about a beer?"

"Yeah, sure."

Devon strolled to the refrigerator, pulled out two beers and
returned to the workstation. He handed a bottle to Peter. They
sipped silently, occasionally casting a wary eye toward the monitor.

"Can I ask you a personal question?" Peter asked, his beer already
half-consumed.

Devon shrugged.

"What happened between you and David?"

Devon tipped a swallow of beer into his mouth. He rolled the
bottle in his hands and scrutinized the label as if it held some
wisdom he had yet to discover. He set it down again and spoke.

"You know David built this as an exact replica of the one where
we spec'd out the first Trxton PC." Devon waved his hand around
the lab.

"Maybe he thought it would bring him luck. Shake off the demons
from Falcon."

"Maybe so. He was due." Devon lifted the beer, drained it and
pushed the bottle aside. "We were a team when we started. Just like
HP. David and I had the usual arguments, hardware versus software.
We were the pioneers. Microprocessors were brand new. Nobody
really understood them, or how to code for them. We made it up
as we went along. We had problems, of course. But David only saw
one solution. His solution. He had to control every detail. Nobody
slept when David was around. He was like some fanatical general,
always on the attack. Charge of the light brigade." Devon chuckled,
retrieved two more beers and sat down again.

"I needed a weekend off here and there. It was personal, but to

David and maybe to the others, the ones who never left the lab, it was mutiny." He studied Peter, sipping slowly. "You have brothers, sisters?"

Peter took a long pull on his beer. "I have a sister," he said in a low voice, realizing that for the first time the word didn't send a shiver down his spine.

Devon nodded. "I've got two sisters and four brothers. We stick together. Our little guy—well, he's not so little anymore. He's close to my size. But he's…" Devon paused and focused on the blank wall above the blinking monitor. The reflected light seemed to drain the color from his face.

"The term they use today is mentally challenged. In the old days, they called him a retard. The label hardly changes the life."

In the dim light, Peter saw Devon reach inside his pocket and pull out a dog-eared set of photos. He lowered them slowly, as if exposing them to another pair of eyes was something he had to ease into.

"That's Ian at six." Devon held the picture out.

Peter noted the untainted grin and wide, innocent expression. He thought of Henry and his boys. It was odd how many lives he had entered, recently, by the simple sharing of a photograph.

"We took this one last Christmas." Devon pointed to another shot. The gentle expression on the man's face was the same, though the flesh surrounding it had hardened and lined and the hair was tinged with gray.

"There's a lot he's missed." Devon dropped the photo on the table.

"And a lot he hasn't."

Devon turned his gaze back to Peter. "One thing he's never had a chance to miss is me. I promised him I'd be there for him and I've never broken that promise." Gathering up the photos, he shoved them back in his pocket.

"And David didn't understand that?"

"I didn't tell him. We were partners. I wasn't going to beg for a few hours of personal time."

Anger crackled across Devon's features like ungrounded electricity. "One Sunday night, I got back to the lab and David was waiting for me. Marched me straight into the conference room like I was some kid. Like the priests in school used to do. He started in on me the same way. I could fool the others, he said, but I couldn't fool him." Devon's voice sharpened. "He accused me of outsourcing the code! Me!"

"Outsourcing the code?"

"Getting someone else to write the software and claiming it as my own. When David said it and I could tell he believed it, I knew we'd never work together again."

"So you walked out."

"Yeah. But first I cold-cocked him. Juvenile, I admit, but satisfying at the time." Devon smiled ruefully.

Peter returned his smile. "But now you're back. Why?"

The workstation hiccupped. Devon tapped out another sequence and refocused on Peter.

"You want to know why I came back?" Devon leaned against the chair, legs outstretched. "Because of Falcon."

"I didn't know you were involved in that project."

"I wasn't. But I could have been. David was wearing both hats for Falcon. No more partnerships for him. But David's a hardware guy. He doesn't know code. He was in trouble from the start. Alok sent me the software design specs. Wanted to titillate me, I guess. Or maybe he saw what I saw. David had loaded the OS with so many features it would sink any processor. I could have fixed it. Instead, I sent the specs back without a word and ignored Alok's emails. I left my ex-partner to twist in the wind." Devon took another swig of the beer.

"Don't know that I'd do it any differently."

Devon shook his head. "Funny, though. Watching David go down wasn't as satisfying as it should have been."

"It never is." Peter swallowed the last of his beer. He could feel the weight of Devon's gaze. He looked up with a slight smile. "What about Sapphire?"

"A good design. Great, really. Just like I heard through the grapevine. I joined Draco because I was bored, and I thought catching David in a fair fight would be a kick. But as we know, the boys at Draco weren't playing fair. I couldn't stomach seeing that weasel Kavanagh get the best of a design as good as Sapphire. So I contacted Alok and he arranged a meeting with David. Luckily, David and I had both grown up over the years."

Peter turned toward the monitor as they heard the quiet hiss of the modems disengaging.

"Looks like we're ready." Devon faced the monitor and tapped the keys. Jake Mullens appeared on screen. Peter, frozen, stood resolute, staring into those turbulent black eyes. "Meet Toby Eastman," he said calmly.

"What!" Devon exclaimed.

"Jake Mullens is Toby Eastman."

"That's impossible. I was there. Working right beside him." Devon's expression was incredulous.

"It's the truth," Peter said, sliding wearily into a chair. "He nearly beat me to death. I never saw his face, but I will never forget that voice."

Devon peered at the face on the screen, his brow furrowed. "I can't believe I didn't recognize him."

Peter stood. Anger flooded him, and with it the courage to face the man who had brutally assaulted him. "He's obviously had surgery. And it's been eighteen years. Let's see what else Michael has to say. Maybe we can catch this son of bitch."

Devon nodded and turned back to the keyboard. Peter watched as Henderson's secret accounting transactions, the ones he and Charlie had found, appeared on the screen, followed by dozens of others. With Michael's help, the pattern in the movement of the money was now obvious. Corporate collusion was the least of it.

Michael Lee knew. He knew it all. Now, Peter realized, bile rising in the back of his throat, so did he.

33

HIS TOWNHOUSE STOOD DARK AND SILENT. PETER PARKED HIS CAR in the driveway and headed up the walkway, gathering up an accumulation of newspapers. His key twisted in the lock. Opening the front door, he flipped the light switch and illuminated the hallway.

The sound was faint, no more than a rustle. Peter looked up and was trapped by a pair of cold, merciless black eyes. The formidable barrel of a Glock 17 was pointed at his chest.

"Hello, sweet cheeks."

Peter nodded. Despite the peril facing him, he felt only the challenge, the expected rush of adrenaline preparing him, pre-tournament, for play with a worthy opponent. Last time he'd been caught unawares. This time he was ready.

"Been waiting long?" he asked drily.

Toby watched him with the calculating eyes of a predator, his body tuned to the familiar scent of the clash. Peter exuded neither fear nor anger. He sensed that Toby was pleased.

"I thought it was time that you and I had a little chat."

"I'm surprised you feel you have the luxury." Peter ignored the tempo of his heart and kept his body erect and still.

"I detest unfinished business."

"Like David Lockwood? Nothing else mattered, did it, once you had Lockwood in your sights again? Just getting Lockwood. No matter what it cost."

"I know what it cost David." Toby flashed a row of perfect white teeth and lifted Peter's pack of Camels from the coffee table. "May I?"

"Help yourself."

Holding the gun steady, Toby tapped the pack and pulled out a cigarette with his lips. He lit it with a practiced, one-handed gesture and held the pack toward Peter. Peter shook him off.

"You really should, you know. That last cigarette. It's tradition."

Peter's smile was nearly inadvertent. "There's a lot of cigarettes left in that pack. I don't intend for any of them to be my last."

"Optimistic, aren't you?"

Peter ignored the bait. The predator before him, like others of his ilk, would try to goad him into action and attack his vulnerability; whether through anger or fear was immaterial. Peter had resorted to this strategy himself in many a tennis match, to drive his opponent to the net or the line before closing in. It had never been so important to keep steady.

"Where have you been? Colombia, trying to square it with Valdez? Or the Caymans, looking for some place to hide when Valdez figures out how badly you screwed him?"

Toby shrugged. "Doesn't matter, does it? The real question is, what are my plans for you?"

"That's pretty obvious. You're planning to blow my brains out."

"Too easy. There are lots of ways to kill, sweet cheeks. Fifty ways. You know, like leaving a lover. For the same reason, an end to unfortunate entanglements." Toby's lips curled, teeth exposed in a hyena-like smile.

"There are the quick kills: a knife, a bullet, a snap of the spine. No one feels much. Death goes on. Then there are the long kills. Like slicing a throat in the jungle. The insects descend in seconds. You lie there, blood oozing to the surface, flesh agape, gargling speech.

You feel the step of every fly that lands to suck your blood for hours, afterward. It takes a long time to die." Toby drew deeply on the cigarette, his eyes dark coals of menace.

"I'm going to enjoy seeing you die, but not as much as I'll enjoy watching you watch her die. Our party's already started. I'm here to persuade you to join us."

Peter's bland expression was purchased with a twisting pain in his gut. *Jordan.* He'd been calling her for hours. She hadn't answered her cell. Neither had Taylor or Josh.

"Where is she?"

"You'll know soon enough."

Toby was watching him closely, sensors patrolling for his reaction. A bead of sweat on his upper lip, an apparent flash of shock would be enough for Peter to lose his edge. Toby didn't just want to kill him. If he did, he would have fired the moment Peter walked through the door and then disappeared into the night. Nor was Toby simply playing cat and mouse. His toying had a more subtle purpose. He wanted to see Peter defeated, his will consumed by a steady deterioration of self until at last, in hollow futility, he leaned on Toby for sustenance, unable to protect himself or the woman he loved. Then and only then would Toby kill him, and savor his victory in a way no mere shooting could provide.

Toby's eyes lasered into him. "I've got a cabin upstate. Where no one will hear you scream. Imagine her long, luscious body stretched out, open, waiting for me. You can watch me take her again and again until she's all used up. Then I'll start cutting. A slash on her ankle, a nick on the wrist. Slice off a nipple, maybe two. Just enough to make sure she bleeds out slow. You'll be staring hopelessly from across the room. Her life force slipping away. Those pretty brown eyes, so full of life and light, dimming, the darkness descending. She'll turn to you, eyes pleading. But you can't save her. You won't even be able call her name."

Peter quelled the rolling waves of panic and rage within by sheer force of will, hardening his face and heart to the taunts from a voice that could still make his skin crawl. Shutting his mind against the perversions Toby threw at him, just as he did the noise of the crowd during tournament play, he focused only on the game at hand. Toby's arrogance, his narcissistic denial of his own weaknesses, was Peter's only chance. *Fuel the anger without getting burned.*

Peter smiled, speaking seductively. "Ah, if only we had world enough and time." Then his voice turned steely. "But you don't. Time's run out."

He took a deep breath and continued. "It doesn't matter that it wasn't your idea to skim the money. Arnold was the fool who thought he could checkmate the king. But once you found out about it, you had to protect him. The way you did in 'Nam. Maybe you could have squared it with Valdez. You were his best pilot. But his men got there first and took care of Arnold. You had to protect yourself and you ran to Carl."

Toby's confident sneer veered toward agitation. He dropped the cigarette in the ashtray. Peter turned up the heat.

"He got you a new name, new face, new job. All you had to do was keep the heat on Henderson, keep him in line. Simple. Only you couldn't stop there, could you? You were the one who went rogue, who used Draco's war chest as leverage to force Henderson to buy flawed companies at sky-high prices. You forced him to go after a controlling interest in Sapphire. You had no problem driving MediaBuilders into bankruptcy if it meant killing Sapphire, and destroying David Lockwood once and for all."

Toby chuckled. "You're spinning quite a fairy tale there, sweet cheeks. Maybe you should get out of the news business and start writing fiction."

"Oh, there's plenty of news here," Peter snorted. "Like the story of how you betrayed Carl and ruined his well-oiled money laundering operation."

Toby's face registered surprise. Peter pressed his advantage. "MediaBuilders' global empire was the perfect place to launder Valdez's dirty money and Henderson was the perfect patsy. His son owed Valdez hundreds of thousands in gambling debts and drug buys. He'd do anything to protect his son."

"Unlike some fathers we know," Toby jeered.

"I'm not finished yet." Peter shifted his weight, prepared for a solid return to his serve. "Except that Carl didn't know you took out an insurance policy when you left Colombia. You had the list of all Valdez's operations, key contacts, the businesses he used as fronts for money laundering, and you sent it to the only man you thought you could still trust. But Henry didn't keep the disk safe. He put it in play and forced you to waste all that valuable time chasing down his boys."

"And things started falling apart. Michael Lee found your Trojan horse. Henderson couldn't get his hands on Sapphire. Carl warned you Valdez was getting nervous. But you still couldn't stop. You had to get Lockwood and you did. It only cost you five lives. I suppose you know the FBI has Carl."

Toby's face darkened in anger. His finger brushed the trigger of the gun. Peter felt the tightrope he was walking start to give way. He forced himself to relax, focus on the endgame.

"Tell me something, Toby. Why do you hate David Lockwood so much? After all, you were the one who wrote the bad code. Not David."

Toby's eyes narrowed. The question seemed to throw him. He hesitated briefly before chuckling. "I could tell you, but I'd have to kill you."

Peter held his ground. "Well then?"

Toby studied him for a long moment, too composed for Peter's purposes. Peter waited, inhaled and watched Toby watching him. Neither man was giving an inch. In the silence, Peter saw a tiny crack in Toby's calm demeanor: anger welling up, edging toward the surface. Though Toby tried for a smile, his face tightened with the memory.

"Because he stole my idea. The Trxton PC was my concept, not his. All he did was add a few frills to the design."

Toby reached into his back pocket and pulled out a single sheet of paper, yellowed and stained with age. It had been torn and taped several times. He tossed it at Peter's feet.

Peter lifted the sheet from the floor and opened it. The similarity to Lockwood's crude sketch—the one that had appeared in the company's advertising for years—was unmistakable. Shock rippled across Peter's features.

"Yes, that's right. It was mine."

Peter shrugged nonchalantly. "You could have picked that up anywhere in '77."

Toby's face contorted. His fingers flexed around the Glock, his knuckles whitening, his anger sliding toward unpredictable fury. He stepped closer to Peter. The gun was inches from his chest now.

Peter stepped back, intent on that moment of rage he could exploit. "Don't you want to know how the story ends?" He took another step back, willing Toby over the line.

"I know how it ends." Toby stepped forward. "It's time to go. She's waiting."

Peter felt the chill in the words, a blunt thrust. At the thought of Jordan and her possible fate, he knew he had to finish it. "You lost. David won. Victor Henderson was arrested in New York yesterday, and David Lockwood used Sapphire to bring him down."

"You're lying," Toby retorted.

"See for yourself." Peter pulled the advance copy of the *Tribune* from his jacket pocket and tossed it toward Toby. The headline "Victor Henderson Arrested" glared from the page. Next to the headline was a picture of David Lockwood standing center stage at the press conference, holding his laptop.

Toby's eyelids fluttered, his mouth twisted. His hold on the gun relaxed almost imperceptibly. Peter kicked out hard and fast, the tip of his shoe connecting with Toby's groin. Toby moaned and doubled over, dropping the gun. Peter dove for it as Toby recovered and lunged for the weapon. Peter stretched his arm, his fingers encircling the butt, and pulled the gun from Toby's reach. The gun felt heavy in Peter's hand. He stepped back and saw Toby standing, a glint of steel in his palm. Crab-like, knife in hand, he came at Peter.

"You know you have to kill me, sweet cheeks," Toby snarled, stepping forward. Peter moved left. His finger found the trigger.

Toby edged closer, circling him. Peter aimed low and squeezed. The sounds rushed at him. A crack. A yelp of pain. The thud of a body falling. Peter stared at the floor. Toby lay prone on the carpet, blood streaming from his right leg. Toby tried to rise and fell back. Keeping the gun trained on Toby, Peter saw the knife and kicked it behind him.

"Where is she?" Peter demanded. Toby snorted. Peter moved forward, crouched over Toby, and aimed the gun directly at his head.

"Go ahead, kill me," Toby urged. "You know you want to."

"Tell me where the hell she is!" Peter's voice was soaked in the fear he'd been holding back for so long.

Toby merely smiled. Peter held the gun steady, finger twitching on the trigger. Time stopped. They stared at each other, at the impasse between them.

"Peter!"

The shout broke their concentration. Devon had thrown the door wide open. He filled the frame with his bulk. His gaze traveled from Peter, still holding the gun, to Toby, half-sitting on the floor, bleeding profusely. Toby's face widened in surprise, and his features melted in an agony that had nothing to do with the pain in his leg. As Toby looked up at Devon, his face crumbled. "I believed in you. And you betrayed me," he groaned.

Devon shook his head. "No, Toby. You betrayed yourself."

PETER RETRIEVED THE KEY FROM TAYLOR'S HIDING PLACE. WITH NO moon or porch light to illuminate his way, he grabbed his flashlight from his car and used it to navigate the flagstone path to the front door. He turned the key in the lock, cracked the door open and stood still, letting his eyes adjust to the darkness.

He heard a low moan. His heart quaked. The moan ended in a stifled cry. His skin shrunk from his frame. The hairs on his arms felt singed. He flipped the wall switch and flooded the room with light.

Two alabaster bodies pulled apart and swiveled toward him, four eyes blinking rapidly in the harsh glare. A young girl with a wild mane of tawny hair sat up, pulling a couch pillow across her naked chest. The boy still sprawled across her hips and legs looked over his shoulder with a baleful stare.

"Who the hell are you?" she glowered at Peter, her voice filled with haughty distain.

"I'm looking for Jordan. Who are you?" Peter met her gaze. She looked down at the boy, readjusted her pillow and glanced back up at him, a little less confident.

"Taylor's niece. They're all at the club. Some special event."

Peter exhaled. "Thank you," he murmured to no one in particular. The boy nodded. "Hey, turn off the light, man, you're ruining the mood."

May 4, 1994: San Francisco, California

An oversized blue and white banner across the entrance to Blue Note West proclaimed *The Battle of the Bands*. Peter turned the collar of his raincoat up against the heavy fog. His blue dress shirt, dank with sweat, clung to his torso. He was still wearing the suit he'd put on nearly eighteen hours ago for the press conference. He could feel the itchy sprout of a five o'clock shadow on his chin.

"Screw that," he muttered, taking in the queue that stretched around the block as people streamed through the doors to catch the midnight show. He turned into the alley and strode to the stage door, flashed his press credentials at the guard and got the wave-through. He'd never been backstage before, and the maze of doors and dressing rooms confused him. He caught the attention of a passing stagehand. "I'm looking for Jordan, with The EJs."

"Third door on the right." She pointed down the hall and kept on walking.

Peter hesitated in front of the door, then knocked.

"Who is it?" her sweet voice asked.

"Peter." He replied, opening the door. She was sitting at the makeup table. Startled, she turned and dropped the eyelash she was applying. Blinking rapidly, she jumped up and threw her arms around him. He tasted her throat, consumed her lips.

"What are you doing here?" She pulled back, her eyes questioning.

"We got them, Jordan. Henderson's been arrested in New York, and the police should have Eastman by now."

Her mouth crinkled upward. "I knew you would."

She surveyed him. He was suddenly conscious of how disheveled he looked. She pressed her palm against his face. "I want to hear every detail, but we're on in about ten minutes. I have to get ready."

"What is this?" he asked, squeezing her hand.

"Battle of the Bands. It's a charity event. The club asked its top five bands to play. The winner gets a recording contract. There's a lot of A&Rs here. Eric's got that record gleam in his eye again."

She turned back to the table and bent down to retrieve her eyelash.

"Jordan." He stepped up behind her as she put the eyelash in place, blinked and looked up at him in the mirror.

He placed his hands on her shoulders. "I love you. Marry me."

Her eyes widened. "Are we doing this now?"

"Yes. Now."

She turned, staring at him in wonderment. Peter tensed as footsteps approached the door. A quick knock. "Five minutes, Ms. Langley."

Peter's arms encircled her waist. Pulling her close, he pressed his lips to her ear. "Light and life."

"What?" She cocked her head, perplexed.

"Light and life. That's what you are to me. I need to know what I am to you."

She bit her lip. Her cheeks flashed pink. "You're the most important man in my life."

"I am?" His eyes sparked with pleasure and relief.

The lights from the mirror shimmered on her face. She nodded. Her eyes were moist. "You have to promise me something first."

"Anything."

"Stop smoking. Now. Tonight. I lost my mother to cancer. I don't want to lose you too."

"Of course."

She smiled up at him, her eyes caressing his face. "Then yes, Peter Ellis. I will marry you."

"Jordan! We're on in two minutes." Eric's voice was harsh. He rapped the door twice.

"Coming."

"Tell him tonight." Peter kissed her forehead.

She shook her head. "Not until it's official."

"What do you mean, official?"

"I need a ring." She stepped away from him, rubbing her ring finger. Her familiar wicked grin flashed. Merriment lit her features. She had never looked so beautiful.

"So the ring makes it official, huh?"

"It does."

He hesitated. She watched, amused, as he looked around the room for inspiration. He had to think of something: a rubber band, anything. What? Then it hit him. Grinning, he pulled his Harvard class ring off his finger and slipped it on hers.

"All I got," he said with a shrug.

She held up her hand to examine it. "I love it."

"I love you." He leaned in to kiss her.

Eric pounded on the door. "Jordan. Now!"

"Gotta go." Her lips brushed his cheek.

"I'll be waiting."

• • • •

Peter leaned against the back of the bar as The EJs took the stage. He noticed Taylor and Josh at a table in the front row. He'd join them in a minute. As he looked back up at the stage, Jordan caught his eye and smiled. Then she raised the sax to her lips and turned to face Eric. The crowd erupted as Eric strummed the familiar opening notes to "Lily Was Here." Jordan answered with her sax.

Their chemistry onstage was better than ever, but now Peter didn't care. She belonged to him. To him alone. Nothing was ever going to change that.

THE END

ACKNOWLEDGMENTS

The manuscript that became *Web of Betrayal* was originally written in 1994. I took the traditional publishing route, got an agent and a publisher, and the book—then entitled *Conflict of Interest*—was scheduled for release in the spring of 1998. Sadly, before the book could be published, the publisher went out of business. My agent said not to worry. We would find another publisher. A few weeks passed and she called me to say that she had talked to all the publishers she knew and they all said the same thing: "Nobody cares about this technology stuff."

Well, that was then. This is now. The Internet—the Web and the Internet Streaming Video product that David Lockwood strove to create then—is a part of everyday life. What would we do without it?

In 1998, I chose not to take the vanity press option, the only one open at the time to those who did not have a traditional publisher. Instead I put the manuscript on the shelf until, at the urging of my counselor and friend, Laura Faudree, in 2011, I started to rework it: keeping true to the times, but now with the clarity of hindsight that, I hope, makes the story more enjoyable and memorable.

I am especially thankful for the wisdom and support of my dear friend, Peggy Harper Lee, author of *Spoiled,* who provided much-needed encouragement through the many recent drafts of this manuscript, and shared her experience and some great writing resources with me.

I owe much of the feel of the times in fashion and décor to my sister, Cathy Nadel, whose eye for detail helped bring the 1990s back to life. And great thanks to Keith Nadel, formerly of the Los Angeles Police Department, for his expertise in police tactics and weaponry. I owe special gratitude my editor Elizabeth Hennies for her encouragement and perseverance in helping me take a "work in progress" to the final outcome. I am thankful for her inspiration and clarity in deepening my characters and keeping a twisty plot on course. And many thanks to my copyeditor, Zoë Bird, who polished this manuscript with a careful and true hand.

In the journey from 2011 to 2014, so many people provided support, wisdom and guidance. I especially want to acknowledge my "support group" of early readers and advisors for their ideas, creativity and feedback: Marti Avery, Beth Caputo, June Bogdan, Keith Nadel, Mary Johnson, Greg Garry, Jake Tuschinski and Leslie Fisher. Special mention goes to the members of the Davis Writer's Salon (2011), who read and critiqued many pages of this book and provided invaluable advice.

Thanks to those whose expertise and skills made the production of this book and its promotional platform possible: to Peter from BespokeBookCovers.com for the cover design, Joy Porter for my author photo, Phi Schmidt of The Project Shaman for a thrilling book trailer and Carol Lynn Rivera of Ravalor Interactive for the wonderful Website.

And, finally, to my mom and dad: thank you for encouraging my dream of being a writer from an early age.

ABOUT THE AUTHOR

Clare Price has been a business journalist, tech industry journalist, Internet industry analyst and the VP of marketing for several software startups. She is the author of five books on marketing and the creator of a unique market development product: *Five Easy Pages: The Essential Marketing System.*

Clare saw the birth of the commercial Internet firsthand as a research director with the Gartner Group, the global leader in information technology consulting. As a principal analyst in Gartner's Internet Strategies Service, Clare assisted many of the world's biggest technology companies (IBM, Microsoft, Cisco, HP, Sun Microsystems, Oracle) in their bid to make the information highway a reality.

An Ohio native, Clare began writing at age five with her short story, "My Dog Nicky." She later graduated from the University of California, Berkeley, with a B.A. in rhetoric. She currently lives in Sacramento, California with her two Shetland Sheepdogs, Dan and Toby. This is her first novel.

www.ingramcontent.com/pod-product-compliance
Lightning Source LLC
Chambersburg PA
CBHW060141260626
47160CB00001B/75